W9-CDJ-393

ALSO BY KRISTIN HARMEL

THE
PARIS
DAUGHTER

KRISTIN HARMEL

G
GALLERY BOOKS
New York   London   Toronto   Sydney   New Delhi

G

Gallery Books
An Imprint of Simon & Schuster, Inc.
1230 Avenue of the Americas
New York, NY 10020

This book is a work of fiction. Any references to historical events, real people, or real places are used fictitiously. Other names, characters, places, and events are products of the author's imagination, and any resemblance to actual events or places or persons, living or dead, is entirely coincidental.

Copyright © 2023 by Kristin Harmel Lietz

All rights reserved, including the right to reproduce this book or portions thereof in any form whatsoever. For information, address Gallery Books Subsidiary Rights Department, 1230 Avenue of the Americas, New York, NY 10020.

First Gallery Books hardcover edition June 2023

GALLERY BOOKS and colophon are registered trademarks of Simon & Schuster, Inc.

For information about special discounts for bulk purchases, please contact Simon & Schuster Special Sales at 1-866-506-1949 or business@simonandschuster.com.

The Simon & Schuster Speakers Bureau can bring authors to your live event. For more information or to book an event, contact the Simon & Schuster Speakers Bureau at 1-866-248-3049 or visit our website at www.simonspeakers.com.

Interior design by Jaime Putorti

Manufactured in the United States of America

10 9 8 7 6 5 4 3 2 1

Library of Congress Cataloging-in-Publication Data is available.

ISBN 978-1-9821-9170-2
ISBN 978-1-9821-9172-6 (ebook)

To my mom, Carol, and my son, Noah, from whom I learned the exquisite and endless joy of the bond between a mother and her child—the most complex and, at the same time, somehow the simplest love in the world.

PART I

Motherhood: All love begins and ends there.
—ROBERT BROWNING

CHAPTER ONE

September 1939

The summer was lingering, but the air was crisp at the edges that morning, autumn already tapping at the door, as Elise LeClair hurried toward the western edge of Paris. She usually loved the summer, wanted it to last forever, but this year was different, for in just four months the baby would be here, and everything would change. It had to, didn't it? She cradled her belly as she slipped into the embrace of the shady Bois de Boulogne.

Overhead, chestnuts, oaks, and cedars arched into a canopy, gradually blotting out the sun as she took first one winding trail and then another, moving deeper into the park. The same sky stretched over all of Paris, but here, beneath it, Elise was simply herself, not a woman defined by her neighborhood, her station, her husband.

When she married Olivier four years earlier, she hadn't realized that the longer she stood by his side, the more invisible she would become. They'd met in New York in early 1935, and she had been awed by his raw talent—he did things with brush-strokes that most artists only dreamed of. He'd been twenty-nine to her twenty-three, and it was the year he'd first been splashed across the magazines. *Art Digest* had called him "the next great artist hailing from Europe"; *Collier's* described him as having "the brush of Picasso with the looks of Clark Gable"; and even the *New York Times* had declared him "a Monet for a new day," which wasn't quite right because his style didn't re-semble the French master's, but the point was clear. He was the toast of the art world, and when he turned his gaze on Elise, she couldn't look away.

She was an artist, too, or rather, she wanted to be. She loved to sketch, she loved to paint, but her real medium was sculpture. Her parents had died when she was nineteen, leaving her lost and adrift, and Olivier had offered her a raft to a different life. He had been the first one, in fact, to introduce her to wood as an alter-native to clay. With a mallet and a chisel she could work out her grief, he'd told her, and he'd been right. When he proposed to her two months later, her reaction had been one of gratitude and disbelief—Olivier LeClair wanted to marry *her*?

Only in the years since had she realized marriage was sup-posed to be a partnership, not a practice in idolatry, and as she gradually got to know the Olivier the world didn't—the one who snored in his sleep, who drank too much whiskey, who slashed canvases in a rage when the images in his head didn't match the ones he'd painted—he had begun to slip off his pedestal. But in time, she had come to love him for the darkness as much as for the light that sometimes spilled out from him, eclipsing everything else in his orbit.

The problem was that Olivier didn't seem to want a part-ner. She'd thought he'd seen in her a raw talent, an artistic eye.

But now, with the clarity of hindsight, it seemed that he'd only wanted a qualified acolyte. And so life in their apartment had grown tenser, his criticisms of her carvings more frequent, his frowns at her work more obvious. Even now, with his baby growing in her belly, changing the shape of her from the inside out, she felt corseted by her marriage to him, choked by the lack of oxygen left over for her in their large sixth-floor apartment in Paris's tony *seizième arrondissement*.

It was why she had to come, as she often did, to the sprawling park that spilled over into Paris's western suburbs. Here, where no one knew her as the wife of Olivier LeClair, she could feel the corset strings gradually loosening. She could feel her fingertips twitching, ready to carve again. Only once she walked through their apartment door would the tingling stop, the creative spirit in her retreating.

But the baby. The baby would change everything. The pregnancy hadn't been intended, but Olivier had embraced the news with a fervor Elise hadn't expected. "Oh, Elise, he will be perfect," he had said when she delivered the news, his eyes shining with tears. "The best parts of you and me. Someone to carry on our legacy."

She sat heavily on a bench beside one of the walking paths. Her joints ached more than usual today; the baby had shifted and was sitting low, pressing into her pelvic bone. She bent to pull her sketch pad and a Conté crayon from her handbag, and as she straightened back up, she felt a sharp stab of pain in her right side, below her rib cage, but just as quickly, it was gone. She took a deep breath and began to sketch the robin on a branch above her, busy building its nest as it paid her no mind.

Her sketches always looked a bit mad, even to her, for she wasn't trying to commit precise images to paper, not exactly. Instead, the sketches were to capture the complexities of angles, of curves, of movement, so that she could find those same shapes in the wood later. As she quickly roughed out the right wing of the robin, she was already imagining the way the thin ribbons of wood would peel away beneath her fingers. The bird turned, laying some sticks at a different angle, and at once, Elise's hand was tracing its neck, the sharp, jerky movements as it shortened and elongated.

As the day grew brighter, she lost track of time, sketching the bird's beak, its inquisitive eyes. And when it flew away, as she knew would eventually happen, she found another robin and flipped the page, once again tackling the delicate perch of its wings, the way they were folded just so against its wiry body. And then, suddenly, that bird, too, lifted off, glancing at her before it soared away, and she looked down at her pad expectantly. Surely she had enough to work with.

But instead of the crisp avian sketches she expected to see, her page was filled with an angry tangle of lines and curves. She stared at it in disbelief for a second before ripping it from the pad, balling it up, and crumpling it with a little scream of frustration. She leaned forward, pressing her forehead against fisted palms. How was it that everything she did seemed to turn out wrong these days?

She stood abruptly, her pulse racing. She couldn't keep doing this: going for long walks that led nowhere, returning home with her thoughts still tangled, her hands still idle. She took a step away from the bench, and suddenly the pain in her midsection was back, more acute this time, sharp enough to make her gasp and stumble as she doubled over. She reached for the bench to steady herself, but she missed, her hand slicing uselessly through the air as she fell to her knees.

"Madame?" There was a voice, a female voice, coming from somewhere nearby, but Elise could hardly hear it over the ringing in her ears.

"The baby," Elise managed to say, and then there was a woman standing by her side, grasping her elbow, helping her up, and the world swam back into focus.

"Madame?" the woman was asking with concern. "Are you all right?"

Elise blinked a few times and tried to smile politely, already embarrassed. "Oh, I'm fine, I'm fine," she replied. "Just a little dizzy."

The woman was still holding her arm, and Elise focused on her for the first time. They were about the same age, and the woman's face, though creased in concern, was beautiful, with the kinds of sharp, narrow lines Olivier loved to paint, her lips small and bowed, her eyes the slate gray of the Seine before a storm.

"*Maman?*" The voice came from behind the woman, and Elise peered around her to see a little boy of about four with chestnut curls standing there in blue shorts and a crisp cotton shirt, his hand clutching the handle of a carriage that held a smaller boy with matching clothes and identical ringlets.

"Oh dear," Elise said with a laugh, pulling away from the woman though she still felt unsteady. "I've frightened your children. I'm terribly sorry."

"There's nothing to apologize for, madame," the woman said, flashing a small smile before she turned to her sons. "Everything is all right, my dears."

"But who is the lady?" the older boy asked, looking at Elise with concern.

"My name is Madame LeClair," Elise replied with a smile she hoped would reassure the child. Then she glanced at the mother and added, "Elise LeClair. And truly, I'm perfectly fine."

"Juliette Foulon," the woman replied, but she didn't look convinced. "Now, shall we go, Madame LeClair?"

"Go?"

"To see a doctor, of course, Madame LeClair."

"Oh." Olivier would be worried if she didn't return to the apartment soon. She had already stayed out longer than she'd intended. "That's very kind but no, thank you. I need to get home, you see."

Madame Foulon took a step back, and it was only then that Elise noticed the bulge in the other woman's belly, slightly bigger than her own. She was expecting a child, too. "We can call you a car after we've called a doctor," she said calmly. "But . . ." Something flickered in the woman's eyes. "Well, I couldn't live with myself if I let something happen to you. When is your baby due to arrive?"

Elise hesitated. "January, the doctor says. Yours?"

Madame Foulon's eyes lit up. "January, as well! I think it will be a girl this time; I can feel it. Who knows, perhaps they will even be friends, your child and mine. Come now, my shop is very near the park. You can lean on the carriage if you need support." She was already herding Elise away from the bench, and to her surprise, Elise found she was relieved to be led.

"If you're certain," Elise said. "I don't want to be an inconvenience."

"No inconvenience at all. In fact, I insist. Now come, boys," Madame Foulon said to her children. The older one trotted after his mother; the younger one craned his neck to look back at Elise from his carriage, his eyes daring her to disobey. "We're taking Madame LeClair home with us."

CHAPTER TWO

Juliette could tell, even before the woman collapsed, that something was wrong. Juliette's pregnancies had come in rapid succession, enough to make her an expert in such things. Claude, who was now four, had arrived first, followed quickly by Antoinette, who had died just thirteen days later and who now lay beneath the cold dirt of a cemetery just south of the park. Alphonse, who was two now, had arrived next, a surprise borne of grief, and now Juliette was pregnant once again with a child she knew was a girl, a child she was terrified of losing just as she'd lost Antoinette. She couldn't bear that kind of pain again, and so she prayed each night for the gaping hole in her heart to one day be filled.

The other woman—Elise LeClair—had reminded Juliette of a nervous colt, her motions jerky, her muscles tensed to run. But Juliette had plenty of practice in coaxing Claude and Alphonse to do what she needed them to, so it was not difficult to cheerfully nudge the woman toward the path that led to the southern edge of the park while keeping up a steady stream of chatter.

Madame LeClair had likely thought it was merely an expression when Juliette had said she wouldn't be able to live with herself if she let something bad happen. But it was quite true. Even before she'd had children of her own, Juliette had always been drawn to lost children, maimed birds, stray cats, anyone who might need her help. It was one of the things her husband, Paul, said he loved about her. In fact, they had first met in this very park, the sprawling Bois de Boulogne, five years earlier when Juliette was spending the summer with her elderly *grand-tante* Marie, her mother's aunt, who lived in the seizième, just east of the park. She'd been strolling down a wooded path that day when she'd come across a tiny, injured sparrow. She'd scooped it up with tears in her eyes and looked around quickly for help, her gaze landing on a tall, broad-shouldered man walking toward her. His hair was sandy with flecks of gray.

"Excuse me," she'd said in her very best French. Her mother, who had died a few years earlier, had insisted she learn the language of her ancestors, though her family had been in the States for two generations. "Do you know whether there might be someone who could help me save this bird?"

The man had stopped and stared at her before breaking into a kind smile. "*Américaine?*"

Evidently her French hadn't been as flawless as she'd hoped. "*Oui, monsieur.* I am just visiting, but this poor bird . . ."

"Come with me," the man had answered, his English slow and deliberate. "I will take you and your bird to Docteur Babin."

Docteur Babin, it had turned out, was not a veterinarian, but rather a general physician and a frequent customer of the small bookshop the handsome man—who introduced himself as Paul Foulon—had taken over just the year before, following the death of his parents. Juliette's parents had died, too, she told him, and he'd given her a tender smile before saying, "I'm sorry," in English, and, gesturing back and forth between the two of them, *"Deux orphelins."* Two orphans. In French, it didn't sound quite as pitiful.

By the time Grand-tante Marie died of pneumonia two months later, Paul, fifteen years Juliette's senior, had already proposed, and by the end of 1934, they were married and Juliette had reorganized the bookshop into one that carried both French books and English-language classics, a destination for local residents of Boulogne-Billancourt and western Paris's thriving expatriate community.

Later, Docteur Babin had delivered her two boys—Claude in 1935 and Alphonse in 1937, but between their two births had been the tragedy of Antoinette, who had simply ceased breathing in her sleep. Juliette had never forgiven herself, although Docteur Babin had assured her it wasn't her fault. "Sometimes, Madame Foulon, these things simply happen," he had said, but she had known the words were a lie. Juliette was Antoinette's mother, and she had failed to keep her child alive.

So no, she could not bear the thought of leaving another pregnant woman alone if her baby was in peril. What if something went wrong? Perhaps this was a test from God. She would not fail, not this time.

"Come, then," she said, slowing slightly so that Madame Le-Clair, who had paused with a gasp to clutch her belly again, could keep up. "We're nearly there, and I'll send my husband to fetch Docteur Babin right away. Hurry along now, Claude!"

Claude looked up at her, his big gray eyes, which matched hers exactly, wide with concern. "Is the lady going to be okay?" he asked in a loud whisper.

"She'll be just fine, dear," she reassured him cheerfully, glancing over his head at Elise. "Nearly to the shop!"

"What kind of shop?" Madame LeClair asked, putting a hand on the carriage to steady herself as she kept pace.

"It's a bookshop!" Juliette kept her voice deliberately bright, for she had always felt that sunny chatter had the power to distract. It was what she employed each time one of the boys came to her with a skinned knee or a bruise. She simply pretended until things were all right. "It belonged to my husband's parents, and we've worked so hard to make something of it. We've even put in a children's section, because children need to fall in love with words, don't they? If you give a person a book, you give him the world. And children deserve the world, don't you think?"

Madame LeClair was staring at her, and Juliette wondered if her attempts at sunny chatter had instead made her sound like a raving lunatic.

"I must apologize," Juliette said. "I tend to warble on sometimes."

"No, it's not that. It is just—am I mistaken?—your accent sounds American."

Juliette groaned. "Is it that obvious?"

"No." Madame LeClair smiled and switched to English. "It is just that I am American, too."

"Well, what are the odds?" Actually, come to think of it, the chances were decent. Juliette had read in the newspaper that there were now nearly thirty thousand Americans living in or near Paris. It was why it had seemed so important to include English-language books; for Americans and Brits on the western side of Paris, it was more convenient to come to her store than to trek to the more well-known Shakespeare and Company on rue de l'Odéon near the Jardin du Luxembourg, more than an hour's walk away.

They emerged from the edge of the park near the Stade Roland Garros and hurried down the avenue Jean-Baptiste-Clément.

"Almost there!" Juliette declared brightly, hurrying Claude along. "La Librairie des Rêves, here we come!"

"La Librairie des Rêves?" Madame LeClair repeated, panting.

"Oh yes. The Bookshop of Dreams. It was my idea; we renamed the store the year after we married, when we were living the kind of life we always imagined. I've always believed that books are simply dreams on paper, taking us where we most need to go."

They turned left on the small rue Goblet, and the bookshop loomed ahead of them on the left. Juliette breathed a sigh of relief. "Here we are!" She pushed the carriage through the door and held it open for Claude, and then for Madame LeClair, who entered tentatively. Madame LeClair stared around, taking it in, and Juliette wondered what the other woman was seeing. She knew the store was a tangle of shelves, but she loved them all deeply; they carried new books and used books alike, for the age of a book was of no importance; all that mattered was that stories could belong to each of us in individual ways. Still, some might call it cluttered or chaotic. She hoped Madame LeClair was not that sort of a person.

"I love it," the other woman said in a whisper, gazing around, and Juliette felt her own shoulders sag in relief.

"Thank you. Now sit, sit. I'll send my husband out to retrieve Docteur Babin, and in the meantime, Claude will fetch you some water." Her older son raced off immediately toward the door in the back, the one that led to the family's apartment behind the store. A split second later, Paul emerged from the same door, glancing first at Madame LeClair, and then at Juliette.

"What's all this, my love?" he asked, approaching and kissing her, a full second longer than what might be considered obligatory. She loved that whenever she was gone, even for an hour or two, he always greeted her return with the same relief and happiness. She loved him more each day, and he her; she could feel it in the heat of his gaze, the way he touched her, the way he kissed her.

"This is my new friend Madame LeClair," Juliette said brightly, nodding at the other woman, who looked embarrassed. "I was hoping you might go fetch Docteur Babin, my dear. Madame LeClair is just fine, I think, but she was feeling a bit unwell, and it's better to be cautious."

"Yes, of course. A pleasure to meet you, Madame LeClair. I'll be back as soon as I can." He cast a worried look at Juliette, who nodded her encouragement. He hurried out the front door of the shop just as Claude emerged from the door that led to their apartment, carrying a glass of water he'd filled to the top. He handed it to Elise carefully, spilling a few drops on her dress, but she didn't seem to mind.

"*Merci beaucoup*," she said, smiling kindly at him, but a few seconds later, it was clear that another wave of pain was traveling through her body; she set the water down and clenched her teeth, looking away.

Her concern growing, Juliette lifted Alphonse from his carriage, ruffled his curls, and asked Claude to take him to the children's section to play. Claude headed off, clutching Alphonse's hand as he pulled the unsteady toddler behind him. "Will this be your first?" Juliette asked.

The other woman smiled shakily. "Yes. And I'm certain he'll be all right. I think I was just winded."

Juliette accepted this with a nod, though they both knew one didn't get winded simply from sitting on a park bench. "You think he's a boy, then? Your child?"

"My husband is certain of it."

"And what do you think?"

"I think—I don't know yet." She hesitated. "I'm afraid a daughter would disappoint him."

"Nonsense." Juliette reached over and squeezed Madame LeClair's hand, which was cold and trembling. "Fathers fall immediately in love with their little girls." She had to blink back tears for a second as she thought of Paul's face when he first saw Antoinette, tiny and quiet. Claude, their firstborn, had come out screaming; Antoinette had emerged like a startled butterfly not yet ready to leave the cocoon.

Madame LeClair gazed around the store, and then another wave of pain seemed to hit her. Her face went white, as she bent to cradle her belly once more.

"They're getting worse, aren't they?" Juliette asked as calmly as she could, looking toward the front window, praying that Paul would return with the doctor soon.

"I'll manage," Madame LeClair rasped, straightening back up again.

"Well, of course you will. But you're about to be a mother, and soon, you'll realize that mothers need all the help they can get." Juliette took Madame LeClair's hand again. "Being a mother is well worth it, of course, but it can be difficult," she added, glancing toward the children's section, where Claude was playing quietly with Alphonse, their heads bent conspiratorially together. She felt guilty saying the words aloud, for her children were a great blessing, and she knew she'd found her place in the world, but in becoming a mother, she'd lost so much of herself, too.

"More difficult than being a wife?" Madame LeClair gave her a wan smile, and Juliette swallowed a lump of unease in her throat. Juliette couldn't imagine thinking that being a wife was difficult, but she also understood that not everyone had what she and Paul had. That kind of love came along but once in a lifetime.

"I think that love is always difficult, because it requires us to lose a bit of ourselves to gain so much more," Juliette said at last. "But I believe that whatever we give up is worth it in the end, if we give those pieces to someone who loves us back just as fiercely." She meant the words as a comfort, but they seemed to trouble Madame LeClair, who looked quickly away.

CHAPTER THREE

Where was she? This bookstore, La Librairie des Rêves, felt like something out of a dream, making its name seem all the more appropriate. The shelves towered around them, chaotic and beautiful, and even from her perch near the front of the store, Elise had already spotted a few of her favorite titles, including *La Condition Humaine* by André Malraux, to whom Olivier had introduced her once; they knew each other through their work with the now-defunct left-wing Front Populaire. It was one of the few books on which she and Olivier agreed.

Elise used to read all the time, and she'd loved it, for doing so always transported her to worlds far away. When had she stopped? It had been sometime after she'd married Olivier, who wanted her to read the books he was reading so they could discuss them over long, wine-fueled dinners, and so she'd be conversant with his friends and their wives. And it wasn't that she didn't want that; she longed to be a part of his world, to have him look at her the way she'd seen Monsieur Foulon gaze at his wife. It was just that she had little interest in the books he gave her, books written by socialists such as Marx and Cabet. They felt like assignments she was bound to fail, not least of all because she didn't agree with the things they said.

At parties, Olivier was fond of explaining to people that true art was found in life's difficulties, but as she looked around now—at this perfectly imperfect shop overflowing with stories, at the two brothers playing together quietly among the shelves, and at Juliette, a woman who didn't know her but had gone out of her way to care for her—she wondered, not for the first time, if perhaps life didn't have to be hard to be beautiful.

But the thought was lost in another wave of pain, and the bookstore spun around her as she clutched her belly. All that mattered was the new baby, who might be coming into the world far too soon.

By the time her vision cleared, Monsieur Foulon was hurrying back through the front door with a balding, bespectacled middle-aged man in tow. He had evidently summoned the man in the middle of his lunch; there was a large crumb hanging conspicuously from the left corner of his lip, and he still had a napkin half tucked into his collar.

"Madame LeClair, this is Docteur Babin." Monsieur Foulon was breathing heavily as he made his introduction.

"*Bonjour, Docteur.*" What if this was nothing, if she'd interrupted Madame Foulon's day in the park and this poor man's lunch for no reason at all? "Thank you for coming, but I'm certain I'm fine."

"I'm glad to hear that you're certain, Madame LeClair." The doctor's eyes were kind as he bent beside her. "But perhaps you should let me be the judge of that. Otherwise, those years at medical college would be quite a waste. Now, shall we take a look?"

Elise let Monsieur Foulon help her up, and she leaned into him

for support as he led her through the store's back door into an apartment with a kitchen and small sitting room on the ground floor and
a stairway leading up. "The rest of our apartment is upstairs," he said
conversationally, guiding her first around a pile of blocks, and then
past a toy bunny with one ear ripped off. "But as you can see, the
boys bring their toys down here. You'll have to excuse the mess."

"It's no mess at all," Elise said. "It's beautiful."

Monsieur Foulon smiled as he helped Elise settle down on a
small settee. "I'm not sure I'd call it beautiful, madame, but it's a
nice thought." Then he backed out, gesturing to the doctor, who
had trailed behind them. "Let us know if you need anything, Docteur Babin."

"Certainly."

The doctor knelt beside her as Monsieur Foulon retreated to
the bookstore. His hand was warm, even through the cotton of
her dress, as he palpated her belly, pressing first on her lower right
side, then her left. "When was your last contraction, madame?"

Elise struggled to sit up, propping herself on her elbows, as her
heart thudded. "Contractions? Is that what these are? I can't have
the baby, you see. It's far too early."

He looked calm, which reassured her slightly. "I suspect these
are false contractions, but let's check. When did they begin?"

"About an hour ago. In the park."

"And how many have you had since then?"

She thought about this. "Five, I think. Every ten minutes or so."

"They're not coming closer together?"

"No. I don't think they are."

"And have you had plenty of water? Sometimes false contractions are triggered by dehydration."

She couldn't actually remember the last time she'd had a drink
prior to Madame Foulon's older son bringing her water in the

bookshop a few minutes earlier. She was just about to say so when another wave of pain began. The doctor must have seen it in her face and in the way her body suddenly tensed, because immediately, his hands were on her belly again, and as she fought through the uncomfortable spasms, he closed his eyes and felt around her midsection, pressing here and there. When the pain subsided, he was smiling slightly and nodding to himself.

"Just as I thought," he said, stepping away from her. "Practice contractions."

"Pardon?"

"You are not having a baby today." His tone was firm, reassuring.

"Are you certain?" Elise struggled back into a sitting position, unsure of whether to feel relieved or dismissed.

"Quite. In fact, Madame LeClair, it means your body is preparing for the birth. Like calisthenics for the big event." He brushed his hands off. "Have a few glasses of water and rest here for a bit, then you can be safely on your way home."

Though Elise was disinclined to believe the simple explanation, she did feel better after finishing the first glass of water, and better still after drinking a second glass at the small dining table while Madame Foulon fluttered around.

"I'm very sorry," Madame Foulon said after refilling Elise's glass once again. "You were fine on your own, and I should not have intervened."

"I'm glad you did." Elise realized she meant it. "I was frightened. I still am, to be honest. Do you think the doctor was right? That it's nothing to worry about?"

"I do, yes. I should have realized." A shadow swept across

her features as she hesitated. "You see, I lost a baby. I—I tend to overreact sometimes. But you can't imagine what it felt like. I—I wouldn't wish that on anyone."

"How *did* it feel?" Elise asked softly, but when Madame Foulon didn't answer right away, Elise realized she'd said the wrong thing. Sometimes, she thought too much like an artist, fixating on feelings and how she could render them rather than remembering her manners. "I'm very sorry," she added hastily. "That was terribly rude of me."

"No, it's all right. Nobody has ever asked me that before." Madame Foulon finally looked up and met her gaze, her eyes damp. "It was the most helpless I've felt in my life." She hesitated and glanced at the floor. "And the grief, it felt like a flock of birds, so many of them, taking flight with nowhere to go." She looked back up. "Goodness, I sound mad, don't I?"

Elise thought of the birds in the park, the ones whose movements she'd been trying to capture. Somehow, Juliette's words brought them alive in a way her crayon hadn't been able to. "Not at all. You sound like you've endured a great loss." She felt something within her stir, an urge to pick up a chisel, to give form to the symbol of anguish. "I'm very sorry, Madame Foulon."

"Please, call me Juliette." She wiped away an escaping tear.

"Only if you'll call me Elise."

Juliette smiled. "Perhaps you could come back sometime, Elise?"

"I'd like that," Elise said. "I'd like that very much."

Juliette called a car, and after saying goodbye to the magical bookshop the family called home, Elise found herself in the back of a black Citroën headed to her own apartment on the tree-lined avenue Mozart in the seizième. It was a quick ride, and she bore it in silence, staring out the window at birds streaking by overhead, wild and free. She heard Juliette's voice in her memory: *It felt like a flock of birds, so many of them, taking flight with nowhere to go.*

Before long, the car pulled to a stop outside her building; Elise took the rickety lift to her sixth-floor apartment in silence. It was empty, Olivier likely out at one of his meetings, and Elise made her way into her studio, a tiny, windowless room in the back that had once been a large storage space. Olivier, of course, had chosen for his studio a bedroom that looked east over the sunbaked zinc rooftops to the Place Rodin, but he'd been reasonable when he relegated her to what was essentially an oversize closet.

"You don't need the windows like I do," he'd said. "Wood is wood in any light. I need the sun, though, Elise, to ensure that I'm capturing exactly the right blends of colors on the palette."

Of course he was right, but sometimes, in this space that he never entered, she felt lost. If she never emerged, would he find her here, or would she simply disappear into the apartment itself, absorbed into its walls?

For the first time in a while, she was feeling something, really feeling something. Meeting Juliette had opened a floodgate she hadn't known was closed, and now, as she pulled out a block of limewood the size of a pile of Juliette's books, a current passed through her fingers. She breathed deeply and leaned into the wood, absorbing its leafy, nutty scent, and then, without conscious thought, she reached toward the carefully arranged line of tools on her workbench. The chisels, gouges, and rasps, all of varying sizes and shapes, were laid out in neat rows, the blades facing toward her, an old woodworker's trick so she could identify the instruments by their shapes without having to stop and think.

Now she wrapped her left hand around the smooth shaft of a large, curved gouge and picked up her wooden mallet with her right. Standing with her legs bent slightly to brace herself, she positioned the gouge and used the mallet to drive it into the wood block once, and then again and again, removing big chunks at the edges, already seeing the shape it would take in her mind's eye. Before she had learned to work with wood, she had always imagined that carving, like sculpting in clay, was primarily a job involving the hands as they found the shape in the material. But this was a task that required her whole body, and while she worked, her shoulders ached from the effort of slicing form from a shapeless hunk, and the muscles in her back sang from the exertion. It was cathartic, becoming one with the art she was making, and she felt alive in a way she didn't in her daily life. Here, her whole body knew what to do. Here, there were no wrong moves.

She had worried when she first found out that she was pregnant that her growing belly would get in the way while she carved, but she had learned to work around it, and besides, her belly had nothing to do with the strength in her arms and shoulders. If anything, it was invigorating to know that she was capable of creating life in both wood and her own body at the same time. And strangely, the more exhausted the pregnancy sometimes made her feel, the more the exertion of carving seemed to revive her.

She paused now and then to adjust the angle of her arms, or to grab a differently shaped gouge, as the figures of tiny birds began to emerge from the wood. Eventually, she put down the mallet and worked only with the sharp tools, moving from one stroke to the next. Her blades zipped effortlessly through the blond wood as paper-thin curls fell away.

As the afternoon wore on, she lost all sense of time. Somewhere outside, the sun was tracking toward the horizon, but she was blind to it in this dark room with no view of the world beyond her doors. All that mattered was that for the first time in a long while, she was creating again. She could feel the emotions that had churned within her bubbling up, funneling into the tools, slicing into the grain, and when she finally finished and sat back to look at what she'd done, it felt as if a great weight had been lifted.

Birds, dozens of them, hewn from the forgiving limewood, rose up from a marshy riverbed, their wings spread wide, their faces turned toward the sky. But narrow sinews, threads to the ground, held them firmly in place, and she had found the sadness in their eyes, the shock in their beaks, as they realized they were forever bound to the earth. It was Juliette's grief, spilling from Elise's hands—*a flock of birds, so many of them, taking flight with nowhere to go*—and she knew she had, after a long drought, shaped something special. She felt, for the first time in a while, that everything might be all right.

But as she emerged into the salon, depleted, the muscles in her arms, shoulders, and back singing in relief and distress, she could hear excited shouts from the street below, sounds that hadn't reached her while she was in her closed studio. The herringbone oak floor was cold beneath her bare feet, though the breeze through the open double windows was still balmy. Night had fallen while she'd worked, and as the baby shifted in her belly, Elise felt uneasy. She looked to the ornate clock above the marble fireplace. It was past eight o'clock, and Olivier still wasn't home. Something was wrong.

Elise crossed to the windows and pushed them open a bit wider, gazing over the wrought iron balcony. Below, on the usually quiet avenue Mozart, people milled about, some waving French flags, some arguing loudly, one man on the corner drunkenly singing "La Marseillaise" while embracing a lamppost. Elise watched, her stomach swimming. There was no reason to think that the stir below had to do with Olivier and the small circle of artists he huddled with in cafés, discussing their hatred of Daladier's government. There were rumors of retribution against agitators, and Olivier wasn't always as circumspect as he should be about his leftist leanings. Could there have been a police action tonight, ordered by the government?

But then she heard the key turning in the lock to their apartment door, and her whole body sagged with relief as she turned and saw Olivier enter, his dark hair, usually swept back by pomade, loose and unkempt, his eyes bright. His shirt was half tucked, torn at the sleeve, and his expression was wild, filled with a strange brew of fear and exhilaration.

"Darling?" she began, striding toward him, her concern spiking when she saw a thin ribbon of blood above his right eyebrow.

"It has happened, Elise." He tripped forward into the apartment, flinging the door closed behind him, and it was then that she realized he was drunk.

"Olivier . . . ?" She reached out for him, wishing to comfort him, whatever it was that was wrong, but he impatiently swatted her hand away. He didn't want comfort; he didn't want her.

"The war, Elise," he said, his eyes glimmering with something dangerous. "Where on earth have you been all afternoon? Hiding under a rock? Hitler has invaded Poland. The war has begun!"

CHAPTER FOUR

Two days after Germany invaded Poland, France and England had declared war, and though not much had changed in the French capital yet, Juliette could feel it, the palpable tension, the shift in the air, the way people cast their eyes downward now when they passed each other on the street. A week later, she and Paul were still walking around in a daze, waiting for something terrible to happen.

War has come to Europe again. The thought of what was to come paralyzed her, because in war, no one was safe. She knew that firsthand; she had been only five in 1918 when her mother had received the telegram saying that her father had lost his life somewhere near the Marne and wouldn't be coming back to their little blue cottage in Connecticut. Juliette had watched her mother struggle, and then later marry a man simply because she needed someone to take care of her and to keep a roof over the head of her daughter.

Paul had known war, too; he had been seventeen when the

Great War began, and he'd enlisted just after. He had fought for nearly the entirety of the conflict before his right leg was injured by an explosion in his trench in 1918. He'd been sent home, and even now, he wouldn't talk to Juliette about the things he'd seen. "It is too painful," he told her sometimes. "I don't want my nightmares to bleed into your dreams. I am lucky to have come home."

With Paul, Juliette had found family. Belonging. The other half of her soul. She had never believed in things like that before she met him; all-encompassing love was something for novels and stage plays, not something one could find in real life. Certainly her mother and stepfather had never had it. But Paul was as real as they came, and somehow, she fell a little more in love with him each day. She kept waiting for her fluttering heart to level out and settle into a familiar rhythm, but then she'd see him whispering conspiratorially with Claude or rocking Alphonse to sleep, or she'd catch him staring at her with wonder from across the room or caressing her pregnant belly while he thought she was asleep, and her pulse would quicken once more, just like it had when they first met.

Did Elise LeClair have that, too? Juliette wasn't sure why she was still thinking about the woman so many days later, when the specter of an oncoming conflict should have pushed everything else aside.

"Will France go to war?" Claude had asked that morning, his eyes as round as saucers. Paul and Juliette had exchanged concerned looks, and then Juliette had said brightly, "It is nothing for you to worry about, my dear! We are safe and sound!" Claude had seemed appeased, but then she'd caught Paul looking at her again, and the doubt in his expression took her breath away. They *would* be all right, wouldn't they? After all, the fighting was far away, to the east. And the borders of France were fortified, impenetrable.

But one of her best customers, Ruth Levy, a widow who lived a few blocks away, had come in that morning with her children, Georges and Suzanne, and was now pacing the aisles nervously as the children played with Claude and Alphonse. Ruth had come from Germany after the Great War to marry her French husband, who had died just a few years ago. She had been talking about the prospect of war since the night the previous November that rioters across Germany had destroyed Jewish homes, businesses, and synagogues with the encouragement of the Nazi Party. *Kristallnacht*, she'd called it. The night of broken glass. "Hitler is getting bolder," she had said then, her voice trembling. "He won't stop, Juliette."

Ruth and her children were Jewish, Juliette knew, and this morning, Ruth had told her that she hadn't slept since war had been declared. "If the Germans invade," she had said when she came into the shop, her voice hushed, "I fear the children and I aren't safe anywhere."

Juliette had tried to reassure her, but Ruth had shaken her head, her lips pressed together, and wandered off to browse.

Now Juliette was distracting herself by reshelving the books in the children's section, placing them back in alphabetical order by author, when she heard the soft ding of the bell on the front door. She stood and brushed the dust from her knees, relieved to have another customer to focus on.

"I'm coming!" she called out as she rounded the corner from the children's section into the main room of the store. She broke into a grin when she saw who was standing there. "Elise!" she exclaimed. "I wasn't sure you'd return!"

"I have been eager to come back," the other woman said, her

smile not erasing the lines of concern on her face. "To be honest, the last time I felt like myself was here."

Juliette smiled, trying to understand how it was possible not to feel exactly like oneself all the time. The two women exchanged kisses on both cheeks. "I've been worried about you," Juliette said as she stepped back. "How are you? Have you had any more frights since that day in the park?"

Elise put a hand on her growing belly. "I think the baby is fine. I really must thank you for what you did for me. It was truly kind of you to—"

"Nonsense." Juliette cut her off with a smile. "It was the least one mother could do for another. And how fortunate for me to have met a fellow American." Juliette beckoned for Elise to follow her as she began moving into the store. "Come. One of my regular customers is here with her children. I'll introduce you."

Ruth was gazing absently at a row of travel guidebooks as they approached. "Ruth," Juliette said. Ruth turned, her expression far away. "I'd like you to meet my new American friend, Madame LeClair. Elise, this is Madame Levy."

"*Bonjour*, Madame Levy," Elise said politely.

"Bonjour." Ruth gave Elise a polite nod, but she still looked lost in her own world.

Juliette put a gentle hand on Ruth's arm. "Let's go see what the children are reading. Elise, you can meet Georges and Suzanne."

Both women followed Juliette to the children's section, and they all watched as Georges read dramatically to the other children from *L'Oeuf magique*, one of Claude's favorite picture books.

"He can read?" Elise asked, and when Ruth smiled, a genuine smile, Juliette's heart felt a bit lighter.

"He is very proud of himself," Ruth said, her eyes never leaving her son. "I am proud, too."

When Georges finished his story, he snapped the book triumphantly closed. The three women burst into spontaneous applause, and Georges laughed and came over to wrap his arms around his mother's waist. His sister followed him over, as did Juliette's two little boys.

Juliette put a hand on each of her sons' heads. "Alphonse, Claude, my darlings, do you remember Madame LeClair?" Alphonse nodded, and Claude continued to stare at Elise.

"You're all right, madame?" Claude asked Elise, worry shining in his eyes.

"I am," she assured him. "Thank you, Claude, for being so kind. The water you brought me helped very much."

His cheeks turned pink. "Good," he mumbled.

"Georges, Suzanne, this is Madame Foulon's friend, Madame LeClair," Ruth said to her children, who looked up at Elise with curiosity. Suzanne gave a shy little wave, and Georges seemed to be assessing her.

"You look very fancy," he said, which made Elise laugh.

"I promise you, I am not fancy at all. You are a very good storyteller, by the way."

He waved her words away. "Do you live in a grand apartment, then?" he asked. "You look like you live in a grand apartment with lots of fancy dishes and maybe even a maid."

"Georges!" Ruth chided. "That's quite an impolite question!"

"It's perfectly all right," Elise said with a laugh. "My apartment is large, Georges, but not especially grand, and to be honest, I tend to drop fancy dishes when I'm washing them. It's my curse."

Georges regarded her suspiciously. "So you don't have a maid to do your washing up, then?"

"Georges!" Ruth chided again, color rising in her cheeks, but Elise brushed the protest away.

"No, we haven't a maid," she said. "And the only reason our apartment is large is that my husband and I are artists. We both have studios there."

"You're an artist?" Georges echoed, his eyes wide now. Juliette was looking at Elise in surprise, too. "What do you paint?"

"Actually, my husband is a painter, but I carve things from wood."

"You said your last name is LeClair?" Ruth was staring at Elise, too, something in her expression having shifted. "You're not the wife of Olivier LeClair, are you?"

Elise went pink, and her smile wobbled a bit. "Yes, in fact, I am. You know of him?"

"Yes, of course." Ruth looked impressed. "My husband—who died when the children were small—was an art collector. Olivier LeClair was one of his favorites. He would have loved to meet you."

"I'm very sorry to hear about your husband, Madame Levy," Elise said.

"Thank you. But to be honest, sometimes I think that if we were going to lose him anyhow, it's good that he was gone before the world entered into another war. He fought for France in the Great War, you see, and when we first married, he told me he was frightened that our countries would once again be at odds. I fear what will happen now that they are."

Elise didn't seem to know what to say to that, and neither did Juliette, but finally, she said, "Please, Ruth, try not to worry. France will not go the way of Germany. You are safe here."

"For now, Juliette." Ruth held her gaze. "For now. But the Germans are coming for all of us, no matter what the newspapers say."

• • •

That evening after closing up the bookshop, Juliette stood at the stove of their small kitchen, absently stirring leek soup. She couldn't stop thinking about Madame Levy's words.

"You look as though you are carrying the weight of the world," Paul said, entering the kitchen with Alphonse in his arms and Claude trailing behind. He set Alphonse down gently in his wooden high chair and came up behind Juliette, putting his hands on her shoulders and squeezing her tensed muscles. He nuzzled her ear, sending a shiver of pleasure down her spine. "What is it, my love? Are you all right?"

Juliette glanced at the children; Claude was scribbling stick figures on a sheet of paper and showing his creations to Alphonse. "Ruth Levy came in today. She's very worried about the war."

Paul's hands on her shoulders stilled, and he was silent for a few seconds. "I am, too."

Juliette turned and locked gazes with her husband. Paul's brown eyes always darkened, the pupils dilating, when he was concerned, and now, they looked black as night. "But surely our soldiers will turn the Germans back," she said.

"What if they don't? We will survive. But Madame Levy . . ." His voice trailed off in anguish. "I don't know, Juliette. I don't know. I fear she is in a bad position."

Later, after Paul and the children had gone to bed, Juliette sat in the kitchen, her battered copy of Fitzgerald's *This Side of Paradise* opened in front of her. Reading usually brought her comfort, but tonight, she couldn't focus. Ruth's words continued to march through her head. *The Germans are coming for all of us, no matter what the newspapers say.* What if she was right? What if this quiet, this normalcy, this stability they took for granted now was simply the calm before the storm?

"Maman?" Claude's little voice came from the doorway, and Juliette turned to see her oldest standing there, his worn, brown mohair teddy bear clutched protectively under one arm. "Maman, are you all right?"

She set the book down and stood up, crossing the kitchen and kneeling down so that they were eye to eye. "My darling, why aren't you asleep?"

"I heard you." He sniffled and wiped his nose with the back of his free hand. "Maman, what's wrong?"

"It's nothing, sweet boy." She pulled him into her arms, feeling his heartbeat against hers. "There is nothing you should worry about. Go back to sleep, my love."

He let her hold him for a few seconds, but then he pulled away. "Maman, I am big. You don't have to protect me anymore. Is it Madame Levy? Is she in danger?"

Claude seemed to see everything. "Not right now, my love. Not right now."

"But I heard you and Papa talking . . ."

Juliette felt a pang of guilt. She knew better than to speak of worrisome things in front of the children; Claude was always listening, even when he seemed to be occupied with something else. He would grow up one day to be a kind, thoughtful man, like Paul. "My darling boy, everything is fine just now. We are safe, all of us."

She could feel him tense, and then relax as he leaned into her shoulder. "Do you promise me, Maman?"

"I promise. Now, let's get back to bed, shall we?" But as she picked him up, his body heavy in her arms, she felt a chill.

She sat beside him on the edge of his bed, rubbing his back until he fell asleep, but in the silence, with his heavy breathing and an occasional sleep-soaked mumble from Alphonse the only sounds, her skin prickled with the sense of something terrible coming their way. She put her hand on her belly, trying to comfort the baby, who was kicking now, as if she wanted to get out. "It's okay, my love," she whispered into the darkness. "I will protect you." But when the words went nowhere, impotent in the stillness, she wondered whether she could really promise anything when the future was unknowable, the storm clouds rolling in.

CHAPTER FIVE

Now that the war was on, Olivier had become a new man whose eyes always glittered, who barely slept, and who rarely inhabited the bed he shared with Elise anymore.

"You must be careful," she told him over dinner one night in early October, the first night he had deigned to make an appearance at their table in weeks. Each day, she prepared a meal, hoping he would talk to her, and each night, he came in the door later and later, usually past midnight, often mumbling about Communist Party meetings he'd attended in secret. Sitting across from him now, over a roasted chicken nestled on a bed of greens, she could practically feel him vibrating, humming with anger.

"Careful?" He looked up at her, his eyes glinting. He brandished the knife in his hand and then sliced through one of the juicy legs of the bird without moving his gaze from her face. "*Careful*, Elise? Do you hear yourself?" He looked down at the steaming chicken, pulled the leg onto his own plate, and then, after a pause, sliced a small piece of the breast meat for her. "Daladier is going to roll right over, the old bastard. Don't you see it?

We're all that's left. People like me, we're the only ones standing up to what's coming! You want me to be *careful* rather than doing my duty to France? To mankind?"

"No," she said quietly as he pushed her plate across the table to her and dove into his own chicken leg, not bothering with a knife and fork, eating like a caveman gnawing on a bone. He looked wild, his hair askew, his whole body jittery, as if he wanted to jump out of his own skin. "I want you to remember that you're about to be a father. That your duty isn't only to France. It is to this baby. And to me."

He paused, the chicken leg suspended in air, as he glanced first at Elise's belly, then at her face. She couldn't quite read his expression, but then he blinked a few times, and when he looked up again, there was something softer in his eyes. "I know, Elise. I know."

She waited for him to say more, but that seemed to be it. He ate the rest of his chicken leg in silence, then he reached for the other leg, sliced it cleanly off, and ate that one, too. She took a few bites of the breast on her plate, not because she was hungry, but because she knew she needed to feed the growing baby. She rubbed her belly, feeling a strange blend of emptiness and fullness at the same time.

That night, Olivier finished his work early; he had vanished into his studio to paint, so she had assumed she wouldn't see him again, but as she nervously cleaned the kitchen top to bottom, the clock ticking past ten, he appeared in the doorway, the sharp scent of turpentine clinging to him like a layer of armor.

"I've done it, Elise," he said, his eyes burning with something different now, something like hope. "Come see."

She set down her dishrag and walked after her husband, real-izing as she moved in his shadow that she would follow him anywhere. Was that a sign of strength or weakness, the fierce loving of someone who didn't let you in? He took her hand and smiled at her, a real smile, not one twisted with the anguish and fire of chasing a cause, and then opened the door to his studio.

The acrid smell of fresh paint assaulted her nose and made her stomach lurch, a side effect of pregnancy that had startled her when it first appeared, but as she followed him into the room, she quickly forgot the discomfort as she gazed around in awe.

There were four large easels set up, one in each corner of the studio, each holding a large canvas. What Olivier had painted on them over the course of the past few days was breathtaking.

In the north corner of the room, a tangle of broken chains snaked through a burning battleground, a discarded Phrygian cap, the color of blood, with its singular bent apex, in the corner of the frame, smoke rising from it. "*Liberté*," Elise murmured, turning to the painting in the east corner, which seemed set on the same flaming field, the French Revolution's winged woman rising from the ashes, a teardrop of blood falling from her right eye as she reached in vain for a stone tablet. "*Égalité*," Elise said, turning once more, to the painting in the south corner. In it, a bundle of rods wrapped in torn ribbons of blue, white, and red, representing France, sat in the center of the fiery field, the symbol of unity born from the French Revolution, representing the strength of togetherness. But in Olivier's painting, the rods were burning, and the soldiers standing around the bundle were tossing logs into a pyre, feeding the flames. "*Fraternité*," she whispered.

But it was the fourth painting, the one in the west corner of the room, that left her short of breath. It was a heavily pregnant woman, standing in the same burning battlefield, one hand on her rounded belly, the other clutching a sickle by her side as she looked toward a rising sun to the east. From this angle, one could see that beyond the battlefield lay endless fields of grain. From the woman's eyes fell tiny red tears in the shape of stars, forming a pool of blood beneath her feet. She was looking skyward, her face anguished, toward dark clouds gathering on a sunrise horizon. It was the most overtly communist thing Olivier had ever painted—the stars and sickle left no doubt—and though it was stunningly beautiful, it would spell the end of Olivier's career, and perhaps even his life, if it was ever displayed.

"You can't. . . ." It was all Elise could manage to say as she turned to him, her eyes damp, her heart thudding with something she couldn't quite name.

"Why can't I?" Olivier asked, his voice low and thrumming with anger.

"You will put yourself in danger," she said at last. She looked back at the woman in the field. "You will put *us* in danger."

Olivier took a step closer and folded his hand around hers, following her gaze to the painting. "She is you, you know. You were the inspiration. You inspire me."

The woman didn't look like Elise, except for the swollen belly, and she wondered if the words were a lie to placate her. She wanted to be by her husband's side, fighting for France, fighting for a path forward, but this wasn't the way. This was a road that would destroy them both and harm their unborn child in the process, for if the baby was born into a world in which his parents were marked as traitors, there would only be grief and despair ahead. Already, there were rumblings that Daladier's government would ban communist propaganda, perhaps even impose the death penalty for those found guilty of creating it. And while the first three paintings could be construed as nationalist, the fourth was undoubtedly a nod to Moscow. "No," she said. "No, my love, you have not painted me. I would protect my baby at all costs."

"But don't you see, Elise? That's what I'm trying to do!" He pulled away from her, raking both hands through his thick hair, disappointment radiating from him. "You act like this art is self-ish, but it is what is inside me, Elise, all of it. It is what I'm called to do. It's my duty."

"But your duty has already alienated you from your peers," she said. "Your dedication to the party and their ideals of art and culture have forced us out of the circles we used to be a part of. Think of what Picasso said the last time we were there!"

When Elise had first arrived in Paris, she had been welcomed with open arms at the studio of the famed Spanish painter on the rue des Grands-Augustins. Olivier hadn't been part of Picasso's inner circle, exactly, but he'd been an accepted member of Paris's artistic community. Elise used to dream that one day, the artists who gathered in Picasso's salon would see her as belonging, too, but in that orbit, women were too often treated as subjects rather than creators, with few exceptions. She had said that to Olivier once, and he had bristled, defending Picasso and bringing up Picasso's respect for his partner, photographer Dora Maar, as an example; but as Olivier's relationship with the painter had soured over their difference of opinion about art as a social statement, he had admitted to Elise that he'd seen her point.

Anger flashed across Olivier's face. "They're all communists, too, Elise, even if they can't admit it to themselves."

"Do you even know what you're fighting for, Olivier? Do you even understand this movement you seem so willing to lay your life down for?"

Olivier didn't seem to hear her. "Pablo has André Gide in his ear anyhow, mumbling about censorship and freedom."

As she looked around at the paintings again, she felt the baby stir. Until now, Olivier had kept his communist leanings to himself, attending party meetings in secret, managing to keep the imagery out of his art. But letting the world see this painting, as the continent slid into war, would put them in great danger. She imagined this moment as a tiny snowball clutched in Olivier's fist at the top of a mountain. If she let him release it, it would roll down the incline, gathering size and speed, until it flattened and destroyed everything in its path.

"Olivier . . ." she began, reaching for him, and then his lips were on hers, and his hands were under the cool cotton of her nightgown, ice on her hot skin, and as he led her from the studio toward the bedroom, his fingers painted the curves of her body, and she forgot, as she often did, just what she was fighting for. As he fell on top of her on their bed, pulling her gown over her head and tangling his fingers in her long hair, she pulled him closer, imagining that with the warmth of her body, she could keep them all safe against the gathering storm.

Later, Olivier snored peacefully beside Elise while she wiped tears of despair away. He only seemed to see her these days when he wanted the closeness of her; at all other times, his indifference cut her to the core.

She owed Olivier everything, and perhaps that was what made it so difficult when it felt to her, sometimes, that he was trying to erase her.

When they'd met at a meeting of the Artists Union in New York, back in 1935, she'd only been in the city for a couple of years. She was trying to make her way as a clay sculptor, but the Depression had hit artists hard, and she was barely scraping by. She knew she had more in her, but she couldn't seem to coax her visions from the clay. She'd been on the verge of giving up and returning to Kansas, where her only living family member, her great-aunt Berthe, had told her she would be welcome as long as she pitched in around the farm. It would have meant giving up her dream, but perhaps it was the responsible thing to do.

She's been attending Artists Union meetings every Wednesday night for more than a year, hopeful that she'd feel inspired by being among a group of her peers, praying that their advocacy for government funding of the visual arts would buy her more time. But at those meetings, she often felt overwhelmed, out of her depth. Artists like Byron Browne, Bernarda Bryson, and Annelies Cash were already doing incredible things, and who was she? Just some nobody from Kansas with oversize dreams and a dwindling bank account.

But then Olivier LeClair—already a big name in the Parisian art scene—had appeared at her side. He was in town for an exhibition of his work at the new Museum of Modern Art, and he had come to the Artists Union meeting to see what it was all about. Everyone knew who he was, of course, and so Elise was acutely aware of him as the crowd shifted, parting like the Red Sea. Somehow, he wound up standing beside her as Byron droned on and on about government responsibility in work relief for artists.

"You're too pretty to be an artist," he had whispered in her ear, his breath warm, his accent tantalizingly French, though his English was flawless.

She was too shocked to respond at first. Olivier LeClair was talking to *her*? Besides, how was one supposed to reply to a statement like that? She was fairly sure it was meant to be a compliment, but she felt a strange urge to defend herself.

"*Je suis sculpteuse*," she whispered back, her cheeks flaming. She had taken French classes all the way through school and was proud of her fluency, but the moment the words were out of her mouth, she felt like a fool.

He didn't say anything for a moment, and she was certain that she'd said the wrong thing. Then he leaned in again, his lips brushing her ear. "I'd like to see your work," he said in English, his voice like honey. "If you'd show me."

She'd felt hundreds of eyes on them as they crept through the crowd a few minutes later, leaving the meeting early. It was a snowy January day, and as they walked the dozen blocks to the apartment she shared with two other female artists—both of whom were still at the meeting—she felt warm beneath her coat, even though the night was frigid.

In her apartment, he'd been a perfect gentleman as he'd walked around the sculptures on her worktable—a dancing woman, an old man working in a cornfield, a child chasing a ball—examining them carefully, reaching out now and then to run his fingers over the curves of the bodies she'd brought to life.

"Would you care for a drink?" she'd asked abruptly, breaking the silence between them.

He'd looked up sharply, almost as if surprised to realize she was still there. "You're good," he said instead of answering, sending another wave of heat to her cheeks. "But you sculpt with grief, and grief doesn't serve clay well."

She blinked at him a few times. No one had ever said anything like that to her before, nor had she ever considered that her sadness was pouring from her fingers. "I—" She hesitated. "My parents were killed in an automobile accident a few years ago, when I was nineteen, back in Kansas. They were all I had. I moved to New York after that."

"Have you tried sculpting in wood?" he asked, finally looking at her. His eyes seemed to penetrate her soul.

"Wood?"

"I think you'd be good at it. Grief, I think, coats the clay. But wood absorbs sadness and anger and loss. And there's something about the physical act of chipping away the layers, of using your whole body to coax form from nothingness, that allows you to work out your pain."

"Oh." It had been all she could think of to say.

"If you'll allow me, I'll return tomorrow with some chisels. You'll see."

"All right," she had said, completely confused. Olivier LeClair was going to teach her to sculpt wood? Why? It seemed like something out of a dream.

He stepped closer to her then, close enough that he could have kissed her. She wanted him to, she suddenly realized, wanted it with every fiber of her being. But instead, he just looked into her eyes and, without breaking a smile, said, "Good night." And then he was gone before she could move.

Within a week, he had given her her first dozen chisels and gouges—a beautiful gift for a beautiful artist, he'd said—and she had moved into his bed at the Algonquin. He had added an extra month onto his stay in New York, and by the time he was due to depart that April, she had become both a wood-carver and his wife. When he went back to Paris, she went with him, leaving behind everything she had once been, and transforming herself— like a carved block of wood—into something entirely new.

CHAPTER SIX

Over the next months, autumn rolled toward winter, the leaves crisping on the trees before fluttering to the ground, and though the world was at war, there was much joy within the walls of the bookshop on the rue Goblet. Juliette's belly swelled, and by the time December arrived, she felt like she was the size of the ship that had brought her to France from America back in 1934. Paul doted on her now, bringing her glasses of water, asking every hour or so if she might prefer to sit. And though Juliette was exhausted, her feet tired and swollen, she didn't want to miss a moment with her children.

Elise came by more often now, too, at least once a week. The other woman was convinced that she was bearing a boy, but the more heavily pregnant Elise grew, the more obvious it was she was carrying very high, a sure sign of a girl.

"What shall we name the baby?" Paul asked one quiet day in early December as Claude played with Alphonse in the children's section and he and Juliette shelved books. A small fire crackled in the hearth, spilling warmth into the cold store. Outside, icicles clung to the window frames.

"I was thinking perhaps Lucie," said Juliette instantly. "It means light. And we need that right now, don't we? Light in the darkness."

"Lucie." Paul smiled. "You're so certain the baby is a girl?"

"I am."

"And if it's not?"

"Oh, but it is."

Paul smiled and pulled her into his arms, then kissed her tenderly on the top of the head. She leaned into his chest, listening to his heartbeat, feeling the baby safe and warm between them. How lucky this child would be to be born into a family so full of love, even if war threatened outside their borders. Already, she felt they'd dodged a bullet, as Paul's age and injured leg had kept him from being conscripted. As long as they had each other, they'd be safe, wouldn't they?

On the sixteenth of December, the third anniversary of the day Antoinette had slipped quietly from the world, Juliette was opening the store like usual, straightening the rows and tidying the register while the boys played, when Ruth Levy bustled through the door, Suzanne and Georges in tow.

"Hello, Ruth," Juliette said, stepping from behind the register to kiss her favorite customer on both cheeks. She had rather hoped that today would be a slow day, with few patrons, but if the shop was to be busy, there was no one else she'd rather start the morning with. She smiled slightly as Ruth's children bounded over to Alphonse and Claude and began chattering excitedly.

"Juliette," Ruth said, taking Juliette's hands. "I'd like to offer to watch over your children and the store for a little while."

Juliette frowned, confused. "But why?"

"Because today is the day, is it not?" she asked gently.

Juliette pulled away, the words searing her. "You remembered?"

"Of course I did." Ruth's voice was so warm, so full of concern, that it broke the false dam Juliette had constructed, and before she knew it, there were tears pooling in her eyes. "The losses never leave us, Juliette," Ruth said. "They make us who we are." She paused and added, "Where is Monsieur Foulon?"

Juliette glanced toward the children, who were playing happily together. "He went out this morning to queue at Monsieur Lychner's butcher shop. I'm certain he'll be back soon."

Ruth clapped her hands together, and then made a shooing motion toward the door. "Go, my friend. Go to the cemetery. We must honor those we've lost. I will look after the children until you return."

Juliette wiped fresh tears from her eyes. "Are you certain? I would never ask you to—"

"You haven't asked," Ruth interrupted firmly. "I have offered. We will be fine."

Juliette lingered for only a second longer before nodding, grabbing her hat and coat, and hurrying toward the door. But when she got there, she found an invisible string holding her back. She glanced once more at the four children. "Ruth?"

Ruth looked up.

Juliette didn't quite know how to put her question into words. "The Jewish situation here in Paris . . ." she began. Though the Germans hadn't tried to invade France with their armies, it seemed they had sent their propaganda to stake a claim instead. Just days before, Juliette and Paul had walked past a large poster with an exaggerated caricature of a man with a huge nose, his face obscured by a big red X, the word JUIF printed below in huge block letters. Paul had glanced around, and then quickly ripped it down, crushing it into a ball.

A shadow moved across Ruth's face. "Go see your baby, Juliette. There will be plenty of time to talk later."

As Juliette donned her hat and stepped outside into the sharp December wind, she was already chilled to the bone, not by Ruth's words, but by the deep sadness in her eyes.

The dark sky and icy air signaled a coming snowfall, and Juliette's cheeks and nose were already numb with cold as she hurried toward the cemetery where her little girl slept forever beneath the frozen earth.

What good was looking backward when life stretched before you, when there were so many beautiful things to reach for, to strive for? When she cracked and allowed herself a moment of grief, she always wondered if this would be the time she'd break, if she'd be swept away by the deep and swirling current of sadness that lived within her, the one that tried, from time to time, to pull her under.

The walk to the cemetery, near the spot where the Seine curved to cradle the southern end of Boulogne-Billancourt, took twenty minutes, but Juliette was lost in her own thoughts, her own memories, and so it seemed she arrived in no time.

Entering through the gates, she could feel a tightening in her chest. In her everyday life, she could set aside her failure as a mother. But here, it was all she could think of, the way she had not done enough to keep her daughter safe and well. How could a mother live with that?

As she rounded the corner past the mausoleum that sat just

beside her own modest family plot, Juliette stopped in her tracks. There was already someone there, standing over Antoinette's grave. "Paul," she said, and her husband turned, his eyes bloodshot, his face damp with tears. He swiped at his cheeks and tried to rearrange his features, but then his face crumpled.

"I—I thought you were coming later," he said.

She approached, and he put his arm around her, pulling her close. "Why didn't you tell me you would be here, my love?" she asked.

He was silent for a few seconds before speaking. "I didn't want you to see me in pain. I must be strong for you."

Seeing Paul this way shook Juliette, but not because she needed his strength. It was because she hadn't realized he'd been feeling this way, too. She hadn't seen him shed a tear over Antoinette after the week they'd lost her. She'd assumed he'd put it all behind him in a way she hadn't been capable of. "You needn't be strong. I only want you to be *you*."

She looked up at him, and then, as they stared into each other's eyes, the rest of their conversation unfolded without a word.

Later, leaning into Paul as they headed back toward the bookstore along the winding paths of the cemetery, Juliette put a hand to her belly and made a silent promise to the baby that she would protect her, always, whatever it took.

"If war comes to France," she said after a few minutes, and Paul pulled her closer, "what will we do? How will we keep the children safe?"

He stopped short, bringing her to a halt with him. The sea of people on the sidewalk, laden with holiday presents and bent against the snow, parted around them as Paul moved his hands to cup Juliette's face. His gloves were cold, but somehow, his touch warmed her. "I won't let anything happen to you, my love. I would fight with my last breath for you and the children."

"But what if . . . ?" She could hardly bring herself to complete the sentence. "What if something happened anyhow? How would we bear it if we lost another child, Paul?"

"We would break on the inside," Paul said at last, his hands falling helplessly to his sides. "We would shatter, wouldn't we? But we would do our best to mend the broken pieces. We would put one foot in front of the other until we learned to walk again. And then we would go where the road took us. There is no other way forward in life, Juliette. We must play the hand we are dealt. But, my love, the children will always be here, and I will always be by your side. I promise."

Tears welled in Juliette's eyes. She knew as well as Paul did that he was making a vow he might not be able to keep. But she couldn't say that. Instead, she whispered, "How did I get so lucky?"

"I'm the lucky one, my Juliette," Paul replied. He gazed into her eyes once more and then leaned down to touch his lips to hers. The snow drifted down and they stood frozen in time, clinging to each other, until finally they pulled apart and headed for the bookstore, where Alphonse and Claude—their reasons for living—were waiting.

CHAPTER SEVEN

Elise went into labor on the first day of 1940 and delivered her baby twenty-four hours later, on the second of January. To her surprise, Juliette had been right; it was a girl after all. Olivier's dark eyes twitched, his eyebrows pitching together in the middle when he held his daughter for the first time, and Elise could feel the weight of his disappointment.

"Mathilde," she said from her bed in the Le Belvédère clinic as he inspected the baby, as if checking for flaws. Elise already knew their daughter was perfect. "Let's name her Mathilde. It means strength."

"You've thought about girls' names," Olivier said, and she could hear the accusation in his voice, as though she'd borne a daughter rather than a son simply to spite him.

But she was too exhausted to engage, and so she simply nodded and held out her arms, already missing the tiny weight of her daughter. Olivier handed the baby back and took a quick step away.

"Mathilde will do," he said. "When you are well enough, Elise, we will try for a boy."

"Such romantic words of seduction, my darling," she said under her breath, but if he heard her, he gave no indication. Instead, muttering that he needed to tend to some matters, he gave her a perfunctory kiss on the cheek and, without looking at his daughter again, headed for the door.

Elise gazed down at the newborn in her arms, her limbs still red from the exertion of her entrance into the world, her skin loose like the folds of a puppy's neck. She was no larger than a loaf of bread, and much more delicate, and though Elise had seen very young babies before, she had never held one, never realized how simultaneously light and heavy a newborn would feel in her arms. If she moved incorrectly, would she hurt her daughter? What if she dropped her? The thought paralyzed her at first, but as the baby blinked up at her with clear blue eyes, she gradually relaxed. She was this child's mother. She would keep her safe, always.

"Mathilde," she murmured. "Welcome to the world."

But what sort of world was she welcoming her daughter into? The future was suspended in air like a feather on the breeze, slowly, slowly drifting down.

"I will keep you safe, little one," she murmured, kissing her daughter's forehead. "I swear it." She inhaled deeply, filling herself with the scent of her child, and when the midwife came in and offered to take the baby so that Elise could get some rest, Elise refused to let go. No, the only way to protect Mathilde against whatever was coming was to hold her tight for as long as she could.

Three weeks later, Elise bundled little Mathilde into her wicker bassinet carriage, which had been a gift from Constant Bouet, the smarmy, well-dressed art dealer Olivier sold most of his work to.

She didn't care for him—she had never understood how Olivier couldn't see that he oozed disingenuousness—but she had to admit that he had good taste in presents. She took the rickety lift down to the ground floor and walked out into a blustery January day, heading west. Mathilde began crying immediately, but Elise tucked the blankets around her more tightly, and the infant gazed up at her, soothed.

"It's all right, my sweet girl," she said, bending to kiss her daughter on the cheek. "We are going for a short walk to meet a friend."

Twenty-five minutes later, she pushed through the door of the Librairie des Rêves bookshop and was thrilled to find Juliette behind the counter, cradling a tiny baby the same size as Mathilde.

"Oh, she's perfect!" Elise said, pushing the carriage over to the counter and reaching for Juliette's newborn daughter. Juliette had sent word two weeks earlier that she'd given birth to a healthy baby girl she'd named Lucie. Juliette handed the baby over without hesitation, smiling as she reached into the bassinet to carefully pick up Mathilde.

"Lucie, meet Mathilde," Juliette said, holding up Elise's daughter as she supported her warm head with the crook of her elbow. "Mathilde, this is Lucie."

"My goodness, they could be sisters," Elise said, stroking Lucie's dark hair, as soft as peach fuzz.

"Is it terrible of me that I think all babies look rather the same at first?" Juliette asked with a small smile, touching one of Mathilde's cheeks. "They don't really become themselves until they're older, do they?"

After a while, they each took their daughters back and went to sit in the two armchairs in the children's section. Claude and

Alphonse ran over to get a look at Mathilde before returning to the puzzle they were putting together. "I don't get it," Elise heard the older boy mutter to his brother. "They just look like babies. Big deal."

"He's jealous," Juliette said, her eyes sparkling with amusement as she looked pointedly at Claude, who was grumbling at the puzzle pieces now. Alphonse had picked one up and was gnawing on it. "It was the same when Alphonse was born. It's an adjustment to have another sibling."

"Olivier is hoping we'll have another as soon as possible," Elise said after a pause. "He wishes for a boy."

"Men and their sons. Don't worry. He'll fall in love with his daughter soon enough."

"And your Paul? He is excited about Lucie?"

Juliette's eyes misted over. "He's over the moon. For both of us, I think it feels like a second chance. After Antoinette . . ." She trailed off, and both women bowed their heads. "I wish Lucie could have known her sister."

"I wish I'd known her, too." Elise knew no other reply; to lose a child would be unimaginable, and she held Mathilde a little closer, vowing once again never to let her go.

In the coming weeks, there were many changes within the apartment on avenue Mozart. Foremost was the transformation Olivier seemed to be undergoing. After having mostly avoided his daughter for the first several days of her life, he seemed to have suddenly realized not only that Mathilde was here to stay but that she was his own flesh and blood. He had even begun sketching her, in broad, soft, indistinguishable strokes first, and then in more finite detail, getting the pitch of her forehead, the point of her chin, the curve of her cheeks, the line of her tiny nose just right. And Mathilde, in turn, seemed enamored with her father; she cooed each time he held her, and she stared at him in wonder, tracing the shape of his face with her eyes.

"Are you still disappointed that she's a girl?" Elise asked a month after their daughter had been born.

Olivier looked up at her in shock. "Disappointed? Certainly I never felt that way, Elise."

The infant had, it seemed, given him a case of amnesia, but Elise knew better than to argue. Instead, she stole away to her studio whenever Olivier felt the urge to rock their daughter to sleep, and she used those fleeting moments to begin carving again.

The birds she'd made a few months ago still sat on the shelf, where they reminded Elise that when her heart was awakened, she could do incredible things. And now, just as Olivier sketched the curves of Mathilde's features, Elise had begun to carve them, too, the gentle bow of her daughter's lips, the twin crescents of her brows, the rounded almonds of her eyes. What emerged from the wood during Mathilde's first few months was breathtaking; not only were there nearly endless studies of her daughter's face, which seemed to mature by the day, but there were also carvings of running water, great forests, wise owls, silent doves. There were intricate bowls, elaborate renderings of children playing, lanterns suspended over the earth. Elise felt grounded in a way she hadn't since marrying Olivier, and she wondered if maybe, just maybe, it was a sign that good things were coming, that her world was righting itself. Mathilde was a light in the darkness, a flame in the cold, a magnet drawing Olivier back from the edge.

By the time spring arrived, Elise had almost come to believe that praying away the darkness would be enough, that this would be the year the war ended, that the world might return to normal, sparing France, sparing her, sparing her child.

Maybe for once, hope would be enough. But at night, when Mathilde awakened, mewling for milk, Elise would nurse her daughter at the window, the blackout curtain lifted just a bit, and she'd peer east into the impenetrable darkness, wondering what was out there, what was coming. She could feel danger lurking on the horizon, just out of sight.

CHAPTER EIGHT

On the tenth of May, just after Lucie turned four months old, the Germans invaded Luxembourg, Belgium, and the Netherlands, catching troops by surprise and overrunning their forces almost immediately. By the time the French army made it across the border to try to hold off the onslaught, it was too late; the Dutch were already in full retreat. Four days later, the Netherlands surrendered, followed two weeks afterward by Belgium. Now, nothing stood between the Germans and the French border but the Maginot Line, which the French government continued to proudly tout as the solution to everything.

But there were many who didn't believe it, including Paul, and Ruth Levy, who appeared at the doorway to Juliette's shop on the first of June, her face white, her hands trembling. Juliette set Lucie down in her small wooden playpen behind the counter, the same one Claude and Alphonse had used, so she could assist a shaky Ruth in entering the store. Georges and Suzanne scrambled behind their mother, attempting to hide in the folds of her skirt, until Claude beckoned them away by holding up a copy of *Babar en Famille*, featuring the elephant king all the children had fallen in love with.

"What is it, my friend?" Juliette asked, showing Ruth to a chair beside the counter and returning to Lucie to pick her up. Ruth sat down heavily and wiped damp eyes before reaching out her arms for little Lucie.

"Please," she said. "Let me hold her. It always puts me at ease."

Juliette handed Lucie over and watched with concern as Ruth put her nose to Lucie's head and inhaled deeply, pressing the girl to her bosom. Lucie whimpered a bit but then seemed to adjust to the generous curves of the older woman's body, sighing contentedly. Juliette could feel herself relax a bit, but the grief on Ruth's face was enough to keep her mostly on edge. "What has happened?" she asked.

Ruth's eyes filled. "It is not what *has* happened, but what is about to."

"But Prime Minister Reynaud says—"

"Pfft." Ruth cut her off with a dismissive burst of air. "The government tells us what they want us to hear."

Juliette didn't say anything. The store's grandfather clock ticked the seconds loudly in the quiet, and behind her, she could just hear the soft cadence of Georges's voice as he read the Babar book to the other children. She gazed at Lucie, held in her friend's arms, and felt a pang of deep worry.

Ruth's gaze never left Suzanne and Georges. "In Germany," she said, "the only way to save the children was to send them away."

Her voice was barely audible, but it sent a shiver of foreboding down Juliette's spine anyhow. She reached for Lucie, and Ruth handed her back wordlessly. Juliette pulled her daughter to her chest as if holding her close could protect her from what was to come. "Away?" she finally echoed.

"There are organizations," Ruth continued, her voice flat and so soft that Juliette had to strain to hear her. "They give the children false identities and take them somewhere safe."

"But how are they reunited with their parents, then?"

Ruth studied her hands. "Juliette, the parents are not returning. But the hope . . ." She drew a ragged breath. "The hope is that the children live. That they will survive and tell the world who they really are one day. In that, they will honor their families."

Juliette stared at her friend. The things she was saying couldn't be true. She tried to imagine handing Claude, Alphonse, and Lucie off to a stranger, knowing she might never see them again. But how could she do such a thing? How could anyone? A mother's job was to stay with her children, to protect them at all costs, wasn't it? "The world has gone mad," she whispered. The grandfather clock ticked into the quiet, and Juliette could just hear the cheerful cadence of Georges's voice, reading about elephant royalty, an imaginary world that suddenly seemed more reasonable than the real one. "Such things will not happen here, though," she added with more ferocity than she intended.

"Juliette," Ruth said, her tone as gentle as if she was talking to a child. "Such things can happen anywhere as long as good people look away. It is what happened in Germany. By the time anyone thought to stand up on any large scale, it was too late."

"But here, we still have a chance."

Ruth looked away, to where Claude, Alphonse, and Suzanne sat crowded around little Georges. "Here, we still have a chance," she repeated, but the sound was hollow, and Juliette feared that perhaps the words were, too.

• • •

That night, Juliette lay beside Paul in bed, Lucie's bassinet beside them. Lucie was whimpering in her sleep, and the sound made Juliette want to awaken her daughter, to soothe her, to promise that everything would be all right. She wanted to tell them all—Claude and Alphonse and even Paul—that she would protect them from whatever was coming. But could she?

"I have been hesitating to say this, my darling, but I think perhaps you should leave France," Paul murmured into the darkness sometime past midnight, and Juliette startled at the sound of his voice, which had broken the silent flood of her own worries. She had known that he was awake beside her, but she couldn't bring herself to tell him that she was also staring at the ceiling, wondering what would come.

"Paul, you can't mean that," she said, rolling to face him.

He, too, turned onto his side, and they searched for each other's eyes in the darkness. She could feel his breath on her cheek. "There might still be time."

Juliette closed her eyes, feeling a familiar stab in her gut, the sharp blade of regret and indecision. "I cannot, Paul. Even if there was a way . . ."

"You could save yourself." His voice was barely audible.

"But the children . . ."

"They would go with you." They both knew the words he wasn't speaking. Paul was French; he would not be able to get papers to come. They'd been over this a hundred times in the previous year.

"Not all of the children, though," Juliette said softly.

Paul's breathing grew heavier. "Her soul is not here anymore, my love."

"We don't know that." Juliette thought of little Antoinette's grave, the tiny casket the priest had recited prayers over, the cold earth that had been shoveled on top of it. "I cannot leave her. What kind of a mother would I be? And I will not leave you."

"If something should happen to me one day, my love, you must go. Even if it means leaving Antoinette behind."

"I know." But Juliette couldn't imagine a world without him in it, a world in which she could not visit the grave of her lost child, a world in which she was once again on American soil, her feet planted an ocean away from her destiny.

Paul's words swirled in Juliette's head all week, so she was glad when, on Friday, Elise bustled through the door, pushing Mathilde in her elaborate baby carriage. After they'd exchanged kisses on the cheek, Juliette gestured toward the sales counter. "There's something I'd like to ask you."

Claude and Alphonse were happily playing with toy soldiers in the children's section across the store, which was otherwise empty. Their business had slowed recently as many expatriates fled home, and money tightened for those who stayed.

"What is it?" Elise asked as she settled the carriage beside the counter and reached inside to pick Mathilde up. The girls were five months old now, both of them with heads of thick, dark hair and inquisitive blue eyes. Mathilde looked around, her gaze settling on Lucie, who was sleeping in a bassinet behind the cash register. She cooed in delight and reached out for her friend, which made Juliette smile. In such a short time, she and Elise—and now Mathilde and Lucie—had become inseparable, their friendship cemented by war.

"Paul thinks I should take the children and go back to the States," Juliette said. "Has Olivier said the same to you?"

"No. In fact, he believes the opposite—that if I left, it would be a betrayal of him, that I should stay by his side and stand ready to fight for France." She half smiled to lighten the words, but Juliette could see the concern in her eyes. "Are you thinking of leaving, then?"

Juliette glanced over at Claude and Alphonse, who were thoroughly involved in their game of make-believe. This shop was their world, all they'd ever known. "No."

"Because of Antoinette?" Elise guessed, bouncing Mathilde a bit to soothe her restlessness.

Juliette nodded, relieved that her friend understood her so well. "But not only that. I just have the sense that this is where I'm meant to be. Besides, it's almost certainly dangerous to try to leave now, and Paul couldn't come with us. If there was an opportunity to go, I fear we've already missed it."

"And with Lucie and Mathilde so young, how could we take them away from their fathers? That thought has haunted me, too."

"But have we made a mistake? What if we're not safe here? What if something happens, and we could have made a different choice?"

Mathilde whimpered a bit, distracting them as she reached out and grabbed a clump of Elise's hair, pulling hard. Elise gently unwrapped Mathilde's fingers and went back to bouncing her. "I think that life is full of roads not taken. And perhaps we're safer here anyhow. There shouldn't be fighting in Paris now that France has fallen, but what if we try to leave and our ship is bombed?"

"There are no good answers."

"Not in the midst of a war." They were both quiet for a moment, and then Elise added, "I also wonder what we'd have to return to, if we went back. My whole family is gone."

"As is mine, except for an aunt I hardly know."

Elise smiled at her. "So we will be each other's family, Juliette. Here we are across an ocean, facing the unknowable. But I have you, and you have me, and our children have each other."

Juliette impulsively reached out and wrapped her arms around Elise. Mathilde, suddenly sandwiched between them, giggled with surprise and pulled Juliette's hair, which made them both laugh. "I've always wanted a sister," Juliette said as she extricated herself from Mathilde's grasp.

"As have I." Elise's smile faded, her expression growing resolute. "Whatever comes, you'll always have me to rely on."

As they held each other's gaze, Juliette felt a great peace settle over her. This was what was meant to be. They would all be safe here, and one day, the war would end, and the Occupation would be just a terrible memory. She put one hand on Mathilde's little cheek, and the other on Elise's shoulder as she looked into Elise's eyes. "And you'll always have me."

❧ CHAPTER NINE ❧

By the following summer, it was too late. Too late to turn back, too late to leave France, too late to claim a future different from the one Elise was blinking down. And it was too late for Olivier to change his fate, too; Elise could see that clearly now. For a while, his meetings with his socialist friends had subsided as they waited for Soviet ideals to come to France, but as time had gone by, the only thing that had happened was that the Germans had pressed their thumbs harder and harder on the backs of the French people.

The previous year, Olivier had begun working with an underground communist group that opposed the Occupation, although the party's official policy was still to support Germany. But by early 1941, the Germans were arresting communists en masse. It was no surprise, then, that when Germany invaded the Soviet Union in June and Stalin ordered all communists to take up arms against them, Olivier had eagerly followed, contacting Picasso's friend Jean Cassou and plunging headfirst into the resistance movement that had been forming since 1940.

He often vanished for days without a word of explanation, and when he returned, always full of apologies, she did her best to forgive him, to hold on to him a little tighter, to make love to him with more passion in hopes of making him stay. But it never worked, and she knew it in her bones that one of these days, he would walk out the door and never return.

"Think of Mathilde," Elise said one balmy August night, their blackout curtains drawn, as they lay atop the rumpled covers of their bed. "Think of the risk to her, should you be discovered. Please, Olivier."

Olivier didn't respond right away, but his fingers trailed absent circles up her inner thighs, under her nightgown. It was hot, the night still, and with the blackout curtains drawn, the air inside their apartment was stagnant and spiked, as always, with turpentine. Olivier had been locked in his studio all day, and he had emerged, paint streaked and buzzing with energy, after Elise had already put Mathilde to sleep. At nineteen months of age, their daughter slept soundly now, except when the night was punctuated by air raid sirens or the percussion of bombs falling in the distance.

"I think of you both," Olivier said. "All the time. It is why I fight, Elise. How else will we reclaim the life we are owed?" His hand was moving higher up her leg now.

"Why must *you* be the one to reclaim it? People *know* you."

"I cannot fail to stand for beliefs simply because I have had success," Olivier said, grunting as he raised himself up on an elbow to look at her. "I must stand for my country. For my wife. For my child. If I cannot do that, how can I look myself in the mirror?"

"But how could you look yourself in the mirror if a choice you make endangers us?" Elise protested, pushing away his hand.

He didn't answer. He shifted his weight onto her, and she could feel the length of him pressing into her thigh. He covered her mouth with his, but her body didn't respond as it normally did, arching into him. This time, she couldn't quiet the voices in her head saying that this was wrong, all wrong, and that his ego would be their downfall. When she didn't kiss him back, he pulled his face away, though he kept his weight on her body, pinning her to the bed. "You worry too much," he said, his voice an angry rumble from somewhere in his chest.

"And you do not worry enough."

"Elise, when I first met you, you took chances. You followed your heart. Your passion. Your *art*." Olivier still hadn't shifted his weight, and now, his nose was just inches from hers. She could taste the whiskey on his breath, could see the dilated blackness of his pupils. "What happened to that woman?" he whispered.

"She became a mother—and she realized there was more to life than trying to make a mark on the world." She twisted away, but Olivier pulled her back, his eyes flashing, and pressed his lips to hers again until she relented and kissed him back. She always did, and somehow, their arguments always ended with them falling into bed, the only thing they seemed to do well together anymore, the only way she knew to cross the widening gulf between them.

Afterward, with Olivier snoring, Elise crept into her studio, and by the light of an oil lamp, she gazed around her. The shelves were stacked with her carvings, but behind them, the walls were bare.

This room had never felt like hers, because she was most at home surrounded by trees and sky. It was why she still ventured to the Bois de Boulogne when she could, often bringing Mathilde there on their way to Juliette's bookshop. She wanted her daughter to know, as Elise did, that she would always be at home under a canopy of nature, the trees living and breathing around her. But it was the star-speckled sky, stretching to infinity, that had always moved Elise the most, for it reminded her that God watched over them all wherever they were. They'd been living under curfew orders for Mathilde's whole life, and her daughter had never seen the stars. Elise missed the grounding force of standing outside on a clear night and simply breathing in and out as the sky twinkled above.

All at once, Elise knew what she had to do, for both herself and Mathilde. First, she moved the shelves out from against the wall. Then, she crept quietly into Olivier's studio, where she selected several jars of paints and some brushes, large and small. Before she'd met him, she had dabbled in painting, too, and though she had never been as adept with a brush as he was, she had enjoyed it. When she had dared to paint canvases a few times in their first year of marriage, though, Olivier had laughed at her work, telling her—like they were on the same side of an inside joke—that she should stick with wood and clay. It had hurt her, but they had been too new and fragile for her to say anything, and gradually, she had simply stopped painting.

Now, as she touched a broad brush to the vibrant colors and then to the wall, she realized she had missed it. And as she began to fill the walls with a forest of her own making—the old-growth oaks and chestnuts that surrounded her each time she walked through the Bois de Boulogne—she felt a little lighter, and the more she painted, the more the weight lifted from her shoulders. As the minutes, and then the hours, ticked by, she roughed out wood and painted the narrow veins of individual leaves, gradually bringing the holt of bark and branch alive. She stood on chairs to reach all the way up the walls, and then on the top of her workbench to reach the ceiling, which she painted in the beautiful deep twilight hue the French called *l'heure bleue*, the blue hour, the short period at the end of the day when the last of the light was fading from the sky and the stars were peeking through. She dotted the heavens with tiny pinpricks of light, sparkling like a faraway dream, and when she was finished, she climbed from her workbench and stared around at all she had done.

It had been six hours, maybe seven, since she had started working. But in that time, Elise had brought the world inside, turning her studio into a glimpse of the heavens. She sat down on the floor, light-headed from the paint fumes, and gazed up at the ceiling. Once the paint dried, she would bring Mathilde here each day to remind her of the world outside their doors, and of the beautiful night sky, even though they were forbidden from seeing it now. "Under these stars," she murmured, "fate will guide you home."

It was something her father had whispered to her once when she was young, when he had taken her outside with his prized telescope to stare at the sky. The heavens over Kansas were deep and endless, and Elise had asked him if he ever worried that they would get lost in a universe so vast. "On the contrary," he'd said, putting an arm around her. "The universe always leads you to exactly where you're meant to be, for though it may be endless, there is a place in it for each and every one of us."

When the oil lamp finally burned out, Elise put her head in her hands. She stayed that way in the darkness until Mathilde, just waking up, began to call out for her, and reality came marching back in.

The walk the next day to Boulogne did little to clear Elise's head, for the heat remained oppressive and sticky. Before the war, she and Olivier had left Paris in the summers, seeking relief in the countryside. But now, there was no thought of holiday, of escape. An invisible boundary pinned them all in place, making it hard to breathe.

"Maman?" Mathilde hurried along beside Elise, her little legs pumping quickly beneath a cotton frock, her glossy walnut curls bouncing around her tiny shoulders. Her cheeks were pink from exertion, but she was determined to walk herself, though Elise knew she would eventually end up picking her daughter up and carrying her the rest of the way. Now, though, the little girl's attention was on a huge poster that took up most of the outer wall of the building to the left of them. "*Qu'est-ce que c'est?*" she asked in French, adding in English, "That?"

Mathilde was just learning her words, but she understood and spoke both her mother's native tongue and her father's. It hadn't been a deliberate decision on Elise's part at first, but as the war had inched closer to France, and as Olivier had slipped further away from them, Elise had begun whispering to her daughter in English, knowing that one day, God willing, they might leave this country behind and return to the States.

Elise's eyes followed her daughter's to a ghastly illustration of an enormous, emaciated buzzard, his claws like curved daggers, poised over the body of a man. The words *Français! Au Secours!*—Frenchmen! Help!—screamed over the bird's head, and the Star of David around its neck left little doubt as to the purpose of the image. She resisted the urge to cover Mathilde's eyes but instead tightened her grip on her daughter's hand and quickened their pace. "It is nothing, my darling," Elise said. "Just a drawing by bad people."

"Star?" Mathilde asked, craning her neck to look over her shoulder at the poster disappearing behind them. "I like stars."

"I like stars, too, my darling," Elise said quickly.

Mathilde's nose scrunched in confusion as she turned back around to focus on the road ahead. "Bad bird."

Elise wiped a tear away with one hand and pulled Mathilde close with the other. "The bird isn't real, my sweet girl. It is something drawn to scare us."

"Bad bird," Mathilde repeated solemnly.

"Sometimes, art is used to bring good into the world," Elise said, perhaps more to herself than her daughter. "And sometimes, it is used to do bad things. Artists have the power to influence the way people think and feel, and sometimes, they don't use that power responsibly."

Mathilde looked up at her, perplexed, but Elise glanced away, because she didn't want her daughter to see the tears in her eyes.

Twenty minutes later, they walked through the doorway to Juliette's shop, and it felt like a bit of the weight had lifted. Elise always felt freer here, her shoulders loosening, her hands unclenching. How was she more herself in this bookshop than she was in her own home, or in her studio, where her art was supposed to be an extension of who she was? The problem was, she wasn't quite sure who that was anymore. But here, she knew. She was a friend. She was a mother. She was a person who wanted nothing more than to see all the people she cared about survive.

"Maman?" asked Mathilde, tugging at Elise's hand. "Where they?"

Elise looked up and realized with a start that Mathilde was right; Juliette was normally in the store this time of day, as were the children, but today, it was so quiet and still that she could hear the sound of her own breath. "I don't know." She tightened her grip on Mathilde's hand and pulled her quickly toward the door at the back, which led to Juliette's apartment.

"Juliette?" Elise called as she pushed the door open a crack. "Are you there?"

There was noise from inside the apartment, and then Juliette emerged, her face white. "Elise. I didn't know you were coming today."

"Is everything all right?"

Juliette's eyes flashed to Mathilde before returning to Elise. "Yes, yes, of course," she said, but Elise could hear the lie in her friend's words. "Come. Ruth Levy and the children are here." She glanced behind Elise, blinking a few times as she seemed to register where her friend had come from. "Was the door unlocked?"

Elise nodded, and Juliette muttered something under her breath, and then hurried past Elise and Mathilde to lock the front door of the shop, turning the sign in to the window to indicate that it was closed. When she rejoined them a moment later, she beckoned them to follow her. "What is happening, Juliette?" Elise asked, but Juliette didn't reply.

They emerged a few seconds later into the parlor, where Madame Levy sat, holding a cup of steaming ersatz coffee in her shaking hands. Paul sat opposite, frowning, while Georges and Suzanne played quietly with Alphonse, Claude, and Lucie on the floor, their faces as somber and drawn as their mother's.

"What is it?" Elise asked, looking from Paul to Madame Levy to Juliette as Mathilde tottered off to sit beside Lucie, who was squinting in concentration as she tried to build a tall stack of wooden blocks.

"There's been another police action," Paul said after a long, awkward pause. "You haven't heard?"

Elise shook her head slowly, a knot forming in her stomach. "Where? What happened?"

Paul opened his mouth to reply, but Madame Levy spoke

first, her tone flat. "The onzième arrondissement, on the other side of Paris. Early this morning. There was an arrest order. All Jewish males between eighteen and fifty, except for Americans. They closed the metros, barricaded the streets, went door-to-door before dawn. If the men weren't home, they took another family member. Women, children."

Elise glanced in horror at Juliette, who looked down.

"The operation isn't done," Paul said, his voice low. "But we're hearing as many as three thousand Jews are on the list in the onzième alone."

Elise struggled to catch up. "But . . . why?"

"They mean to do here just what they've done in Germany." Madame Levy wiped a tear away.

"It's not possible." Elise looked at Juliette and then back at Madame Levy. "Not in France."

"Elise," Madame Levy said, the gentleness of her tone breaking something in Elise. "It was the French police leading this raid. This is what the Germans do. They make things terrible for everyone, and then by the time they begin removing us, no one notices. No one cares. Fewer mouths to feed."

"Certainly no one feels that way," Elise said, turning to Juliette for support. As Elise looked back at Madame Levy, a chill ran through her. "Madame Levy, surely you'll be safe."

"It is not myself I worry about. It is the children," Madame Levy said, her voice barely audible now. "It is why I came to see Juliette today." She glanced at Juliette. "I've received an offer to help Georges and Suzanne."

"Help them?" Elise repeated. She glanced over at the Levy children, who were more subdued than usual, their voices low as they talked to Claude and Alphonse. Lucie and Mathilde were working together now on the stack of blocks.

Madame Levy cleared her throat, but it took a few seconds for the words to come. "Take them away from here. Move them somewhere safe."

"But you . . . ?" Elise asked.

"The offer is only for children. But it would give them a chance to live. I—I think it might be the only choice."

Paul was nodding, Juliette staring at Madame Levy blankly, but Elise couldn't accept it. "No, no. That can't possibly be. They're your children. They should be with—"

"They should be alive," Madame Levy interrupted, her voice shaking. "That is all that matters now—that they live."

Slowly, she explained the situation. The Oeuvre de Secours aux Enfants, the OSE, had been established before the Great War to assist Jewish children and to provide medical services in communities suffering from persecution. Since the start of the war, it had set up a network of children's homes to take in young refugees, mostly from Central Europe and Poland, who had nowhere else to go.

"But you have a home here," Elise said when Madame Levy paused to collect herself. "Your children aren't refugees."

"I'm a foreign-born Jewish widow, Madame LeClair. If I'm not on a list already, I will be soon—and then my children will be alone." Tears pooled in Madame Levy's eyes. "This isn't a decision I make lightly, but being a parent is not about doing what is right for ourselves, is it? It's about sacrificing all we can, big and small, to give our children their best chance at life."

"But there must be another way, a place for all three of you to go together." Elise thought fleetingly of suggesting they come stay with her, but with Olivier's activities and his increasing carelessness about the expression of his political views, she would only be moving the Levys from the frying pan to the fire. She glanced desperately at Juliette, who pressed her lips together and shook her head. "Perhaps at my apartment . . ." Elise said, despite her misgivings. Surely they could figure something out.

"Juliette suggested this, too, and it's very kind," Madame Levy said. "But it is impossible. Your husband is well-known, and there are many people in and out of this bookstore. One of the things the Germans excel at is turning man against man, you see. When people are hungry, they will betray their neighbors for the price of a few meals. We would be too conspicuous at your apartment, Madame LeClair, or here above the bookstore. It is a risk I cannot take for my children, though it means very much to me that you offered."

Elise looked helplessly at Juliette, who appeared just as lost as she felt. "There must be something we can do."

"There is," Madame Levy said. "You can pray for my children. And you can talk to yours about never turning their back on their fellow man. Maybe one day, we'll all live in a better world."

CHAPTER TEN

On the day the following week that the woman from the OSE came to take Georges and Suzanne away, Juliette left Paul in charge of the store and the children and went to spend the afternoon with Ruth, who was inconsolable. There was nothing Juliette could say to make it better. Her grief over losing Antoinette existed always at a low hum in the core of her heart, allowing her to empathize with the devastating losses of others, but this was something different. And though Juliette understood that Ruth had done what she thought was best, she couldn't imagine sending her own children off to the unknown. How could Ruth live with it?

"It's not fair," Juliette whispered, settling for the most obvious thing she could say while she rubbed Ruth's back. The older woman was bent over in grief, a cup of tea, now cold, before her on her small table. She hadn't spoken in more than an hour, had hardly moved a muscle.

"The war will be over soon," Juliette tried again after a while. "You'll see. The children will return home safe and sound."

Finally, Ruth looked up. It was almost as if she was registering for the first time that Juliette was even there. "You can't possibly believe that."

Juliette's smile of comfort froze on her face. "That the children will be safe? Of course I do. You must, too."

"No. That it will be over soon. This is just the beginning, Juliette. Don't you see? By the time it's all over, there will be no home for them to return to."

Juliette looked around her. This was the first time she had seen Ruth's apartment, which made her feel ashamed. Yes, Ruth had started out as a customer, but over time, she had become a friend. Why hadn't they shared coffee in each other's home? Why hadn't she asked the obvious when Ruth had stopped making purchases at her bookstore, when it had become clear that her children were still wearing clothes they had outgrown? She'd been so buried in her own concerns about the future that she had neglected to see what was happening right in front of her. "You can't afford the apartment anymore, can you?"

"No." Ruth didn't meet her eye, and in the silence, Juliette studied the small room, where it appeared all three of the Levys had slept. She had imagined something different, especially since she knew Monsieur Levy had been reasonably successful, but he'd been gone for years, and this apartment was hardly bigger than Juliette's kitchen. Life, it seemed, had been letting Ruth down for longer than Juliette had realized. And so, too, had she, by failing to notice.

"We can help you," Juliette found herself saying, though she couldn't imagine where she would find the money. No one was buying books anymore, and she was already worried about how she and Paul would feed the children and keep them warm this winter. But she could talk to Paul about it. They would find a way. "Let us help."

Ruth blinked at her, her eyes bloodshot, her gaze unfocused. "I've already made my decision, Juliette. I need to leave Paris."

Suddenly, though the summer heat was oppressive, Juliette felt very cold. "But where will you go?"

Ruth wiped her eyes. "South. Now that the children are safe, I need to make sure that I survive, too, so that they have someone to come back to. I'm all they have."

It felt like the world was spinning out of control. "You're safe here, Ruth," Juliette said. "There's no reason to think there will be more roundups coming."

"Juliette, there's every reason to believe that. The Union Generale des Israelites de France is helping people like me." She wiped her eyes again. "I don't want to go, Juliette, but it is my best chance of survival, and I must take it."

Juliette went quiet as she stared at her friend. "How could it come to this?"

"The world is crumbling all around us, and no one is doing a thing to stop it." Ruth smiled sadly. "How could it *not* come to this, Juliette? How could it not?"

By the following month, Ruth was gone, too, having left with a whisper in Juliette's ear that she would pray for her each day. At night, sleep no longer came easily. As Paul snored beside her in the bed they shared, she stared into the blackness, thinking of the vanished Levy family—and of the impossible choice Ruth had made to let her children go.

The winter passed, dark and cold, and there was never enough food for the children, never enough fuel for the fire, but they were here, and they were safe and together. Elise came by at least once a week, and Juliette's children delighted in seeing

Mathilde. There were dark circles under Elise's eyes now, and though she rarely spoke of her husband, Juliette knew that Olivier was the cause of her friend's deepest concerns. Elise was in a better position financially than Juliette—she often brought bread and cakes for the children, thanks to Olivier's art dealer and his black market contacts—but Juliette knew that it weighed on her friend heavily that Olivier's activities were growing more and more dangerous.

"I'm not even certain he knows what he's fighting for anymore," Elise confessed one day at the beginning of March, her tone weary. "At this point, he merely seems to enjoy being in the middle of the action."

"And you've talked to him about this?"

"More times than I can count. He doesn't see the danger he's putting Mathilde and me in, Juliette. He thinks he's invincible, that we all are. But no one is invincible in war."

That night, after Juliette and Paul had put the children to bed, Paul sat quietly in the parlor, reading a book, and Juliette puttered around the kitchen, washing and putting away dishes, full of nervous energy she couldn't quite place. The winter had been long, and the nights seemed endless, especially with the blackout curtains drawn. That's what she was thinking about—the blackness of the night—when suddenly, a bright burst of orange appeared at the very edges of the window shades, startling Juliette so much that she dropped the plate she'd been drying. It shattered on the floor.

"Juliette?" Paul's voice was full of alarm as he appeared in the doorway. "What is it?"

"Something outside," she said, moving closer to the window, which provided a full view of the building across the street and a glimpse of the rooftops that rolled east. She put a hand on the blackout shade, but Paul stopped her. "Turn the lamp out first," he warned, and she quickly extinguished their light, plunging them into darkness.

Slowly, quietly, Juliette pulled the shade aside, and she and Paul gasped in unison, staring in disbelief at the wild landscape before them. All across the night sky, bright lights—some orange, some white—drifted slowly down, like fireworks in slow motion, a million candles floating in from the heavens. At first, Juliette couldn't understand what was happening. "Paul?" she said, her heart hammering in both fear and exhilaration at the breathtaking show.

He was as frozen in place as she was for a second, and then all of a sudden, he gasped. "My God, Juliette, it's an air raid!" he said, springing to motion, pulling her along with him.

She was already running up the stairs toward the children's rooms behind him, his hand still on her arm. "But the sirens didn't go! It can't be—"

"They're markers!" he shouted. Panic had erased all sense of volume, and his voice woke the children; she could hear all three of them crying as he flung open the door. "They're dropping phosphorescent markers so they can see their targets in the dark!"

And all at once she understood as the light outside their window grew brighter and brighter, setting the sky on fire. The clouds over the city reflected the colors back like a terrible furnace surrounding them, and as Paul grabbed the boys from their beds, scooping them effortlessly into his arms, terror snaked itself around Juliette's limbs, freezing her in place. "Get Lucie!" he cried, already running from the room and heading for the stairs. "Juliette, now!" he barked.

She snapped out of it, grabbing her wailing two-year-old and stumbling after Paul. "The gas masks!" she screamed.

"I'll get them! Just get to safety!"

Down the stairs they all flew, through the bookstore, through the children's section, to the narrow door against the opposite wall that led to the small, private basement beneath, which they used mostly as a storage area for books waiting to be shelved. "I'll come back up for the masks!" Paul called over his shoulder as they clambered down the cellar stairs, all three of the children crying now. "Juliette, get on top of the children!"

In the darkness, Juliette pushed the sobbing children to the floor and shielded them with her body as Paul ran back up the stairs, returning a few seconds later with the five gas masks the local prefecture had provided. They'd had to queue for hours to receive them, and Juliette had been forced to return twice to argue that the children needed smaller masks, for the adult ones would swallow their faces but offer no protection. The result was that Paul, Juliette, and Claude had adult masks, and they'd been granted two smaller masks for Alphonse and Lucie. It would have to do.

The children cried and protested as she and Paul wrestled them now into the large masks, which smelled like rubber and made them all look like bug-eyed aardvarks. In the light of day, when they'd practiced putting them on, the boys had laughed about how funny they all looked, but now, it all felt terrifyingly real. The masks would protect them if this was a gas attack, and the beams of the cellar should protect them if it was a bombing, but there was no way to know what was coming.

"It's the Allies," Paul guessed after he had secured the masks on the boys. Lucie was wailing as Juliette secured the mask to her tiny face. "They won't hit us here. They're after the Renault factory."

"The Renault factory?" Juliette asked as she struggled to put her own gas mask on. The strap caught in her hair. "But the factory is French!"

"They're repairing German tanks, Juliette! They have no choice!" And then Paul's mask was on, obscuring his face, and as Juliette pulled hers on, too, the world went dim, and she felt like she was in a terrible nightmare. She could hear the rush of her own strained breathing, the muted sounds of the children crying and whimpering in fear, but she couldn't soothe them with her words, for they wouldn't be able to hear her. So instead, she held tightly to their little bodies, and then Paul wrapped all of them in his arms, and they stayed that way as the whistling sounds overhead began.

When the first bomb hit, somewhere far away, the earth trembled, and Juliette clung to the children more tightly and began to pray, begging God to spare them. In the near blackness of the basement, which rattled each time a bomb landed nearby, Juliette squeezed her eyes tightly closed and tried to understand what was happening. The *Allies* were bombing them? How could they do such a thing, even if the Germans were in control of the Renault factory? Didn't they understand how close the factory stood to civilian homes, how none of the innocent French people in the paths of the bombs that night had anywhere else to go? That most of the citizens on the ground here hated the Occupation, too? And why were the explosions so nearby? The factory was a thirty-minute walk away. Even in the smoke and darkness and confusion, how could the bombers be missing their targets by so many kilometers?

The cellar shuddered, the children screamed, and the world shook again and again, as their muffled cries, the shrieks of falling bombs, and the roar of aircraft engines went on for what felt like an eternity. Juliette could smell smoke and gasoline, and the terror of being blown up by an errant bomb was suddenly riding tandem with the dread that they might all burn to death down here if a fire began above them. Eventually, the bombing subsided, and Juliette felt her shoulders sag in relief. It was over. They had survived.

She began to remove her mask, but Paul grabbed her arm.

"No!" he said, his voice muffled behind his own mask. "That was just the first round."

He was right. A moment later, the whistles and the blasts began again, the bombs shrieking down from the sky with an audible, whining crescendo. This time, there was the *ratta-tat-tat* of return fire, of Germans on the ground desperately trying to shoot down the planes, a symphony of destruction. On and on it went, in waves, for two hours, glass breaking, the earth quaking, the sounds of their terror filling the cellar.

And then, finally, it really was over. They clung to each other in the silence for five full minutes before Paul removed his mask. "I think it's done," he said, and Juliette removed her mask, too, and breathed in a glorious mouthful of stagnant cellar air.

They helped the children remove their masks, and all of their faces were wet with tears, their noses red, their eyes bloodshot. "Maman!" they all cried, refusing to let her go, and she couldn't move because the mere fact that they had all survived seemed impossible.

"I'll go check upstairs," Paul said.

Juliette nodded, terrified of what he would find. Was the store still standing? Was the world on fire? Would their little cocoon fill with black smoke? But when Paul made his way back down the stairs a few minutes later, carrying an oil lamp, the look on his face was one of relief.

"No damage," he reported.

"None?" Juliette couldn't believe it. "But it felt like the bombs were falling just above us."

"I know. But all the buildings on our street look untouched. Monsieur Lychner's butcher shop has a broken window, but that's all. And our store is fine, Juliette. Not a book out of place. It's a miracle."

"A miracle," Juliette echoed. So why didn't she feel better? Her children were here, safe and sound, as was Paul. She had prayed to God, and he had spared them.

But there was no escaping the new reality. Their lives could be shattered at any time. Airplanes could swoop down from clear skies, destroying everything in their paths. And now that Juliette knew, she could never look at the world the same way again.

"Shall we get the children back to bed?" Paul asked. "Maybe I should go out and help Monsieur Lychner."

"No." The children were still in her arms, and though she knew she was fooling herself to imagine that she could protect them, she couldn't let go. "No, please. Stay. Let's spend the rest of the night here, just in case."

Paul looked at her contemplatively before nodding. "All right." He leaned down to kiss her on the cheek, his lips lingering, a tattoo of tenderness. "I'll go get some blankets."

The bombs didn't fall on Boulogne-Billancourt again as the winter turned to spring, and the spring to summer. But that didn't mean Juliette could relax. The Germans were rebuilding the destroyed pieces of the factory, and no one beyond their suburb seemed to care that hundreds of people on the ground had lost their lives that March night. A bomb could easily have found their little bookstore on the rue Goblet. Even though Paul reassured her again and again that they were too far from the Renault

factory to have to worry, Juliette knew the truth. There was nowhere one could go in wartime that was completely safe.

Elise's visits to the store grew more frequent, and Juliette
found herself waiting eagerly for them. Lucie and Mathilde were
as close as sisters now, and more often than not, the two toddlers
played happily together, giggling over block towers or rag dolls,
while the boys ran around the store pretending to be pirates or
soldiers. Elise's calm presence was a balm, and somehow, knowing that she would always be back within a few days made it easier
for Juliette to brave the rough waters in between. Since that night
in March, Juliette felt adrift, but Elise always reminded her that
the one thing she could control in the world was how loved her
children felt. Juliette never missed an opportunity now to hold
Lucie, Claude, and Alphonse tightly and tell them how proud she
was to be their mother.

She knew that Elise, too, was doing all she could to make
sure her daughter knew she was a light in the world. But Elise
was swimming through a darkness that Juliette didn't entirely
understand. Her husband was apparently getting more and more
involved with the underground, becoming a louder voice against
the Occupation.

"I'm frightened, Juliette," Elise told her one day, tears in her
eyes. "It's like there's a fire raging through him, and each time I
try to put it out, I only stoke the flames."

"Perhaps he's doing what he thinks is right," Juliette said.
"He's trying to stand up for France."

Elise's tears overflowed. "If that was all this was, I think I
could bear it, even if it put us in danger. But this isn't about fighting back, Juliette. This is about Olivier feeling that he matters,
that people listen to him, that he's an important artist and an

important man." She wiped at her eyes and glanced at Mathilde, playing quietly with Lucie in the children's section of the bookstore. "This is about *him*, not France. And because of that, I fear it's only a matter of time until he does something careless."

That night, Juliette lay in bed with Paul, thinking about how marriages could be so different from one another. Elise had never given her any of the specifics of Olivier's underground activities, so she was vague now when she brought them up to Paul.

"I'm worried," she told him. "He's not thinking of his wife and his child." She felt a soft swell of gratitude for the man beside her, who had, in every day of their marriage, thought of her first. She rolled onto her side and kissed his bare shoulder. "Elise is terrified of what will happen."

Paul was quiet before turning to face her. "It sounds as if Olivier LeClair is already writing the end to his own story."

A shiver ran through Juliette. "But what about Elise? It's her story, too. Hers and Mathilde's."

Paul reached out to touch her cheek in the darkness. "We all have some choice over the way our story ends, don't we, my love?" He leaned forward to kiss her, and even in the tender gesture, she felt a sense of foreboding that matched hers.

"Thank you," Juliette whispered. "Thank you for thinking of the children and me."

"Always, my love." Paul moved against her, pressing his body to hers. "Always and forever."

CHAPTER ELEVEN

It was the second Monday in September and Olivier had been gone for five days.

It was the longest he'd stayed away since the war had begun, and by Sunday, Elise had known that something was very wrong.

She had waited until the next morning to do anything about it, but when the sun rose over the rooftops, making the tiles glow like burning embers, she buttoned Mathilde into a cardigan, and together they walked the twelve blocks to Constant Bouet's gallery. Constant would know where Olivier was.

But Monsieur Bouet just shrugged, his forehead lines deepening with concern as he glanced first at Mathilde and then at Elise. "I haven't any idea," he told Elise, his voice low. "I haven't heard a thing, either. You should go home, Madame LeClair."

"And what? Simply go about my life as if everything is normal?" Elise asked, finding it difficult to match his volume but knowing she must so they didn't attract the attention of strangers. In the corner of the gallery's main room, a wealthy-looking couple browsed, and moments before, Elise and Monsieur Bouet had both watched a German officer stroll into the adjoining room, which held the gallery's premier collection. Several of Olivier's paintings hung on the walls there, and Elise shuddered as she thought about a German walking out with one of her husband's creations—or worse, flagging them as undesirable art and forbidding their display. It was what had happened to Picasso; he'd been forced out of the public eye when the Germans arrived, his art removed from museums and private collections.

"That's exactly what you must do," Monsieur Bouet said, his voice so quiet it was barely audible now. "Do you want to attract attention?" He cut a glance toward the adjoining room, where the German browsed. "Of course you do not. So you and Mathilde will go home. You will act as though your husband is simply away painting. And you will go about your life."

"But he isn't, is he?" Elise asked. "Something has happened. And none of you care enough to tell me."

Monsieur Bouet's expression hardened. "Madame LeClair, I will make inquiries right away and will notify you the moment I hear anything. Now, if you'll excuse me."

She walked the dozen blocks home, holding tight to Mathilde's little hand, knowing that she had been dismissed. But she had seen it on Monsieur Bouet's face, too, the uncertainty, the worry. And that, more than being treated like a dim little woman, gnawed at her. The world was shifting beneath her feet, and she had the terrible feeling that soon there would be nowhere to stand.

"I want to go to the woods room," Mathilde told her once they had walked back into their apartment. It was what Elise wanted, too. Mathilde was two and a half years old now, and the star-soaked sky Elise had painted a year earlier had become their refuge, the place they went nearly every day to imagine a world without war, a Paris without swastikas snapping in the breeze.

Now, she brought Mathilde into her painted studio and cleared a space in the middle of the floor where they could both lie down and stare up at the starlit sky, imagining they were somewhere else, anywhere else.

"Tell me the thing, Maman," Mathilde said as Elise pulled her close, both of them on their backs on the marble floor. "Tell me the thing your papa told you."

"Under these stars," Elise murmured, hoping that somewhere out there, wherever he was, Olivier could hear her, too, "fate will guide you home."

"Fate will guide you home," Mathilde echoed. Elise felt tears in her eyes as she held her daughter tightly. "Don't cry, Maman," Mathilde said after a moment, reaching up to touch Elise's damp cheek. "We are safe here in the woods room."

"We are safe," Elise repeated, and as she stared up at the trees and the stars, she wished she could believe that Mathilde was right.

It was midday on Wednesday when there was a sharp knock on the apartment door, and Elise knew, even before she peered out the peephole, that it was the end of life as she knew it, the end of everything. She just hadn't imagined how quickly it could all slip away, like sand through her fingers.

She paused before answering the door, walking first to Mathilde, who was sitting on the floor, coloring an old, torn canvas with crayons. "Darling," she said, bending to her daughter. There were so many things she wanted to say in that moment, but she couldn't pause time long enough for the words to come.

Mathilde looked up, her lips bowed into a tentative smile. "Maman," she said, holding up her picture. "See?"

The three scribbled figures she had drawn looked a bit like swirling tornados with arms, but Elise knew just what they were meant to be, and it made her heart break a little. "This is you and me and Papa, yes?" she asked, and when Mathilde enthusiastically nodded, her grin widening, Elise had to resist the urge to grab her daughter and flee before the bad news could reach them. But the truth was, she knew both exactly who was knocking, and equally, that she could not run from what he'd come to say. She kissed Mathilde on the head and forced herself to cross the room and open the door.

"Madame LeClair." It was Monsieur Bouet, just as Elise had known it would be, and she could see the truth on his face before he said the words. Something terrible had happened to Olivier.

"Is he in prison, then?" she asked. "Or dead?"

He looked surprised that she had gotten to the point so quickly. He cleared his throat. "I'm afraid he is not coming home, Madame LeClair."

"In prison or dead?" she repeated, hearing her own voice rise an octave. Her hands shook, and she grasped the door to steady herself. "Monsieur Bouet, you must tell me."

Again, he hesitated, at first looking away and then seeming to steel himself for the inevitable as he once again met her gaze. "He was arrested on Friday." His words were slow, too slow. "They caught him at a party meeting. The men he was with were suspected of some sabotage. . . ." The space between his words was lengthening, as if he feared reaching the end of the story, as if he wished to hold it off as long as possible. "They took him to avenue Foch and the SD . . . they tortured him. Nothing you need to know about, Elise. I'm sorry. But when they realized he wasn't going to give them any more names, they—" He stopped abruptly.

"What, Monsieur Bouet?" she demanded.

"They beat him, Elise." The sentence came out in a cruel tumble. "He did not survive."

A tremor moved through Elise, followed by an eerie stillness. She stared at him. "He's dead?" The words didn't feel real. Yet it had been so clear, from the moment he'd decided to walk down this path, how this would all end for him. "Olivier is dead?"

Monsieur Bouet cleared his throat. "He didn't give up any of the others. He was standing for what he believed in. Most men can't say that. You should be proud, Madame LeClair."

"Proud," she repeated numbly.

Monsieur Bouet once again shifted his gaze away from her. He seemed to be looking at Mathilde when he spoke again. "There's more, I'm afraid." He cleared his throat. "They're aware he's married to an American." This time his cough was more pronounced as he looked back at her. "They seem to think that you might have been part of Olivier's actions, that you might know his contacts. That you're working with the communists, too."

"*What?*" The world went still. "Why would they believe such a thing?" When he didn't answer, the puzzle pieces rearranged themselves in her mind, and she drew a sudden breath in, putting her hand over her mouth. "He *told* them I was involved?"

"You must understand, he was being tortured."

She felt ill. "He protected his compatriots by giving *me* up?"

Monsieur Bouet couldn't seem to meet her eye. "I'm afraid it's very likely they will come for you soon. Time is of the essence, Madame LeClair."

"But, Monsieur Bouet, I know nothing of his activities. I didn't support what he was doing. It was one of the things we argued about all the time."

"I'm aware." His voice was tight. "But they will not believe you. Or at the very least, it won't matter. The Germans aren't after truth right now; they're after blood."

"No," she whispered, all of it washing over her in an instant—

what was coming, what it meant, what she would need to do. She turned to look at Mathilde in horror, just as Monsieur Bouet startled her by taking a step into the apartment.

"If you'll let me in, Madame LeClair, I will tell you the plan."

"There's a plan?" she asked weakly, stepping aside, though the way he filled her entryway made her feel like she wanted to retch, because in with him swept grief and danger and things unknowable. Still, she closed the door behind him.

He looked once more at Mathilde and then withdrew from his back pocket a small handful of papers, which he thrust at Elise. "Here. New identity documents."

"Identity documents?" She flipped through them. He had handed her an identity card, ration cards, a library card, and a bicycle ticket, all bearing the name Leona Denaes, though it was her own photograph attached to the identity document. "I— I don't understand."

"Olivier had them made several months ago. Just in case."

"False papers for me?" Elise stared at them for a few long seconds before looking up. "And what of Mathilde? There are papers for her, too?"

This time, when Monsieur Bouet reached into his back pocket and pulled out another small stack, he wouldn't meet her gaze. He handed a baptismal certificate and a birth announcement to Elise, who stared at them, flummoxed.

"But her name doesn't match mine," Elise said.

Monsieur Bouet didn't say a thing.

"Monsieur Bouet, you've given her the surname of my friend Juliette."

In the split second before Monsieur Bouet replied, Elise suddenly understood, and her whole body went stiff and cold. "No. Oh, no, no."

"It was Olivier's idea." Monsieur Bouet effortlessly caught Elise as her knees buckled and she started to fall. He had known, even before her own body did, that she would collapse. He had known, she realized, far more than she did about her own life, her own future, all along. "He told me about the promise you and Madame Foulon made to each other. If he was ever caught, he knew the authorities would come looking for you. And if you fled, they would know you'd be traveling with your daughter. It would make you much easier to find."

"No." It was all Elise could muster, an utter rejection of all that he was trying to sell her.

"It's for the best, Elise. It's the only way to protect her—and yourself."

"No." This time, the word was a low wail, so saturated in grief that it made Mathilde look up from her drawing and stare at her mother.

"Maman?" the little girl asked, and the single word undid Elise. She came apart in huge, heaving sobs, but Monsieur Bouet didn't reach for her or try to comfort her; he merely stood there, staring at her, waiting for the storm to pass. When she forced herself to stand again, Mathilde was beside her, looking up at her with wide eyes.

"Maman?" Mathilde asked again. "Why are you crying, Maman?"

"Oh, my baby, my baby," Elise moaned, and Mathilde, who couldn't possibly understand what was happening, wrapped her arms around Elise's legs and held tight.

"It's okay, Maman," Mathilde whimpered, but nothing would ever, ever be okay again.

"It's the only way," Monsieur Bouet said, his voice flat. He glanced at Mathilde and then back at Elise. "You know that."

Elise could only nod. He was right, of course. Olivier had already thought this through, had already planned for it, had known there would likely be a time when he'd be dead, and Elise would have no choice but to leave her child behind to save them both. He had done this to her, to Mathilde, with his eyes open, and that made it all the worse.

"Olivier said that your friend, this Juliette, sounded like a kind woman. He felt sure she would keep Mathilde safe." Monsieur Bouet's tone had softened slightly, but it made little difference.

"But I'm her mother! It is *my* job to keep her safe, Monsieur Bouet!"

Monsieur Bouet waited until she looked back up at him. "You will return for her one day, when the war is over. But for now, there is no other choice." He hesitated, but only for a second. "I know this is difficult, Elise. But we must pack up and go now, before the Germans get here."

"I can't leave Mathilde. I simply can't. It's out of the question."

"You would prefer to let her die? They will kill you, Madame LeClair." Monsieur Bouet was firm. "And then they will take your child. She will be sent away to a labor camp, which she will not survive on her own. You would prefer that fate?"

Elise's stomach lurched. "Of course not."

"Then come. Pack your things. I'll look after your apartment while you are gone."

"The apartment," she repeated, feeling dazed. She hadn't thought about it; it seemed not to matter at all in the face of everything else. But if she just abandoned it, it wouldn't be here when she got back; she had already watched vultures in the building sweep in and take living spaces that were not theirs.

"I will take care of everything." His stiff smile didn't reach his eyes. "It's the least I can do. Now please, Madame LeClair, hurry."

It took Elise ten minutes to pack up clothes for both of them, the stuffed bunny Mathilde loved, and some baby pictures Elise knew she would look at every night until they disintegrated under the salt of her tears. Constant had told her not to bring anything personal, that if she was arrested, they would use whatever they could against her. But she couldn't go south to an unknown fate without taking a piece of Mathilde with her. As they headed out the door, with Mathilde chattering excitedly about what Elise had framed as a visit to see Juliette, she grabbed one last thing— the little teddy bear Mathilde had snuggled with for the first year of her life, before the bunny had prevailed in her affections. Elise held it to her face and inhaled deeply. It smelled of her daughter— talcum, sugar, and milk.

As they hurried along the tree-lined rue Michel-Ange, Elise scooped Mathilde into her arms and carried her, holding her close. Every pair of eyes that glanced at them felt like a threat, every uniformed German a potential land mine.

"Maman? I walk?" Mathilde asked after a while, her little body hot from the energy radiating from Elise. "I'm a big girl."

"Let me hold you for now. I want to remember this. The weight of you. And I want you to remember, too, the way it felt to be part of me. I want you to remember that I am coming back, and that I will hold you this way again."

Mathilde didn't protest, but the look of worried confusion on her face broke Elise's heart.

When they reached the door of Juliette's bookshop twenty-five minutes later, Elise scanned the street around her to make sure they hadn't been followed, though if someone had wanted to take them, they would have been picked up already. But she couldn't shake the sense that there were bogeymen everywhere. If she couldn't trust her own husband not to betray her, everyone was a liability. Finally, satisfied that there was no one lurking in the shadows, they went in.

"Elise!" Juliette hurried from the back of the shop, her cheeks pink, her smile wide. "I wasn't expecting you today. What a—" But then she abruptly stopped, her gaze traveling first to the valise Elise clutched in her right hand, then to Mathilde, still pressed against Elise like a part of her body. "What is it?" she asked, her tone changing. "What's happened?"

"Everything," Elise replied, and then, because she didn't want to break down again in front of Mathilde, she gently set her daughter down, kissed her sweat-shimmering forehead beneath her brown curls, and rushed through the back door into Juliette's apartment, where Paul was sitting at the table, eating a sandwich. He sprung to his feet instantly, a defensive reaction, and then, blinking rapidly a few times, seemed to register that it was a familiar face.

"Madame LeClair?" Paul asked, taking a step forward, his arms outstretched, as if her imminent collapse was written across her face.

She went down a second later, her knees buckling beneath her, just as Juliette burst through the door.

"Elise, what is it?" Juliette cried as Elise began to wail, an inhuman, unnatural sound.

Elise clapped one hand over her mouth, and then the other, trying to stop the grief from pouring out. She didn't want Mathilde to hear her, didn't want her daughter's last memory of this day to be one in which her mother fell to pieces.

"What's happened?" Paul asked as he helped Elise from the floor to a chair at the table, where she sat like a rag doll.

Elise managed to look up, and then, turning her gaze to Juliette, she forced the words out. "Olivier is dead, and the Germans are coming for me. I need to get away, and I can't . . ." She couldn't push the final words out, but something in Juliette's expression shifted, from compassionate to horrified to resolved, all in the space of a few seconds.

"And you can't take Mathilde with you," Juliette filled in softly.

Elise nodded, her body heavy with grief. She slumped forward on the table and was hardly conscious of Juliette rubbing her back, of Paul leaving the room in a hurry, his brow furrowed. Finally, she forced herself upright and took the deepest breath she could manage. "The art dealer, the one who has always sold Olivier's work, came to tell me. He said they're likely already on the way. That they'll be looking for an American woman with a little girl. That if I keep her, neither of us will survive."

"Oh, Elise."

"Please, Juliette, can I leave her with you? I know what an enormous thing it is to ask, and if your answer is no . . ."

There was silence for a second. "You're certain there's no other way?"

Elise looked at her in horror. How could Juliette think that she had a choice? "No."

"Then of course we will take her," Juliette said. "It is just what we talked about, the promise we made to each other. We are each other's family."

Elise pressed her eyes closed and then forced them open. "Thank you." Grief and gratitude rolled through her in waves. "Thank you, Juliette." She hadn't realized until that moment that there was a piece of her that had hoped Juliette would say no, and that Elise would be left with no choice but to take Mathilde with her. But that would be for her own sake, not her daughter's, and right now, she had to choose Mathilde's survival. *Being a parent is not about doing what is right for ourselves, is it?* Ruth Levy had said the previous summer, before sending her children away. *It's about sacrificing all we can, big and small, to give our children their best chance at life.* The words had moved Elise to tears then, but she hadn't truly understood until now just how true they were, or how deeply they would hurt.

She hesitated only a second longer before pulling Mathilde's false papers from the waist of her skirt. She thrust them at Juliette, her hand shaking so violently that the papers fanned the air like the wings of a hummingbird.

As Juliette took them from her and skimmed the page on top, her brow furrowed. "You already have identity papers that make her mine?" Her expression was unreadable as she looked up.

"Olivier had them made, Juliette. I had no idea."

"How will I explain why she has suddenly materialized here? A daughter from nowhere?" Juliette's tone was laced with fear.

"She is Paul's cousin's daughter," Elise said slowly, flatly, the story Constant Bouet had repeated to her quickly before departing. "Her husband died at the front, and his cousin died suddenly of influenza. There was nowhere else for her child to go, so you did the charitable thing and adopted her. The last page there is a death certificate for this cousin."

Juliette looked back at the documents in her hands. "She has kept the name Mathilde?"

"Olivier's art dealer said it would be less confusing for her. He said he'll have his contact forge and file the adoption paperwork this week so that if anyone comes looking, there will be a proper trail."

Juliette stared at the papers for what felt like an eternity. "Yes, all right," she said at last. "All right."

She looked up and met Elise's gaze once more, and Elise could feel the weight of the moment. This was the instant all of their lives would change forever. "Tell her about me. Please." Elise reached out to grasp Juliette's hand, squeezing so tightly that her knuckles turned white, the skin on a few fingers cracking into hairline rivulets of blood. "Whatever happens, don't let her forget me."

"She will never ever forget you," Juliette replied, and this was when Elise realized that her friend was crying, her tears coming just as fast as Elise's. "I will make sure of it. A mother is a mother forever."

CHAPTER TWELVE

Ten minutes later, Elise had dried her tears, but Juliette could still feel her friend's grief rolling from her in waves as they made their way back into the store, where Mathilde was playing with Lucie, Alphonse, and Claude. Mathilde fit in with Juliette's children so perfectly, and Juliette knew from looking at them now, at their closeness, that the ruse would work unless anyone had a tangible reason to be suspicious. She was very nearly a member of their family already.

What would it be like to be in Elise's shoes right now, to have no choice but to give up one's child to keep her safe? It was as unimaginable to Juliette as it had been to lose Antoinette several years earlier. She understood all too well, though, what it felt like to have fate steal a child, to leave one no control over a destiny already etched in the stars.

She squeezed her eyes closed and then forced them open again, pushing thoughts of her own lost daughter from her mind. She put a hand on Elise's back, hoping that her friend felt her encouragement, just as Elise bent to Mathilde, who threw her arms around her mother's neck.

"I love you, Maman," the little girl said into her mother's shoulder as Elise crushed her daughter to her.

"I will love you forever and ever," Elise said, pulling back far enough to look into Mathilde's eyes, but not letting her go. Mathilde squirmed a bit, and Juliette could tell that the girl had sensed that something was wrong. "Remember the stars, my love. They will lead us back together, just as we always say. As long as the stars are above us, I am out there thinking of you."

"Fate will guide you home," the girl mumbled, glancing up at Juliette. Juliette forced a smile, but it must not have convinced Mathilde, for she turned her attention back to her mother with a frown. "You're sad, Maman. Why?"

"Well, my darling, it's because I have to go away for a little while." Elise's voice trembled, but she kept her smile bright. "But you will be very safe and happy here with the Foulons. Think how much fun it will be to play every day with Lucie and the boys."

Mathilde glanced up at Juliette, suspicion in her eyes, before looking back at her mother. "I go with you, Maman."

"No, my darling." Elise's voice broke. "I cannot take you with me. But I will come back for you. I promise."

Juliette looked away, before the child could see her choking on a sob.

"I go with you!" Mathilde repeated, her voice a bit higher and more frantic.

A tear slid down Elise's right cheek, and she swiped it away quickly, replacing it with an even brighter smile. Juliette could see the pain in her eyes. "It isn't possible, my love," Elise said.

The little girl finally seemed to understand, her eyes welling with tears. Elise embraced her again, pulling her close against her bosom, and Juliette could see that it was taking every ounce of her friend's willpower not to break down and cry.

Near the front of the store, Paul suddenly cleared his throat loudly, and Juliette looked up. Her eyes met his, and he lifted his chin toward the store windows. Outside, a German soldier lingered, peering in. Juliette's heart skipped in terror for a few beats until it registered that he was studying a book in the window, a first edition of Gide's *Les Faux-monnayeurs*. His gaze drifted up to find her looking at him, and then something like regret flashed across his features before he spun on a heel and strode quickly away.

"Did he see Elise?" Juliette asked as she moved closer to Paul.

His face clouded over as he looked down at her. "We are in danger as long as Madame LeClair is here." Paul stole a glance at Elise, who was whispering in the ear of a sobbing Mathilde.

Paul was right, but how could she wrench Elise away from this moment, from the last time she might look upon her daughter's face in months, years, maybe forever if the worst came to pass? She hesitated, and Paul nudged her, nodding pointedly in Elise's direction.

Slowly, Juliette crossed back to Elise and Mathilde. "It is time," she said, and Elise glanced up.

Realization seemed to cross her features, and after a second, she stood, her hand still on the shoulder of a sniffling Mathilde. "You're right. I'm very sorry."

"No," Juliette said quickly. "I should be the one apologizing, for rushing you through this, but . . ." She let her voice trail off. They both understood the reality, that Elise would not be coming back for Mathilde for a long while.

"Promise me," Elise said, stepping closer. Mathilde grabbed her mother's hand and held tight. "Please, Juliette. Promise me you will protect her."

"I will protect her as I would my own children," Juliette heard herself say, and in that moment, she knew it was the truth, that she could not absorb Mathilde into their family without loving her as her own, without vowing to shelter her as her own. "I promise you, Elise."

"And I promise you, Juliette, that I will do the same for your children if they ever need me." Elise looked fiercely into Juliette's eyes.

"There's no need to—"

"No. I understand the situation I am putting you and your family in, Juliette. I want you to know that whatever happens, I will do whatever I can to help you, and to help your children, until my last breath."

Paul approached from the front of the store. "It is time, Madame LeClair," he said, his tone both firm and gentle, his eyes filled with compassion. "I am sorry, but you must go."

"Yes," Elise agreed, but she seemed unable to release her daughter's hand. "For the rest of my life, I will be in your debt."

"You owe us nothing, Madame LeClair," Paul said. "Just do your best to survive."

"I will return for her." Elise's voice had turned hard as steel. She looked at Juliette. "I *will* return."

"I know." Juliette stepped forward and hugged her friend tightly.

"Mathilde, my love," Elise said, pulling away. Juliette could see her friend struggling mightily not to cry. "I will see you soon. In the meantime, be very good for Madame and Monsieur Foulon." Elise bit her lip. "You must call them Maman and Papa."

"But *you* are my maman." Mathilde's voice was so small it was almost lost.

"I will *always* be your maman. But this is something you must do. You must pretend that Lucie is your sister, that Alphonse and Claude are your brothers. You are part of this family now, until I come back for you. Do you understand?"

Slowly, Mathilde nodded, glancing at Juliette in fear.

"Madame LeClair," Paul said, his tone a warning.

"I know, I know." Elise glanced at Juliette. "How can I ever thank you enough?"

"Just live, Elise. Live, and I will see you soon."

"Godspeed," Paul said, and then, because Elise would never have had the strength to leave on her own, he put a hand on her back and guided her to the door. "We will pray for you."

Elise turned once more. Mathilde was rooted to the spot, staring at her mother. "I love you, Mathilde," she said. "I will love you forever. Remember the stars, my love. Under the stars, Mathilde, fate will guide us both home." And then, before the tears could spill over, she turned and walked briskly away, out the door and into the obstinately sunny day without looking back.

"Maman?" Mathilde whispered, and then, as the air seemed to go out of the room, the little girl deflated, falling to the floor with a scream of anguish, and Juliette fell beside her, pulling the child into her arms and holding her tight as she cried out in vain for her mother.

It took two weeks for Mathilde to stop crying, and a third week for her to say her first word in Elise's absence, but within a month, the girl was smiling again, if only occasionally. Children were resilient that way, Juliette knew. She envied them that strength sometimes, especially Claude, who had at first been struck by the loss of his baby sister but who now seemed to rarely think of her at all. What must it be like to be a child, to put aside the memories that were difficult, and to walk into the light of the future unencumbered?

It was for that reason, a desire to remove pain, that Juliette soon broke the promise she'd made to Elise. *She will never ever forget you*, she had vowed. *I will make sure of it.* She had meant it when she'd said it, but now she understood that keeping her word would make things not only more painful for Mathilde but more dangerous for all of them. The more Mathilde remembered about her mother, the more trouble they could be in if anyone began asking questions.

So each night, swallowing her guilt, Juliette said in Mathilde's ear over and over, "We are your maman and papa now, my child. You are a Foulon."

Most nights, half asleep, Mathilde mumbled a foggy assent, but one night in November, as the other three children drifted off, Mathilde burst into tears at the words. Juliette pulled the sheet up farther to cover Alphonse and Claude in the bed they shared, and then quietly crossed the room to where Mathilde lay weeping into her pillow.

"You must be quiet, my child," she said in the darkness, stroking the girl's silky curls. "Your brothers and sister are sleeping." For a second, she allowed herself to imagine that the head she was caressing was Antoinette's, that her little family was complete after all. It was easier to believe such things in the dark.

"I want my maman," Mathilde whimpered, loudly enough that Lucie, who was sharing her bed, stirred and mumbled in her sleep. Juliette put a comforting hand on her daughter's shoulder and waited for her to resettle before speaking.

"I am your maman now, Mathilde," she said, her voice soft but firm. "We have talked about this. I am your maman, and Monsieur Foulon is your papa."

"No. My maman and papa went away."

"No, child. We are right here. We will never leave you." She stood and smoothed the front of her dress without another word. Mathilde was still whimpering, but what could Juliette do? The sooner Mathilde forgot about Elise and Olivier, the better it would be for all of them. When Elise returned—*if* Elise returned—there would be plenty of time to right the wrong, but for now, this was how things had to be. Besides, Elise had left of her own accord. The more time that passed, the more Juliette's stomach swam uneasily with the knowledge. How could a mother who really loved her child do such a thing? Juliette wanted so much to understand, but she couldn't.

The next night, before putting the children to bed, Juliette gathered them all in the boys' bed and sat beside them to tell them a tale. It had been a while since she'd lulled them to sleep this way, but she knew she needed to do so now, to remind Mathilde of the new story of her life.

"Once upon a time, there were five birds who lifted off into the sky," she began, but the words stuck in her throat.

"What comes next, Maman?" Alphonse asked, his voice already thick with coming sleep.

Juliette cleared her throat. "The first bird was big and strong and took care of his brother and sister birds. The second bird fell from the sky, but she found a place to sleep, and she was at peace. The third bird was wise and kind."

"That's me," Alphonse piped up.

"Yes, my love. The fourth was a girl bird, very brave and imaginative. And the fifth bird was the littlest sister, the one all the other birds loved. The mother bird and the father bird loved them all very much."

Mathilde made a noise and Juliette glanced over to see the tears rolling down the little girl's cheeks. Her own heart squeezed, and she resisted the urge to pick the girl up and pull her close. No, that was something the other children, her little birds, would need to do, to remind Mathilde that she was part of this new family now. After a moment, it was Alphonse who reached across Lucie and squeezed Mathilde's chubby little leg in comfort.

"But I don't want to be a bird," Mathilde sniffled.

"It's all right, Mathilde," Alphonse said. "Maman's stories always have happy endings."

Mathilde glanced at him and wiped away her tears. Claude murmured, "Brave girl," with an encouraging nod, and Juliette's heart felt as if it might explode.

"Tell us more, Maman!" Lucie chirped, and Juliette smiled at the children and dove back into the story.

"One day, the birds went flying over Paris," she said. "And do you know what they saw?"

"The Eiffel Tower?" Claude guessed.

"Notre-Dame," Alphonse said with a yawn.

"Roofs!" said Lucie, and Alphonse gave her an encouraging pat on the head.

"Mathilde?" Juliette asked.

Mathilde licked her lips a few times, then, with a glance at Claude for approval, she murmured, "Stars. The moon and stars and trees."

"Very good, Mathilde." For a moment, Juliette could breathe again. Her family was here, and tonight, she would tell them the story of the family of birds who found their way across Paris to the Bois de Boulogne, where their mother and father waited for them with a loaf of bread. Tomorrow, the Foulon family of six would go back to their normal lives, their perfect lives, in the bookshop, where they would always be safe and well, and soon, Mathilde would stop crying for the past and would see only the future stretching before her, open and bright.

PART II

Good night, then. Sleep to gather strength for the morning.
For the morning will come.
—WINSTON CHURCHILL,
TO THE PEOPLE OF FRANCE,
OCTOBER 1940

CHAPTER THIRTEEN

November 1942

Juliette thought of Elise often, but there was no talk of her permitted in the store. She thought of Ruth, too, and of her children, and each time she did, she felt a swell of guilt. After all, a world in which she and her family were safe and fed while the others ran for their lives was madness.

"Do you think we should have done more?" she asked Paul one morning in late autumn, two months after Elise had fled, as they worked side by side in the store, realphabetizing shelves that had grown disorderly. Their French customers had a habit of sticking books back wherever they pleased, while the small German section they now carried at the front of the store, a concession to ensure they stayed on friendly terms with the occupying forces, was always perfectly in order. The Germans were the most meticulous people she had ever encountered.

"Done more about what?" Paul asked absently as he studied the spine of a book of poetry that had somehow landed in their small biography section. On the other side of the store, in the children's area, Claude was showing Alphonse and the girls how to play jacks. Lately, Juliette had found herself relaxing more and more into this new life as Mathilde was absorbed into the family. The girl rarely asked about her mother anymore, and Juliette knew—to both her relief and sadness—that Mathilde was slowly forgetting Elise.

"About all of it." She hesitated and waited until he looked up from the book. "About Ruth and the children. About Elise."

"But what could we have done that we did not do, my love?" Paul's expression was sad. "We could not have saved Ruth and the children. And we have done what we could for Elise. We have another mouth to feed now, a child that could be a danger to us if she says the wrong thing to the wrong person."

"She will not." Of this, Juliette felt certain. The child understood now that the past was gone.

"Nevertheless, she is a liability."

"She is our daughter," Juliette answered sharply.

Paul seemed to be choosing his words carefully. "But she isn't, my love. She is not Antoinette. She is not a sister to our children. She is a child we are looking after until her mother comes home."

Juliette could feel her shoulders tighten, her lungs constrict. "She *is* our daughter," she repeated. She hadn't realized until that moment how much she needed it to be true, and when Paul didn't respond, she decided to take his silence as agreement. After all, he, too, had come to love Mathilde. She could see it in his eyes, hear it in the surprised delight of his laugh when she amused him, see it in the way he lifted her onto his shoulders, just as he did with the three other children, to let them place the highest books on the shelves.

"And what will happen," he asked after a while without looking at her, "when Madame LeClair returns?"

From the corner drifted the sound of Mathilde's delighted giggle, joined a second later by Lucie's. "I think we must be equally prepared for the eventuality that she will not," Juliette replied.

"If I didn't know better, I would fear that's what you're hoping for."

"Paul!" Juliette could feel her cheeks flaming. "How could you say such a thing? Of course I want her to come home. She is my dearest friend."

He merely shrugged, his expression concerned, and so she stepped off the shelving stool and crossed quickly to where her four children played, letting the sound of their laughter drown out the voices of doubt in her head.

In November 1942, the German and Italian armies invaded the Unoccupied Zone, bringing all of France under German military administration. Juliette found herself thinking often of Elise. Had her old friend headed for the Swiss border? Tried to cross the mountains into Spain? Or had she found a way to become someone new; to smooth the edges of her lingering American accent; to blend into a town somewhere across the demarcation line? What would become of her now?

Juliette tried not to think of it, for what good would it do? Instead, she threw herself into preparing for the children the best Christmas she could under all the restrictions. The boys cut strips of paper from old copies of the *Journal Officiel* and helped the girls fashion them into ring chains. Paul lifted them all up onto his broad shoulders, one by one, so they could decorate the shop, and a day later, he went out for a few hours and returned, his cheeks pink from the cold, with a small Christmas tree that wasn't any taller than Lucie and Mathilde, but that may as well have been the grand evergreen from the Galeries Lafayette. He set it in the center of the bookshop, nailing a few pieces of wood to the base to steady it.

"How did you manage this?" Juliette snuggled up against Paul as the children danced, giggling, around the tree.

"I have my ways," he said, pulling her close. She knew from the way he avoided meeting her eye that he had done something unsavory—perhaps offering free books to the enemy—to get it, but at that moment, it didn't matter. "I love you, Juliette."

"And I, you," she murmured, closing her eyes briefly and trying to fix the moment in her mind. It was perfection; snow drifting down outside the window, the small, slightly lopsided tree, the children dancing happily around. Claude began to sing "Mon Beau Sapin," and Alphonse joined in, as the scent of pine wafted through the store.

But then the spell was broken as the front door of the store opened, letting in a burst of cold air along with a German soldier, his uniform perfectly pressed, his posture as rigid as a board. Mathilde made a little crying noise in her throat, and Lucie gasped as the soldier looked down at her, his expression unreadable. Juliette felt frozen to the spot, and Paul didn't move either, so Juliette was grateful when Claude, seeming to recognize the danger, quickly shooed the other children into the back of the store, where they exited into the family apartment. The soldier, who still hadn't spoken a word, watched them go.

"*Guten Morgen*," Juliette said, finding her voice, though it trembled.

The soldier raised an eyebrow and turned his attention to her. "Oh, so you speak German, yes?" he asked in perfect French. A smile played at the corner of his lips, but she wasn't sure whether it was sinister or pleasant.

"Only a few phrases," she said, making sure to pronounce her French carefully, in the accent she'd been practicing for months. It would be no good to anyone if she stood out as an American. She could feel herself trembling.

"I see." Hands clasped behind his back, he began to stroll, scanning the shelves. "You love literature, yes?"

Paul was still standing behind the counter, but the German was speaking only to her.

"I do," she said. "We have some German books just here." She gestured to the small German-language section, but his gaze didn't follow. He was still staring at the door in the back, the one through which the children had disappeared.

"And four children, I see. Many mouths to feed at a time like this." The German's affect was flat, and Juliette's heart thudded. Had he noticed something amiss? Did he know that she was only supposed to have three? She nearly blurted out her well-rehearsed lie, that Mathilde was the daughter of her dead cousin, but what if he knew nothing of her? That would only give him reason to be suspicious.

"We manage," she said.

After what felt like several minutes, he turned to her, speaking quickly. "Do you have any copies of *Die Kapuzinergruft*? I was told I might find it here."

All at once, the reason for his strange behavior became clear. The book he was asking for was by Joseph Roth, a Jewish writer who'd fled from Berlin to Paris, and though Juliette had enjoyed an English translation of an earlier book by the same author, she knew better than to carry something that might antagonize the enemy. It wasn't worth risking the children's lives simply to make a point.

"I'm afraid we don't carry any books by Roth." She watched his face closely as he absorbed the news, trying to decipher whether he'd really hoped to find the book, or whether this was some sort of a test. From the brief flicker in his eyes, she guessed it might be the former, and she felt a surge of pity for him, for all readers, despite her fear.

"Good. Very good," he said. "Well. I thank you for your time."

She never took her eyes off him as he headed for the door. Once he reached it, he turned around, meeting her gaze. "Keep your children safe, madame," he said, his expression grave. "It is dangerous out there."

And then, in another swell of icy air, he was gone, but the chill in his wake remained. The words hadn't felt like a threat, but rather a warning from a place of concern. Did he know about something that was coming? Were she and the children in more danger than she thought?

"Strange fellow," Paul said after a few seconds of silence.

"Yes," Juliette agreed, but had he been strange? Or had he merely been human, someone who longed for a book he was forbidden to read, someone who worried for the children he couldn't save?

After a pause, though, she shook herself out of it and went to retrieve the children from the apartment. Claude had been brave and wise to get the others out of sight right away, and she intended to tell him that. She only wondered whether next time such quick thinking would make a difference at all, or whether the dangers that lurked outside their door would be too great for them to escape.

CHAPTER FOURTEEN

Christmas was lonely that year for Elise, lonelier than it had ever been.

Her only comfort was imagining Mathilde protected and warm and surrounded by the other children in the little bookshop. Had Juliette kept her promise? Was she telling Mathilde stories of Elise right now? Did Mathilde dream at night of the mother she had once known, the mother who would do everything in her power to return to her? Did she remember the painted stars above her, looking over her always, guiding her forever home?

Elise could only hope the answer was yes, that her daughter was safe, was waiting, was remembering the mother out there who thought of her with every breath, every moment, every fiber of her being.

After leaving Paris in September, Elise had taken a train south, crossing into the Unoccupied Zone. She'd been astonished that her papers had so easily passed inspection at the checkpoint in Moulins, but Monsieur Bouet had done that for her, at least. They were flawless, as was the travel permit he had given her, which said she was bound for a village in the hills called Aurignon. Though she'd never heard of the place until she studied a map, she dutifully stayed aboard until the train reached Clermont-Ferrand and then bought a bus ticket to take her the rest of the way. Monsieur Bouet had given her no assistance beyond that, though, so once she arrived in town, she had no idea where to go.

Drawn by the light reflecting from the stained glass windows of a church, she made her way up a small hill. It was a Catholic church, and childhood memories came flooding back as she pushed open the large front door. A faint scent of frankincense lingered in the air, and above the altar straight ahead, a gilded Jesus hung on a cross, face tilted toward God.

Elise crossed herself, surprised by how familiar the motion felt. She had stopped attending church after marrying Olivier because he didn't believe in organized religion, and the few times she had attended mass, he had acted aggrieved, as if her faith was a betrayal. Now she realized in a wave of guilt how wrong that had been—all of it. Not just abandoning her roots, but letting Olivier's opinions slowly become her own, gradually allowing him to erase her. But had he been the one to delete who she'd once been, or had she done that to herself, so eager to become part of his world?

She took a deep breath and walked farther into the church, which was empty. She chose a pew midway down the aisle and sat, feeling the scratched wood beneath her fingertips. How many generations of parents and children had worshipped here? After a moment, she closed her eyes and slid onto her knees. She recited the Lord's Prayer once, twice, and then again, and as a feeling of peace settled over her, she began to speak to God, to ask him, no *beg* him, to protect Mathilde.

She was so immersed in the prayer that she didn't hear approaching footsteps, nor did she notice a shadow looming over her. When she opened her eyes, she was so surprised to see a tall, middle-aged priest gazing at her from just a few feet away that she let out a small scream.

"I'm terribly sorry," he said, taking a step back. He was standing in the aisle, and he looked embarrassed. "I thought perhaps you were here to see me."

It was a strange thing to say; weren't priests supposed to leave you alone with your prayers? Still, his eyes looked kind, and gradually, she relaxed. "No, Father," she answered. "But thank you."

He studied her for a few more seconds. "Well then. I apologize for the interruption. Peace be with you, my child." Without another word, he walked up the aisle, limping slightly, toward the back of the church, where he entered a small room that Elise recognized as a confessional. She stared at the door after he'd closed it. Had he assumed she was here for confession?

But perhaps the priest had seen something in her that she hadn't been able to recognize herself. Of course she needed to go to reconciliation, to confess her sins to God, to ask for his forgiveness. She had so much to be sorry for, starting with her complicity in drifting away from the church, and ending with her failure to protect her daughter. Perhaps God would hear her prayers then.

Shakily, she stood, mentally preparing herself for her first time in a confessional in years. Before she could take a step in that direction, though, the main door of the church opened, and a man about her age slipped in.

Elise couldn't put a finger on what it was that struck her as strange about him. Perhaps it was the way he didn't look toward Jesus on the altar, as she had instinctively done, and didn't cross himself. Maybe it was the way he met Elise's gaze, his eyes narrowing slightly, though he didn't acknowledge her. Or was it the way he averted his eyes, ducked his head, and hurried into the confessional, slamming the wooden door behind him?

She hesitated, and then, her heart thudding, she began to walk quietly toward the confessional. Something felt wrong.

Suddenly, raised voices came from behind the wall, first from the side the man had entered, then from the side of the priest. Elise tensed. Should she do something? Then again, she knew that if this confessional was anything like the ones from her youth, there was a wooden screen separating the parishioner from the priest, and since she hadn't heard anything crack, she assumed the priest was safe for the moment on his own side of the partition. Still, she continued to move closer.

Her eyes darted around as the man inside yelled something unintelligible. There was nothing that looked like a weapon nearby, and Elise feared that if she ran all the way down the aisle to the altar to grab a candlestick, she'd be too far away to help if the priest needed her. Her gaze landed on a Bible sitting on a nearby pew, and after a second, she grabbed it and raised it up to feel its weight. The cover was thick and solid, the words of God giving it several pounds of heft. If she flung it at the man with all her might, she might stun him long enough to let the priest get away, if indeed he was in trouble.

She had barely formed the intent when suddenly the door to the confessional burst open, and the man strode out, hardly glancing at her as he hurried toward the main entrance of the church. It was only after the door had banged open, letting a burst of sunlight in, that she realized she'd hoisted the Bible up defensively over her right shoulder, ready to strike.

"What were you planning to do with that?" the priest asked mildly, and she spun around to see him emerging from his side of the confessional, eyebrows raised.

Guiltily, she lowered the Bible and slid it back onto one of the pews. "I—I don't know. I heard raised voices, and I—" She didn't know how to finish.

He studied her. "You were prepared to help me. Why?"

"I—" she began again, but then faltered. "It felt like the right thing to do, I suppose, though now that I think of it, perhaps using a Bible might have been sacrilegious."

The priest's lips twitched, as if he was fighting back a smile. "Had you saved me, I suspect God would have understood. In fact, you could have confessed it in there." He gestured toward the booth he'd just emerged from. "If you're the confessing sort." She could hear the question in his words; he wasn't sure if she was Catholic. But she also had the sense that she would still be welcome here, even if she wasn't.

She smiled slightly. "I haven't been the confessing sort in a while, though I once was. I don't remember yelling at my parish priest in the confessional, though."

He laughed at this, a surprisingly joyous sound, given the situation. "I assure you, yelling is still not the preferred method of reconciliation." He watched her for a few seconds more, and he seemed to be struggling with something he wanted to say.

"What is it, Father?" she asked after a moment.

"You are not French." He said it without malice, but she froze, suddenly aware of how foolish she had been to drop her guard. In Paris, since the start of the Occupation, she'd been terribly careful to ensure that she spoke to strangers as little as possible, and that when she did, she spoke with an impeccable French accent. But here, perhaps in thinking about the church of her youth, she had been careless and had apparently let some of her American *r*'s and careless *ou*'s slip through.

"Of course I am," she said, but she couldn't meet his eye, couldn't say it convincingly, because she was acutely aware that she was lying to a priest in a church.

"What brings you to Aurignon?" he asked, his tone unchanged. He still sounded kind and gentle, so she snuck a look at him. He didn't appear to be plotting her demise.

"I needed to . . ." She trailed off. "I had to leave my home."

"I see," he said, and when she glanced at him again, she could tell he understood what she was saying, that she was running from something, and it was this, more than anything else, this act of being *seen*, that brought tears to her eyes. Quickly, she wiped them away, but he had noticed. "It is difficult to leave home," he said gently.

"Yes," she agreed, tears rolling down her cheeks now. She was unable to stop them. "I'm sorry for this."

"There's no need to apologize." He cleared his throat and seemed to be considering something. "Do you have a place to stay?" he asked.

She shook her head, the tears coming faster. "I was told only to come to Aurignon, but . . ." She hesitated, unable to explain more without saying too much. "No. No, I do not."

He was silent for a while and seemed to be thinking about something. "Do you have any experience with children?" he asked.

She blinked a few times. "I have a daughter," she whispered. She shouldn't have said it, but it was the only response in the moment, and it cracked something wide open in her. The tears flowed faster and after a few seconds, she doubled over, the pain of it all too much to bear.

She felt the priest's hand on her back, solid, comforting. "She is not with you," he said, a statement rather than a question.

All Elise could manage was a brisk nod, and the priest seemed to make up his mind about something.

"There is a house on the edge of town, just down the hill, past the fountain. Take a left on the rue de Levant, and keep walking for thirty minutes or so until the roads ends. They have a spare room, and a need for some assistance. Tell them Père Clément sent you, and that Madame Roche should come see me as soon as she's able. Do you understand?"

Confused, she nodded. Perhaps it was a family in need of an au pair. Was that why he had asked her about children? In any case, she wasn't sure whether being around someone else's sons and daughters would help ease her pain or would make it worse, but she had nowhere else to go. "Why are you helping me?"

"It felt like the right thing to do, I suppose," he said with a small smile, and she smiled back through her tears in recognition of her own words from moments earlier.

"Thank you." As she turned to go, she could feel his eyes on her back. She walked a few steps up the aisle before turning back around. "I'd like to return for confession at some point," she said. "If that's all right. It's just that I don't think I'm ready yet."

"Of course," he said, and she could see that he understood. She was grateful for that, and as she began to walk away again, she heard his voice behind her, and it stopped her in her tracks. "Madame, I will pray for your daughter—and for you."

She didn't turn. She couldn't, for fear that she would shatter completely. Feeling the eyes of the priest, and perhaps even the eyes of God, on her, she made her way to the door and left the church, moving into the warmth of the autumn sunshine.

Madame Roche turned out to be something entirely different from what Elise expected. An older woman living alone in a large, isolated farmhouse in need of repair, she had at first tried brusquely to turn Elise away, but after Elise had explained that a priest named Père Clément had sent her, the woman's attitude changed. "Is that right?" she asked, peering at Elise over the top rim of thick glasses. "Well then, you can make yourself comfortable here on the step while I go speak with him. My farmhand, Bernard, is around. He says little, but he will notice if you're snooping, so don't get any ideas. He sees everything."

The woman, who had to be at least seventy, pedaled off on a rusty bicycle, heading for town, before Elise could say another word. Elise watched her go, a million questions running through her head. Surely Madame Roche was too old to have children in need of care. Still, she had nowhere else to go, so she settled onto the front step and waited.

The house was silent, but after a time, there was a noise from the direction of the barn, and a man emerged and stopped, staring at her. He was huge, easily two heads taller than Olivier, and solid as a wardrobe. He was about her age, his hair a deep chestnut brown, his skin tanned as leather. She stood and gave him a polite wave, but he didn't acknowledge her. He merely stood there, looking at her, before turning back toward the barn, his shoulders squared like he was preparing for battle.

Bernard, she thought. He hadn't seemed dangerous, exactly, but his very presence felt like an ominous warning, and she shivered, suddenly feeling cold.

Nearly an hour later, just as the sun was setting, Madame Roche pedaled back up the lane and dismounted with surprising agility. She walked her bike up toward the house and beckoned to Elise. "Père Clément said I could trust you," she said. "But I have a few questions of my own."

She brushed past Elise and unlocked the front door. She gestured for Elise to go inside, but Elise hesitated on the doorstep. "I hardly know Père Clément," she said honestly. "I—I don't want to mislead you. I'm not certain why he vouched for me."

"Because Père Clément has a better sense of people than anyone I know," the old woman snapped. "If he says you are trustworthy, you are trustworthy. Now are you going to take the opportunity or discard it? The clock is ticking."

Indeed, a grandfather clock inside the front hall tracked the seconds loudly, its rhythmic clicks echoing in the silence. The woman closed the door and brushed past Elise, gesturing that she should follow her. The long hallway opened onto a dining room where a table sat surrounded by eight chairs. Madame Roche pointed to one of them, and Elise obediently sat while the old woman began to pace.

"Père Clément says you have just arrived in Aurignon," she said, the words sounding like an accusation.

"Yes, madame."

"And that you have no place to stay."

"Yes, madame."

"And that you have a daughter."

Elise bowed her head. "I do."

"So you left her."

Elise didn't look up. She should never have mentioned to the priest that she was a mother, nor should the old woman be aware of it now. She had only been gone from Paris for a day, and already she was failing. But the mistake had already been made, and so she saw no point in lying now. "Leaving her was the most difficult thing I've ever done. But it was the only way to ensure that she survived."

Madame Roche stopped pacing and studied her. "You are telling the truth." She seemed to be considering something. "Père Clément thought you might be able to assist me with something. But I would be remiss not to tell you that there is a possibility there may be danger in it."

The words sent a shiver up Elise's spine. She needed only to survive until the war ended, and then she would return to Mathilde. Deliberately imperiling herself ran contrary to that goal, didn't it? It was just what Olivier had done. "Madame, I'm not sure—" she began, but Madame Roche held up a hand to stop her.

"You are a mother," she said. "And you are relying on another person to care for your child, yes?"

"Well . . . yes."

"You see, *we* are those people for other mothers."

Elise blinked at her. "Pardon?"

"We keep the children of others safe. You can do for other parents what someone, right now, is doing for you. This is life and death, madame. And I believe firmly that it is our duty, to our fellow man and to our God, in this time of darkness."

"You're—you're saying that you shelter children here?"

The woman didn't answer. Instead, she stared long and hard at Elise. "What is your name?"

"Leona Denaes." It was the name on the identity documents Constant had given her, and though she'd practiced saying it under her breath, it still felt strange.

"Not your real name, I imagine," Madame Roche said

brusquely. "Very well, Madame Denaes. I will make this simple. There are no Germans here, not yet. When they do invade the Unoccupied Zone—and make no mistake, they will—they'll pay little attention to this town. You are safe here, for now. And so are the children who need to hide. But I am an old woman. I cannot do this alone. I take a tremendous risk by telling you this, and I'm certain you understand that if your answer is no, Bernard will deal with you, and you will be in no position to report us. Children's lives are at stake, and frankly, madame, so is yours. Are you with us or against us?"

The words had all poured out in a hurried tumble, and now the silence felt pregnant with danger. The sound of the ticking clock wafted in from the hall.

"I am not against you," Elise said at last. "But I must return to my daughter. If something happens to me, she has no one."

"And if we do not play a role in fighting back, you will not be able to return to her anyhow," Madame Roche answered immediately.

Elise considered her words. "My husband is the one who put us in this position, by joining an underground movement. Wouldn't I be making the same choice? To put myself in danger in a way that could change the course of my daughter's life?"

"No." Madame Roche's expression softened a little. "Had your husband not made his decision, you would not be here now. You would be with your little girl. Her life has already changed forever. But now that you are here, this is a way to *do* something— and to find a place to stay in the meantime, with people who will protect you. It seems to me, Madame Denaes, that the best way of finding your way back to your daughter is to help see an end to this war."

Elise understood what the woman was saying, and a part of

her agreed. The other part of her, however, wanted only to vanish, to curl up in a ball somewhere, to pause time until she could return to Mathilde.

But she had felt something in the church, a sense that stirred something within her. Maybe she was meant to save other people's children, as a penance for the danger to which she'd exposed her own child. Maybe, just maybe, if she did this, God would lead her back to Mathilde.

"Madame?" Madame Roche nudged her, after Elise had been silent for what felt like too long.

Elise focused her gaze on the older woman, an unfamiliar peace settling over her. "Yes," she said. "I will help you."

Madame Roche's smile was small, but Elise could feel the relief in it. "Good," she said. She turned and walked away without another word, but Elise sat frozen in place. "Well?" Madame Roche asked, turning as she reached the stairway. "Are you coming? Or are you planning to sit there until the Germans arrive?"

She didn't wait for an answer, and after a few seconds, Elise found herself scrambling after the woman up the stairs.

CHAPTER FIFTEEN

"Time for a drill!" Juliette clapped her hands together as the children finished their breakfast on an icy morning in March 1943. "Grab your masks, everyone! Off to the cellar!"

"I don't like drills, Maman!" Lucie said, standing from the table and stomping her foot. "Mathilde and I want to play!"

Mathilde glanced at Juliette, seeking approval before she hopped up and stood beside Lucie. "We want to play," she echoed uncertainly, and Juliette had to hide a smile. The girls, who were three now, had become more than just sisters; they were near clones of one another. Wherever Lucie led, Mathilde followed. Juliette was glad they had each other, for she could see the sadness sometimes in Mathilde's eyes. She missed her parents, and no matter how hard Juliette tried to make her feel at home here in Boulogne, she couldn't quite mend the broken pieces.

Still, there was plenty of laughter and joy in the bookshop, even with the war dragging on outside their doors, and Juliette knew they'd done the right thing by welcoming Mathilde into their family. She had been there for six months now, and already, Juliette had trouble imagining life without her.

"There will be plenty of time to play after we practice, children," Juliette said brightly. "Now come along! Pretend the sirens are going!"

"But the sirens didn't even go last time," Claude grumbled. He had just turned eight, and he had begun to push back against his parents, already testing boundaries. He was kind and gentle with the girls, and a best friend to Alphonse, who was six. Juliette could already see the man he was going to be one day.

"Well, that's why we have to be ready at a second's notice," she said, keeping her voice cheerful. She'd tried to make a game of this monthly practice, so the children wouldn't be frightened, and they'd know not to panic if real bombs ever fell again. "So off to the cellar, now!"

Still grumbling, Claude took Lucie's hand, and Alphonse—the only one among them who always seemed perfectly happy to practice for potential bombings, because he thought the masks were funny—grabbed Mathilde's. Together they dashed into the store, where Paul was already waiting for them at the basement door against the far wall.

"I'm timing you, children!" Paul singsonged, glancing at his watch. "Can you beat your record?"

This spurred Claude to action, and he grabbed his mask from the pile by the door and then picked one up for Lucie, too. Alphonse did the same, grabbing masks for himself and Mathilde before the four of them raced down the stairs, Juliette right behind them carrying a lantern. Paul was the last one in, holding masks for Juliette and himself. He pulled the door closed behind them.

"Twenty seconds if you want to win!" he called, and Juliette bit back her laughter as Claude hurriedly wrestled his sister into her mask before pulling his over his head. Alphonse did the same, a bit more awkwardly, with Mathilde, and Paul had to step forward to help, since Alphonse had put her mask on upside down, but seventeen seconds later, by Paul's count, all six of them had their masks on.

"*La famille oryctérope* is victorious again!" Paul cried, his voice muffled.

The children laughed, and all of them took their masks off, their faces red where the rubber had imprinted their skin. "We do look like aardvarks!" Mathilde exclaimed with a giggle, and as Juliette removed her mask, too, she smiled at her little family. As long as they were together, they would all be safe and well.

That night, after the children were asleep, she and Paul quietly made love, and they lay in bed afterward, holding each other. Juliette knew how fortunate she was to have a husband who was still here, a husband who hadn't been conscripted, a husband who adored her and the children so fully. She loved him so much that it sometimes hurt.

"Where do you think Mathilde's mother is now?" he asked, breaking the easy silence between them.

"I don't know," Juliette said after a moment. "Do you think . . . Do you think she's still alive?"

Paul seemed to be considering this. "I do."

"Can you imagine it, Paul?" she asked after a moment. "Leaving our children like that?"

She could feel Paul tense, ever so slightly. "Juliette, she did not have a choice. You know that. We all agreed it was the only option. The war has forced us all to make choices we couldn't imagine."

"But our children are the very essence of us. They are our hearts. Our souls. How could we survive without them?"

"By knowing that we have done the best we could to keep them safe, Juliette, just as Elise LeClair did. Just as Ruth Levy did. I can only imagine how painful it must have been for them to walk away."

"Well. I could not do it." While at first she had pitied Elise, that feeling had begun to turn the longer that Mathilde was a part of their family. As Mathilde had begun to forget her parents, Juliette sometimes caught herself thinking of Mathilde as a true daughter. "So you still believe Elise will return?" Juliette asked.

"I do." Paul didn't elaborate, and Juliette didn't respond. But as his breathing slowed and grew more even, she rolled away from him and lay on her back, staring at the ceiling.

In the morning, Juliette arose before Paul and the children and let herself out into a quiet, fog-draped dawn. Boulogne was just beginning to stir, blackout curtains opening, people stepping onto balconies to water spring blooms, the sound of a baby crying from an open window. Head down, she hurried to the cemetery where Antoinette was buried. It had been nearly a month since she had visited, and the guilt of that sat heavy on her shoulders, like a funeral shawl.

As she knelt by her daughter's grave, she began by apologizing for her absence. "I think of you each day, my darling," she said, brushing the dirt from the headstone. It always seemed too permanent, too stark, to see her daughter's name etched in the marble, the year of her birth and death tragically the same: *1936–1936*. "I'm sorry I haven't visited, but the other children have needed so much, and there have been days when we haven't had enough to eat. Your father had to take a second job to help us along. He repairs furniture for Monsieur Simon, who pays him far less than he's worth, but you remember how wonderful he was at building the bookshelves in our store, don't you? Oh yes, he's very good at building things, and I think this is good for him, to work with his hands."

Juliette couldn't remember when she'd started talking to Antoinette this way, as an older child rather than a helpless infant, but it comforted her to think of Antoinette continuing to grow up, just as her other children did. She would be seven years old now, and Juliette could imagine exactly who she would have become: kind like Claude, bright like Alphonse, inquisitive like Lucie.

The wind rustled in the trees, and a few leaves danced by. Juliette watched them go and chose to believe that it was Antoinette moving them, a sign to Juliette that she was still here.

"I'm sorry," she repeated. As the wind picked up the leaves again, surely a response to Juliette's words, she closed her eyes and put her hands on the cold earth. The world was not a fair place, but she was doing all she could to get by, to protect the children she had left. "I'll return soon, my love," she promised, and then she stood, and quickly dusting the dirt from her knees, hurried away, back to her real life, once again leaving her first daughter behind.

Three weeks later, on a warm April Sunday, Juliette awoke to all four children—Alphonse, Claude, Lucie, and Mathilde—standing at her bedside.

"Please, Maman!" Lucie begged. "May we go see the horses?"

"Please, Maman, please, oh, please!" the other children echoed, clamoring for her attention as she struggled to consciousness and pulled herself upright.

"The horses?" she asked, looking at their little faces, all bright with hope.

"At the racecourse, Maman!" Claude piped in.

"They're running today!" Alphonse added.

"Ah." Juliette had known this, of course. It was all anyone had talked about for the past week, the opening of the season at Longchamp. It seemed ridiculous to Juliette that something like horse racing would continue to go on in the midst of a war, but it wasn't really for the entertainment of the conquered, was it? She knew as well as anyone that a sizable portion of the audience would be made up of German officers, oblivious to—or, more likely, unconcerned about—the fact that their very presence had decimated the racing industry. Many of the country's prize horses had been killed in bombings during the initial invasion in 1940, and a substantial percentage of those who survived had been seized from their French owners and shipped to Germany, just like everything else France had to offer.

"My darlings, we have talked about this before. The racetrack will attract many German officers. It is simply not safe." She glanced quickly at Mathilde, who of course made everything just a bit more dangerous for all of them.

"But there will be many French people there, too," Mathilde said.

"But not us," Juliette said. "*We* will not be there. We will be safe and sound in the store."

By lunchtime, the streets outside were filling with spectators and horse enthusiasts coming and going from the nearby Pont de Sèvres metro station, and the children were swept up in the excitement of a busy day. For the first time in a year, their shop was bustling, and Paul happily manned the till, ringing up more sales than Juliette had imagined possible, enough that she knew they'd be comfortable for at least another month, even if Paul didn't find much furniture repair work on the side.

"Shall we let the children go have a look at the action at the track?" Paul asked once the flow of customers had died down. The race would be starting soon. "They've worked so hard today. I'm certain all the German officers are inside by now. It should be safe enough to let them enjoy the festive atmosphere for a bit."

Juliette hesitated. "You're right. I'm being too cautious."

Paul smiled. "They'll be very happy."

Together, they ushered the children into the apartment for a late lunch, which they wolfed down hungrily. "My darlings," Juliette said, casting a smile at Paul, as Alphonse, Claude, Lucie, and Mathilde looked up at her. "Your papa and I have a surprise for you. Would you like to go see the festivities at Longchamp?"

The room exploded in excitement, all four of the children leaping up and dancing around, hooting and hollering. Juliette laughed, tickled by their joy, and exchanged another look with Paul.

"Papa and I just need to wash the dishes. Claude, can you mind the younger children for a few moments?"

"Of course, Maman. We will play in the bookshop until you're ready." He led the other three through the door to the shop in an exaggerated horse trot. Alphonse and the girls giggled and galloped along as Juliette watched with a smile.

"We really are fortunate, aren't we?" she asked. "Four children, perfectly healthy."

Paul crossed the room and kissed her tenderly on the forehead. "And a perfect, beautiful wife," he said. "We are lucky to have each other, Juliette."

She tilted her face up to his, and their lips met. In that moment, she had nearly everything she could have wished for. The silence in the apartment felt magical, loaded with possibility, and as she pulled away from Paul and began to gather the children's plates from the table, she was overwhelmed with gratitude for this life she'd been granted, even in the midst of chaos and pain.

And then, in an instant, everything changed.

Juliette wasn't certain whether it was Claude's scream of warning or the sharp knife of the air raid siren that cut through the quiet first, but suddenly, the world was filled with sound, too much sound, and as the siren shrieked its plaintive, deafening wail, Juliette pushed off from the sink and stumbled toward the door leading to the bookstore. "The children!" she cried, and Paul answered something unintelligible, his voice lost in the siren's swell.

She could feel him behind her, his breath on her neck, as they pushed through the door. Panic rose in her throat when she didn't immediately spot them.

"Claude! Alphonse! Lucie!" she screamed, her voice hoarse as she stumbled, in a panic, toward the children's section.

"They're in the children's section!"

"What about the gas masks?"

"Forget them!" he shouted back as they hurtled through the store. "Just get the children to the cellar! Hurry!"

Just then, there was an explosion outside, very close, too close. The ground rolled, nearly throwing her off her feet, and over the din of the siren, she could hear the girls screaming, Claude yelling at everyone to get down, Alphonse calling her name. "I'm coming, children!" she screamed, and it seemed like time slowed to a crawl as she lurched around the corner, past their shelves of children's books, Paul just ahead of her. None of it made sense; the warning had sounded less than a minute earlier. The Renault factory was kilometers away; what were the planes doing bombing a residential area again? And in broad daylight?

"Maman!" Alphonse called again through sobs.

"Juliette, get the boys!" Paul called at the same moment, and she saw him hoist Lucie and Mathilde, one in each arm, the three of them backlit by a sudden burst of light flooding through the window as another bomb exploded so nearby that their front window shattered, sending a spray of broken glass into the store.

This time, it was she who screamed. All she could think about was getting to Claude and Alphonse, shielding them with her body, making sure all of them made it to the cellar door. Paul was already running that way, the girls wailing in his arms. "Maman is coming!"

"Maman!" Alphonse's face was splotched and streaked, his eyes wide with terror.

She was a millimeter away from grabbing his hand, a centimeter away from Claude, when a sudden whistling sound above turned to an urgent shriek, and in the millisecond before the world went black, she knew exactly what was about to happen, though there was nothing she could do to stop it. It was already too late.

In the instant that existed between light and dark, between life and death, between the before and the after, the roar grew deafening, the flash of light eclipsed everything, and Juliette's bones felt as though they'd been reduced to dust as the world around her disappeared.

CHAPTER SIXTEEN

By the time spring arrived in 1943, Elise had been apart from Mathilde for more than six months, and her daughter's absence still felt like a gaping wound that would never heal. Was her daughter safe? Did Mathilde remember her? Was Juliette making her feel as loved as one of her own children? Elise worried for Mathilde every day, and once a week, she attended mass at the Église Saint-Alban and begged God to protect her daughter, and to spare her, too, so she could return for Mathilde.

During the days, she swept Madame Roche's floors, did her best to keep two skinny hens alive, hidden, and producing eggs, and cooked meals for the children who moved in and out of the secret attic above Madame Roche's bedroom. Once a month or so, new children arrived, some of them frightened, some resolute. Some had been recently separated from their parents; others hadn't seen their mothers or fathers in more than a year. Many cried at night when they thought they couldn't be heard; all of them had eyes darkened by the weight of the lives they now knew. None of them had come with their real names, and despite herself, Elise found herself feeling a maternal sort of tug toward each and every one. Perhaps if she cared for them, gave them a piece of her own heart, God would ensure that Juliette was doing the same for Mathilde, making her feel loved and whole.

It had become Elise's job to queue for food in town and then, upon returning to the farmhouse each day, to climb into the attic to help the children with their lessons. Madame Roche was adamant that to let the children's minds grow idle would be doing them a great disservice, and so Elise came up with exercises about math and history and literature for the oldest ones, and about letters and shapes and the world outside for the youngest. Madame Noirot at the bookshop in town had once been a schoolteacher, and she'd procured several textbooks for various ages. Perhaps it was futile to worry about an adequate education for the children when their attention should be focused mostly on surviving, but knowledge was everything, and besides, learning was a distraction from fear and loneliness.

At night, she had begun to paint again. She had mentioned in passing to Madame Noirot, on one of her excursions to purchase textbooks, that she had once been an artist. She hadn't elaborated, hadn't said that she was a woodworker, and certainly hadn't mentioned that she had been married to a painter, for fear of betraying her own cover. The next time she'd come to the store, Madame Noirot had given her a box wrapped in tissue, and Elise had opened it to find a beautiful set of acrylic paints and brushes. "It is the least I could do," Madame Noirot said with a smile, holding her gaze. "After all, look at what you do for us."

Elise had thanked her profusely and walked back to the farmhouse feeling enormously grateful. Though she hadn't painted professionally in years, she had filled Mathilde's world with stars and sky and darkened trees, brought to earth with a paintbrush, and as she let herself into Madame Roche's house, she knew suddenly that the way to bring Mathilde back to her, even when she was many miles away, was through bringing the heavens here, too.

"May I paint the ceiling of my room?" she asked Madame Roche that night over a simple omelet dinner. It was just the two of them sharing a silent meal, as it often was. Bernard, who slept in the loft above the barn when he was here, was mostly living in the woods with a group of *résistants* by now; he surfaced from time to time to offer help with manual labor but was otherwise scarce. And it was too dangerous for the children to be out in the main house, in case an unexpected visitor dropped by. So they took their evening meal in the attic, while Elise ate silently with her gruff host, who still hadn't warmed up to her.

"Paint your ceiling? Whatever for?" the old woman snapped.

"To remind me of home." Elise pushed her eggs around on her plate, her appetite suddenly gone. "I used to paint my apartment, for by the time my daughter was born, there was already a curfew, and we were not allowed to be outside at night. I wanted her to know the way the trees looked in the moonlight, the way the clouds were lit from within, the way the stars glowed like floating lanterns from another world."

Madame Roche noisily chewed a mouthful of food. When she swallowed, she glowered at Elise. "Do you know what you're doing?"

"I—I was an artist," Elise said after a moment, and the words felt strange between them, because after that first day, when Elise had told Madame Roche she had a daughter, they had never spoken again about who or what they had been before the war. "I carved wooden sculptures, actually, but sometimes, I painted, too."

Madame Roche looked at her for a long time. Perhaps it was

Elise's imagination that the woman's stern face softened slightly. "We were all something else in our past lives," she said at last. "I suppose what matters, though, is who we choose to be now. Just don't do anything garish."

That night, Elise lit a lantern and began to paint, just as she had in her studio on the avenue Mozart during the summer of 1941. First, the blue-black sky over the Bois de Boulogne, the particular hue that only Paris had, a magical glow born of the Seine and light and air. The next night, when the paint had dried, she began dotting the stars, white as a fire's heart, across the sky, tears streaming down her face as she recalled lying with Mathilde on the floor, talking about the vastness of the heavens.

"Under these stars, fate will guide you home," Elise whispered. When she'd said the words to Mathilde, in the room she'd painted for just the two of them, she had meant them as a meditation to soothe her daughter with a promise that God looked over them all in the vast universe. But now, as Elise looked up at the star-speckled sky, she hoped the words meant something else: that the stars, watching over them all, would bring Mathilde back to her, that fate, in all its mysterious ways, would save them both and put them on a road back to each other. "Under these stars," she murmured again, because she had to find a way to believe it, "fate will guide you home."

By the beginning of April, the attic was empty, but the sky over Elise's room was full, the leaves of the Bois de Boulogne reflecting the clouds and the stars and a slivered moon back up at the velvet heavens. The most recent batch of refugees—a boy of twelve and two girls, ages three and eight—had been sent on with a courier to the next stop of their journey after receiving false papers, and now, she and Madame Roche had been told to expect four new children, who had been hiding in plain sight as the Christian nieces and nephews of a widow several towns over. Their identities had been betrayed by a classmate's suspicious mother and they had been moved quickly, in the middle of the night, just hours before the Germans had arrived at the home of their protector. The soldiers had arrested the widow, and no one had heard from her since.

"How old are they?" she asked absently as she and Madame Roche swept out the attic and unrolled fresh blankets and bed-sheets for the floors.

"The boys are eight and six, I'm told, the girls six and four."

"Young," Elise said.

Madame Roche sighed. "Too young. All of them are too young."

"It will be a change for them, living in an attic."

Madame Roche's lips were compressed into a thin line when she turned to Elise. "At least they're alive. Don't forget that, Leona."

Elise suppressed a groan and turned away. Even though she'd been here for months, Madame Roche still seemed to misinter-pret everything she said as a criticism. "Yes," she agreed after a moment, resisting the urge to explain that she only meant that she pitied the children. Madame Roche would simply say that she should save her pity for the ones who were dead, and then they'd argue, and Elise would politely back down while Madame Roche regarded her smugly. It had become a familiar dance.

"You will make a stew," Madame Roche said when they were done tidying. "They'll be hungry when they arrive."

Elise nodded and headed down the ladder from the attic and

into the kitchen, where Bernard stood, smoking a cigarette. He had been here more often since January, when he'd arrived one day looking as though someone had rearranged his face. Shocked, Elise had rushed to him and asked what had happened as she instinctively tried to blot away the dried blood on his cheeks and forehead. He had told her gruffly not to worry about him, that he'd met a man in the woods who didn't like him much, a collaborator who was presently at the bottom of a riverbed.

"Bernard," she said now, smiling at him. "What brings you here?"

"Chicken," he grumbled, making the word—*poulet*—sound like it consisted of a single syllable. He gestured to the table where, spread on a strip of butcher's paper before him, a dead chicken lay, more bone than flesh beneath its paltry feathers. "You are cooking?"

Elise nodded and crossed the room to reach for the chicken, but Bernard shot a big hand out to stop her. "I will pull the feathers," he said. Without waiting for a reply, he began to pluck the bird.

"Thank you." Elise went into the cupboard and emerged with several starchy Jerusalem artichokes, knobbier and more tubular than potatoes, and set to work boiling a pot of water. "You're all right, Bernard?"

He grunted an affirmation, which she assumed was all she would get from him. He was a man of few words, and she had gotten used to his near silence. But now, it seemed something was weighing on him. "Your daughter," he said, and she was so surprised that she almost dropped the knife she'd picked up to cut the vegetables. "Madame Roche told me you are a mother. Do you think of her often?"

It took her a moment to answer. She had never discussed Mathilde with either Bernard or Madame Roche. "Every moment of every day," she said, returning to her chopping.

"You are good with the children," he said after a moment. "I can see it. I know you are a good mother."

Elise stopped cutting again and closed her eyes. "But would a good mother leave her child behind?" It was a question she'd been asking herself a lot lately, but to hear herself speak the words so plainly made her heart ache.

"Of course." Bernard's answer was instant. "All the children who come through, you think their parents were not good parents? No, those parents did all they could to save their children. It is why they are still alive." It was the most she'd ever heard him say at once, and she felt mildly stunned by the conversation.

"But what if there was more I could have done? More any of these parents could have done?"

"Do you think we'd all be here if it was as easy as that?" Bernard asked. "No. That's why we do what we do, Madame Denaes. To put it all back together."

"To put it all back together," she echoed. "Do you really think we can?" she asked after a moment. "Can we ever fix what is broken?"

"The world breaks all the time," he said without looking at her. "And always, always, it is put back together again. You'll find your way back to your daughter, and she will be waiting."

The words replayed in her head long after Bernard had slipped the chicken, which he'd cleaved into quarters, into the pot and headed outside without saying another thing. She could hear him chopping wood outside the barn, and the rhythmic *thwack-thwack* of the axe was strangely comforting. For the first time in months, her fingers itched. How freeing it would feel to carve some wood, but here, there was so little to spare. It seemed indulgent to ask.

She was still lost in thought a few hours later, just past sunset, when she glimpsed through the kitchen window an old farm truck rattling up the lane toward the house. She recognized it; it belonged to Monsieur Léandre, the butcher from the next town over, a man who sometimes delivered batches of children. Their occasional emaciated chickens and sausages of questionable construct came from him, too; he gave Madame Roche whatever he could spare, since the children in the attic had no access to rations.

Elise watched from the window as Madame Roche emerged from the house and strode toward the approaching vehicle, scanning the horizon all around to make sure that no one was watching. The farmhouse was situated in the perfect place for clandestine comings and goings, for the land around sloped gradually down, leveling out into fields and, in the distance, trees lining the road toward town. There was only one way to approach by vehicle, and it was easy to see for several kilometers in each direction, so one would spot a surprise visitor many minutes before he arrived at the door.

The truck squealed to a halt in front of the house and Monsieur Léandre alighted and exchanged a few words with Madame Roche before crossing to the bed of the truck and lifting a large blanket, which he'd held in place with a few barrels. He said something, and from beneath the cover scrambled four children, two boys and two girls, who looked quizzically up at Monsieur Léandre. He gestured to Madame Roche and said something else, and nodding, the children followed, the tallest boy leading the way. Elise couldn't see their faces from the window, but they all looked healthy and well-fed, which was a relief. In the half year she'd been here, only two of the children had arrived ill or terribly malnourished, but both had been difficult to nurse back to health.

She turned back to the stew, tasting it for seasoning—it was predictably, unavoidably bland—and began to ladle servings into dishes. The children would be hungry, and welcoming them with food would go a little way toward indicating that this was a home where they'd be cared for. It was a crucial first step to building trust.

The front door opened and closed, and she could hear Madame Roche's voice, as devoid of warmth as always, and the children's timid footsteps as they all approached the kitchen. "Madame Denaes," Madame Roche said, and Elise turned with a welcoming smile, holding a steaming helping of stew, as though filling their bellies could erase the loneliness that came from leaving home, the fear that came from not knowing where they were headed next.

Later, in the attic, with Madame Roche in the barn speaking to Bernard about something, Elise was helping the children prepare their makeshift beds when the older girl, who went by the name Thérèse, reached out to touch her cheek, as if afraid she wasn't real. "How many children have come through here, Madame Denaes?"

Elise wasn't supposed to discuss the specifics with any of them, for if they were captured, any information they possessed could be used against them, and against the network. "Too many," she said.

"How long do they stay?" the smallest boy, who went by Roland, asked. "Will we be here for a long while?"

"I don't know," Elise answered honestly as she turned to help him tuck his sheets in around the corners of his straw mattress. "You'll be moved as soon as the network can get you out safely."

"Where will we go?" Thérèse asked.

"I don't know that, either. But you will be safe."

"How can you promise that?" Thérèse's eyes filled with tears. "My mother promised it, too—that we would be safe. That our family would be all right as long as we followed the rules. She was nearly first in line to pick up our stars. And then she was one of the first the police came for."

Elise blinked back tears. "I'm so sorry, Thérèse."

"That's not my name," the girl said. "That's just the name they call me. It cannot erase who I am, though. I won't let it."

"No one wants to erase you, dear girl," Elise said instantly. "But we're not our names. We are who we are in the core of our beings. And God will always know you, wherever you go." She thought fleetingly of Mathilde, living with a name that wasn't entirely hers, with parents she didn't belong to, and she cleared her throat before she could burst into tears, which would only frighten the children.

"I want to stay here for a long time," little Roland murmured as he climbed into his bed with a yawn.

"Get some sleep," Elise said. "I am not going anywhere tonight, and neither are you. You are safe here, all of you."

That night in her own room, she lit a candle and added a sweep of white clouds to her ceiling, along with four new stars, twinkling among the masses. Then she lay on her back and stared up at the darkness, imagining that she and Mathilde were together, gazing at the same sky, waiting for exhaustion to overtake them.

It took hours for her to fall asleep, but when she did, she dreamed of Mathilde, floating in the sky above Paris, as ephemeral as a wisp of smoke. "Mathilde!" she called to her daughter, as loudly as she could, desperate to bring her back to earth.

But Mathilde just smiled and tilted her head heavenward, float-ing away until she disappeared entirely, leaving Elise screaming below her on the ground.

A week later, the children were gone, and the house was empty again. Madame Roche had gone into town, and when she heard a truck rumbling up the drive, she went to the window to peer out. It was Monsieur Léandre, the butcher, and as he drew closer, she could see from the window that Bernard was in the passenger seat. Were there more children coming without warning?

She walked to the front door and let herself out, just as the truck pulled to a stop and Bernard hopped down. "Everything all right?" she called, her stomach swimming uneasily.

"Just a delivery," he replied, crossing to the back of the truck.

She took a few steps forward, expecting a few children to tumble down from the truck bed, in need of shelter. Her mind was already spinning with thoughts of what she could prepare for dinner with so little notice and almost no supplies.

But instead of children, Bernard began unloading big, thick hunks of wood, pieces of tree trunks that had been cut into neat logs three feet high. "Where would you like them?" he shouted to her.

"What is all this?" she asked.

"It's wood," he told her, unnecessarily.

"Are you building something?" she asked, still confused.

He stopped and squinted at her. "No, you are. Madame Roche didn't tell you?"

"About what?"

"She asked me to go out into the woods and find you some wood suitable to work with. Something about your being a carver? I've brought some tools for you, too—Madame Noirot ordered them."

Elise's mouth fell open as she stared at him. "Madame Roche and Madame Noirot did that? For *me*?"

He shrugged. "I hope walnut will do. I'll bring them to the barn."

Stunned, she followed behind him. Once he'd set down the first pile of logs, he straightened and pulled a fabric roll from his back pocket. "Chisels," he said. "Madame Noirot gave me a sharpening stone for you, too. It's in the truck."

"I don't know what to say."

Bernard shrugged. He didn't seem to have a response either. "What are you going to make?" he asked, nodding at the raw wood.

Elise stared down at it. She had worked mostly in limewood; walnut would be a new beast to tame. But the familiar energy sizzled through her fingers now, and she felt drawn to it. She bent and stroked it along its rough edges, feeling the heat radiate from it, the potential. "My daughter."

Bernard nodded like he understood, and then he was walking away, toward the truck to bring the rest of the materials in. Elise turned back to the logs in awe, already imagining Mathilde's face in the swirls and knots, already planning how she would coax her daughter from the wood, which would have to be enough until the stars led her home.

❧ CHAPTER SEVENTEEN ❧

The world swam into gradual focus, dust hanging in the air like a fog, the acrid smell of smoke tickling Juliette's nose as she forced her eyes open. Where was she? All around her, the world was broken and gray, and her head throbbed. From far away, she could hear shouts, sirens, wailing, but in this space, the silence was a wool blanket, muffling everything else.

Her whole body hurt, and there was something heavy on her left leg. She sat up to push it aside but realized that she could barely move it. She blinked into the darkness, her eyes burning with the smoke, until she could see the outlines of the room. Where had all the light gone? Where were the windows? Where was the *store*?

That's when she realized that the heavy object weighing on her leg was a bookcase that had somehow fallen over backward on her, the shelves faceup, still holding their books, as though the world had simply tilted sideways. None of it made any sense.

"Paul!" she called, choking on dust and smoke as she took a great gulp of air. She clawed at the books in the case, flinging them out, trying to make the heavy piece of furniture light enough to move. "Paul, what has happened?"

But there was no answer. Where was Paul? Her head throbbed and her vision swam as she tried desperately to put the pieces together. Just before the world had gone black, she had been in the children's section, just about to grab the boys. Suddenly, her heart skipped a beat, then two. Surely Paul wasn't answering because he had reached the children, had gotten them to safety in the cellar, right?

"Paul?" She could hear the panic in her own voice, desperate and raw now as the pieces began to rearrange themselves in her head, forming a picture she couldn't bear to imagine. "Claude? Alphonse? Where are you?"

There was still no answer. The silence pressed down, and through her rising terror, the room gradually swam into focus. "Lucie?" she called, her voice cracking. Paul had reached the girls, hadn't he? They had been in his arms. Surely they were all in the cellar, worrying about her. "I'm fine!" she called out, trying to make her voice bright. "Just hold on, my loves! I'm coming!"

But the store was as quiet as a crypt. "Children?" she called, once again choking on all the destruction in the air. Outside, the noises of rescue, men's shouts and sirens, seemed to be coming closer, but they still sounded like they belonged to another world.

Her rising panic gave her strength, and with a grunt and a heave, her whole body throbbing, Juliette managed to lift the bookcase just enough to free her leg. It hurt so much that it made her dizzy, but she was so desperate now to get to the children that she didn't care. She began to drag herself across the mound of rubble, toward the cellar door, moaning as pain radiated up and down her left thigh. "Children!" she called again. "Paul! I'm here! Please!"

It was at that moment, the plea still on her lips, when she saw the first sign of them: Alphonse's shoe, tattered and too small for him. She had hated that she couldn't buy him a new pair, that there weren't leather soles to be found anywhere anymore. That was no way to live, but Alphonse had seemed to understand and had cheerfully insisted that he loved these shoes, even when his big toe began to poke out of his left one. That was the foot she saw now, the faded brown leather, a toe just visible. "Alphonse!" she cried, scrambling toward him. Why hadn't Paul protected him? Gotten him to the cellar? The boy must be terrified. "Alphonse, Maman is here!"

When she reached him, she grasped his foot. "I will get you out!" she called. "Hold on, my darling." But there was no reply. His foot didn't move. Trembling, she pushed books aside, noting numbly that some were just covers, their pages blasted out. She put her hand on his little calf, and squeezed, but still, there was no response. He was cold, too cold, and she couldn't understand what was happening. He didn't feel like her little boy, not at all; he was stiff as a marionette, but that wasn't possible. "Alphonse!" she cried out, and some part of her must have understood, because already, her throat was closing, and she was choking on the grief, the horror, the disbelief. *No, God, no.*

She clawed through the pile now, no longer aware of her own pain, her shattered leg, the screaming ache in her head, the way her vision was still blurred. The only thing that mattered was getting to Alphonse, pulling him out of this hell, breathing life back into his lungs.

But then, there were his shoulders, and then his little head, turned to the side, his sandy brown hair mussed, and as she pulled him up, her own limbs shrieking in protest, he was cold, his skin too gray, his lips the color of the Seine's waters on a dismal day.

"Alphonse!" she screamed, pulling his limp body toward hers and shaking him, because this was impossible, this couldn't be happening. "Alphonse, breathe!" she commanded, but he wasn't listening, because he wasn't here anymore.

She parted his cold lips, his little body flopping against hers, and blew her own breath into his lungs, willing his chest to rise, willing him to wake up and come back to her. But when she took her mouth away, he was silent, still. "No!" she cried to the sky, to God, before breathing once again into him, trying to give him life, trying to turn back the clock, trying to deny what she already knew. She put a hand on his neck, feeling for a pulse, then, when she couldn't find one, to his wrist. When there was no motion there either, she moaned and lifted him up, pressing her head to the left side of his chest, searching for a heartbeat she already knew wasn't there. "Alphonse!" she screamed, crushing him to her own chest. "Come back!"

But it was too late. His soul had flown, taking all his laughter and joy with it, and she thought for an instant of the flock of wooden birds Elise had once shown her, rising to the sky, grief and hope in their wings as they lifted toward the heavens. Just as quickly, just as fleetingly, she felt a hot surge of anger toward Elise. Could Paul have saved Alphonse if he had grabbed him rather than Mathilde, a child who wasn't his? But then the anger was gone, vanishing into the rubble, as Juliette gently lowered Alphonse's body back to the floor, his resting place a pile of pages. "Paul?" she called out, but the panic had drained from her, and all she felt now was grief as the realization slowly dawned on her. There was a reason for the silence, the stillness here. They weren't in the cellar, were they? Paul would have heard her. He would have done all he could to reach her, to reach Alphonse.

Still, the truth was too terrible to face.

Slowly, she dragged herself through the rubble, pulling her limp leg behind her. She saw a hand beneath a pile of books, and sobbing, retching, she moved toward it, already knowing it was Claude's, already knowing he was dead. She grasped it and found it cold and still, with no pulse. How long had she been unconscious? How long had it taken for all the warmth to leave her sons? How long ago had their souls left their bodies? Was it day? Was it night? She had no sense of time, little sense of place. How could their safe, beautiful bookstore have been transformed into this hellscape?

Howling, she dug through the rubble until she could see Claude's face, his eyes open, his lips parted. Had he called for her? Had he died with fear in his heart, believing she had abandoned him, or had he gone instantly, without pain, without terror? "Claude," she whispered, but when she pulled him up and pressed him to her breast, where he'd nursed as an infant not so very long ago, he was just a shell, just an empty vessel that had once held the soul of a boy who was supposed to have a beautiful life.

Near the cellar, Juliette could see another form in the darkness, and after guiding Claude's lifeless body back to the floor, she crawled toward the shape, pain still radiating up her left leg, all the way to her broken heart. It was Paul—she could see him lying on his back before she got there. He was splayed out like a snow angel, piles of rubble on either side of him, his empty eyes looking up at the darkness, his skin unnaturally pale, his mouth just slightly open. Juliette pulled her body beside his and laid her head on his chest, listening for a heartbeat she knew wasn't there. "Paul, please, come back to me," she begged, but he was gone, and she wondered about spirits and souls and whether he was with the boys, if he was holding their hands wherever they were, telling them it would be all right, which was a lie. It would never be all right, none of it.

But Lucie. Where was Lucie? If Lucie had survived, Juliette would go on. She couldn't simply close her eyes in this terrible hell and wait for death to reunite her with her family. "Lucie?" she called in the darkness, and there, just to the right of Paul, she saw another hand reaching out from the rubble, a tiny hand, with tiny fingers and tiny nails, and suddenly, as she dragged her own body toward it, she was desperate to remember which of Paul's strong arms had held Lucie and which had held Mathilde, but then she was squeezing the hand in anguish, and it was just as cold as Claude's had been, just as devoid of life, and she wept as she dug through the rubble, trying to reach the girl entombed beneath, though she could already feel that her pulse was forever gone. Was it Lucie? Juliette would die if it was; she was certain of it. But just as she found a cold, lifeless leg beneath the books that had once sustained them, there was a noise behind her, a rustling, and then a cough.

"Maman?" whispered a tiny voice in the darkness, the most beautiful sound Juliette had ever heard. It was Lucie. The other girl's hand, which she was still clutching though it was cold and lifeless, belonged to Mathilde, and she let go of it instantly, shaking off a ghost. Her heart lurched in pain and guilt for a skip of a second, but the crushing weight of her own loss was unbearable, and there was not room enough on her shoulders for regret over not protecting her friend's child when she could not even save her own. What mattered now was that Lucie was still here. Her daughter was alive; her daughter was calling for her; her daughter was still on this earth.

"Lucie!" she called, choking on the lump of grief and hope

that had lodged itself in her heart, and then she was pulling her little girl from the rubble, and it was indeed her, her hair matted, her face gray with ash, her arm streaked with blood, but she was here, and she was alive, and there was hope for them both, and Juliette had a reason to live.

"Maman!" Lucie kept saying, over and over, and Juliette pulled her close and buried her face in her brown curls and breathed all the hope and the life and the love she'd had for the others into the living body of her one remaining child.

"Lucie, it's going to be all right," she lied. "Maman will make everything all right."

And then, though her throbbing leg shouldn't have supported her own weight, let alone the weight of two, she pulled herself up and hoisted her daughter into her arms and stumbled her way across the destruction, past the hand of Mathilde still reaching up from the rubble, toward the shattered front of the store, where a door still stood, a door to a life beyond this hell, beyond these ruined walls. The grief of losing Paul, Claude, and Alphonse would break her, the guilt of losing Elise's daughter would bow her, but Lucie was still here, a gift from God, and Juliette knew in that moment that they would both go on, even if the future ahead of them was something they wouldn't recognize, something they couldn't bear. They would do it together, a mother and daughter, emerging from the ashes like a pair of phoenixes, though Juliette feared grief would tether her to the ground no matter how wide she spread her wings.

An ambulance arrived at some point and brought them to the hospital, where both Juliette and Lucie were forced to stay for months. Juliette's leg had been broken, and her head injury was

significant; the doctors couldn't figure out why sometimes she
fainted out of the blue, and sometimes she couldn't sleep at all,
for days on end. Lucie had broken an arm and a collarbone, and
once she was healed, the nurses let her sleep by Juliette's bedside,
where the nights were punctuated by screams from her recurring
nightmares.

Paul, the boys, and Mathilde LeClair were buried alongside
Antoinette, in the cemetery on the southern end of Boulogne-
Billancourt, and after she and Lucie were released from the hospital, a priest from the Paroisse Sainte Cécile performed a funeral
mass that no one else attended.

For the first year, Juliette and Lucie went every day to visit
the graves, but by April 1944, a year after the blast, there was no
longer a place for them in Paris. The government had no interest
in supporting an American-born widow and her daughter, and
there was no money to help rebuild the store.

Juliette finally wrote a letter to her father's estranged older sister, her aunt Sally, who lived in New York. She wired them some
money, but it was only enough to rent a small room in a farmhouse outside Paris. They were always on the verge of starving,
and slowly, slowly, Juliette came to hate the France she had once
loved, the place she had thought of as the embodiment of all her
dreams. It had taken everything from her, and now, in her most
desperate hour, it refused to give anything back.

After the Liberation, she'd had no choice but to write to her
aunt again, begging her to take them in. She couldn't bear the
thought of leaving Paul, Claude, Alphonse, and Antoinette behind, but it was only their bodies here. She knew that now. Their
souls were with her always, and lately, she'd been hearing Paul's
voice in her head, urging her to make something of her life, for
Lucie's sake.

"Begin again," he'd been whispering to her. "Begin again for her."

When she'd told her doctor that her dead husband had suggested she return to America, he had replied by recommending a psychiatric evaluation. But it wasn't crazy to believe that the love of her life was still with her, or that she could hear the voices of her children every time she closed her eyes. Paul had promised never to leave her, to always keep her safe, and he had always been a man of his word. Why would he abandon her now, when she needed him most?

And so, just as Paul had urged her to do, she and Lucie climbed aboard an ocean liner bound for New York Harbor to begin a new life, leaving the ruins of their bookshop of dreams behind them forever.

CHAPTER EIGHTEEN

Mathilde.

It was all Elise could think about as she rode in the passenger seat of Monsieur Léandre's borrowed truck, the first week of September 1944, with Bernard at the wheel, the wind whipping her hair. *Mathilde.* The word rang again and again through her head like church bells on a wedding day, a sound of joy, a sound of hope, a sound of a future beautiful and bright. Mathilde would be there. Mathilde would be waiting. Mathilde would be in her arms again, safe and sound.

The war still raged in the east, and there was still fighting in the south, but Paris had been liberated the week before, and the Germans were gradually retreating from the rest of France, too, pushed back at every front by the unstoppable Allied advance that had begun in June with the landing at Normandy. Elise had never imagined that the war would last this long, but as 1943 had turned cold and bled into 1944, she had felt some of the light go out of her. She had helped to protect hundreds of children who came through Aurignon, but each one had reminded her anew of her distance from her own daughter. Would Mathilde remember her?

She had imagined their reunion so many times, the feel of Mathilde's heart beating against hers, the familiar scent of her, the way Mathilde would have grown from a toddler into a child by now. It had been nearly two years, each day of distance almost unbearable. There would be so many things to share, so many stories to tell, though Elise knew she would only recount a fraction of what she'd gone through. She would never tell Mathilde about the Resistance fighter who died in her arms from a wound she couldn't patch, or the woman she'd seen shot in the face in the streets of Aurignon by a German whose hand trembled as he pulled the trigger. She would not tell her of the blood she had helped scrub from the church floor after a man took his own life there, nor would she tell her of watching Père Clément dragged away and thrown into the back of a transport truck. He was surely dead by now, and she prayed for his soul every night.

But the war in France was over, and Bernard was driving her north to Paris, to a life where she would reunite with her daughter and return to her apartment and try to become Elise LeClair again.

"You will see your daughter soon," Bernard said without looking at her as they drove. His eyes were on the road, which was shredded and lined with stalled cars and the occasional body. Though the devil had receded with the occupiers, the trail of his destruction remained.

A car honked behind them, urging them to hurry, and Elise wanted to beg Bernard to drive faster, too, but she already knew that was futile. Now, as he narrowly missed steering the truck into a bomb-hewn ditch, she understood why. This wasn't the

France she and Olivier had driven through years ago on their way back from a rare holiday in Vallauris. This was a hellscape out of a nightmare, something she couldn't have imagined before seeing it with her own eyes.

"Will she remember me?" Elise asked after a time, once the impatient driver at their tail had attempted to whiz around them and had instead wound up veering off the road and sideswiping a tree.

"A child always remembers," Bernard said. They were quiet for a moment more, and then he added, "My mother died when I was eight. I remember her still, every curve of her face."

"I'm sorry." Elise knew how lucky she was to still be alive. God had shown her favor, had spared her, and she knew that it was because she was meant to return for Mathilde.

Bernard waved the condolence away. "Your daughter will know you."

"But she was so young. It's been two years, Bernard. I don't know if I would have strength enough to bear it if she were to look at me like a stranger."

"Your daughter will know you," he repeated. "And you're stronger than you think."

She wished she could feel as confident about the future as Bernard seemed to be, but surety eluded her. The only thing she knew was that Mathilde was still out there, and she would find her, and nothing else would matter. "Bernard," she said after a while. "I don't know how to thank you."

He glanced at her briefly and then returned his gaze to the shattered landscape beyond the windshield. "What for?"

"For believing in the future when I cannot seem to. For taking me home."

He didn't answer, and she didn't speak again. Instead, she

wrapped the silence around her like a blanket, muffling the world that rolled by outside the windows.

Darkness fell before they reached Paris, and though Elise wanted nothing more than to get to Mathilde as quickly as possible, she couldn't argue with Bernard, who pointed out how dangerous the damaged roads would be in the blackness. They slept in the truck, hot and restless, and set out again at dawn, fueled by a canteen of water, a hard loaf of bread, and some potatoes Madame Roche had packed for their journey.

It was just past ten in the morning when Bernard steered the truck north from Issy, crossing one of the twin bridges over the sparkling Seine. As they approached the capital, the streets took on a festive feel, with the tricolor waving from balconies and flying from rooftops. American and British soldiers lined the roads, talking and laughing. Here, for the moment, these boys who had risked their lives to turn back the Germans were enjoying the fruits of their labors. Paris was free.

"Shall I bring you straight to your friend's bookstore?" Bernard asked, glancing at Elise. She couldn't tear her eyes away from the joy, the celebration.

"Please." The closer they drew to Juliette's street, the harder it was for Elise to breathe. There was evidence of fighting here, bullet holes in walls, burned buildings, pockmarked streets. But Boulogne-Billancourt was still standing, having survived the worst. Elise's heart thudded in anticipation.

"Bombs," Bernard said after a while as he steered the truck carefully around haphazardly parked automobiles and overturned scooters. Somewhere in the distance, a crowd sang "La Marseillaise."

"Pardon?"

"Bombs," he repeated, his eyes never leaving the road. "This area has been hit."

Elise swallowed a sudden lump in her throat. "Recently?"

"It's difficult to tell." He paused and scanned the neighborhood as he waited for a woman and child to cross the road ahead of them. "No. I don't think so. But there was a lot of damage."

"The Renault factory," Elise said. "It was struck in March of '42, before I left."

The concern didn't slip from Bernard's face.

"You don't think the Allies hit it again, do you?" Elise asked.

"I don't know. It depends whether the factory went back into service, I think."

Elise could hear the fear in her own voice as she said quickly, "The bookstore is nowhere near the factory."

"That's good, then."

But as they drove west and then north through the suburb, Elise began to notice signs of ruin that weren't there before: charred trees, broken pavement, buildings with jagged bites taken out of their roofs.

Finally, the road ahead of them ended abruptly in a pile of rubble so thick it appeared that a truck had simply dropped a load of shattered cement, concrete, and bricks in their path. They both sat staring at it for a few seconds before Elise spoke. "The bookstore is just ahead, I think, a block or so down."

Without looking at her, Bernard put the truck in reverse. "I will find a way around."

But Elise was filled with a sense of sudden desperation. "No. I'll get out. It's only a short walk from here."

"I will come with you."

"No." Elise looked at him, an unexpected sadness sweeping

through her, mingling with her panic. "You've already done so much."

Bernard frowned. "And if the bookstore is closed?"

"Then I will ask around until I find someone who knows where the family has gone."

"And if—"

Elise cut him off, unwilling to hear whatever he was about to say. "I will find them, and then I will bring my daughter home."

Bernard watched her closely as she opened the truck door and climbed out, closing the door lightly behind her. "Be well, Leona."

"Elise," she said through the open window. "My real name is Elise."

He smiled. "Elise, then. I am François."

"François," she murmured. "It is nice to meet you."

"And you." And then, with a nod, he backed up, turned the truck around, and was gone, cleaving the past two years of her life away, as if they had never happened at all.

She watched until his truck vanished around a corner, and then, squaring her shoulders, she set down the path that had been cleared to the right of the rubble. She had the strange, disorienting feeling, as she wove her way around a bend and over a pile of jagged stone fragments that dug into her shoes, that she was on another planet. The destruction here was so complete, civilization so obscured by the mounds of ruin, that she couldn't recognize it as any version of earth she knew, never mind a familiar suburb of Paris. Dust kicked up with her every step, swirling into the air like devastated clouds, but then there was light on the other side of the ruin, and her heartbeat quickened. She was almost there, almost to Juliette's street, where she would find the bookshop standing, and Mathilde safe and sound within its walls.

She picked her way with effort over a final mountain of rubble, breathing hard, and as she descended the other side, she stopped short, her heart squeezed by an icy fist of fear. "No." The word escaped her lips, a choked sound of grief, as she stared.

Ahead of her, the row of buildings where the bookstore had once stood now loomed like jagged, angry teeth against a gray sky, roofs missing, walls collapsed inward, sharp edges scraping nothingness. Gone were the bakery, the hat store, the antiques store. Gone was the green door across the way with the crooked 10 listing to one side, the geraniums in the pots that bloomed in the spring. In place of all that was familiar, there was only waste and ruin. The rubble she had just clawed her way through, she realized with a sudden jolt of horror, was the detritus of the world she'd once known, the world she'd assumed would be waiting when she returned.

Shaking, Elise spun around in a circle, searching for something she recognized. Surely she was on the wrong block. Bernard had dropped her in the wrong place, or perhaps her memory had been faulty after all the time away. But there, at the end of the street, was the familiar bell tower of the Paroisse Sainte Cécile, and perpendicular to the ruined lane was the still-standing butcher shop that had belonged to Monsieur Lychner.

Elise put one foot in front of the other, her whole body shaking as she approached what had once been the bookstore. There was no door to push open, so she stepped over the ruined threshold and gaped at the emptiness. Gone were the shelves, the books, the desk Juliette sometimes worked behind, the children's area where Mathilde had played with Lucie and the boys. Bile rising in her throat, Elise took a few more steps inside, noting the sky above her where the ceiling—and the apartment above it—had once been. In the middle of the room that was no longer a room at all, on a pile of rubble, lay a splintered piece of wood with the letters *Li* in faded blue and gold—all that was left of the Librairie des Rêves sign that had hung just above the door.

Elise's stomach lurched, and she folded in two, her body rejecting what her eyes were telling her. She allowed herself a brief moment of collapse before she wiped away the tears and stood, scanning the devastation. *Breathe*, she reminded herself. *You would feel it if your daughter was dead.* But would she? Or had that connection been severed the day she walked away from Mathilde, the day she entrusted her child's life to someone else? She moaned and fell to her knees, still gazing around in disbelief at the wreckage of the store. In the far corner, she could make out the icebox that had once lived in Juliette's apartment, the armchair where Paul read his books at night, now flattened to a pancake.

"Madame?"

The voice came from behind her, and Elise spun around to see a tiny, stooped old woman standing there, her dress gray with dust. "It is not safe," she said. "You can't be in there."

"What happened?" Elise whispered. "To the bookstore owners? To their family?"

The woman glanced behind Elise, as if waiting for Juliette and the children to emerge from the rubble, and then she refocused on Elise. "The Allies bombed the Renault factory on a Sunday last April. There were several bombs that missed. They had terrible aim, you know. Imagine missing by so many kilometers!"

Elise's throat was dry. "But there was enough warning for everyone to get to safety, yes?"

The woman shook her head slowly. "Less than a minute. In broad daylight. By the time we understood what was happening . . ." Her voice trailed off.

"The children? What happened to the children at the book-store?"

The woman didn't meet her gaze. "The husband died."

"Paul. My God, Paul."

"And three of the children."

"No." A dark tide of foreboding rolled through Elise. "My God, no. Which ones?"

"There was a fourth child here, too," the woman went on. It was like Elise's panicked questions were simply sailing over her head. "The little girl of Monsieur Foulon's cousin, I believe, an orphan already. Sweet little soul."

"Yes, Mathilde." Desperation clawed at Elise's throat. "Mathilde survived? Please, you have to tell me! Is Mathilde alive? Is Juliette alive?"

"Madame Foulon lived, yes." The woman sighed and gestured toward the bookstore. "I have never seen someone so broken. Her daughter was the only one of the children to live."

"No." Elise was struggling to put together what the woman was saying, though it was already clear. "Do you mean Lucie? Not Mathilde? Lucie?"

"Blessed be to God." The woman crossed herself. "A miracle."

"But the other little girl . . . Mathilde . . ."

"I'm afraid not." The woman pressed her lips together. "The priest reminded the congregation that week that the orphan had gone to be with her parents, who had already departed this earth. Part of God's plan, he said. He encouraged us all to find peace in that."

The woman delivered the last words with a singsong note of hope, and if Elise hadn't been so paralyzed by horror, she would have reached out and slapped her. "Mathilde is dead?"

She grieved for Paul and the boys, too, ached for Juliette's loss, but she couldn't process what the woman was telling her. Mathilde couldn't be gone.

The woman looked at her more closely now. "Did you know the child yourself?"

"I am her mother," Elise whispered.

The woman began to protest that it was impossible, and in some corner of her consciousness, Elise could hear her asking questions about why the Foulons had said Mathilde was an orphan, but she was already turning her back, already walking away, her feet carrying her down what remained of the street, right at the corner, and east toward the graveyard near the Seine where she knew Juliette's first daughter was buried. Had she laid the others to rest in the same place? Had Mathilde been buried with them?

She felt like a dead woman herself as she staggered into the cemetery twenty minutes later. She had been here once with Juliette, to lay flowers on the lost baby's grave, so she knew the general area of the Foulon family plot. Still, her vision was blurred by shock and grief, so it took another ten minutes before she found the familiar gravestone of little Antoinette Foulon, and beside it, four new headstones, their lettering stark and unmistakable.

Elise was aware, on some level, of the graves marked for Paul, born in 1897; Claude, born in 1935; and Alphonse, born in 1937. But it was the fourth headstone that brought her to her knees. *Mathilde Foulon, 1940–1943.* There it was, chiseled into stone. It was the final resting place of Elise's daughter, and it didn't even bear her real name.

Elise placed her hand on the cool grass in the headstone's shadow and retched until her body was exhausted. She was hardly aware of the tears streaming down her cheeks, or the moans rising from her throat in the shape of her daughter's name. She clawed at the earth, not caring that people were stopping along other paths in the cemetery to stare. She wanted to bring her daughter back, to hold her, to breathe life back into her. That's what a mother was supposed to do, and she had failed. She had been many miles away, living a different life, when a bomb had fallen from the sky and ripped the soul from her daughter's tiny body. How would she live with herself?

"Madame?" Strong arms wrapped around her and pulled her from the ground, and as she fell backward, the arms held her, not letting her go. It was a man, a stranger, and he didn't say another word as she sobbed and screamed and cursed the heavens. He simply braced her with his own body and waited until, like a spent balloon, she deflated and fell limply forward, still in his grasp. "Are you all right, madame?" he asked when she went silent.

A laugh bubbled up in her throat. How could he ask such a thing? How could he imagine that she would ever be all right again? "No." She pulled away and turned to look at him. He was perhaps ten years her senior, with a scar down his right cheek, and a closely trimmed mustache. His eyes were kind and full of pity that she didn't deserve.

"Your family?" he asked, gesturing to the grave markers.

"My daughter." Another tear slipped down her cheek.

"I lost my girls, too. Both daughters and my wife."

Elise realized then that it wasn't just pity she saw in his eyes; it was recognition. He, too, had a well of raw grief within him. "When?"

"March of '42. The first bombing. I—I was at work at the factory. I was supposed to protect them, you see."

"I'm sorry." She searched his eyes again. "I'm very sorry. How do you move on? How do you . . . How do you believe it? That they're gone? I don't feel it, you see. I don't feel it here." She tapped her empty heart.

"I have a son. He needs me to return to life. There must be someone who needs you, too, isn't there?"

"My husband is dead. Mathilde was all I . . ." Her voice trailed off into a sob.

"Still, you must go on, madame. There is no other choice. You must live to honor her."

Elise didn't say anything. How could she honor her daughter with life when all she wanted to do was curl up beside her grave and die?

"Can I help you home?" he asked after a time.

Slowly, she shook her head.

He studied her, perhaps evaluating whether she was a risk to herself, before nodding. He put a hand on her arm for a few seconds and then withdrew without another word, trudging out of the cemetery without a look back.

Slowly, Elise turned back to her daughter's grave and traced the letters of her name—*Mathilde*—with a shaking hand before curling up on the cold earth and closing her eyes, praying that God would see fit to take her, too.

CHAPTER NINETEEN

Elise slept atop Mathilde's grave for two nights before the cemetery's caretaker made his way over, his mouth turned down at the corners, to tell her that he would call the authorities if she did not move on. She had explained that her daughter was here, and that she could not leave her alone.

"This place is full of sons and daughters, madame," he said, his expression as flat as his tone. "I can't have people sleeping in my graveyard, though. Move along."

And so she had dragged herself back outside the cemetery walls to a world that was still in existence, though she could hardly believe it. How could life go on without Mathilde? But her stomach rumbled, reminding her that she hadn't eaten in more than two days, and finally, she began to walk east, back toward Paris, crossing the Seine on the Pont Mirabeau and making her way slowly up the avenue Émile Zola.

It was strange how familiar Paris was, how undamaged, how much like its old self. In Boulogne, just across the river, hell had come to earth, but here, flowers bloomed cheerily from window boxes, and the women strolling the streets wore rouge, lipstick, and heels as they walked briskly along. Did they not know that the rest of France had been shattered? That people had lost husbands and wives, daughters and sons? That as she hurried along, Elise felt no sense of belonging, though not so long ago she had been one of them? She resented their happiness, the lightness of their expressions, the intact homes they were likely returning to with baguettes and sunflowers tucked under their arms.

She turned from the rue Jean de la Fontaine onto the avenue Mozart and found her old building just as she'd remembered it, white marble, gilded edges, a soaring mansard roof. A doorman she didn't know stood in front of the door, blocking her way rather than ushering her in as he gazed at her suspiciously.

"Madame?" he asked, the word a question. He wrinkled his nose slightly.

"I live here." She knew she looked a fright, but so would he if he'd just traveled from the south and learned that his daughter had died. His family was probably safe and whole, and she instantly hated him for it with a ferocity that surprised her.

He narrowed his eyes slightly. "I have never seen you before."

"I have not seen you, either," she answered reasonably. "I have been gone for two years, but a friend has been keeping my apartment."

When he didn't say anything, she added impatiently, "Monsieur, I am Elise LeClair. I live on the sixth floor."

"And you have identification proving this?" he asked, still not moving. It was clear he did not believe her.

"Of course." She dug in her handbag and withdrew her papers, only to realize just before thrusting them over that they identified her as Leona Denaes. She yanked them back before he could take them, and he raised an eyebrow at her.

"Perhaps your *friend* can vouch for you," he said in a tone that clearly mocked her. "Until then, though, you'll need to step away from this building."

She wanted to spit at him, but that would do her no good. Instead, she whirled on her heel and walked away with as much dignity as she could toward Constant Bouet's art gallery nearby. He would help her sort things out.

She was relieved to find it standing, the Galerie Constant Bouet shingle still hanging outside. In the window, among several paintings she had never seen, she spotted one of Olivier's works, an abstract piece he had done the year they married. On it was a tag with a price that seemed unimaginable; it was three times what one of his paintings would have sold for two years earlier.

A man she'd never seen before emerged from the back of the immaculate gallery and looked at her the same way the doorman outside her building had. Before he could turn her away, she spoke. "I'm looking for Constant Bouet."

"I'm afraid he is not here, madame."

Elise felt a rising sense of desperation. "Do you know when he'll be back?"

The man shook his head and took a step toward Elise, waving in her direction with the backs of both hands, shooing her away. "As I said, he is not here."

Elise took a few steps backward as he stepped closer, but then she stopped. She was done with being pushed out, done with having things taken from her. The world had stolen her husband, her daughter. She would not let it take her dignity, too. "Monsieur, I am Elise LeClair. Monsieur Bouet was keeping my apartment for me in my absence. He is expecting me."

The man's expression immediately changed. "Elise LeClair?"

Something flickered in his eyes, and his mouth twitched. "You're the widow of Olivier LeClair."

Even two years after his death, he defined her. "Yes."

He stared at her for a moment more. "Monsieur Bouet left word that you might return, but I didn't expect . . ." His voice trailed off.

"You thought I was dead." Elise took a step toward him. "But I am not. I am alive, and I am here, and I want to go home. Now, I will ask you again: Where is Monsieur Bouet?"

The man held her gaze. "He departed just a few weeks ago. For New York."

Elise blinked at him, sure she had misunderstood. "New York?"

"Yes. He is planning to open a gallery there." He said it as though it was as reasonable and expected as Constant having gone to the market to buy milk. Instead, he had apparently immigrated to another continent while a world war still raged.

"But how is that possible?" Elise sputtered.

The man rubbed his thumb over the tip of his index and middle fingers, the universal sign for money. "He has acquired much valuable art, which has earned him some influence."

Elise looked around the store and realized for the first time how empty the walls were. Her vision blurred for a second as she turned back to the man. "He took my husband's paintings with him."

The man had the decency to look away. "Many of them, yes. But of course he paid for them years ago, didn't he? That was his arrangement with your husband." His gaze slid back to her. "Now, shall we find your apartment key?"

He turned without waiting for an answer, and she watched as he slipped behind the desk in the main room and unlocked a drawer. He rummaged briefly before emerging with a key in his hand. "This is it, I believe."

Elise stepped forward and plucked it from his grasp. It felt hot and unfamiliar, a portal to a life that had long since vanished.

"Your daughter?" he asked, breaking the silence between them and startling her.

"Pardon?"

"You have a daughter, yes? She is all right, too?"

Elise couldn't look away, though she wanted to. "No. She is dead," she said, and the sudden pity in his eyes burned a hole in her.

"Madame, I'm terribly sorry. If there's anything I can——"

"I—I'll need your assistance with the doorman," she said quickly, cutting him off. She didn't want any of his sympathy.

"I see. Let me just close up, and I will accompany you."

Five minutes later, he had closed the gallery doors and flipped the sign. Olivier's painting seemed to watch them from the window. "I did not introduce myself," the man said as they began to walk. "My name is Roland Vasseur. I never had the chance to meet you or your husband, but Monsieur Bouet spoke of you. I joined the gallery as his business partner in November of '42."

"Not long after I left." Elise pushed away thoughts of what she was doing in the fall two years earlier. She had been huddled beneath blankets in Madame Roche's guest room, crying herself to sleep, dreaming of returning to Mathilde.

"Yes." Monsieur Vasseur cleared his throat. "He had just come into possession of an artist's collection, and he needed someone to manage the gallery for him while he showed her art to various clients and tastemakers. She made him a fortune. He hired me at first as a manager, but when he left for New York, he sold his gallery to me with the condition that I keep his name on it."

"You've done well for yourselves, it seems," Elise said. She did not mean it as a compliment, and it irked her to see his chest swell with pride. "Who was the artist whose work made him such a success?"

"A woman named Anicette Rousselle. Did you know her? I believe she was part of your husband's circle."

Elise ticked through Olivier's acquaintances and shook her head. "No. But I wasn't very included in my husband's world during the last years of his life."

Monsieur Vasseur looked sad. "I'm sorry, Madame LeClair. You have lost much."

She bowed her head. The exclusion from Olivier's social group paled in comparison to the loss of her daughter.

"In any case," Monsieur Vasseur continued after a few seconds of silence. "Madame Rousselle died during the war, leaving behind a great trove of art that came into Monsieur Bouet's possession."

"I see." Other people's misfortune, it seemed, had been Constant's enormous gain. "How sad for her."

"How sad for all of us. So many great artists lost."

They turned the corner onto her block, and Elise stood back while Monsieur Vasseur exchanged words with her doorman in a low tone. He ushered them past without looking at her, but she stopped in front of him and stood there until he was forced to make eye contact. "Bonjour, Madame LeClair," he grunted.

They took the lift to the sixth floor, and as they approached her door, her hand was shaking so uncontrollably that after a few seconds, Monsieur Vasseur took the key from her and inserted it into the lock himself. He opened the door and stood aside to let her enter first.

She was hardly aware of him as she walked into the dark, shadow-cloaked apartment. Dust hung in the air, and furniture was draped in blankets, making the interior look ghostly, haunted. As if sensing the same, Monsieur Vasseur strode across the floor, his shoes clicking against the polished wood, and rolled up one of the heavy curtains, flooding the space with light. "No need for these anymore," he said brightly, gesturing to the blackout shades, but Elise hardly heard him.

She was immediately aware of the emptiness, the spaces where her belongings should have been. The dining table and sofas were still there, under sheets, along with a few lamps, the outline of beds in the bedrooms. But the place had been stripped of everything else: books, the old typewriter she had once used to write letters, even the family pictures of Olivier, Elise, and Mathilde that had once graced the end tables. Most striking, though, was the lack of art. The walls had once been lined with Olivier's work, framed paintings and sketches, and the shelves had been filled with her wood carvings. Now, it was like they had never existed at all.

"Where is everything?" she asked, turning to Monsieur Vasseur. Perhaps he and Constant had moved the things for safekeeping.

But his expression was blank. "Everything?"

"The art," she whispered. "All the art. My *life*."

He looked around, confused, and she could see him registering the blank spaces. "Madame LeClair, I have been in this apartment only once, and it looked just as it does now. Monsieur Bouet mentioned that there had been a German raid in this arrondissement in the fall of '42, and that he lost several paintings himself. It is likely, I'm afraid, that your art was taken."

"Taken?"

He nodded. "The Germans sent teams of art experts to, er, *borrow* works to take back to Germany. That is what they called it when they came. Your husband's address was almost certainly on their list because of his renown."

"But those paintings were ours. The sculptures were mine." In a daze, she crossed the parlor to her studio and opened the door. A few of her pieces remained—a few attempts at Juliette's birds, a side profile of her father's face. But every carving she'd made of Mathilde—the sculpture of her hand when she was a newborn, the dozens of times Elise had coaxed her daughter's face from wood, were gone. She moaned and felt her knees give out.

"Madame LeClair?" Monsieur Vasseur was at her elbow, helping her up. "I understand that this is a lot to take in. Let's get you seated, shall we?" He helped her back into the parlor, where, still supporting her by the arm, he used his other hand to whisk a sheet from the sofa. Dust flew everywhere as the faded blue of her familiar furniture emerged, and she allowed herself to be guided onto a cushion. "Now, what is missing? Perhaps we can make a list, and I can assist you with a formal claim."

She shook her head, looking around at the emptiness. It was the final droplet of water that had broken the dam. "Please, just go."

He looked startled. "You're certain? I can stay and help you get things in order."

"I only want to be alone."

"Very well, Madame LeClair." He shifted awkwardly from one foot to the other. "You can find me at the gallery if you need anything. I'm certain Monsieur Bouet would have insisted I do all I could to make you comfortable."

"Thank you." It was entirely beyond this man's understanding that she would never be comfortable again. He hesitated awkwardly, then slid her key onto a table and headed for the door, which he pulled shut with a thud of finality on his way out. Afterward, she sat on the couch in the stillness for hours, until the sun began to set, and then, numbly, she stood, her legs shaking beneath her, and made her way toward Mathilde's nursery.

She turned the knob and entered. The room was dark, and she crossed to the window to lift the shade up. Amber light poured in, coating the space in honey, and a sob caught in Elise's chest. Mathilde's infant bed was still here, along with the tiny pillow over which her curls had once fallen. Elise touched it, and she could almost see Mathilde's rosy cheeks, her lips parted in a rose-bud bow, her eyes closed in slumber, as her little body rose up and down with the steady breath of sleep.

But Mathilde wasn't here. No part of her remained in this room.

Next, Elise moved back to her studio, where she'd spent so many hours with her daughter, showing her the world outside their doors. She looked up at the ceiling and was startled to see the paint intact, the trees of the Bois de Boulogne beneath a star-dotted twilight sky. Her eyes welled with tears; of course there would have been no way for the Germans to steal this. It felt like a gift from God, this reminder of Mathilde's sky, which Elise had imagined connecting them while she'd been gone.

She lay down on her back on the floor, her whole body aching, grief burning through her. In the silent emptiness, she stared up at the ceiling and willed sleep to take her, even for a little while, into oblivion.

Instead, she was still awake beneath the sea of stars when morning came, and as the sky above her began to glow in the light trickling in from the open door, she squeezed her eyes closed and tried to see Mathilde's face. But all she could see was the headstone in the cemetery, beneath which her daughter would sleep forever.

• • •

Elise forced herself to bathe, to change into some of her old clothing, which still hung in the closet, and to go out that day for food. Realizing she had neither money nor identification, she returned to the gallery, where Monsieur Vasseur looked like he was expecting her.

"I know Monsieur Bouet bought my husband's work outright, and you don't owe me anything," she said quickly. "But I see how much you're selling his paintings for now. Far more than Monsieur Bouet paid him for them, now that Olivier is dead. I'm hoping you'll consider loaning me a bit of money to get by on until I am back on my feet. I wouldn't ask, but right now I have nowhere else to go."

She was expecting an argument, but the gallery owner simply handed her a neat stack of bills, along with a satchel. Suspicious, she looked inside and found bread, cheese, a sausage, and three apples, a small bounty. "That is to take with you," he said. "I have biscuits and coffee in the back room for you now, if you'd like. I was hoping you would return."

He led her to the back room, which was saturated with the scent of coffee beans, real ones. Her stomach growled, and he motioned for her to sit down at the small table, where a plate of biscuits awaited her. She hesitated but then took one, gasping with delight at the buttery taste.

"Where did you get these?" she asked.

"A baker who owed me a favor."

"And the coffee?"

"Another favor." He smiled as he poured her a steaming cup.

She took a long sip, savoring the taste, which brought her back to a time when the world was at peace and the future had stretched before her like a grand illusion. "It seems you are owed many favors."

"I suspect life owes you some favors, too, Madame LeClair. How else may I help you?"

"First, I must have Monsieur Bouet's address in New York," she said when he sat beside her with his own cup of steaming coffee. "I have some questions for him about the disappearance of the art."

"Of course. I will write it down for you."

"And my identity card. When I fled, it was with false papers, and now, well, I need to be myself again."

"I will take care of that. Is there anything else you need, Madame LeClair?"

"Yes." She hesitated. "I need to find Juliette Foulon."

He looked at her blankly.

"She is the woman who cared for my daughter. There was a bomb . . ." She drew a shaking breath. "Only she and her daughter, Lucie, survived. I don't know where she has gone, but I need to hear how Mathilde—" She stopped abruptly, unable to complete the sentence. "I need to know. And I need to see if she needs my help." It was foolish, she knew. What could she do? But she had promised Juliette on the day she left Mathilde with her that she would help her if ever she needed it. She still owed her that, and though she was still reeling from her own loss, Elise's heart broke thinking of what Juliette had endured, too, and how devastated little Lucie must be. Juliette was Elise's family. She had to find her.

"Of course, madame. I will make inquiries."

"And there are two children. Georges and Suzanne Levy. They were separated from their mother. I need to locate them if they return to Paris."

"Jewish?" he asked, and for a second, she bristled. "I only ask because it will help me to find them. The Jewish children who have begun to return are being assisted by an aid organization. I will make some inquiries there, too."

"Can you connect me with them?" she asked. "The aid organization? Perhaps I can do some good there."

He seemed to consider this for a few seconds before nodding. "Certainly. But are you sure you wouldn't prefer to simply take some time to reacclimate?"

"No." She thought of all the children who had passed through Madame Roche's home, all the children who might be returning to find their families gone forever. "I think this is something I need to do."

"Very well, then. I'll place some calls, Madame LeClair."

"Why are you helping me?" she asked after a pause. "You don't owe me anything."

"Because it is the least I can do as a human being, madame. And I know how important your husband's work was to the establishment of this gallery's reputation. If I can do anything to help you, I will."

"Thank you," she said, taking the final sip of her coffee and standing. For now, it was enough to have Monsieur Vasseur feeling that he was in her debt. "Please let me know the moment you have any news of Juliette Foulon."

"Yes, madame." Monsieur Vasseur stood, but Elise was already striding out, the gallery owner's satchel of apology slung over her shoulder, her belly full but her heart as empty as it had been since she'd seen the ruins of La Librairie des Rêves.

CHAPTER TWENTY

Elise's days took on a familiar rhythm as 1944 bled into 1945, winter into spring. Elise volunteered twice a week with the Jewish children's aid organization Oeuvre de Secours aux Enfants, the OSE, occasionally making the journey to Andrésy, a commune northwest of Paris, to visit the children housed at the orphanage there. She scanned the rosters of returnees for Georges and Suzanne in vain and cried herself to sleep at night, depleted by the constancy of telling children that though they'd survived against impossible odds, there was no sign of their parents. Often, there were cousins or aunts and uncles or sometimes even grandparents who could be found to take them home. But for many of them, it had already sunk in that it was likely their parents would not return.

The tales from the east that had begun to flow back to France were horrific: camps where children and the elderly were murdered on arrival, showers that pumped poison gas, mass graves in picturesque summer resorts. The horror of it all sat within Elise like a weight; otherwise, she might have floated away like an untethered balloon, nothing grounding her to earth.

Monsieur Vasseur had insisted on loaning her a bit more money to get by on, and he had given her the address of Constant Bouet in New York, but her letters to him had all gone unanswered. She wondered if her words were even reaching him; mail service was still wildly disrupted. Still, his silence felt like a severing of the final threads connecting her to her former life. No one she had known well before the war was here anymore, and sometimes it felt as though the past had been a dream.

On her days off from her work with the OSE, she began visiting the Hôtel Lutetia in the sixth arrondissement, which in April had become a processing center for the men, women, and children returning from concentration camps. And each morning, no matter what the rest of her hollow day held, she greeted the sunrise by kneeling beside Mathilde's grave.

On a sunny afternoon in May 1945, she had just walked through the door of the orphanage in Andrésy when she heard a small voice call her name.

"Madame LeClair?"

She looked through the doorway to the large front parlor where, to her astonishment, she saw Suzanne Levy seated beside her brother, Georges, both of them reading books. She gasped and took a few steps toward them, catching the children in her arms as they threw themselves at her, all of them talking over each other. Finally, they wriggled out of her grasp and stood grinning at her.

Both had sprouted since she had seen them last, and Georges, who was now nearly thirteen, stood nearly as tall as Elise. Both children looked malnourished, dark circles under their eyes, hair hanging in strings around their narrow faces. But they were here, and they were alive. "Georges," she whispered, reaching out to touch his face, and then his sister's. "Suzanne."

"Is it really you, Madame LeClair?" Suzanne said. "Where is Mathilde? How are Madame Foulon, and Lucie and Claude and Alphonse?"

The jubilation of finding the children was replaced immediately with a deep swell of grief, and Elise put her hands over her mouth to keep a sob in as she tried to force a smile. Georges and Suzanne had already seen too much sadness, and with their own mother still missing—which she must have been, if they were here in the orphanage—they didn't need to shoulder her grief, too. "Mathilde did not survive," Elise managed to say without breaking, though she could hear the wobble in her voice. "There was a bomb . . ."

And then, despite her best effort, she was crying, and Suzanne's arms were around her waist, pulling her into a tight hug. After a moment, Georges wrapped his arms around both of them, and they stood like that for a full minute, drawing comfort from each other.

When they pulled away, Elise explained what had happened to the bookstore, adding that Juliette and Lucie had disappeared.

Suzanne stared at Elise in disbelief. "And Madame Foulon left no word for you?"

Elise could only shake her head. "I assume she thought I had died, too. There isn't a day I don't think of her, though, and worry for her and for Lucie."

"I am sure she thinks of you, too," Suzanne said.

Elise wiped her tears away and forced a smile. This was, after all, a joyous reunion, even with all they'd lost. The children had, like Elise, survived the war against the odds.

"Madame LeClair?" Georges asked after a moment. "Have you had any news of our mother?"

His voice was high with hope, and Elise hated that she had to let them down. "I have been checking often, but there are many

people still missing. I feel certain that she will return for you."
She didn't know why she had said it, for she had begun to lose
hope that Ruth Levy was still alive. The sadness in Georges's eyes
was deep as an ocean, and in that moment, Elise made a decision.
"Come, children. I will sort things out with the OSE, and we
will go to my apartment. You will be safe with me until your
mother comes home."

Suzanne accepted this with a teary nod, and after Georges
nodded his assent, too, Elise went off to speak to the woman in
charge of the orphanage, who would push back because Elise was
not Jewish, but who would have to see that the children would
be loved and that she would promise to honor their past and their
heritage until their mother returned.

Georges and Suzanne slipped easily into Elise's life, sharing the
room that had once been Olivier's studio. It would have been
easier to give them Mathilde's old room, but Elise couldn't bear
to change a thing about it. Each night, when sleep eluded her,
she crept into her studio and by candlelight added clouds or stars
or wisps of smoke to the sky, keeping it alive and ever changing.
Georges and Suzanne seemed to understand that more than anything, Elise needed to continue living in the past.

They told her that they'd spent most of the latter half of the war
on a farm in Saint-Agrève, where they helped out with chores along
with two other children, and were rewarded with a warm place to
sleep, food to eat, and false papers that declared them Christian.
Their mother's choice to send them away had saved them.

As the summer rolled on, Elise bought them new clothes,
cooked for them, and promised that she would enroll them in

school in the autumn, but they were all living in a fog of grief. She could never take the place of their mother, and they could never fill the gaping hole in her heart that Mathilde had left behind. They were puzzle pieces that didn't fit and never would. But she could give them her love, and by late that summer, they were a family, cobbled together from the remnants of loss, glued fast by grief.

Elise wrote sixteen letters to Constant Bouet in New York, inquiring after the works that had disappeared from her apartment, but he never replied, and by late July, the funds Monsieur Vasseur had given her had nearly run out.

"I must go to the gallery," Elise said one day over a meager breakfast of bread and preserves. It was still impossible to obtain real coffee, but she'd found a grocer who sold a convincing duplicate made of acorn and chicory, and with a bit of milk, it was possible to swallow it.

Georges took a gulp of his small glass of milk. "We are out of money, aren't we?"

Elise looked away. "It's nothing for you to worry about," she said lightly. The children had already been forced into early adulthood; she couldn't bear the thought of burdening them with this, too.

"I will find work," Georges said, sitting up a little straighter.

"You are thirteen, Georges." She reached across the table and put her hand on his. "Please, don't worry. I will come up with a solution."

The obvious answer was that she should sell the apartment. They didn't need a space this large, and it would fetch them enough to keep them comfortable for some time. But that would mean losing her last physical connection to Mathilde, the place she'd brought her newborn daughter home to, the place she'd nursed her, the place she'd imagined the future she would have. She couldn't do it.

After breakfast, she walked confidently to the Galerie Constant Bouet, noting that Olivier's paintings still hung in the window. Just before eleven in the morning, Monsieur Vasseur arrived to open up, and when he saw her, he stopped and stared.

"Madame LeClair," he said, his smile tight. "To what do I owe the pleasure?"

"I'm supporting two children now, and I'm afraid I'm nearly out of money," she blurted out, not bothering to sugarcoat it. "I need a job, Monsieur Vasseur. Is there any chance I could work here as an assistant?"

"I do wish I could help you." He frowned. "But Madame LeClair, this gallery is hanging on by a thread. People simply do not have the funds, or desire, to acquire art at the prices we reasonably ask."

"Can't you offer my husband's paintings for a bit less?"

He looked horrified. "And sell off the last remaining works by one of Paris's greatest artists for a song? Surely not, Madame LeClair."

She bristled at his description of Olivier, whose ego would have ballooned at such words. Olivier hadn't been considered one of the city's greatest artists while he was alive; it seemed unreasonable that death should elevate him. "Please, I'm begging for your help," she said.

Monsieur Vasseur studied her skeptically for a long moment. "You are an artist, too, yes? I believe Monsieur Bouet said as much."

"I was."

He arched an eyebrow. "Madame LeClair, artists don't simply cease to be."

"But when their hearts are broken, things change, you see."

"With all due respect, Madame LeClair, grief has shaped some of our greatest artists. They simply learned to harness that pain." He said it clinically, as if creating art from a well of sadness wouldn't be like poking oneself in the eye again and again. "What is your medium?" He looked hungry now, a predator sniffing out a potential source of income.

"I was a wood-carver."

"Well, do you have any of your old pieces for me?" He took a step closer, his eyes gleaming. "I could evaluate them to determine their merit. You are not known like your husband, but perhaps the cachet of the LeClair name . . ."

So she would be sold not on the basis of her talent but on the strength of her dead husband's famous name. It rankled her, but it mattered little, for there were no works of art to be handed over anyhow. "When our apartment was looted, they took everything."

"Yes, of course, all your husband's paintings. You've said this."

"And nearly all my carvings, too." Her heart ached as she thought of Mathilde's face, sculpted again and again, pieces she had never sold for they were too personal.

"They took *your* work?" He seemed to be evaluating her. "So the Germans saw something in you. They thought your work was worth bringing home to their führer."

She didn't say anything; his obvious surprise was insulting, as was the fact that he was only looking at her this way now because German thugs had found her work desirable.

"How many pieces did they take?" he continued.

She bit her lip; it was still painful to think about. "More than two hundred."

"The Germans stole more than *two hundred* wood carvings from your apartment?"

He looked like he didn't believe her, so she added in explanation, "Most were small."

"I don't understand why there were so many of your pieces being stored there. Were you unable to sell them?"

"Monsieur Bouet was not supportive, nor was my husband."

He looked at her for a long time. "I see." He seemed to be considering something. "Well, Madame LeClair, I will send you some wood. Do you still have your tools?"

She thought of the chisels and gouges lying under a layer of dust in her studio and nodded.

"Well then, make me something new. If you're as good as the Germans evidently believed you to be, perhaps we've both found a solution to our problems."

A shipment of limewood blocks arrived at Elise's door the next day, delivered by a blank-faced young man who rolled the large box through her door on a cart and then scurried backward down the hall.

"What is this?" Georges asked, jumping up from his place on the couch to help her. He and Suzanne had been reading in silence, but this was more interesting. Elise opened the studio door for him, and with dust particles hanging in the air, illuminated by slanted light, Georges wheeled the cart in.

"Limewood," she told him, her heart thudding. She reached for a knife and sliced into the box, then she inhaled deeply, nearly knocked off her feet by the way the fresh, leafy scent of the familiar wood brought her back to another life.

"What will you do with it?" Georges asked, watching her with a perplexed expression as she bent to breathe the wood in, closing her eyes.

It struck her then that neither he nor Suzanne knew that she had once been an artist, had once coaxed form and substance from wood. She opened her eyes and smiled at him. "I'm not entirely sure yet. But I used to carve things all the time. I will see if I remember how."

He looked at the wood and then back to her. "What will you make?"

"I don't know."

"How do you make things from this?" he asked, stepping back as he wiped his hands on his trousers.

"Those are my tools." She gestured to the chisels and gouges lined up like a surgeon's implements on her workbench, waiting to be brought back into service. "Maybe I will teach you someday."

"I think we won't be here much longer. My mother will be back for us. I know she will." He held Elise's gaze. "But you don't believe she is coming back, do you?" His voice broke on the last word.

"Georges, I'm not sure what to believe."

"But I would feel it here, you see." He tapped his chest. "Suzanne would, too. We would know it. We would feel it in our bones if she was dead."

Elise took a deep breath. She had wanted to believe, too, that we could feel it when our loved ones slipped from the earth, that she would have known it the moment her daughter had died. But she hadn't felt a thing, hadn't sensed the ripping of the cord, the shifting between this world and the next.

"I know that our mother is alive," Georges said after a moment. "You must believe me, Madame LeClair. Please, you must believe it, too."

She forced herself to smile. "I pray every night, Georges, that she will return to you and Suzanne."

He nodded, relief in his eyes, but as he turned away, she let out a sigh. The Hôtel Lutetia, she had heard, would be closing as a center for returnees soon, for the flow of prisoners returning home had slowed to a trickle. If Ruth Levy had indeed survived the war, she would almost certainly be back by now, and there had been no trace of her at all.

CHAPTER TWENTY-ONE

At first, the limewood refused Elise's advances, failing to give beneath the sharpness of her tools, obstinately standing still when she needed so desperately for it to dance. She tried to re-create Juliette's birds, thinking now of the Foulon family rising up in a flock toward the sky, but the result was so childish that she chiseled straight through it in frustration, splintering it into lifeless chunks, and then slammed her fists on the table.

Next, she tried something simpler—to shape the farmhouse where she'd stayed near Aurignon. She could still remember each angle and curve, could see it clearly in her mind's eye, but the wood continued to taunt her. She tried the faces of Georges and Suzanne, the face of Olivier, even the faces of Bernard, Madame Roche, and Père Clément, but they emerged looking like theater masks, false and empty-eyed. She tried the bedraggled mutt that lived within the florist's stall on the corner, a pigeon on the terrace rail, even a garden of poppies, which should have been simple.

But everything she did looked like it had been created by a first-year art student, someone who hadn't yet learned how to work with the grain rather than against it. Each evening, she emerged from her studio, her eyes bloodshot, her cheeks streaked with tears, and Georges and Suzanne politely averted their eyes and bustled about, setting the table for dinner, while she washed up.

On her eighth day with an unyielding block of wood, her failures splintered around her on the floor, there was a light knock on her studio door. She slammed down the piece she'd been working on—her attempt at a tangle of trees in the Bois de Boulogne—and called, "Yes?"

The door cracked open and Suzanne slipped inside, her eyes downcast. "We can get jobs, you know," she said without bothering with pleasantries. "Georges and I. We have talked about it. It's not right that you're here trying so hard to make money, while we do nothing."

"You're eleven," Elise said. "That is all you two should be focusing on. Being children."

Suzanne smiled sadly. "Madame LeClair, we have not been children for some time."

"That is a tragedy, Suzanne, and one that I won't contribute to. I don't want you to worry about a thing. It is time to begin again."

"Is that what you are doing, Madame LeClair? Beginning again?"

Elise looked pointedly around at the ruins littering the studio floor. "I think it's quite clear I'm not certain *what* I'm doing."

Suzanne looked at the carving Elise was working on. "What are you making now?"

"I had intended this to look like trees."

"Did you always carve trees?"

Elise chuckled. "No."

"What did you make, then?"

"Different things."

Suzanne blinked at her, waiting.

"Before Mathilde was born, it was whatever inspired me," she added after a few seconds. "I tried to give shape to the words people said, the things I'd read. I carved faces, expressions, the way a mouth turns up at a lie, and down with sadness. I tried to soak in life and to let it out through my hands into the wood."

"And after Mathilde was born?"

"The war had started by then. There was a sense of false comfort, a forced calm, but we could feel the storm coming. It was right there, on the horizon, the clouds looming, electricity crackling. Sometimes I sculpted that—things that represented the storm, the way we all felt about it." She paused and touched the block of wood before her. "But mostly I carved Mathilde."

"When she was a baby?"

"I carved everything. I would sit down to create something different, and instead, I would find the curves of Mathilde's face. I carved her as she was—but I also found, in the wood, what she might be one day. I carved her as an older girl, imagining the future she would have." Elise paused and blinked a few times to clear her vision. "I let the wood show me what she would look like as a woman. I saw her whole life ahead of us."

"Were those the carvings that were stolen?"

Elise hung her head and nodded. They were all she had left of her lost daughter, and the Germans had taken them all, every last one, in one final, horrific blow.

"So why not try again? You see her all the time, don't you? In your dreams?"

"How do you know that?"

"Because it is where I see my mother, and sometimes, my father, too. They're so real that sometimes I reach out to touch them, but they always disappear. But you, you can bring Mathilde back. Carve her, Madame LeClair. Don't let the Germans take her from you forever."

Elise looked down at her useless hands. "But I need to make money. If I carve Mathilde, I won't be able to part with her. I won't sell those pieces."

"Then start with Mathilde. And let her lead you into something else. But begin with her."

Elise stared at Suzanne. "How did you become so wise?"

"The war made us all wise, Madame LeClair."

Elise swallowed the lump in her throat. "I'm sorry, Suzanne. I'm so sorry for all the things that have happened to you. None of it is fair."

"This isn't the life any of us were meant to have. But we are still the people we used to be. Don't you think we are?"

She slipped out before Elise could reply, and in her wake, Elise felt a surge of power. *We are still the people we used to be*, the girl had said. How had Elise forgotten that? Once upon a time, she had been strong. She had known how to let life flow from her fingertips. She had been able to pick up a block of wood and see the potential within it.

She sighed and returned to the sculpture that was meant to be a cluster of trees. Slowly, her hands roamed over the surface, feeling the swirls in the grain push back against her fingertips, stubborn and with a mind of their own. This time, though, rather than letting her conscious thought dictate shape, she took a large, curved gouge and let her body do what it knew how to. Tapping her mallet against the base again and again, she cleaved off the treetops she'd already hewn, took the branches away in big chunks until she had reduced the wood to a shapeless lump, much smaller than the one she'd started with. And then she set the mallet aside, picked up a smaller gouge, and began to slice in tiny, gentle strokes, letting the grain itself guide her.

The wood was warm and responsive, forgiving under the sweeping cuts, and she found herself breathing more quickly as she chiseled and refined the slope of a forehead, the aquiline slope of a nose, the roundness of eyes that had once looked back at her with such trust. Her gouge found the bow of lips, the line where the mouth had once parted to make the sweetest sounds Elise had ever heard. She shaped cheeks that were as full as apples, and she peeled away layers to reveal the waves and curls of a silky cascade of hair.

Elise had learned long ago that while clay went wherever one's fingers led it, sculpting in wood was a dance between two masters. The wood-carver always led first, working in broad strokes and big lines, but as the shape emerged, the wood itself took over, pushing back, objecting when it didn't want to be led. Sometimes the wood broke, and sometimes its protests were softer—a refusal to yield the right angles against the grain. It had taken years for Elise to learn the complicated tango, the way she needed to listen not just to what she wanted to create, but to what the wood itself was willing to become.

This particular block, though, seemed happy to acquiesce now that it was no longer destined to be a tangle of trees. It had pushed back as her blade forced branches and leaves, but now, as her chisel zipped over the last familiar angles, the wood gave itself up entirely to her, letting her know that this time, it was a willing partner in the dance.

When she stepped back hours later to look at her progress, her breath caught in her throat. She had done it. There, before her on the worktable, lay her daughter's face, just as she had looked when Elise last saw her. The lines were right, Mathilde's mouth forming the beginning of a smile, her eyes wide and inquisitive. Elise slowly ran her thumbs over her daughter's cheeks, and she choked on a sob.

"You came back to me," she whispered. The wood was smooth, alive. It was Mathilde, gone forever, but still, somehow, right here. She stared, tears clouding her vision, as hope fluttered up in her chest. She could bring Mathilde back, and knowing that opened a floodgate within her, letting a river of pain and regret pour out, washing her clean.

Finally, setting the piece aside, Elise reached for another block of wood and began anew, something in her untethered from the present. This time, her gouge found Juliette's birds of grief, and quickly, they soared up from the wood—a father bird at the head, the baby birds flying behind, safe and free, their beaks pointed to the heavens.

The fifth of August began like any other day. Elise walked to the cemetery alone in the morning, knelt and spoke to Mathilde, and then returned to the apartment. She took the carvings she'd done the week before and brought them to Monsieur Vasseur, who gave her a small handful of francs from the previous two weeks' sales. Her pieces never brought in much money, and he insisted on paying her on commission rather than purchasing her pieces outright as Constant Bouet had done with Olivier, but it was enough to pay for new wood, as well as the food and milk the children needed, and the other bills she had fallen behind on. Her most precious work, her Mathildes, she kept for herself, but collectors on a small budget were interested in her birds and her trees, her solitary forms on horizons, and the faceless dancing girls she had begun to create. As her chisels and gouges found her way over their forms, she imagined an older Mathilde, her face always obscured by windswept hair, twirling in the breeze, the wind ruffling their dresses. This is how her daughter came to her now in dreams, always dancing, her face always turned away, and when Elise brought those forms to life, she didn't feel guilty about giving them away, for Mathilde was meant to be in the world, dancing through life.

"Shall we go?" she asked Georges and Suzanne after she'd put the money away in the box where she kept it, hidden behind her blocks of wood.

The children followed her out of the apartment and down the stairs, into the sunlight. This was their routine; each afternoon, they walked down the rue de l'Assomption, crossed the Seine, and turned left on the avenue Émile Zola, making their way through the fifteenth and seventh arrondissements, over to the Hôtel Lutetia, which loomed like an oversize ship on the corner of the boulevard Raspail and the rue de Sèvres. The art deco–style palace had once been a haunt for artists and writers; she'd heard that Joyce had written *Ulysses* while staying in the hotel, and that de Gaulle had reportedly honeymooned there before he was the hero of France.

Now it was a place of both joyous reunion and repeated tragedy. While at first the place had bustled with people, today it was much quieter, awash in sadness rather than hope, resignation rather than desperation. People still milled, checking lists, sighing to themselves, trudging away in despair. Returnees moved up and down halls, many of them with haunted eyes that had seen too much, all of them with sallow skin that hung limp from protruding bones.

While Elise scanned the lists, looking for the name of Ruth Levy, the children searched faces, trying to recognize something familiar in features that had been forever changed by horror, grief, and starvation. Once, they'd spotted a man all three of them had known, a shoemaker from Boulogne, who had been arrested early in the Occupation and had never come back. Georges had let out a yelp and run to embrace the man, almost knocking him over. It had taken Elise much longer to realize who it was, but when she did, she had stepped forward, tears in her eyes.

"Monsieur Kopelman," she'd said, and he had looked at her with empty eyes.

"Do I know you?"

Georges's arms were still wrapped around the shoemaker, but he didn't seem to notice. Beside him, Suzanne was shifting from foot to foot, her arms hugging herself.

"I am Elise LeClair. A friend of Juliette and Paul Foulon."

When he continued to stare at her blankly, she clarified, "They owned the bookstore near your shop."

Something in his eyes flickered and he looked away. "That was another life, madame. One in which my family existed. Now, if you'll excuse me." He slipped from Georges's grasp and moved past Elise. If he hadn't brushed against her, she might have wondered whether he was real at all, or whether they'd all just seen a ghost. She wanted to run after him, to tell him that her family had been lost, too, that she understood him, that she was here to help if he needed anything. But she knew from the look in his eyes—from the look in all the returnees' eyes—that their loss was different, the well of their grief and suffering deeper than she could imagine.

It had been more than a month since they'd seen Monsieur Kopelman, and there hadn't been another familiar face since then. The few refugees who trickled through now, most of them scanning the faces of waiting family members with terror, afraid of whom they wouldn't see, were mostly those who had been too ill to travel home at first.

Elise had given up hope that Ruth Levy would ever walk through the halls of the Lutetia, but Georges and Suzanne searched the incoming faces just as carefully as ever, their eyes cataloguing each detail of the women who walked by. Was this just repeated torture for the children to be disappointed again and again? Or did they need this as a way to let go of their grief, to begin to heal? She had, at first, leaned toward the latter, but as the weeks had turned into months, she had begun to question herself, and lately she hurried them through these painful moments of disappointment, eager to return home and put distance between the children and the thoughts of what could have been.

But something felt different today; there were more family members waiting than there had been in weeks, and there was a frisson in the air. "Is something happening?" she asked a harried-looking woman jotting things down on a notepad.

"A busload of women from an American army hospital," she said, her words staccato. "They're in bad shape, I hear." She was gone before Elise could ask more.

"What is it?" Georges asked.

"Women," Elise said, keeping her tone flat so as not to spark false hope. "From an American army hospital."

"American women?" Suzanne asked, confused.

"Women the Americans helped, I think."

Hope lit up in Suzanne's eyes and then in Georges's, and Elise hated herself for playing any role in instilling it in them. Optimism felt vulgar here.

"Do you think our mother might be among them?" Suzanne asked, and Elise couldn't muster words of denial over the sudden lump in her throat. She decided in that moment that this would be their last day here. It was damaging to the children, and she'd done them a disservice by letting them believe there was a chance.

A door opened at the end of the hall, and a woman walked out, so stooped and frail that at first glance, Elise took her for a very old woman. But as she moved closer, she scanned the faces of the waiting family members, searching for someone who belonged to her, and Elise could see that she was, in fact, quite young. Her skin was sallow and loose, but it wasn't lined, and it still had that impossible bloom of youth. She was perhaps twenty-two or twenty-three. Elise held herself still so the woman wouldn't see the grief shudder through her as they locked eyes.

"The Ducelliers?" she asked, the words directed at Elise.

Elise looked around her, but it was clear the woman was speaking to her.

"The Ducelliers," she repeated. Her eyes darted around. "They are my parents, my brothers, my sister. Do you know them?"

Elise just shook her head now, too shattered to speak for a second. The woman had survived the unimaginable and had come home, hoping to find her family, and none of them were here. Elise prayed that the Ducelliers were simply elsewhere, with no idea that their daughter was coming, but the reality was that they'd probably died long ago. "There are lists," she managed to choke out. "Down the hall. Names of family members looking for loved ones. Maybe you will find their names there."

The woman was already moving away by the time Elise croaked out, "Good luck."

Her eyes followed, which is perhaps why she didn't see the next woman shuffling toward them, her pace picking up as she approached. Georges was the first to recognize her, and his grunt of surprise was enough to trigger a second look from Suzanne, who gasped and then gave a little scream.

Elise turned, expecting to see another shopkeeper from the old neighborhood, someone the children had known in their old life, someone who would ensure that their false hope would survive for a little while longer. Instead, in the shell of an unfamiliar, stooped figure, on a face transformed by hunger, Elise recognized Ruth Levy, her skin nearly translucent, both cheeks scarred, but her eyes bright with hope and brimming with tears. "Children?" she whispered, limping over. She dragged her left leg, which seemed shorter than her right now. "Are you really here, or am I dreaming?"

And then the children were in her arms, and she swayed on her feet, but she stood strong, and the three of them held each other and sobbed, rocking back and forth as a single unit, as Madame Levy repeated over and over, "Georges, Suzanne. Georges, Suzanne. Georges, Suzanne."

The broken record should have been the most beautiful symphony Elise had heard in months, so she was ashamed when a fresh wave of grief swept over her. A reunion with their mother was all the children wanted, and Elise hadn't believed it possible. In her mind, their future would include her in it, as a woman who loved them, who would care for them, who would belong with them. And now, underneath this joyful reunion was a renewed and sweeping sense of loss.

Madame Levy's gaze finally met hers over the heads of the children. "Madame LeClair? Is it really you?"

Elise took a hesitant step forward. All at once, she was acutely aware that she did not belong in this moment, that this had nothing to do with her. She had only been deceiving herself when she'd imagined she wasn't all alone. "Madame Levy," she said. "Thank God. You are home."

"Maman," Suzanne said, her voice muffled. She was still crushed against her mother. "Madame LeClair took us in. She has been caring for us these past months."

Madame Levy's eyes met Elise's. "This is true?"

Elise nodded.

"And your husband, Madame LeClair? Your daughter? They are alive and well, too?"

Elise looked down without a word, and in Madame Levy's sudden inhale, she heard understanding and compassion. She was still looking down and blinking back tears when Madame Levy's slender hand shot out and grabbed Elise's wrist, pulling her in with a surprising amount of strength. She was pressed against Georges and Suzanne, Madame Levy's arms encircling the three of them, squeezing them close.

"Then you are our family now," Madame Levy said simply, and Elise felt a strange peace settle over her as she relaxed into an embrace she hadn't known she so desperately needed. "You are our family," Madame Levy repeated, and Elise's tears fell for the first time in months.

CHAPTER TWENTY-TWO

Madame Levy, who insisted now that Elise drop the formalities after all they'd been through and address her as Ruth, moved into Elise's apartment on the avenue Mozart, and it somehow felt just right to have all three Levys living there. The place was alive in a way it hadn't been when it was just Elise and Olivier, and it was full in a way it hadn't felt when it was just Ruth's children and Elise. She understood now that in order for a place to feel like a home, it needed to be full of love, equally given and received by all within it.

It took two months before Ruth was able to tell Elise her story, and in the weeks before she spoke of what had happened to her, she writhed in bed each night, moaning, awash in nightmares. She cried out, "Stop!" and, "No!" and Elise sometimes tried to wake her, but Ruth always arose to consciousness with glassy eyes and a faraway expression, part of her still in the past. Elise knew that whatever she had gone through had been horrific, but she hadn't imagined just how awful it had been until Ruth began to speak one night, after the children were asleep.

"I almost got away," she said, her voice hoarse as she broke a comfortable silence between the two women. They'd been sitting in front of the fire, the first they'd lit that autumn as the weather grew cold.

Elise turned to look at Ruth, who, in the past few weeks, had begun to gain weight, the color gradually returning to her cheeks. "You *did* get away. You're here now, my friend."

Ruth didn't look at her. She was staring into the embers as if hypnotized by their glow. "I mean, before the war ended. I never made it out of France, but I was safe. I was living in a village near Chartres, in a banker's cellar, along with two other women, all of us from Germany. With our accents, we could not blend in, could not live in public, so we were grateful for the protection. We heard about the invasion at Normandy, and we knew it was only a matter of time before France was liberated. But in the chaos, we were betrayed by a neighbor. The banker and his wife were arrested; I don't know what happened to them. And then they came for us."

Elise felt bile rise in her throat. "You were so close to the end of the war. So close to being safe."

"Yes. We were on one of the last convoys east, more than a thousand of us packed into a few train cars."

She paused, and against her heavy silence, Elise could hear the crackling of the fire and the ticking of the grandfather clock. "I'm so sorry," she said, knowing it was not nearly enough.

"When we arrived, they separated us, selecting some for labor." She coughed. "I was sent with many others to work in a textile mill. I still don't know how I survived. I suppose it was because I was not in my right mind. I dreamed every night that I was holding tight to Georges and Suzanne, and in the mornings, I woke in a daze, not fully in my body, but somehow able to go through the motions."

She paused to wipe her eyes, but they were dry. She had used her tears up long ago. Elise, on the other hand, was crying, tears falling so quickly that she couldn't stop them.

"The winter was terrible. Snow and ice everywhere, no proper clothing to keep us warm. People freezing to death, dying of illnesses, starving. It was hell, Elise. Hell. In January, the camp was evacuated. Everyone who could walk was sent marching west, guarded by the SS. But I was very ill by then. I had tuberculosis. I could hardly breathe, couldn't walk. It's a wonder I wasn't shot; perhaps they thought I'd be a waste of a bullet. Instead, they simply left several very ill prisoners behind. On their way out, they blew up the crematoria, trying to destroy the evidence of what they had done, but they forgot about us, the witnesses who could speak the truth. When the Red Army arrived a week later, I was delirious, so much so that I didn't know we had been saved, not for many days.

"I was taken to a hospital, and I remember nurses speaking over me in a language I did not understand, but I knew, from the tone of their voices, that they did not believe I would live. I could not open my eyes, but I knew then and there that I had to prove them wrong. I had to survive. I *had* to. For Georges and Suzanne. And because someone had to tell the world what the Germans had done."

She stopped talking abruptly and looked again into the fire. Elise's tears were still coursing down her face, and she couldn't find the words to say in response. Ruth's voice had remained flat, emotionless during the recounting.

"How?" Ruth asked, her voice so low it was barely audible.

"Pardon?"

"How?" she repeated. "How could they do those things to us? I have been over it so many times in my mind, Elise, and still, I do not understand. Are we not humans to them? I cannot understand what would make man turn against his fellow man this way." She drew a trembling breath. "The children, Elise. So many of them dead. How could they kill children?"

"I don't know," Elise whispered.

Both women fell silent after that, lost in their own thoughts.

"I'm terribly sorry about Mathilde," Ruth said after several moments, breaking the silence. "The kind of loss you have suffered, well, there are no words that can ease it, I think."

Elise felt guilty for accepting sympathy from someone who had been through so much. "I would give anything to know," she said, choking on the final word. She had to pause to collect herself. "To know what happened in her final moments. To know whether she was happy. Whether she was frightened or whether she went too quickly to know what was happening." She paused to draw another breath, her whole body shaking. "I don't know what her last months were like, Ruth. How can that be? I'm her mother. I'm her mother, and I don't know who she had become. How can Juliette simply have left without leaving some word for me?"

Ruth looked down at her hands as Elise began to cry again, silently. She felt another wave of shame roll over her. She was being a terrible friend to Ruth now, just as she'd been a terrible mother to leave Mathilde behind. But when Elise finally dared look up to read the judgment on Ruth's face, she found none. There was only sadness there.

"Elise, think of the loss Juliette suffered. Her husband, two of her children—all gone in the blink of an eye." Ruth spoke gently. "How does a person move on from that? She must have believed, Elise, that you did not survive, and that she had nothing to remain here for. Who can blame her for wanting to run? If I had lost my children, I would have run, too, imagining that putting distance between myself and the past would ease the pain."

"Would it, do you think? Ease the pain? Do you think the distance helps, the starting anew?"

Ruth sighed. "No."

"So what do I do? How do I close the door on the life I had when I don't know what happened to my child?"

"That will come in time," Ruth replied. "Until then, my friend, you must keep moving forward, however difficult the road may be. You must live, and one day, you will realize that the future lies ahead of you, and it is time to let the past go."

The next two years passed in a blur. The children adjusted to life in Paris, going to school, making friends, as their mother healed. They celebrated a bar mitzvah for Georges in the summer of 1946 and a bat mitzvah for Suzanne in the spring of 1947, and by May of that year, Elise could sense a shift in the household. She had become a part of the Levy family, entirely bonded to them, but she could feel them pulling away, could feel a restlessness within the walls of the apartment they shared.

"We must go," Ruth said abruptly one night in mid-May, the air sticky and still outside the open windows as the children slept.

Elise was working on a large carving of a bird's wings, which had become her trademark in the past year. She certainly wasn't setting the art world on fire, but her pieces had begun to command more money at Monsieur Vasseur's gallery, enough that she worried less about making ends meet and knew she could keep the apartment for as long as she wanted it. Perfecting her wings—sinewed muscles, delicate feathers—had kept her from carving faces, too, which helped maintain her sanity. She was only tempted to bring the curves of Mathilde's face to life every few months now.

She looked up and was startled to see Ruth's eyes glistening with tears. "Go where?" she asked, her heart already sounding a drumbeat of alarm.

"Away," Ruth said, her gaze sliding away. "It is time, Elise. You know it is."

"No," Elise said, standing abruptly. "Ruth, this is your home." Ruth still had terrible, debilitating dizzy spells, and she hadn't been well enough to get a job. How would she support the children if they left? Still, Elise could see the sad resolution in Ruth's expression, and she knew that somehow, the woman's mind was already made up. "This is your home, Ruth," she repeated feebly.

"No, this is *your* home," Ruth reminded Elise. "And we have imposed for far too long."

"It has never been an imposition."

Ruth looked down. "It isn't only that, Elise. It is that this country no longer feels like a home for us. How can I ever forget that it turned its back on me, and on my children, in the first place? I've been thinking about this for some time, and I simply cannot stay, cannot let my children become adults here. What if France turns on us again? How can we ever feel safe?"

"Such things will never happen again," Elise protested.

"You cannot know that, Elise."

"But . . . where will you go?"

"Your country, actually." Ruth smiled slightly as Elise felt her throat go dry. "America. My father's second cousin Julius has agreed to sponsor us."

Elise knew that Ruth had been in touch with an American relative, a distant relation who lived in New York, but she had assumed it was simply a desire on Ruth's part to reconnect with family after so many of her loved ones had been lost. She hadn't imagined that it was a silent escape hatch, a plan in the making. "How wonderful," Elise managed to say.

"Why don't you come, too? Start anew along with us."

The thought of leaving France, returning home, had crossed Elise's mind many times over the past two years. After all, she had moved to France to marry Olivier, and now she was alone. Her parents were gone, and she had lost touch with all her old friends back in the States, but there would be something comforting about being back on American soil, starting over in a place like New York where she could be anonymous. But then who would tend her daughter's plot in the cemetery? "I can't leave Mathilde, Ruth."

Ruth took her hands. "You know she is not here anymore. Her grave might be, but Mathilde herself—"

"France is the only home Mathilde ever knew," Elise said, cutting her off. "I—I simply cannot. I'm sorry."

Ruth released her, and Elise could see in the other woman's eyes that she'd known the answer all along. "Come visit us, then. When we get settled."

"I will." She knew it was what she was expected to say. Her heart ached as she realized that for the second time this decade, she was about to lose her only family. "When do you leave?"

"In two weeks' time."

"Two weeks?" Elise sat back, stunned. "Do Georges and Suzanne know?"

"They do. None of us quite knew how to tell you, Elise. You've been very good to us, but we need to stand on our own now, a fresh start."

Elise arose from the table. The half-finished wing seemed to be beckoning to her, but was it telling her to stay or to walk away? She blinked at it a few times, but there were no signals from beyond hiding in her art. A wing was just a wing, and a broken heart was just a broken heart. "I'm going to bed," she said, trying to keep her voice from wobbling, but Ruth must have heard it, because her eyes filled with tears again.

"Thank you, Elise. For everything."

Elise forced a sad smile and then turned to go. She didn't look back, but she could feel Ruth's eyes on her as she walked hurriedly away.

The Levy family sailed for America on the first Wednesday in June.

"We'll write to you, Madame LeClair, we promise," Georges said, squeezing her hands and then kissing both of her cheeks.

"Will you come to visit us? In America?" Suzanne asked, her eyes wet as she hugged Elise goodbye.

"I will one day," Elise said, though she wasn't sure the words were true. Still, she would miss the children terribly, and she knew she would regret it if they had become adults by the time she saw them again. Time moved too swiftly, too relentlessly. "Are you sure there's nothing else you need?"

"Elise, you have given us more than enough," Ruth said. She put a hand on each of Elise's arms and looked into her eyes as Suzanne stepped back. "You kept my children safe and helped bring me back to life. You have already given me the greatest gift anyone could give."

"You have done the same for me," Elise said. "You gave me a place to belong."

Ruth waited until Elise was looking at her again. "We will always be your family, my friend. Always."

Elise nodded, too choked up to reply, and then she watched as Ruth, Georges, and Suzanne, the only people she had left in the world, turned and walked toward the ship that would bring them to a new life, one that did not include her.

She took the train back to Paris the next day and went straight to Monsieur Vasseur's gallery on her way home. "Ships," she said when he opened the door to her. He looked at her blankly, but she pressed ahead. "If I could sculpt great ships, the kind that take souls away from us, would you be able to sell them?"

In his eyes, she could see his mental calculations unfolding. "I believe I could. People like ships."

"Good." She was already imagining the way her hands would find the vessels in the grain of the wood, the way she would make the passengers wisps with wings. The sculptures would represent the actual departing of people—like the Levy family—to another land, but also the crossing from this world into the next, and the irreversible movement of time, passengers moving forward with the tide whether they like it or not.

"Madame LeClair?" Monsieur Vasseur interrupted her train of thought, and her attention snapped back to him.

"Yes?"

"Are you all right?"

She forced a smile. Just as she changed blocks of wood into something different, perhaps she could shape herself, too, chiseling the edges, stripping away the grief. "Perfectly fine, thank you," she said. "I'll have some new work for you next week."

"Very well." Monsieur Vasseur smiled back at her, but he couldn't hide his concern, and Elise turned away quickly before she had to face her reflection in his eyes.

She knew, even before she had ascended the stairs to her apartment, which now lay silent and empty, that the first piece of wood would transform in her hands to become the ship that had carried Juliette and Lucie away, wherever they were.

Maybe if her hands could find them in the wood, there was still hope. She had to know what had happened to Mathilde—what her last months had been like, whether she'd died alone, whether she'd missed her mother—but more than that, she needed to make sure Lucie was all right.

Five years earlier, Elise had shown up at Juliette's door and begged her friend to protect Mathilde. It was more than anyone should ask, but Elise hadn't had a choice. Juliette had said yes without hesitation, and even through the fog of her own grief, Elise had known then that she was making a pact that could never be broken. Juliette had been there to help her child; Elise would always owe the same to Lucie.

The girl would be seven years old now, four years older than Mathilde would ever be. She was still out there, still alive, and Elise wouldn't be able to rest until she found her and made sure she was all right.

PART III

Do not be afraid; our fate cannot be taken from us;
it is a gift.
—DANTE ALIGHIERI, *INFERNO*

CHAPTER TWENTY-THREE

September 1960

Until the day Ruth Levy walked in and ruined everything, Juliette Foulon had managed to build a life that was exactly the way she wanted it to be.

Well, not *exactly*, of course. *Exactly* would have been living a life where Paul, Antoinette, and her boys were still alive. Claude would be twenty-five now, Antoinette, twenty-four, and Alphonse, twenty-three. Juliette couldn't imagine them as adults, and it hurt too much to force herself to try. They were forever frozen in her mind at the ages they were when they were taken from her. Claude would always be eight, and when he came to her now, dancing on wisps of light, his smile was just as bright as it had been in the seconds before the bomb fell. Alphonse had just turned six when he died, and he would forever stay that way, innocent and laughing. Antoinette would always be an infant, so tiny she could nearly fit into Juliette's palm, and sometimes, Juliette held out her hand to catch the sunshine streaming through the windowpanes and imagined that the warmth there was the weight of her sparrow daughter.

And Paul. Oh, her Paul. Fifteen years her senior, he would be sixty-three now, his skin creased with time, his laugh lines deeper. She could hardly imagine it. But she had aged, too—impossibly, she was forty-eight, two years older than Paul had been when he died—and each time she saw herself in the mirror, she looked quickly away, rejecting the passage of time. But she could not forget that she was seventeen years and an ocean away from her buried family. All she had now were Lucie and memories of a life that no longer existed.

She had remarried, not for love, but because that was what her mother had done, what she herself was expected to do. She had become quite adept at doing what was expected, and she found it easier than trying to chart her own course. It was, she supposed, one of the things that had appealed to her most when Arthur Lawrence Wolcott, a wealthy industrialist old enough to be her father, had proposed marriage four months into her stay in New York.

She and Lucie had moved in with her aunt Sally—her father's sister—who lived on Manhattan's Upper West Side. The old woman hadn't been too pleased to have them, but for goodness' sake, she had a three-bedroom apartment just a few blocks from the park, and she was living there alone. She let them know at every opportunity what an inconvenience it was to have two quiet, shell-shocked houseguests, and that she expected them to move out just as soon as Juliette found work. But Juliette found Arthur first, and that had been that.

Arthur later told her that he'd been drawn to her when he spotted her hurrying across the park one day because she was so effortlessly beautiful, a knockout without even trying. She remembered it differently; she'd been wearing the only nice dress she owned and was on her way back from yet another unsuccessful job interview. No one, it seemed, wanted a shopgirl on the wrong side of thirty.

Arthur stopped her as he passed and asked spontaneously if she would care to accompany him to lunch, and because she hadn't eaten since the previous day, she said yes, though she didn't know him from Adam.

"My husband died," she found herself telling him over a tender steak at an upscale French bistro on East Sixtieth, where he'd brought her after she told him she'd spent years living in France.

"I'm very sorry. He died in the war, I imagine?"

She'd nodded, looking down so she would not need to explain.

"A hero, then, God rest his soul. My wife passed, too," Arthur said. "I've been surprised to find myself quite lonely since she's been gone."

"You should know I still love my husband," she blurted out, already feeling guilty for accepting a free steak under false pretenses. "And I have a daughter."

He'd chewed thoughtfully before saying, "Children can be amusing."

Later, when he'd called her aunt's apartment to ask her on another date, she had been perplexed. "I told you how I feel about my husband, though."

"Yes, but I suppose we all come with complications," he'd said. "And to be frank, Juliette, I've had the love of my life. Now, I'd simply like someone to have a nice meal with once in a while. You strike me as an intelligent woman, and that's something I value."

She hadn't known what to say to that, but he had clearly taken her silence as a tacit agreement, for in the weeks to come, he wooed her with flowers and fine dinners, and he had even brought dolls for Lucie to play with and chocolates for her to eat. He proposed marriage on a snowy day in January, on a carriage ride through the park.

"But I've told you, Arthur, I still love my husband," she had said quietly.

"And I still love my wife. But they're both gone, Juliette, and I enjoy your company. I have the means to give you a good life, you know."

"I have only one request," she said after a moment, having weighed her options carefully. "I had a bookstore in France. I would like to open one here."

"That can be arranged," he replied. "If you say yes."

Less than a year later, she had a new husband, an apartment on the Upper East Side, and a bookstore on East Fifty-Sixth Street, which she had the budget to stock and design in any way she wanted. She had chosen the spot specifically because there was an art gallery owned by a Frenchman on the corner, as well as a French café on the same block, and she wanted to be able to walk to work and imagine—despite the yellow cabs rattling by, despite the brownstones and the wide, even pavement—that she was not in New York but back in France. *Little Paris*, the neighbors called their block, and she reveled in the title, in the idea that by sheer will, one could re-create a life anywhere.

And so, while Lucie attended kindergarten at a private school Arthur had chosen for her, Juliette spent her days in the bookstore, painstakingly rebuilding a shattered past. With every book she ordered from France, with every shelf she commissioned, with every angle she designed to look just like the old store, she could breathe a bit more easily. She harangued carpenters for making bookcases a bit too high, insisting that they cut them down to match her memory. She stood with her arms crossed at the foot of a ladder several days in a row as a man installed lights, urging him left and right until they hung just right. She even had a painter repaint the counter seven times to achieve exactly the correct hue of brown, but at the end, it was worth it; the interior was an exact duplicate of La Librairie des Rêves in Boulogne-Billancourt. In fact, the first time she brought Lucie to the store after the renovation, the girl began to shake.

"What is it, my darling?" Juliette asked as Lucie cowered behind her.

"It is—it is the scary place," Lucie stammered, and Juliette had to blink several times to clear her tears before bending to the frightened child.

"No," she said. "It is the beautiful place, the place where we spent our days with your father and your brothers before that terrible day. We will have only happiness here."

But Juliette had known, even then, that she was telling lies. She didn't know how to be happy anymore. She could hardly understand how she got out of bed each day and put one foot in front of the other. But she had become adept at pretending to be a doting mother, pretending to be a devoted wife.

Arthur was a good man. He gave her everything she needed and didn't expect a bigger piece of her heart than she had to give. His presence ensured that Lucie would always be safe and fed. And if her only obligations were to smile at the right times, to dutifully join him each night for dinner at seven on the dot, and to lie on her back a few times a month, imagining she was elsewhere while his body moved on top of hers, she could do that. It was a small price to pay.

Lucie grew and grew, as children do, but it was difficult for Juliette to watch as the girl moved from being a child to becoming a young teenager. After all, Claude and Alphonse were frozen at eight and six, and it seemed rude of Lucie to sail right past them and keep going. Juliette knew that was an unreasonable thought, so she kept it to herself. But while Arthur, now retired, puttered around their sprawling apartment doing goodness knows what, and while Lucie attended school, Juliette spent every weekday in the bookshop talking to ghosts. Paul came to her most days now, and Claude and Alphonse were often playing in the back, their giggles wafting up from the floorboards. Though she knew intellectually that they were not real, it did not stop her from eagerly awaiting their visits. In fact, most days, she closed the shop for a few hours because she didn't care about making a profit as much as she cared about making space for the past to join her.

Arthur didn't mind. He had broached the subject of the store a few times, asking if perhaps it might be better to close it and try another venture, given that it lost money each month. But each time, Juliette burst into tears, and each time, he held his hands up in apology and admitted that he should not have suggested such a thing.

All was going as well as expected until the day in September 1960 that the past walked right through her door.

It was an unseasonably warm Tuesday, so pleasant outside that Juliette had propped the front door open to let the breeze in, along with the scent of baking baguettes from the French café down the street. She had found that when the wind was blowing in just the right direction, the odor wafted in and could transport her to France on wings of flour and yeast. This was one of those days, and so when she looked up and saw a familiar face gazing around with astonishment, it took her a few extra seconds to register that she was experiencing anything unusual. She was so accustomed to seeing Paul and the children here that Ruth Levy, though her hair was grayer and her face older, seemed to belong perfectly. But then Juliette realized how strange this in fact was, and she dropped the handful of books she was holding. The tremendous bang they made as they hit the floor seemed to snap Ruth out of her obvious shock.

"Juliette? Juliette Foulon?" Ruth said, and hearing the woman's voice aloud, reverberating through the shop, was strange. Paul, Claude, and Alphonse only spoke to her in her head.

"Yes," Juliette answered evenly, because perhaps if she pretended that this was normal, it would be. Suddenly, she was certain that Ruth was a ghost, too. That would make sense.

But then the woman stepped forward and took Juliette by the arms, and Juliette had to admit that she didn't feel like an apparition. "Juliette Foulon," the woman repeated. "It is me. Ruth Levy. From Boulogne. Don't you remember me?"

"Yes, of course I do," Juliette said.

Ruth blinked at her, and Juliette wondered if she'd said something wrong. "Juliette," Ruth said a moment later. "This store. It is exactly like . . ." Her sentence trailed off.

"Like the original Librairie des Rêves, yes," Juliette agreed. When she found Ruth still looking at her with concern, she added, "It is not the original store, of course. My husband allowed me to open a new one here, in New York."

But Ruth's confused expression didn't clear. "Monsieur Foulon is alive?"

Juliette's cheeks went hot with embarrassment and rage. "No. I am remarried."

"Oh. Yes. I'm so sorry." Then she amended, "I mean, of course, that I am sorry about Monsieur Foulon, but I'm very happy for you that you found love again."

"I did not say that I found love," Juliette said, but when she realized her voice sounded as hard as steel, she softened it. "But my husband, he is a good man."

"Oh. How nice. And Lucie?"

Juliette forced a smile. "Lucie is very well, thank you."

Ruth looked relieved. "Oh, I'm very glad. I've worried so many times over the years about the two of you. She is what, twenty now?"

Juliette had to think about it for a few seconds, and she pushed down her quick stab of anger. It wasn't as though she could complain to Ruth about Lucie's obstinate determination to keep growing older while her siblings stayed the same age. "Yes. That's right. Twenty." She followed the words with another polite smile.

Ruth seemed to be waiting for something else, but Juliette wasn't sure what it was, so she kept quiet until Ruth said, "Georges and Suzanne are also well. Georges is twenty-eight now. Suzanne is twenty-six."

"How wonderful," Juliette said, hoping that rage was not flashing in her eyes. It wasn't that she wished the Levy family ill. But Ruth had sent her children away instead of staying with them to protect them, as Juliette had done. How had all three of the Levys managed to survive intact while her family was ripped apart?

Ruth stared at her for a little while more before her eyes moved away. Juliette could see her gazing around the store, and she felt proud of what she knew the other woman was seeing. She was seeing a piece of her past, a past she thought was gone, but it wasn't, because Juliette had kept it alive. Finally, Ruth's gaze returned to hers. "Juliette, have you never reached out to Elise?"

It felt like Ruth had slapped her. Juliette took a step away, knocked backward by the blow. Her throat suddenly felt very dry, and the floor beneath her seemed to pitch and quake before settling. "Elise LeClair? Surely she did not survive the war."

"But she did," Ruth said. "She has been living in her old apartment these past sixteen years, trying to surround herself with the past. Perhaps much like you are doing." The words were delivered gently, but they felt like another blow, and Juliette bristled. "I think it would help her greatly if you reached out and told her what happened to her daughter. It is a terrible feeling, I think, not knowing. Perhaps your words would give her some peace."

Juliette could feel her lip curling in disgust. It was unimaginable to think that any peace would come with knowing the horrific details of the blast, the way Juliette could still smell singed hair and burned flesh, charred paper and her family's blood. "Her daughter died, Ruth."

Ruth blinked a few times. "Yes, I know. But I think knowing the circumstances would help her to heal."

The idea that Elise LeClair, who had abandoned her child, had any right at all to healing was so laughable it was an outrage. But Juliette knew this would be impolite to say, so she forced a neutral expression. "Perhaps I will write to her one day."

"Juliette," Ruth said after a long pause. "I'm afraid I must insist. You were there for her daughter's last moments on this earth, and she deserves—"

"She deserves *nothing.*" Juliette snapped, cutting Ruth off, and then collected herself, adding more calmly, "What I mean to say is that it is *my* family who sacrificed to give her daughter a home. And if my husband had not tried to protect Mathilde, perhaps he could have saved my boys."

Ruth put her hand to her mouth and looked down, and Juliette knew she had said the wrong thing. Perhaps she should take it back, but she didn't want to. Sometimes, the truth was quite hard to hear.

When Ruth looked back up, her eyes were shining with tears. "I'm very sorry you feel that way, Juliette, but regardless, I think it would be a kindness to another mother. Wouldn't you want to know how your child's last days were spent? Your child's last moments?"

"I *do* know those things about my children, you see, Ruth. I was there to see them all die."

"I'm very sorry," Ruth said again, and at that moment, the front door to the store chimed, and in walked Lucie.

Her brown waves, which reminded Juliette of the young Sophia Loren's style in the Clark Gable movie Arthur had taken her to last month, fell to her shoulders, and she had developed the annoying habit of hiding behind a curtain of her own hair, parting it so far on the left that her right side appeared to be simply a cascade of rippling curls. Her face was partially obscured now, but she peeked out for long enough to get a look at Ruth, and when she did, she stopped short.

"Lucie?" Ruth breathed. "Is that you?"

"Y-yes." It was clear Lucie had a sense of knowing the woman but couldn't place her.

"Dear girl, I am Ruth Levy. I knew you when you were just a small child, in France. It is wonderful to see you again."

"Madame Levy." Lucie said the name slowly, like she was trying to figure something out. "You had two children . . ."

Ruth beamed at her. "I do! Georges and Suzanne. In fact, they live right here in New York. They used to play with you when you were small."

Lucie's eyes were wide. "Yes, Georges and Suzanne," she said softly. She cut a quick glance at her mother and then her eyes went to the floor. "Are they well?" she asked.

"Don't mumble," Juliette reminded her.

"They are quite well, thank you," Ruth said. "Suzanne is a secretary and Georges is the manager of a grocery store. I know they would love to see you sometime, my dear."

Lucie's eyes darted to Juliette, who gave her a hard look. "I would like that," Lucie said, and Juliette narrowed her eyes. She would certainly not allow that to happen. There was no need to go digging up the past. The only pieces of Paris they needed lived right here in the bookshop.

"I was just saying to your mother how much it would mean to Madame LeClair to receive a letter telling her what happened to Mathilde."

Lucie's eyes flashed to Juliette again. "Mathilde's mother is alive?"

"It seems so," Juliette said.

"Then you must write to her, Maman! You were friends once, weren't you?"

Friends. It was ludicrous. Friends didn't abandon each other. Friends didn't put your children in danger and force your husband to choose their child's life over his own. "Once." Juliette knew her voice sounded as cold as the ice running through her veins. "But that was a long time ago."

"You must tell her about what happened to Mathilde," Ruth said again, and though Juliette was refusing to look at either of them, she could feel Lucie's eyes on her, too. "It would bring her some peace, I think."

"Very well," Juliette said at last. "Perhaps if you could send me her address . . ."

"I'll deliver the letter myself," Ruth said instantly. "I will wait right here while you write it."

And though the very thought still made Juliette's stomach churn in distress, Ruth didn't look like she would budge, so after a few seconds, with Lucie still staring at her, Juliette sighed and walked to the desk to withdraw a piece of stationery.

CHAPTER TWENTY-FOUR

While Lucie's mother sat down to write her letter to Elise LeClair, her lips pursed like she'd tasted something bitter, Madame Levy asked Lucie if she might give her a tour of the bookshop.

Lucie looked at her mother for permission, immediately annoyed at herself for still seeking maternal approval so desperately. She was twenty years old, for goodness' sake! Other people her age were out on their own, giving not a fig about their mother's opinions, smoking cigarettes and wearing shorter hemlines and dancing dangerously close to boys while Chubby Checker records exhorted them to do the twist. But perhaps other people hadn't lived their whole lives knowing that their very existence was somehow a letdown. Her mother loved her, of course, but she also seemed determined to remind Lucie at every turn that she had not lived up to her expectations. Antoinette, Claude, and Alphonse all would have been smarter, kinder, more successful than she, and nothing Lucie did seemed to justify being the only one of the siblings to live.

"Go on, Lucie," her mother said now, nodding toward Madame Levy. "What are you waiting for?"

Lucie forced a smile at Madame Levy over the lump in her throat and beckoned for her to follow. Of course Madame Levy wouldn't know how uneasy Lucie felt in the store, even after all these years. While her mother wanted to live in the past, Lucie wanted only to forget it, for her last memories of the store on Paris's outskirts were filled with terror, grief, and loss. Each time she set foot into this newer version of La Librairie des Rêves, her blood felt like ice in her veins, and her stomach twisted in knots of protest. But what choice did she have? The few times she'd dared object to being asked to work in the store, her mother hissed that everything Juliette did, she did for her family, and that Lucie should be more grateful. And it wasn't that Lucie *wasn't* grateful; but she wanted desperately to live in a world in which her mother's whole life didn't revolve around children who had died nearly two decades ago rather than the one standing right in front of her.

"This," Lucie said now as she led Madame Levy past the first set of bookshelves leading away from the register, "is the section where my mother keeps French-language classics."

"I remember," Madame Levy said, her voice a low rumble as she reached out to brush her fingers along a row of spines.

The older woman looked wistful, nostalgic, and for a second, Lucie felt a surge of envy. She wished she could view the store that way, but of course Madame Levy hadn't been there when a bomb had blown it apart. She cleared her throat and went on.

"In the old shop, though we carried many English-language books, my parents liked to stock plenty of books for French speakers, too." The words came out by rote, for Lucie had shown many customers around La Librairie des Rêves at her mother's request. *Tell them about the store in France*, her mother always said. *It will make the Francophiles buy books.* But this was the first time she had ever explained these things to someone who had known her in her previous life, and now she was surprised to find her throat closing. She coughed and went on. "But our real purpose was to serve the English-speaking community of the greater Paris area. Of course you know Shakespeare and Company, run by my mother's contemporary Sylvia Beach, but our store had a larger children's section. It was geared toward expatriate families."

"Dear girl," Madame Levy said, reaching out and putting a hand on Lucie's arm to stop her. "I know all of this. I was a frequent customer of the store, beginning before you were even born. It was a haven for people like me, people who loved to read but who did not quite fit in with their adopted country just yet. At first I bought books to improve my French, but sometimes your mother would order German books for me as well, until my facility with the French language improved."

Lucie stared at Madame Levy. "My mother did that?"

Madame Levy's expression was far away as she glanced in the direction of the register, now hidden behind shelves. "She was different then, Lucie."

Lucie's eyes felt suddenly damp, and she was torn between defending her mother and bursting into tears at the idea that someone understood that things hadn't always been this way. She settled for a quiet bit of honesty. "I remember."

The truth was, she didn't recall much of her life before the blast at all—but she remembered her mother's warmth, her hugs, her love. It all felt different now, and sometimes, Lucie wondered if she had dreamed the *before*, conjured from air a mother who laughed and whose eyes sparkled with pride and affection. But she knew that woman had existed, for there were glimmers of her here and there, always when she talked about the other children.

Claude and Alphonse, whom Lucie had only foggy memories of, must have walked on water, and Antoinette, though she'd lived only thirteen days, had been born a saint. Lucie knew by now that there was nothing she could say or do to live up to memories that grew shinier and more golden with each passing year.

She'd been just three years old when their lives were blown apart. She remembered tumbling into bed with the other children between their mother and their jovial father for story time. She remembered the feel of being sandwiched between all those warm bodies, tickled by Claude, teased by Alphonse, kissed on the top of her head by her father, having her hair smoothed lovingly off her forehead by her mother. She remembered the smell of the store: paper and wood, mixed with the faint scent of her father's musky cologne. She remembered the tinkling bell that announced the arrival of customers, the knotty wood of the floorboards, the sound of Mathilde's giggles when they played with dolls together in the corner of the children's section.

She was not allowed to speak of Mathilde, though, and her mother acted as if the other girl had never existed. She blamed the LeClairs' daughter for the deaths of the other children; if Papa had not scooped her up, he would have reached the boys, her mother had said more than once. Claude and Alphonse would still be alive.

But how could she possibly know that? And if Claude and Alphonse had lived, would Lucie have died? Is that the outcome her mother would have preferred? Lucie had the sense that her mother's answer to that question would have been yes. Sometimes she caught her mother staring at her, the look in her eyes not one of maternal love but rather of sheer disappointment.

"I'm sorry," Madame Levy said now, her tone gentle, and Lucie realized she'd been silent for far too long, lost in her own thoughts. "I'm sorry that things have changed so much. Your mother, I think she is very broken."

"Yes," Lucie agreed, looking at the floor and feeling a surge of guilt at her disloyalty.

"She is not alone in this. Many people who lost everything in the war have had trouble moving forward. But I know she loves you very much, dear. A mother's love never goes away, even if circumstance sometimes forces it into hibernation."

Lucie smiled slightly at this, the idea that her mother's love for her would one day reemerge after a long winter's sleep. It was impossible. "You said you know Madame LeClair?" Lucie asked, changing the subject.

Madame Levy smiled. "She gave us a home after the war. Her kindness, even in the midst of her own pain, made all the difference to my children and me."

"She is all right?" Lucie asked. "It must have been terrible for her to find out that Mathilde did not survive."

Madame Levy's smile was sad, distant. "I do not think she has recovered from it. I'm not sure a mother ever does."

Saddened by the thought, Lucie changed the subject. "What happened to you during the war, Madame Levy?" Lucie asked. Rapt in horrified attention, she fought tears as Madame Levy told a sparse story of being deported to a camp in Poland while her children moved from safe house to safe house.

"I'm so sorry that such things happened to you," she whispered when Madame Levy finished her story, and she knew the words were terribly inadequate. She had read about concentration camps in school, but she had never known someone who had endured such things. Had her mother been so lost in her own grief that she had never stopped to consider what had happened to her old friend? "I'm very sorry I didn't know," she added.

"My dear, you were just a child." Madame Levy paused. "Do you remember Madame LeClair well?"

Lucie tried to conjure an image of the woman, but she couldn't do it. She shook her head. "I remember Mathilde," she said. "She was a sister to me."

"You were very young when her mother left her with your family."

"My mother doesn't like me to talk about her." She swallowed, guilt thickening her tongue. She didn't know what was making her speak against her mother this way, only that it felt like a relief to tell someone who had known them.

"It is hard to hold on to childhood memories we are forbidden from having," Madame Levy said after a moment. "You should know, though, that Madame LeClair is a very kind woman who is broken, much like your mother is, but in different ways."

Lucie couldn't imagine that there were many other ways to break, for it seemed that her mother had shattered in every manner possible. But she felt truly sorry for Madame LeClair, who had lost everything, too. "Is she . . . stuck in the past? Like my mother is?"

"Not exactly. I think Madame LeClair is drowning in regret. She believes that if she had brought Mathilde with her, Mathilde would still be alive today. She feels she made the greatest mistake any mother could make. And there is no way to reason with her, to remind her that she acted out of love and out of a fierce desire to protect her child, and that she couldn't have known what would happen."

"None of us see the past as clearly as we should," Lucie said, and Madame Levy nodded vigorously. "Will she . . . will she be all right?"

"I think the letter from your mother will help. Being granted the chance to close the door on the past lets a person begin to move forward."

Lucie thought about this. Is that why her own heart ached the way it did? But how could she move on from the past when it surrounded her every day? Being in this bookstore—where her mother demanded she work to pay for her classes at Hunter College—was like pouring salt on a wound constantly forced open, but it was all she'd known for the past fourteen years, since Lucie's stepfather, Arthur, had agreed to finance this endeavor. She wondered sometimes whether Arthur realized how strange this all was, but he preferred to remain removed from the goings-on of his family. Perhaps it was easier to let insanity continue to unfold around you if you looked the other way.

"Monsieur LeClair, Mathilde's father," Lucie said after a long silence. "Did you know him, too?"

Unbeknownst to her mother, Lucie had taken some art classes in school, and one of them, which focused on modern European art, had used an Olivier LeClair painting of a winged woman rising from the ashes, reaching for a stone tablet, as a case study in political statement through art. It was part of the Liberté, Égalité, Fraternité series that he had painted before Germany invaded France in 1940. She hadn't spoken up in class, hadn't volunteered the fact that she'd held Olivier LeClair's daughter's hand while she died, but she had felt a surge of pride that she was even tangentially connected to such a legend. The French-owned art gallery down the street from the bookstore featured several LeClairs, too, all going for exorbitant prices, and Lucie had become a fixture at their window, gazing at the artwork and wondering if she, too, could one day create such emotionally charged masterpieces.

"No, I didn't. By the time I met Elise, I think they were moving in different orbits. He was very involved in his politics, and she wanted only to protect their daughter." Madame Levy's voice was heavy with sadness. "You know, Elise is an artist, too. I think that perhaps for many years, his star outshone hers, and so she let hers dim. But she is very talented, perhaps more so than he was, even if she doesn't know it."

Lucie's eyes widened. "She has exhibited her work, too?"

"No, dear. I wish she would, but she has no belief in her own talent, and I think that holds her back. She sells basic pieces in Paris to support herself, but I think perhaps she is still punishing herself for the past. She makes beautiful works of art, but she keeps them to herself."

"I would like to meet her one day," Lucie said, but she immediately regretted the words. Her mother would never allow it. Besides, Madame LeClair was a continent away, and who was to say that she would be any more accepting of Lucie's artistic ambitions than her own mother was?

"I think she would like that very much, my dear girl." Madame Levy smiled. "After all, she knew you many years ago. Now, would you be so kind as to show me the children's section? I have the fondest memories of my own Georges and Suzanne playing there in the old store when they were small."

Later, after she had completed Madame Levy's tour, and the older woman had departed with her mother's letter to Elise Le-Clair in hand and a promise to return soon, Lucie detoured south through Times Square before heading home, losing herself in the chaos. On Fifty-Sixth Street, and in the apartment where they lived, it still felt like Paris, but in the center of Manhattan, with car horns honking and Broadway signs flashing and billboards screaming at her to buy Canadian Club whisky and Admiral televisions and Chevrolet cars, Lucie knew she was firmly on this side of the Atlantic, miles away from the past, which always made her feel better.

An hour later, she sat at the window of her room in Arthur's apartment, looking out across Madison Avenue, just a block from Central Park, a sliver of which she could see between buildings. She still thought of it as Arthur's apartment rather than her own, even though they'd lived here with him since 1946. In fact, she didn't really think of anything in this life as her own, except perhaps for her painting, which she did in secret, because her mother would be furious if she found out. Artists, her mother said, were irresponsible, selfish. They were the type of people who abandoned their children and left them to die.

Sometimes Lucie thought about how differently her life would have turned out if the war hadn't happened. Her father and the boys would still be alive, and her mother would still be whole and happy, not the shattered and bitter woman she'd become. Perhaps Olivier LeClair would have lived, too. Since Lucie was friends with Mathilde, would he have one day spotted her talent and offered to mentor her? Would her mother have let him? Would he have ushered her into his circle of artists, showing her that she could create a life of her own choosing with a paintbrush? She and her mother would still be living in France, the bookstore would still be standing, and most of all, maybe Lucie would feel like she belonged in her own skin.

That's what she was thinking about when a pebble pinged off her window, followed by another. She grinned, and slid the window up to climb out onto the fire escape. "You're early!" she called down to the dark-haired, olive-skinned young man with the easy smile on the street below. He'd been born Tommaso Barbieri in Bologna, Italy, and like her, he had moved here with his family after the war. Unlike her mother, though, his parents seemed to want only to forget their past and assimilate to American culture as quickly as possible. They changed their last name to Barber upon arrival, and Tommaso now went by Tommy; but their lingering accents, and the fact that they lived in Lower Manhattan, with its sizable Italian immigrant population, hadn't helped them to blend in as much as they'd imagined. Lucie found Tommy's dark-haired mother—who was always at the stove, stirring a pot of pasta sauce—and his father, who chain-smoked while listening to baseball on the radio, charming and warm, even if she couldn't understand them when they slipped into rapid Italian.

"I couldn't wait to see you!" he called back, and she reached inside her window for her pocketbook, slid her window shut, then climbed down the fire escape to join him. She had met Tommy last year at Hunter College, and although she had spent many Sundays at his family's apartment, working on assignments for the art class they shared, he had never been inside Arthur's place, nor had he met her mother, who would never approve. It wasn't personal; it was simply that her mother wasn't ready to admit that Lucie was, in fact, an adult and therefore old enough to have a boyfriend. Her mother would consider the blossoming relationship a personal affront, simply because it was one more piece of evidence that Lucie was thoughtless enough to continue growing up while her siblings lay beneath the cold earth.

He greeted her with a long kiss and then slung his arm around her shoulder. "Where should we continue our secret love affair today?"

She knew the sneaking around behind her mother's back bothered him, but he understood that family—especially family that had come through an earth-scorching war—could be complicated.

"I want to go to the art gallery on Fifty-Sixth and Lexington," she said. "The French one."

He whistled, low and slow. "On the same block as the bookstore? Does this mean you're ready for me to meet your mother?"

She coughed and looked away. "I was thinking we would just go to the gallery. I—I met someone today from my past, and it made me want to look at the Olivier LeClairs again. They remind me of the things we left behind."

Tommy shrugged. "Sure. But one of these days, you're going to have to introduce me to her, you know."

"I know," she said, letting an easy silence fall for a couple of blocks. She had never told Tommy the story behind why she and her mother had left France. He didn't know that her father and siblings had died in a blast, or that her mother had spent years nursing a grudge against the LeClair family, though she'd mentioned that the families had known each other. Aside from that, he only knew that her mother was a widow and that she'd once owned a bookstore in France, which she'd replicated here. It was all he needed to know, for who was to say what would happen if Lucie came clean about everything? Would he, too, blame her for having the gall to live while the others had perished?

They avoided the bookstore entirely, walking down Lexington and turning left at the northeast corner of Fifty-Sixth. It was nearly dark by the time they entered the gallery through the double doors.

Lucie had been inside six times before to gape at the impressive collection of LeClairs. They seemed to be the anchor pieces of the gallery, and they were priced astronomically. Since Lucie had begun venturing in, only one of the dozen LeClairs had sold, and it had been soon replaced by *another* LeClair, which astonished Lucie. How did the gallery have access to such a large collection of Mathilde's father's work when he'd been dead for twenty years? Hadn't most of his oeuvre sold to collectors by now? Lucie had spent more than an hour in front of the new LeClair when it had gone up a few months earlier, soaking in all the lines and brushstrokes, before the surly French owner had grunted at her that if she wasn't going to buy a piece, she should move on. He was clearly aware that even the gallery's lesser pieces, by artists no one had heard of yet, were well out of her price range. Then again, what would he think if she casually mentioned that her stepfather was Arthur Lawrence Wolcott? Not that Arthur would be springing for an Olivier LeClair piece anytime soon, but he *could*.

The room was painted white, with white marble floors, and each piece sat in the glow of its own small spotlight. The same twelve LeClairs she had seen on her last visit were evenly spaced on three walls, with smaller pieces from other artists hanging between them. In the back room sat several sculptures on pedestals, by artists including Camille Claudel and Anicette Rousselle, though Lucie had never ventured close enough to take a good look at them. She was much more interested in the LeClairs, which held a link to a piece of her past she wanted to hold on to.

Grasping Tommy's hand, Lucie avoided the narrow-eyed gaze of the owner and drifted to the LeClair just to the right of the entryway, which had always been her favorite. It was a view over the Paris rooftops that had, from the moment she'd first seen it, felt like something she had seen before.

"I wonder," she said now, squeezing Tommy's hand, "if I was ever inside their apartment to play with their daughter. It would explain why this piece feels so familiar to me."

Tommy raised an eyebrow in amusement. "Well sure, that,

or the fact that it looks just like the big LeClair that hangs in the Museum of Modern Art."

Lucie flushed as she heard a low chuckle behind them. She turned to see the gallery's owner, a plump, immaculately groomed man with silver hair and a matching, neatly trimmed mustache. He smelled of cigarettes, whiskey, and expensive cologne, and his enormous belly strained against the buttons of his shirt like it was trying to make an escape.

"Of course LeClair painted this one at the same time as *Night Over Paris*," the man said, his words coated with a slippery French accent. "It is said that this one, in fact, was the model for the one that hangs in MoMA, his first experimentation with that particular landscape, if you will, painted in 1937."

"Does that explain why the price is so whopping?" Tommy asked cheerfully.

Lucie elbowed him hard in the ribs as the gallery owner's eyes narrowed to a glare. "Is this the view from Olivier LeClair's apartment?" she asked.

"It is." He wrinkled his nose. "But as I believe I've reminded you before, young lady, this is a gallery for those with the means to buy art. Those who simply want to gawk at paintings should proceed to this city's great wealth of museums."

Lucie could feel her cheeks burning, and she opened her mouth to reply, but Tommy beat her to it.

"Actually, she knew Olivier LeClair," he said, giving her hand a comforting squeeze. "So I guess you could say she's not simply gawking at paintings."

The gallery owner's eyebrows shot up, and he turned to stare at Lucie. "No. You're much too young to have known him. He died in 1942."

"I know. I was just a little girl," she said. "His daughter

was . . . She was my best friend." Tommy's eyes were on her now. She had never mentioned this to him, and she could feel his surprise. But she held the gallery owner's gaze as she added, "Her name was Mathilde, and she came to live with us after he was killed and his wife had to go away."

Recognition sparked in his eyes, along with something else Lucie couldn't quite name. "Yes, I know the story." He glanced at Tommy, who looked stunned, and then back at Lucie. "I'm Constant Bouet, the owner of this gallery," he said, extending his hand.

"Lucie Foulon."

"Foulon." The blood had drained from his face. "The daughter of the woman who owns the bookstore on this block?"

"Yes."

"Foulon," he repeated, a haunted expression on his face. "I never put two and two together . . ." Constant Bouet looked like he wanted to say something else, but then he clamped his mouth shut.

"Do you know her? My mother?"

"Not exactly."

The silence was awkward, so Lucie filled it. "And Madame LeClair? Did you ever meet her?"

"Of course. I was her husband's art dealer."

This was beginning to feel like pulling teeth. "And was she an artist as well?"

"She dabbled." He hesitated. "She is not in touch with your mother?"

"No." Lucie didn't elaborate, and she could have sworn that Bouet looked relieved, but then his expression quickly cleared and returned to neutral. "Well, Lucie Foulon, you and your friend here may stay and look at the LeClairs. I hadn't realized your connection."

He scuttled away without another word, giving her one last

suspicious glance over his shoulder. He said something to the man behind the counter, who was ruddy-cheeked and middle-aged, with sandy hair and blue eyes. He looked as incongruous in the gallery as Lucie felt. While Constant Bouet was polished, every hair in place, the other man's hair was constantly mussed, his shirts rumpled and tucked into casual slacks. His fingers were always paint-stained, Lucie had noted more than once, a dead giveaway that he was an artist, too. She had seen him here several times before, so she knew he was associated with running the gallery in some way. She locked eyes with him now as Constant Bouet drifted away, and he gave her a friendly smile and then returned to jotting something down in a ledger.

"You were best friends with LeClair's daughter?" Tommy asked in astonishment. "I mean, I knew your family knew the LeClairs, but how come you never told me the rest?"

"It's complicated. Mathilde—she died a long time ago. My mother doesn't like me to talk about it, and so I suppose I've gotten in the habit of never mentioning her."

"Well, you're full of surprises," Tommy said, leaning in to steal a kiss. "What a city this is, where it turns out my girlfriend is practically related to one of my favorite artists! New York, huh? What a place."

"What a place," Lucie echoed, and with one last glance at the LeClair painting that looked over the rooftops of Paris, she grabbed Tommy's hand and led him toward the door. "Let's go paint."

"Let's go paint," he echoed cheerfully, and as she turned to look back, she saw the man behind the counter, the one in the blue jeans with paint under his nails, watching her with a puzzled look on his face. He smiled and gave her a wave just as she exited the gallery, her hands itching to find a paintbrush to transfer to canvas the confusing feelings ping-ponging through her heart.

❦ CHAPTER TWENTY-FIVE ❦

The knock on Elise's door startled her and her hand slipped, taking a chunk out of the smooth blond limewood in front of her. She'd been working on the large sculpture all morning, a commission from a man opening a kitschy new bar on the Left Bank. Monsieur Vasseur had looked out for her these past fifteen years, selling a few of her original pieces in his gallery and suggesting her commissioned work to clients as often as he could. "She can carve anything except for little girls," she had heard him tell a stone-faced banker one day as she slipped into the gallery unnoticed. "Girls remind her of her daughter. Killed in the war. Tragic, yes?" The banker had ordered a wooden peacock, and Elise had gone home in tears.

What he didn't know was that she had actually been sculpting Mathilde all along. Her apartment was overflowing with renderings of her lost daughter, imaginings of how she would look if she had continued to grow up. She would have lips like Elise's were in her youth, full and rounded, and a high forehead like Olivier. Her cheekbones would be sharp and defined, as they had been even when she was a toddler, and her chin would be narrow, giving one the impression of a heart.

At night, Elise lay in bed for hours until sleep came for her, tracing the imagined lines of her daughter's face at seven, ten, fifteen, and now twenty. It was almost inconceivable that her tiny child would be a woman now. The wood beneath her knife had once been alive, too, but Elise's tools could resuscitate it, to give it a second chance at being. She was doing the same for the daughter she would never see again.

And yes, in the past few years, it had gotten out of control. On some level, Elise knew this, and she had taken to hiding the busts of Mathilde—under beds, behind curtains, in boxes—so no one would try to make her stop. Not that anyone other than Monsieur Vasseur came by her apartment anyhow, but she suspected he would worry if he realized what she was doing. She was worried, too, about her own sanity, but it wasn't as though she could stop.

Now, jolted by the knock on the door, she frowned. Monsieur Vasseur had gone to London on business this week, as he did the first week of October every year, and there wasn't another soul in Paris who knew her well enough to turn up out of the blue. Perhaps it was an error, someone at the wrong apartment door, but then the rapping came again, and Elise put down her gouge. "I'm coming!"

She pulled the door open and then blinked into the hallway for a second, trying to make sense of what she was seeing. "Ruth!" she exclaimed, leaning forward to kiss her old friend on both cheeks. "What a surprise to see you! What on earth are you doing here in Paris?"

"I'll explain," Ruth said, her voice tinged with sadness. "Elise, may I come in?"

Elise glanced over her shoulder. The only Mathilde carving on display was one she'd done years ago, what she'd imagined Mathilde would have looked like at the age of four, her face tilted up as she laughed. It was sitting on the coffee table just beside the sofa, where Elise talked to it most nights. The other Mathildes—the embodiment of Elise's inability to move on—were all hidden away. "Certainly." She opened the door a bit wider, perplexed by the tears in Ruth's eyes as she walked into the apartment. "Ruth? Are Georges and Suzanne okay?"

Ruth looked startled. "Yes, they're fine."

"Then what is it?" Elise asked as she closed the door behind Ruth and gestured toward the sofa. "What are you doing here?"

Ruth took a seat and tapped her foot repeatedly against the floor as Elise sat across from her.

"Ruth, you're making me nervous," Elise said.

"I've found Juliette," Ruth blurted out.

Suddenly, Elise's vision felt blurry. "Juliette Foulon? Where?"

"In New York. She has been living there all along, and I—" She stopped abruptly. "She owns a bookstore there." Ruth seemed to be saying the words carefully, unsure how to begin. "It is very similar to the one she and Monsieur Foulon owned in Boulogne."

"She bought another bookstore?" Elise could hardly imagine it.

Ruth frowned. "Not exactly. It seems she married someone wealthy, who encouraged her to rebuild the exact same bookstore she had here. It was strange, Elise. It was nearly an exact replica."

Elise's eyes drifted to the sculpture of the young Mathilde that sat beside Ruth, and she swallowed a lump of shame as Ruth glanced at it. Was it obvious to Ruth that Elise, too, was guilty of trying to seize a past that was gone forever?

"It's different, Elise," Ruth said quietly, reading her mind.

"You are trying to find peace. Juliette seems to be trying to find . . . something else."

"What do you mean?"

"I don't know quite how to explain it, Elise, but this was not the Juliette you and I once knew." She hesitated. "Physically, she appeared fine. But she seemed angry. Or perhaps that isn't the right word. She seemed shaken to see me, unsettled that I spoke to Lucie, put out that I asked her to write you a letter."

"And did she?" Elise leaned forward, still trying to puzzle out how the woman she had once known had become the woman Ruth was describing. "Did she write me a letter?"

"It is why I have come, Elise."

Elise could feel her heart thudding. Ruth had sailed across the ocean to bring her a piece of mail? "Did you read it?"

"It was not mine to read, my friend."

Indeed, when Ruth withdrew an envelope from her handbag, the name Elise LeClair scrawled across the front, it was sealed. Elise took the letter and held it in shaking hands, simply staring at it.

"Would you like me to leave?" Ruth asked. "To give you some privacy?"

"Of course not." Elise wiped a tear away and tried to smile. "This is just very difficult, you see. I've been wondering for so many years what happened . . ."

"And now you will know," Ruth said. "Take your time."

The world seemed to close in around Elise as she ran her index finger beneath the seal and split the envelope open. The single piece of paper crackled beneath her trembling fingers as she struggled to unfold it. Did it take only a single sheet to explain her daughter's fate, the end of her young life? It seemed impossible. She took a deep breath and began to read.

Dear Elise,

    It is with regret that I notify you of the death of your daughter, Mathilde, on the 4th of April, 1943. I understand that you already know the circumstances of the errant bomb, and its subsequent destruction of the bookstore. Perhaps it will bring you some comfort to know that Mathilde died in my husband's arms. Your daughter did not suffer.

    Sincerely,

    Juliette Foulon Wolcott

Elise read the brief, impersonal letter twice before looking up at Ruth with tears in her eyes. "This is *it*? After seventeen years? This is all she tells me of my daughter's life and death?" She handed the letter to Ruth and watched as the other woman scanned it and then shook her head.

"I was afraid of this," Ruth said. "I'm very sorry, Elise. You can see what I mean about Juliette having changed. Does it bring you some comfort to know that Monsieur Foulon was holding Mathilde, at least?"

"It does." Paul had been a nice man, the kind of person Elise wished she'd chosen for herself instead of choosing Olivier. But if she hadn't married Olivier, Mathilde wouldn't have existed in the first place, and a world without Mathilde would have been like a world without birds or flowers or music. No, Mathilde had lived, and because she had, the world would always be a bit brighter, even if Elise's existence had grown as dim as a candle about to burn away. It made Elise's heart ache with gratitude that the man who had taken her child in without reservation had died trying to protect her. "It does," she said again. "And to know that she had Lucie's friendship in those days means a great deal, too."

But she and Ruth both knew the words were empty. The

letter had been sparse and cold, and Elise understood, as perhaps only a mother who had lost a child could, that Juliette had forever been changed at her core, just as she had.

"And Lucie?" Elise asked after a moment. "You saw her, Ruth? How was she? I've worried so much about her over the years. I've wondered how she has coped with being the only one of the children to—" She stopped abruptly, unable to complete the sentence.

"To be honest, I'm not certain. She seemed . . . sad. It was as if Juliette was gazing right through her, right past her, like she hardly existed at all."

"Poor Lucie," Elise murmured. "Poor Juliette."

"They both seemed . . . so lost, Elise."

Elise didn't say anything for a few moments. Her heart ached for her old friend, for the way grief had seemingly transformed her. The coldness that had seeped from the single-page letter chilled Elise, and it made her wonder about the life Lucie had, growing up with a mother who had changed so.

"She asked about you, you know," Ruth said after a while.

"Juliette?"

"No, Lucie. She seemed interested to hear that you are an artist."

Elise glanced in the direction of the peacock carving she'd been working on and frowned. "Am I?"

"Of course you are." Ruth leaned forward to pat her hand. "Lucie said she'd like to meet you."

Elise blinked back tears. "Meet me? I knew her once, so well. She was my daughter's best friend. Doesn't she remember me?"

"She was so young, Elise."

Elise thought for a moment, a feeling of dread and certainty settling in the pit of her stomach. "I must go to New York, mustn't

I?" She nodded to herself. "I have to find out what happened to Mathilde. What her last months were like. Who she had become. And . . ." She hesitated. "I have to see Lucie. I have to make sure she's all right."

"Lucie?"

"I promised, you see. When I left Mathilde with Juliette, I promised that I would find a way to pay her back one day, that I would always look out for her children the way she was looking out for mine." She blinked back tears. "I have thought of that promise every day, Ruth. I have prayed to God that one day I would find her." Elise turned to study the carving of Mathilde. "I think I must try," she said without looking away from her daughter's face. "I think it is the least I owe to Juliette."

Ruth looked troubled. "That would be a great kindness, Elise. I'm scheduled to return in three days' time. Shall we see if there's an extra berth on the ship?"

Elise looked at her hands. "No. I think—I need to spend some time with my thoughts before I'm ready. But I will come, Ruth. I will. And then, perhaps, once I've learned about Mathilde's final moments, once I've repaid the debt to Juliette by making sure that she and her daughter are safe and well, I'll be able to live again."

"Elise . . ." Ruth began, her brows arching in sadness, but Elise waved her away. She knew Ruth worried often about Elise's withdrawal from the world, her reluctance to leave Paris. But Ruth's two children had come home, and the three of them were together. Despite all she'd been through, there was no way Ruth could understand what it felt like to have her whole world taken away forever. Her family had been through hell, but they had survived.

"So," Elise said brightly, clapping her hands together and forcing a smile. "Tell me everything. I want to hear every last detail of your life in New York, and especially what Georges and Suzanne are up to these days. You said in your last letter that Suzanne has a nice boyfriend?"

Ruth looked uncertain, but after a moment, she began to talk haltingly about how embraced she felt by her adopted city, which was filled with glaring billboards and exhaust fumes and immigrants from everywhere, and how readily she had managed to pick up English after all.

As Ruth spoke, telling her first about the young man Suzanne had met at the law firm where she worked as a secretary, and then about Georges's new job, Elise's gaze moved back to the bust of Mathilde on the table, one of her countless feeble attempts to ask herself what would have been if her daughter's life had not been lost to an errant bomb.

But Mathilde was gone. She had died on the fourth of April, 1943, in the arms of Juliette Foulon's kind husband. She had died without her mother there to protect her. And no amount of chiseling her face from wood would change that.

That night, when Elise went to bed, Ruth snoring loudly in the guest room, sleep came to her easily, and for the first time in years, she dreamed not of the lines of her daughter's face but of the terror Mathilde must have felt in her final seconds, held tight by a man who died trying to save her, with her own mother hundreds of miles away.

CHAPTER TWENTY-SIX

Lucie couldn't exactly put a finger on what she loved so much about art, but she suspected it had a lot to do with the fact that her mother was so adamantly against it. She wasn't sure what that said about her. Was she subconsciously trying to make her mother's life miserable? Or was she just desperate to be some version of herself that wasn't dictated by her mother's grief?

When she was ten or eleven, she'd been absentmindedly sketching at the dining room table one day, trying to put to paper two sea lions she had seen at the Central Park Zoo, whiskers waving, mouths open as they bobbed their heads at each other. It had seemed to Lucie that the two were talking to each other, and she'd been fascinated by the idea that animals could seem so human. She had just turned her pencil over to erase an eye she had drawn—it needed to be shaped more like a gumdrop than a teardrop, with brows that made the creature look earnest—when her mother had appeared at her shoulder, gasped, and snatched the paper away.

"What do you think you're doing?" her mother had demanded, staring at the drawing in horror. Even then, Lucie had been aware that the rendering was good—better than the work of an average fifth-grader, anyhow. Shouldn't her mother be proud? Instead, she was acting like she'd caught Lucie swigging from one of Arthur's bottles of Calvert Reserve Whiskey.

"Drawing," Lucie had responded, confused by her mother's reaction. "Well, sketching, really. The big one looked like he was laughing, you see, and I was just trying to see if I could . . ." She trailed off when she saw her mother's horrified expression.

"Laughing *sea lions*?" Under her breath, her mother added something that sounded like, "Not if I have anything to say about it."

"Wh-what did I do wrong, Maman?"

Her mother leaned in, her nose so close that it touched Lucie's as she said through gritted teeth, "Listen to me very carefully, Lucie. Foulons are not artists. *Artists* abandon their children."

At that moment, Lucie understood her mother hated art because she hated the LeClairs. Lucie didn't remember Mathilde well, though sometimes she could recall the feel of the other girl's hand clasping her own, the sound of her laughter, the joy of coloring together with bright crayons on old scraps of paper. She knew enough, however, to know that Mathilde's death had been as unavoidable as that of her brothers and her father. How could her mother still feel such anger toward an innocent little girl, or toward another mother who had lost a child just as tragically as she had?

Now, art was Lucie's only rebellion, her form of denying her mother's version of the past. Her mother had created a prison for her, with rules Lucie had long ago stopped trying to understand, but painting was its key. Art allowed her to fly away from this place, to soar over the ocean to France, to imagine a great, wide world out there that wasn't filled with recrimination and anger over things Lucie couldn't control. It was also the last connection she had to Mathilde; her memories of the months before the bomb were foggy, but she remembered drawing together almost every day.

It was Tommy who had talked her into signing up for an art class when he saw her absently sketching in a notebook while their history professor droned on one day. She had been drawing the world from the bottom up; she'd become fascinated with the act of lying on her back in parks and committing to memory the way the lampposts and trees around her seemed to strain and reach for the sky. "I'm signing up for a modern art course," he had said without preamble, the very first time he'd spoken to her, though she had noticed him and his long, black eyelashes across the classroom. He had noticed her, too; she had felt it.

"That's nice," she had replied tentatively.

"I'm signing up because I heard it was a breeze. You should sign up, too, though," he said. "Since you're an artist."

"But I'm not."

"Sure you are," he said with a grin, gesturing to her notebook, filled with sketches that had simply poured from her mind onto the page. "Obviously. So c'mon. Sign up with me, will ya?"

And so she had discovered a whole new world she hadn't known existed, a world of people who saw life in shapes and colors and sought new and innovative ways to put the images in their heads on paper. Tommy brought her a blank sketch pad on the first day of the next semester, and when she opened the card that went with it, she found herself smiling. *May I take you on a date?* it inquired in polite chicken scratch, and when she'd looked up and said yes, he had grinned and pumped his fist in the air like his Yankees had just won the World Series.

That night, she had sketched the bookshop in France, the one she knew would always be different from the one her mother had painstakingly re-created here. Her mother was obsessive now about having every single thing exactly in its place—books all aligned at ninety-degree angles, the shelves situated just as they'd been in France. But the store that lived in Lucie's memory was perfectly imperfect—dust here, an upside-down book there, a few errant spines leaning at the wrong angles—because Lucie's mother and father had once been too busy living life to worry about perfection. That was the bookstore Lucie missed, the *life* Lucie missed. And with her pencil, she could bring it back.

For months now, she had been going each Sunday to Tommy's apartment just south of Hester Street to paint and to have dinner with his family. She loved how they made her feel like she belonged, even though she wasn't from Italy and often couldn't follow their conversations. But they were loud and warm and made her feel included and wanted.

Most of all, though, she loved that becoming a part of Tommy's life had given her a place to paint, at least on Sundays. Tommy's interest in painting had petered out—he was easily distracted, and his latest hobby was repairing car engines with his cousin Domenico—but he gave her a few hours alone each week in the den to put the thoughts in her head on canvas. It was a cathartic release each week. "I don't mind," his mother had once explained. "If it makes Tommy happy, it makes me happy." She had leaned forward then and kissed Lucie on the cheek, startling her. "And you, *carissima*, make my Tommy happy."

But the third weekend in November, Tommy met her at the door when she arrived, her bag of paints and brushes slung over her shoulder, ready to tackle a piece she'd been thinking about all week. She wanted to paint Paris, like Olivier LeClair had done, but she wanted to do it her way, and she was itching to start.

"We can't stick around here this weekend, doll. I tried to call you, but your stepfather said you'd already left."

Lucie peered around him at his mother, who was puttering around the kitchen, pretending to ignore them while she muttered to herself.

"What happened?" she asked. "What's wrong with your mother?"

"She's sore because I'm ditching the rest of the semester to sell Christmas trees with Domenico."

"What?" Lucie was certain she'd heard him wrong. "But your scholarship—"

He avoided her gaze. "Ah, Luce, school doesn't come easy to me the way it does for you. I got a scholarship for being a poor immigrant kid, but the jig was almost up. C'mon, you didn't know? I'm failing most of my classes. Might as well call it quits before they kick me out."

"But—" She was at a loss. She wanted to tell him he was tossing away a wonderful opportunity, but that would make her sound like her mother, who had such a clear idea of how everyone's life was supposed to turn out. Maybe Tommy wasn't cut out for college. Maybe she wasn't, either. She didn't have the courage to stand up to her mother and tell her she wanted to pursue painting instead, but maybe it was good that Tommy was following his dreams. "Oh," she said, unsure of whether to chide or congratulate him.

"Don't be sore, Luce. Dom has a connection with a tree farm out in Jersey. They're giving us the trees at rock bottom, and he's got us an abandoned lot to set up on in Park Slope with John and Joseph. You remember them? We'll sell a bunch of trees and make some real dough."

Lucie glanced past him, through the doorway into the apartment he'd grown up in. She could smell his mother's sauce simmering already. "And your mother . . ."

"Doesn't exactly see it that way." He frowned. "She says I'm throwing my life away just like Domenico is. But she never sees the big picture."

His mother's muttering got louder in the kitchen, and Lucie could hear her slamming pots around.

"I don't think we're invited to dinner today," Tommy added unnecessarily.

Tears sprang to Lucie's eyes, and embarrassed, she brushed them away while Tommy's face fell.

"Aw, Luce, I thought you'd be happy for me."

"Sure I am. It's just—" She didn't finish the sentence.

"Right. Painting."

"Well . . . yes." His apartment was the only place she could work freely, without worrying about Arthur or her mother catching her, and she hadn't realized until that very moment just how much she needed it each week.

"Look, come see the lot where we're gonna set up. I know you'll see dollar signs, like I do." He reached out his hand, and after a second's hesitation, she took it. "We just gotta take the Brighton Line to Seventh Street station in Brooklyn. It couldn't be easier . . ."

He continued babbling about subway directions as he led her away from his family's apartment, down the stairs, oblivious to the fact that she was still fighting back tears. Where would she paint now?

That night, after she'd dutifully admired the corner of Sterling Place and Seventh where Tommy and Domenico would set up their lot with their two friends next week, Lucie came home early and opened her window. It was freezing outside, the last of the autumn leaves making their final descent from skeletal trees. She breathed in the crisp evening air, spiked with the scent of smoke drifting from chimneys nearby. Arthur was holed up in his study, oblivious as usual. Her mother was still at the bookstore, where she'd likely be for at least the next few hours; she'd been coming home later and later since Madame Levy's visit to the store, as if the collision with the past had accelerated her growing obsession with pretending Lucie's father and brothers were still alive. She thought that Lucie hadn't noticed, but of course she had; her mother talked to them aloud now, even when Lucie was right there. Lucie had tried telling Arthur that she was concerned, but he had barely looked up from his newspaper. "Whatever makes your mother happy," he had said, waving a hand.

There was no one here to catch her in the forbidden act of painting, so she set up quickly, using an eight-by-ten piece of heavy linen paper clipped to a textbook as a makeshift easel. She imagined her Parisian sky much bigger, filling the ceiling above her head, but she was relatively certain that painting a room-wide mural would not be quite as secretive as she needed it to be. She pulled out her Liquitex paints, which she had been buying tube by tube for months now, and several brushes, and she set to work.

She painted from memory and imagination, as she often did. When she was starting out, she had attempted still lifes, trying to capture the things she saw in front of her, their shadows and lines. But she learned over time that when she painted that way, her work always looked forced and flat. Instead, she preferred to think about her project for days ahead of time, sketching the work in her head again and again, erasing lines here, shading curves there, until the image she held in her mind came alive and felt fluid, three-dimensional. Then, and only then, could she commit it to paper, trusting her brush to move swiftly enough to keep up with what she could already see. One of the many questions she would have asked Olivier LeClair if he were still alive was whether he did the same thing. Was it a sign that she was thinking like a true artist? Or was her brain as broken as her mother's?

She had been thinking for weeks now about LeClair's painting of the rooftops of Paris, and for the last two nights, she had dreamed of flying over the city, one with the clouds, as twilight fell. So that's what she began to paint now, roughing out Haussmann buildings with balconies and tumbling roses, treetops in the breeze, slender chimney pots in shades of copper and terra-cotta.

She worked quickly, adding a cat on a balcony, the shadow of a woman in a window. There was the moon, hanging bulbous over a Paris twilight, and there were the mansard roofs. In the distance, the tip of the Eiffel Tower scraped the clouds, and the towers of Notre-Dame hulked, promising a carol of bells. She had lived in the suburbs as a girl, but she knew that before the arrival of the Germans, her mother had taken her for strolls in the city. She had foggy impressions of Paris even after the Occupation had begun, the landscape rolling by outside her baby carriage as she stared in wonder, taking it all in. Paris was gray and solemn, she knew, but it was also filled with color and life, and it was that juxtaposition she aimed for now as she painted smoky shadows of a couple dancing cheek to cheek in one apartment, a pop of red from a window box, the amber glow of a candle burning in a window, the deep cobalt of the sky losing the sun. It was color and light and life, and when Lucie finished, she sat back, breathing hard, and let her eyes rove over what she had created.

It was only a small sheet of thick art paper, but it held a piece of Lucie's world, one that felt long gone, and as she stared at it, her heart pounded. There was room for improvement—the lines of the building on the left were slightly off, the shadows of the roof left of center leaned at the wrong angle, she hadn't captured the exact red of a French rose in the spring—but this was the best thing she'd ever painted.

The longer she looked at it, the more a dangerous thought began to take shape in her head. What if she gave the painting to her mother as a gift? Juliette's heart was still in France, so much so that she had desperately tried to build a duplicate of the old store on this side of the Atlantic. She thought that Lucie didn't care, but of course she did—and perhaps this would be the proof. "You have re-created the store, and I am trying to put my memories on paper," Lucie imagined herself saying. "We're one and the same after all, don't you see?" Maybe her mother would understand, at last, why art meant so much to Lucie, why she *needed* this.

The more she thought about it, the more logical it felt. After all, her mother spent her days speaking to the dead. But this, this was *real*. This was solid, tangible, *here*. Maybe if Lucie could give her this, she could give her back the here and now. She could remind her that there was beauty out there, that this very same Paris still existed, that her mother could even one day return there without feeling the need to travel in time to a lost era.

She was so caught up in imagining her mother's reaction and the bridge it could build between them that she didn't hear her bedroom door open. Only a second later, a shadow fell across the canvas and she froze. She'd been caught.

"Lucie, what are you doing?" It was Arthur standing there, not her mother, which was a relief. "Hasn't your mother forbidden you from painting?"

"Yes, but she's wrong." Lucie felt suddenly emboldened. "I miss Paris, too! I remember the past we left behind, too. But we

don't need to live in it, don't you see? If I give her this, she'll understand. I know it."

Arthur pinched the bridge of his nose. He was twenty-five
years her mother's senior, which made him an old man. Though
he went to the barber each Monday to have his beard and mustache perfectly trimmed, he never seemed to notice the white hairs
sprouting from his ears and his nostrils, and she supposed the barber must be too polite to point them out. He always dressed for-
mally, with crisply ironed trousers, a pressed shirt, and an expensive
leather belt, even when he was simply lounging in his study, and
his eyeglasses seemed to get thicker with each passing year. Now
he stepped closer and studied her painting through his Coke-bottle
lenses before turning to her with sympathy in his eyes.

"I'd hate for you to upset your mother, Lucie," he said.

"But what if it doesn't upset her?" She hesitated. "What if it helps
her to finally *see* me?" She hadn't realized until she said the words
how much she longed for that. But there it was. Lucie was losing
Maman day by day, and she didn't know how to get her back.

Arthur put his hand on her shoulder. "Lucie, it's beautiful,
dear. But your mother already sees you. She's very proud of you.
You can't understand the grief of losing someone as she has,
though. It can't be fixed with a piece of art." He gave her shoulder a squeeze and then strode out, leaving Lucie alone once again.

But he was wrong. He had only known her mother after the
war, but Lucie still remembered the woman who had cared for
her before the blast, a mother who sang and smiled and laughed,
a woman full of joy and wonder. That person was still in there,
in the shell that had become the modern-day Juliette Foulon, and
Lucie wouldn't rest until she had figured out how to bring that
version of Maman back—or until Maman realized that Lucie had
been right here all along.

CHAPTER TWENTY-SEVEN

The bookshop was quiet that afternoon, the autumn light outside the color of honey. Then again, it was always quiet here, which was the way Juliette preferred it. At the beginning, when Arthur had first indulged her desire to rebuild La Librairie des Rêves, she had looked forward to his visits, and even to Lucie's incessant questions. But now, Arthur rarely came at all, and Lucie was grown and hardly said anything to Juliette anymore.

"Perhaps I'm being too hard on her," she said aloud as she reshelved a French-language Babar book that had been difficult to get after the war. It was a first edition, and when a portly, middle-aged woman had walked in that morning, just after the store opened, and manhandled the book, flipping through its pages so roughly that Juliette feared they would rip, it was all Juliette could do to stop herself from snatching it out of the woman's hands. This was, after all, a bookstore, and customers had the right to look through the books if they wanted to. In France, she had been happy to have those who loved words thumbing through pages; it was why bookstores existed, wasn't it? Still, when the woman had set Babar down and walked out, Juliette had been relieved.

"Perhaps you are," came Paul's answer as she reverently slid the book into its spot, aligning its spine with the others in the series and stepping back to make sure the angles were perfectly straight. Reshelving had been Paul's job in the old store, and Juliette knew she wasn't as adept at it as he was.

"It is just that she seems to have no appreciation of how lucky she is," she said, lovingly running her fingers over the spines. She had a sudden flash of Claude in the children's section, dramatically reading *Le Roi Babar* to Alphonse and Lucie, and she had to reach out to steady herself against the shelf. Snippets of memory, as clear and frozen as still photographs, whisked by now and then, nearly knocking Juliette over with the strange blend of grief and nostalgic joy they brought with them. "Perhaps it's my fault. I spend so much time with you, Paul, that I'm afraid I neglect Lucie. I should do better."

"You're doing your best, my love." Paul's voice was deep and soothing. She knew logically that he wasn't here at all, but she could still feel him, could still hear him whispering through the shelves, the very essence of him seeping out of the books he had helped her choose so long ago. That had been one of the reasons she had been so intent on building not only the bookstore of her memory, but a collection of books that mirrored those of the shattered store on rue Goblet. As long as those books were here, Paul was here, too. Arthur couldn't know that she didn't actually *want* to sell the books in her store, but it was better that he believe her to be a bad businesswoman. If he knew she was here each day talking to her husband, he would likely be upset. Perhaps he would even leave her, and then where would she be? That was why it was so important to keep up the pretense of being a dutiful wife, why she never missed a dinner at home with him, why she let him hold her at night before he fell into a state of snoring oblivion.

"It isn't fair," she said as she picked up a copy of *Les Petits Voyageurs*, which another customer had callously abandoned on a table in the children's section. She ran her fingers lovingly over the cover; the book had been Alphonse's favorite when he was a baby, and it was nearly impossible to find here in the States. In fact, Juliette had paid a pretty penny to the stout French art dealer on the corner, who had offered to help her obtain some of the rarer books from France.

"In a fair world, I would still be there with you," Paul agreed.

"And the children," Juliette said, her eyes suddenly damp. "The children would be here, too. Or rather, I would still be in France with all of you, not in this godforsaken city an ocean away."

"You used to love New York," Paul pointed out. "You told me on our first date how much you'd loved going into the city as a girl with your mother. Remember seeing *Animal Crackers* at the Forty-Fourth Street Theater? Or *Fifty Million Frenchmen* at the Lyric?"

"Of course I do." It was just like Paul to hold her memories so dear. "I knew after I saw that musical that I would one day go to Paris, too."

"I know." She could hear the smile in Paul's voice. He knew all her stories, perhaps better than she did. "I owe Cole Porter a thank-you for that, I suppose." The suave composer and lyricist had come into their store twice, and both times, Juliette had found herself starstruck and speechless. "But, my love, you are there now, and you must make the best of it. You must go on, for all of us."

Juliette knew this, of course, but it was so easy for Paul to say. He didn't have to get up each day and face an empty world. "I wish I knew how to stop being angry," she said, tears welling in her eyes again as she moved on to the travel section, filled with French-language 1930s guidebooks. She had paid a great deal of money to the art dealer for these, too, but it had been worth it. Her hand lingered on the book about the Côte d'Azur, where she and Paul had honeymooned, and for a second, she was too choked up to speak. She could see that idyllic time in her mind, another frozen snapshot, the two of them lying side by side in the sand, warm skin turned amber by the sun, the sound of waves lapping. They'd had no idea what life had in store for them or that their time together would be far too short.

"Who are you angry with?" Paul asked, though he knew the answer to the question. They'd had this conversation before.

"Myself," Juliette said. "With you, for not saving all of them, for not saving yourself. With Mathilde, just for being there. And sometimes even with Lucie, for being the one to live so that I had to go on, too." She couldn't believe she'd said the words aloud. How could she still be so angry with Lucie? But if Lucie, too, had perished, Juliette could have closed her eyes in the midst of that rubble and joined her family. Her daughter's survival had forced her into this life she never wanted.

"Oh, Juliette." She could hear the sadness in Paul's voice. "There's no use living with anger like that. How can you be happy?"

"I don't deserve to be. Neither does Lucie." She said the words before she could think about them, and as soon as they were out in the open, she clapped her hands over her mouth in horror. What would Paul think of her? She was wishing unhappiness on their child. "It is just that she isn't who I imagined she would be," she added quickly, trying to explain. "She doesn't think of the other children at all. She is perfectly happy to forget them, Paul, and she asks too many questions about the LeClairs, as if they didn't play a role in ruining our lives."

"It isn't the LeClairs' fault," he reminded her.

But just because Paul was dead didn't mean that he knew everything. Of course it was the LeClairs' fault. Olivier LeClair with his foolish ideals and Elise LeClair with her complete disregard for Juliette's children as she flounced away to the countryside, leaving her own child behind. Certainly the LeClairs hadn't dropped the bomb themselves, but if Mathilde hadn't been with Juliette and Paul, who knew how things would have turned out? "She's obsessed with Olivier LeClair," Juliette said bitterly. "Like he's some sort of god of the art world."

"Martyrdom tends to do that for mediocre artists." Paul sounded amused.

"He's no martyr," Juliette snorted. "And Lucie is a fool to think otherwise."

Paul didn't respond to that, and after a moment's hesitation, Juliette asked, "Paul? Are you still there?"

But there was no answer, and suddenly her head ached as much as her heart did. When Paul came to her now, he didn't stay as long as he used to, and she hardly ever saw the children anymore. What if they were forgetting her, drifting further away from the boundary separating her world from theirs? She couldn't bear it. Or perhaps Paul was simply trying to force her to spend more time with the child left behind rather than the ones who had been taken from her. She wanted to scream at him that he didn't understand, that it was impossible having to carry on day after day without him, but he never seemed to quite grasp how difficult it was for her.

The bell above the door chimed then, and Juliette hurriedly wiped her tears away, then cleared her throat and gathered herself.

She forced a smile as she turned the corner from the travel section toward the front of the store; after all, it wouldn't do to have customers seeing her weep.

But it wasn't a customer standing there. It was Lucie, her dark hair falling over her right shoulder like a river, obscuring one of her eyes. Juliette meant to say hello, but what came out instead was, "Don't slouch," and she hated herself a bit more as some of the light went out of her daughter's eyes. Still, the girl straightened her posture, throwing her shoulders back, and as her hair cascaded out of her face, she held Juliette's gaze.

"I've come to talk with you." Lucie's voice was high-pitched but firm, a girl on the cusp of womanhood. One would hardly know she'd started her life in France; the accent had all but vanished.

"Did your father send you?" Juliette asked before realizing how foolish that sounded.

"Arthur?" Lucie asked, looking confused.

Relieved, Juliette nodded, though that wasn't what she'd meant at all.

"No. I—I wanted to talk to you about something."

It was then that Juliette realized Lucie was holding something behind her back. Had Lucie found one of the volumes Juliette and the art dealer hadn't been able to locate? If Lucie had done so, perhaps it would soften some of the tension between them. It would show Juliette that Lucie wasn't trying to disrespect her past by forgetting it, and that in fact, she was working with her mother rather than against her. "What is it, Lucie?"

"I—I have something." Lucie sounded shy, nervous. "Something that I hoped might remind you of the past—but also of the life that still lies before us. Something that I hoped would show you that the past is important to me, too, just as it is to you."

It *must* be a book. Juliette smiled at her daughter. She had judged her incorrectly. Perhaps Paul *had* sent her here today, to remind Juliette that she and Lucie were in this together, that as mother and daughter, they could focus on making this store an even more perfect replica of the one they'd left behind. "How did you find it?" she asked.

Lucie's forehead creased. "Find it?"

"The book!" Juliette held out her hand, feeling lighter already. "Was it the art dealer? Did Arthur give you the money?"

The confusion on Lucie's face deepened. "Maman, I don't . . ." She trailed off and cleared her throat. "I don't have a book."

"Oh." Juliette let her hand drop. The familiar sting of annoyance had begun to creep back in. "Well then, what is it?"

But Lucie didn't make a move to reveal whatever she was hiding. Instead, she stared at her mother until Juliette was forced to look away. She didn't like what she saw reflected there. "They're perfect, aren't they?" Lucie asked, her voice so soft it was almost inaudible. "They can do no wrong."

"Who?" Juliette asked impatiently.

"Alphonse. Claude. Antoinette. Papa."

Each name hit Juliette like a separate blow to the gut. She put her hands to her belly to protect herself. "What are you saying?"

"They'll always be perfect to you, because they died." Lucie's voice quivered, and Juliette knew that she was supposed to step forward and wrap her arms around her daughter in comfort and reassurance, but she couldn't bring herself to do it. "But I lived. And because of that, you see only the things I'm not, all the ways I've failed you simply by being me."

Juliette felt heat rise to her cheeks, anger at her daughter's audacity, embarrassment at the veracity of her statement, fury at Lucie's inability to understand. She forced herself to breathe, to imagine Paul's hands on her shoulders, comforting her. "That simply isn't true."

"But it is." Lucy's tone wasn't accusatory, merely sad, and perhaps that was worse. "You live in the shadows of what happened, Maman, but I don't want to anymore. I can't. We have to move on, both of us."

"Move *on*?" Juliette's voice rose an octave, and she was aware of the way her anger was leaking out at the seams now, but she wasn't able to control it. "How can you suggest such a thing? Do you know how lucky you were? To have *lived*?"

"Yes, of course!" Lucie shot back. Her hands were still behind her back, and Juliette fought the sudden desire to reach around and rip whatever it was out of her daughter's hands. "But simply surviving isn't everything! We must make a life, and to do that, we must live in the present, not the past. *You* must live in the present, Maman!"

"You know nothing about it," Juliette retorted. "You were a child! You have no idea what I've been through. You hardly even remember them."

"Remember them?" Lucie's laugh was bitter. "Of course I do! I think of them all the time. They were my family, too! I lost them, too! But it feels as if I lose you again and again every day."

"Lose me?" Juliette scoffed. "That's nonsense. I'm right here in front of you."

"Are you? Then why does it feel like you're thousands of miles away?"

"Because I'd like to be! Because I can't stand this life, Lucie! Because I shouldn't be here! I should be dead in the ground in France, and you should be, too!"

Lucie gasped and stepped back, and Juliette immediately regretted the words.

"I didn't mean that the way it came out," she said. "I'm grateful you lived, of course."

"No, I don't think you are." Tears coursed down Lucie's face. "I think you would prefer me frozen in time like the others. Then you could love me, too."

"I do love you," Juliette said, but she could hear how forced the words sounded, and she could see the pain on her daughter's face. She hated herself for inflicting it, but her limbs felt heavy, her feet rooted to the spot, and she couldn't muster the strength to step forward and make it better. "I do love you," she repeated. "I love you very much."

"No, you don't. You love the child I was on an April morning in 1943. You don't love the woman I've become. You want me to stick to a script you have written in your head, Maman, but I am my own person with my own interests. Claude, Alphonse, Antoinette, and Mathilde would have grown and changed and become their own people, too, you know!"

"But they never had the chance! And you insist on becoming someone I hardly recognize!"

"Only because you don't take the time to see me!" Lucie retorted. "You spend all your time here in this store talking to yourself . . ."

Juliette glared at Lucie. "I'm not talking to myself."

"Of course you are. When there's no one here to answer you, that's exactly what you're doing."

Juliette pressed her lips together. Lucie would never understand. No one understood.

"I just . . ." Lucie trailed off, and she shook her head. "Maman, I want you to *see* me. I want you to see who I've become and try to love me for it. I want you to remember that there's a whole world that exists outside the store. We're in New York, Maman!

You could stand on the street here and hear a dozen languages all at once; the lights of Broadway are like a universe full of bright stars; the skyscrapers soar higher than we ever could have imagined when we were in Paris. It's okay to think of the past, to miss it, but it's been seventeen years, whether we like it or not. We're here now, not *there*." Lucie was crying now, but they weren't the tears of rage Juliette expected. She only looked lost, sad. "I want you to realize that you're ignoring the present and throwing away the future." She paused and then added in a small voice, "You are throwing away *me*."

"I'm sorry." Juliette felt a surge of remorse, and that was good, because it meant she was feeling *something*. "I *am* sorry, Lucie. I don't intend to hurt you."

"This isn't about your hurting me. This is about your coming back to me. Coming back to Arthur, even. Coming back to *life*."

Juliette was about to say that she'd never left and that she would try harder to make Lucie see that, but then Lucie ruined everything, for she finally withdrew the item she was holding behind her back and held it up for Juliette to see.

"This is for you." Lucie took a step closer as Juliette stared in horror at the image. Was Lucie mocking her? "I remember, too, Maman. I think of them all the time. Perhaps if we go back to Paris together, if we see it in the present, if we visit their graves, you can put the past to rest and remember what it is you loved about France . . ."

But Juliette was hardly listening to her daughter anymore. She snatched the painting from her hands and stared at it, rage clouding her vision. Who did Lucie think she was? "Where did you get this?" she demanded.

"I—I painted it." But she sounded uncertain now, like a frightened little girl. "I thought perhaps you could hang it in the shop. A reminder that the past shaped both of us, but that we're here now. I thought maybe it could be a fresh start."

"A fresh start." Juliette repeated her daughter's words flatly. The painting was a violation of everything, a betrayal. It showed the rooftops of Paris under a twilight sky, the Eiffel Tower hulking in the falling darkness, the amber and crimson fading from the roofs, life happening in the shadows of the windows. "You thought *this* would be a fresh start?"

Lucie's face had grown red, her eyes glassy with tears. "Why can't it be?"

"Because *this* isn't who we are!" Juliette spit out. "This Paris doesn't exist anymore!"

"Of course it does! It always did. It was always right there, but you wanted to freeze time, to pretend that—"

"Enough!" Juliette roared, cutting her off. She looked again at the image. She could feel white-hot fury rising in her like a terrible tide. "You are forbidden from ever painting again! How dare you?"

Something changed in Lucie's face then, and Juliette didn't like it one bit. It wasn't her daughter's usual sadness and hurt. It was something else, something obstinate, something angry. Lucie drew herself up a bit straighter. "Maman, you cannot stop me from being who I am." Her voice was quiet but firm. "*This* is who I am." She pointed at the painting. "I am an artist, Maman. *This* is me."

"This is *not* who you are!" The air seemed to go still around them. Juliette looked once more at the painting. Lucie seemed determined to spite her at every turn, and now, her stubborn obsession with Olivier LeClair had gone too far. She looked back at Lucie, whose eyes were welling with tears, and for a second, just a second, she hated what she knew she had to do. But there was no choice, not if she wanted to remind Lucie once and for all of who she was. She looked once more at the painting with its violet skies and amber roofs and then, refusing to look at Lucie, she ripped it straight down the middle.

"Maman!" The word was somewhere between a yelp of pain and a cry of anguish, but Juliette ignored it. It was for the best.

She twisted away as Lucie lurched forward, trying in vain to take her vile painting back. But the quiet hiss of the ripping paper had been too satisfying, and Juliette ripped again and again, severing the painting into fourths, then eighths. She was just about to tear it once more when Lucie lunged around her and wrenched the pieces out of her grasp.

"Maman! How could you?" Lucie demanded, her voice choked, and when Juliette finally looked up at her daughter, she was surprised to see tears coursing down her face. All of this over some foolish painting?

"You'll thank me one day," Juliette said. "You'll see."

Lucie's reply was a muffled sob, and she turned quickly on her heel and strode toward the door, clutching the remnants of her betrayal.

"Don't you dare walk away from me!" Juliette called after her. But her daughter was already gone, the door swinging closed behind her. "Well," Juliette said a moment later, brushing off her hands. A tiny scrap of paper on the floor caught her eye, and Juliette picked it up. The image on it looked like a window, a shadow of a woman alone in front of the pane. She looked skyward. "I was right, Paul," she said. "Wasn't I?"

But there was no answer from her husband this time, and as the silence swirled, and the lonesome woman in the window stared up at her, Juliette had the terrible feeling that perhaps she'd gotten it all wrong.

CHAPTER TWENTY-EIGHT

Lucie could hardly see, tears clouding her vision, as she strode quickly away from the store, the pieces of her ruined painting clutched in her fist. *I should have known better.* The words echoed again and again through her head, not anger at her mother, but anger at herself for believing that things could be different. Life wasn't magical, though, and people didn't surprise you. Not in the real world. She was a fool, both to believe that she could be a painter and to think that her mother would embrace the idea.

Sniffling, she opened her hand, spreading her fingers wide, and let the pieces of thick paper fall just as she turned right at the corner onto Lexington. Perhaps it was time to let that dream go, because it wasn't just about the art, was it? It was about resetting the clock, bringing her mother back, taking what she could from the past to move into the future. But the past was as dead as her father and her brothers, and her mother was mired inescapably in it. Those were things Lucie couldn't fix no matter how vivid her brushstrokes were.

"Wait!" a man's voice called out several yards behind her after Lucie had walked another half block. "Miss, please, wait!"

She kept walking, because there was no one who would be calling her, but then there were footsteps behind her, and a shadow at her elbow, and when the voice asked her to wait again, this time, she stopped and turned.

She vaguely recognized the man standing there, panting. He was the other owner of the art gallery on the corner, the one who wasn't French, the one with paint-stained fingers who was always disappearing into the back somewhere without saying a word while the French owner in his immaculate suit oozed charm at wealthy customers.

"Is this yours?" he asked, holding up something in his hand, and that's when she realized, to her horror, that he was holding the pieces of her destroyed painting.

She stared at her torn work. "It was a mistake."

"Art is never a mistake."

A bitter laughed erupted from her throat. "Sure. Whatever you say."

The man was studying her picture, or what remained of it, his eyes roving over the ruined rooftops. Finally, he looked up at her. "Why is it torn?" His tone was so gentle that it brought tears to her eyes.

"My mother," she said simply, and though that wasn't really an explanation at all, the man seemed to understand.

"You're the daughter of the woman who owns the French bookshop, aren't you?" he asked. "Lucie, is it? You've been in several times with a young man."

She nodded, surprised that he knew who she was. Perhaps she wasn't as invisible as she thought. "And you're the man from the gallery."

He nodded, too. "Jack Fitzgerald," he said as he looked back at the pieces of her ruined work. "Lucie, this is very good."

She could tell from the way he said it that he meant it, and the compliment made heat rise to her cheeks. "My mother says painting is a waste of time."

"Well, your mother is wrong, of course. She is the one who tore your painting?"

Lucie hesitated. It felt wrong to betray her mother, but a lie would have felt worse. "She is . . . troubled. It's hard to explain, but my father and my brothers died during the war, and . . . I think she looks at my painting as a betrayal."

She had said too much—and at the same time, not enough—but confusion didn't cloud his features, as she expected. Instead, he simply nodded, still staring at the pieces of her painting like they were tea leaves that would tell him something important. "Above the gallery, we have eight artists' studios," he said simply.

"Artists' studios?" This was news to her. She had thought the gallery was simply a place for beautiful art to find its way into the hands of wealthy patrons, something that felt entirely out of her reach.

Mr. Fitzgerald smiled slightly. "It was my only condition when I agreed to partner and open the gallery. We could display art, but only if we fostered its creation, too. I run the studio space upstairs while my business partner runs the gallery itself."

"The Frenchman in the nice suits?"

Mr. Fitzgerald chuckled. "An apt description indeed. Yes. In any case, two of our studio spaces upstairs are currently open. Would you like one? A place to work?"

Lucie stared at him. "Me? You want *me* to paint in an artists' studio?"

He smiled and made a show of looking around him. "Is there another artist standing here with us on the street?"

"But I'm not an artist, sir."

"Of course you are." He looked at the pieces again and shook his head in disbelief. "Don't you ever let anyone tell you otherwise, Lucie. Now about that studio space . . ."

"I—I couldn't possibly afford it." Her eyes welled with tears again. Her stepfather had the money, but she knew he wouldn't do anything to upset her mother.

"Oh, there's no charge," Mr. Fitzgerald continued cheerfully. "Well, not until you've made a sale. And then you only pay a small percentage until your rent is covered." He leaned in conspiratorially. "It's the only way I could justify the endeavor to my partner, but the rent is only twenty-five cents a day."

"Twenty-five cents? But what if I never sell anything?"

"Then you don't owe me a thing."

"Why?" Lucie asked. "I mean, why do you do this? Run the studios, I mean."

His smile was kind. "Because artists should have a place to be themselves."

Her heart pounded a bit more quickly at the thought. "Are you an artist?"

"I am." He smiled. "And I firmly believe that the only thing more important than art itself is letting an artist know that it's okay to spread his or her wings and fly, even if that flight path doesn't look the way the world thinks it should. Do you agree?"

The words nearly cracked her open. They were the absolute opposite of everything her mother was always telling her. But they felt true and right, and she found herself nodding vigorously. "I do. I do agree."

"Good. Then shall I get you set up?"

Lucie could only nod as Mr. Fitzgerald took one last look at her torn painting. "This is really very good, Lucie," he said, and hope floated up within her like a ghost rising toward the sky.

Walking into the gallery a few minutes later with Mr. Fitzgerald, Lucie felt for the first time as though she really belonged. Although she'd known the LeClairs once, the French gallery owner always made her feel like she was doing something wrong when she dared venture inside to look at the art. It was why she had never even been into the smaller back room, which featured more paintings and several sculptures on white pedestals, illuminated by overhead lights. But now, this place felt like hers in a way it never had before. She'd been invited in. The thought sent a little sizzle of joy through her as Mr. Fitzgerald led her through the back door of the gallery and up a winding staircase to the second floor.

Upstairs, nine doorways flanked a narrow hallway; four on one side, four on the other, and one at the end of the hall. Eight of the doors were labeled with numbers, and Mr. Fitzgerald led her to the one marked with a 6 and withdrew a key from his pocket, unlocking it and pushing it open for her. "Your studio, Lucie," he said, smiling down at her as he flicked a switch, illuminating the small space.

The walls and ceiling were freshly painted white, and the floor, exposed brick, was splattered with paint. In the corner sat an easel, and there was a tiny window on the far wall that let a bit of light in. To Lucie, it looked like heaven.

"The door at the far end of the hall is a supply closet," Mr. Fitzgerald said. "It's full of paints and brushes, watercolor paper and canvases. If you need something else—clay, perhaps, or even if you want to try your hand at wood carving—just ask. I can usually get additional supplies with a few days' notice."

Lucie looked up at him, her mouth agape. "You even supply the materials?"

Mr. Fitzgerald shrugged. "Most of our artists here need the help, and I'm happy to give it. I tell my business partner that it's an investment in our future; if we help foster a new generation of artists, and they eventually decide to exhibit their art with us out of loyalty, we keep ourselves in business, don't we?"

"That's not all it is to you, though, is it?" Lucie asked.

His smile was sad. "No, Lucie, it's not. Art should be something we can all enjoy without worrying about the cost. Now, shall we get you settled?"

It felt like she had stepped into some sort of a dream. "What happened to the person who had the studio before me?"

"He was hired to do a restoration project in London." Mr. Fitzgerald beamed like a proud father. "One of our recent success stories, Lucie. Maybe you'll be the next."

"Mr. Fitzgerald," Lucie said, swallowing back a lump in her throat. "It is already a success to know that there's room here for me to be . . . me."

Mr. Fitzgerald blinked at her a few times, his face registering emotion as if she'd said something profound. Perhaps she had, but to her, it had been simple. It was all she had ever wanted: a place of her own to do what her heart told her to.

"Lucie," he said after a few seconds, "I think that's all you ever need to be."

By the end of the next week, Lucie was fully ensconced in room six above the gallery. She disappeared for hours at a time, and somehow her mother never seemed to suspect that Lucie was just a hundred yards away from La Librairie des Rêves, doing the very thing she had been forbidden from doing.

Mr. Fitzgerald, it turned out, was a talented painter in his own right, and he'd been part of a wave of artists opening studios downtown on Tenth Street a decade and a half earlier. But he hadn't been able to keep the doors open, and he'd told Lucie he'd been just about to call it quits when an art dealer from Paris arrived one day with a proposition: he would save the day financially by bringing in a boatload of French art—including dozens of paintings by Olivier LeClair and sculptures by Rousselle and Claudel—and in return, Mr. Fitzgerald would need only to sponsor his visa application and give him an address in the United States so his papers would be approved. Mr. Fitzgerald had told Lucie he'd hesitated at first, because he believed artists should control their own fate and profit from their own work, but then he'd realized he could use the situation to provide studio space to those who were struggling and just needed someone to believe in them. His new partner's only condition was that they'd need to move uptown, where they could find a wealthier clientele.

"Constant Bouet and I are constantly at odds," he had added. "We have different ideas about what art should be, and who should have access to it. But that's what great art is, isn't it? Light and darkness, color and absence, yin and yang. We balance each other out, I suppose, and maybe that's why we're still afloat."

"That and the Rousselles, the Claudels, and the LeClairs," Lucie had replied with a smile, and Mr. Fitzgerald had laughed heartily.

"Yes, well, I suppose that hasn't hurt," he agreed.

Having the art studio to escape to made Lucie feel like herself for the first time in years, and it changed everything for her. She no longer felt like she was carrying the weight of the world somewhere inside her; having access each day to paints and brushes and space of her own made her feel impossibly light.

Though she hadn't shown her paintings to anyone yet, she had completed seven works she liked enough that she was considering sharing them. Mr. Fitzgerald, who always greeted her with a friendly smile when she arrived, had said he would love to see whatever she had created whenever she was ready, but he had also told her there was no rush. "The space is yours for as long as you need it, Lucie," he'd said more than once. "I mean that."

But it wasn't just the canvases she had brought to life; it was the studio itself. With Mr. Fitzgerald's permission, she had begun to paint the walls, grand buildings at first, then rivers, then trees. She painted over her work again and again, starting from scratch every few days, slowly pulling the images from her mind, making the space feel like a secret retreat from the world, a place that lingered between the past and the present. The more she painted, the more her dreams came alive with images, colors, and light, as if those shapes and shades had been there all along, trying to get out. She put them on canvas when she could, but there was also a great sense of relief in creating a world of her own, using the images from her dream.

The more she brought to life, though, the more she began to remember. And the more she remembered, the less she understood about how her life had come to this, locking her in a gilded cage of her mother's making, with no way out but the secret escape of art.

CHAPTER TWENTY-NINE

The wind whipped through Elise's hair, and she pulled up the hood of her old alpaca-lined wool coat as she shivered on the deck of the SS *United States*, wondering just what on earth she was doing.

It was the second week of December, and she was on her way back to the States for the first time in more than two decades, aboard the fastest ocean liner ever to make an Atlantic crossing. The speed with which the mammoth boat sliced through the water was dizzying, the temperature outside frigid. She was the only passenger crazy enough to be standing at the forward rail, squinting at the western horizon.

Since Ruth's visit in October, Elise hadn't stopped thinking of Juliette, of the coldness of her letter, of the way Ruth had described her. At first, Elise had wrestled with fury; didn't the other woman care about the pain Elise had been in for the past sixteen years, not knowing what had become of her daughter? Why hadn't she written earlier? Why had it taken a visit from Ruth to spur her into action, obviously against her will?

But then the anger had melted, and beneath it, there was an ocean of guilt. What right did she have to feel angry with Juliette about anything? Elise had done what she'd thought was best, but the fact was, she'd left her daughter behind. She'd *left* her, and Juliette had taken her and cared for her and protected her for all those months. It hadn't been her fault that a bomb had fallen from the blue sky, or that Mathilde had been one of the children fated to be in its path. And the anger that oozed from Juliette's letter, well, Elise could understand that, too. She felt it herself sometimes, a great rage at the universe for taking so much from her. But then that fire always turned inward, burning her up from the inside out. *She* was the one who had left her daughter behind. It wasn't the universe's fault, nor was it God's. It was hers.

So she couldn't blame Juliette for her coldness. Juliette hadn't made a mistake, as Elise had. She had simply continued to live her life in a place that she'd been told was safe. And she had lost nearly everything.

But Juliette still had Lucie—and she had the answers to many of the questions Elise had been asking God for the past sixteen years. Since returning to New York, Ruth had written several letters to Elise, explaining that she dropped by the bookstore to check on Juliette and Lucie every few weeks, and that the few times she had run into Lucie, the girl had looked miserable.

"I'm coming," Elise had declared two weeks earlier when Ruth had placed a transatlantic call to her to express her concern. It still felt like a miracle to be able to hear her voice crackling across the ocean. "I need to hear the story from Juliette's lips. And if there's anything I can do to help her and her daughter, it's time."

"Juliette may not be happy to see you," Ruth had responded. "But it cannot hurt to try."

Actually, it could. Seeing Juliette would wound Elise to the core, and laying eyes on Lucie, her daughter's best friend and play-mate, all grown up now, would be a painfully visceral reminder of all that Elise had lost. "I think I must. I'll see you soon," Elise had said, and when she'd hung up, her hand was shaking so hard she knocked the telephone from its place on Olivier's old desk.

She had silently packed a suitcase and bought the earliest ticket available, and here she was, looking west across a seemingly end-less sea, knowing that in just two days' time, the ship would dock in New York Harbor, bringing her home to the United States, and, at last, face-to-face with her past.

Ruth had suggested that Elise stay on the couch in her apartment on the Lower East Side, but Elise knew herself well enough to know that if she was going to summon the courage to do what she'd come to do, she would need some time and space to herself. She would also need to stay close enough to the bookstore on Fifty-Sixth Street so that she couldn't chicken out.

The cab from the harbor took her through Times Square, past billboards for *The Mouse That Roared* with Peter Sellers and *Cinderfella* with Jerry Lewis, past Elvis Presley smoldering beneath a cowboy hat on a poster for his latest movie, past Lucille Ball's face looking down at her from a big sign advertising previews of a new musical called *Wildcat* just down Fifty-Second Street at the Alvin. She remembered seeing *Uncle Tom's Cabin* at the Alvin in '33 when she'd first arrived in the city, wide-eyed and optimistic, just a girl. She'd seen *Anything Goes* there the next year, too, her last show before she met Olivier and left for Paris. The city had changed so much since then that it was almost unrecognizable to her. Then again, Elise herself was nearly unrecognizable, too, an empty husk of the hopeful young woman she'd once been. Part of her felt strangely let down that New York had continued evolving without her while she'd remained frozen in time.

She checked into the Hotel Dorset on West Fifty-Fourth and tried to convince herself to walk the six blocks to the address Ruth had given her for La Librairie des Rêves, but even after crossing an ocean to be here, she couldn't bring herself to do it right away. Instead, she opened her suitcase, withdrew the block of wood and the five chisels and two gouges she'd brought with her, and began to work, coaxing from the limewood the face of her daughter, the face she had imagined so many times, the face Mathilde would have had if she'd lived. She sank into the work, stroking here, chipping there, until the light outside began to fade away. Sweaty and covered in wood shavings, she set down her tools and gazed at what she'd made.

She had carved an adult Mathilde's face a thousand times, but this piece, created much more quickly than usual and with a rudimentary assortment of instruments, seemed to be alive in a way the others hadn't. As Elise sat back, breathless, and stared at what she'd done, she felt a tidal wave of regret over the loss of her daughter's whole life. It wasn't just that Elise had to go on without her; it was all the things Mathilde could have been, could have done, all lost to a single instant.

"Welcome to New York, Mathilde," she whispered.

It was dark outside when she made herself stop staring at the face of her lost child. The truth was that Elise had no way of knowing what or who Mathilde would have turned out to be, how she would have looked, whether she would have tilted her head left or right, whether her eyes would have sparkled with joy or mischief, what her laughter would have sounded like. She would never know, and continuing to coax the ghost of her child from wood, well, it was a fool's errand, wasn't it?

There was a knock on her hotel door then. Elise jumped, hastily wiping the tears from her eyes. She had almost forgotten that she'd made plans to meet Ruth in the lobby at six for dinner. She stood, and then, on second thought, picked up the bust of Mathilde and slid it under the bed. She had the sense that Ruth would not approve, and the last thing she wanted right now was pity.

When she swung open the door to her room, it was indeed Ruth standing there, her hair shorter than the last time Elise had seen her. Ruth took a step over the threshold, and without a word, embraced Elise. "I was worried," she said.

It had been a long time since anyone had held Elise this way, and it was so unfamiliar that she stiffened before forcing herself to relax into Ruth's arms. "I'm sorry I didn't meet you downstairs," she said. "Time got away from me."

"As long as you're all right." Ruth stepped back and studied her. "*Are* you all right?"

"I think so. It's hard being back here. Like a reminder of the life I had so long ago." It had been unexpected, the difficulty of being in New York again. The last time she'd been here, she had just married Olivier after a whirlwind romance, and Mathilde hadn't yet been born. Now she found herself alone again, right where she'd begun, more than twenty years later, and what did she have to show for it? "I had such big dreams once," she said, and Ruth seemed to understand, for she hugged her again.

"You're young, Elise," Ruth said. "And you're so very talented. It's not too late for those dreams."

"Of course it is." Elise wiped her eyes and pulled away. Her friend was being kind, but she didn't understand how the art world worked. If Elise's talent had been real, she would have found her way into galleries by now. She was forty-eight, after all, and she'd been carving for two decades. Thanks to Monsieur Vasseur's compassion—or, to call it what she knew it was, pity— she made enough to get by, but only just. She was a fool for once having believed she could be something special.

"Well," Ruth said. "It's wonderful to see you, and I know we have much to talk about. Shall we go have dinner?"

Elise gathered herself and smiled. Despite the miles between them, Ruth was her family, and one of the few people in the world who had once known Mathilde. It was a comforting thought. "I'd like that," she agreed, and together they walked out the door.

Snow fell as Ruth and Elise made their way to a diner two blocks away, and they watched the flakes drift down outside the window as they ordered patty melts and Coca-Colas and caught up on the past several weeks while a jukebox hummed Elvis and Brenda Lee, the Everly Brothers and Bobby Rydell.

"I worry about you," Ruth said haltingly, her German accent still strong despite the fact that she'd left her home country twenty-five years ago. "Won't you think about moving from Paris, Elise? I worry that being surrounded by ghosts is holding you back, as is the case with Juliette."

At the mention of her old friend's name, Elise felt her heart skip. "It's not the same, Ruth."

"I know. Still, perhaps it's time for a fresh start."

How easy it would be to truly believe in that possibility of new beginnings. "Perhaps," Elise said, and when Ruth smiled at her with pity, she smiled back with pain, and she had the feeling they both knew she wasn't ready to make any sort of change.

After dinner, as they stepped into the snow, which had begun to accumulate, Ruth gently suggested that they stroll by Juliette's bookstore on the way back to Elise's hotel.

"Oh," Elise replied. "I'm not ready for that yet."

"She won't be there," Ruth assured her. "The store is closed. But it might be a good idea to see it, from the outside at least, so it isn't a complete shock when you go tomorrow."

Elise hesitated. "Yes, all right."

Together they walked a few more blocks, turning left on Park Avenue and right on Fifty-Sixth Street. Elise spotted the shingle immediately, hanging just ahead to the right. "La Librairie des Rêves," she read aloud, stunned to see the familiar script hanging over a sidewalk in Manhattan, though Ruth had forewarned her. "But . . . the sign is just the same."

"Wait until you see the store."

A moment later, they were standing in front of the darkened windows of Juliette's bookshop, and Elise couldn't breathe. Ruth had told her that Juliette had somehow created a replica of her Boulogne-Billancourt shop here, a continent away, but she had assumed that it was an exaggeration.

But Ruth hadn't stretched the truth at all. Even in shadow, lit only by the streetlamps outside, the store looked like it had been pulled whole from Elise's memories. The shelves were all spaced exactly as they had been in the old location, and even the spines of the books—or at least the ones Elise could see from the window—looked familiar. If she pressed her face against the glass, she could just make out, in the far corner, the children's area where Mathilde had spent so many hours playing with the others, and before she knew it, there were tears coursing down her face.

When she pulled away to stare at Ruth in horror, the other woman's eyes were shining with tears of sympathy.

"But it's . . . *exactly* the same," Elise said haltingly.

"Didn't I tell you it was?"

"I—I thought you meant it was similar. But she has re-created the past down to the last detail."

"You can see now why I am so worried."

Elise turned back to the window and choked back a sob as she gazed into the darkness. People passing by on the sidewalk created ghosts of movement inside. The real store had been reduced nearly to dust—Elise had seen it with her own eyes—but here, one could almost imagine that terrible day had never happened, that there hadn't been a war, that a bomb hadn't fallen far from its target, taking her daughter with it into the ground. "How did she do this?"

"Her husband is very wealthy."

Elise pulled back from the window. "I still cannot believe she remarried. Paul was the love her of life."

Ruth smiled sadly. "I believe he still is." When Elise gave her a questioning look, Ruth sighed. "She talks to him, you see. I went into the store once to check on her, and she was so immersed in the conversation she was having—with the thin air, Elise—that she didn't even know I was there."

Elise put her hand to her aching heart. "Ruth, it sounds like she's in a terrible state."

Ruth held her gaze. "I hope she will listen to you."

As they walked away from the store, Elise shook her head. She'd been cut from Juliette's life long ago; Juliette's single letter to her had proven it. What chance was there that she'd answer any questions now, or that Elise could do anything to help pull Juliette back from the edge? But if not Elise, then who?

She was so caught up in thinking about how to fix her friend that she almost didn't notice the gallery across the street as they approached the corner of Fifty-Sixth and Lexington. But at the last moment, a flash of bright color in a painting in the window caught her eye, and she looked up. She stopped short with a gasp.

"What is it?" Ruth asked, stopping alongside Elise and looking at her with concern.

Elise didn't say a word. Heart hammering, she took Ruth's hand and, looking both ways, pulled her across Fifty-Sixth Street. "That piece," she said when they were standing before the window of the gallery on the northeast corner of the intersection. "It is one of Olivier's. I—I remember him painting it."

They both stared at the canvas, lit by the streetlights. It was an image, filled with color, of a couple dancing in a brightly lit room, the woman's dress a brilliant blue, the tables of diners around them dotted with candles and fading into a blur as the man gazed down at the woman. She was laughing, her face upturned, her eyes closed. The expression on the man's face was one of pure adoration, and for a second, Elise had to look away. She remembered, suddenly, when Olivier used to look at her that way, like the moon and the stars lived within her and she held the key to the universe. She had gotten so frustrated with him at the end that she had almost forgotten that what had existed between them had once been so pure.

"Is that *you*?" Ruth asked after a moment.

Elise forced her gaze back to the picture. "Olivier took me dancing in Spain once, just after we married. It is one of my favorite memories of him, of us. But this painting, it was ours. He didn't sell this one. It was one of the things stolen from our attic by the Germans when I was . . . away."

"The Germans stole it?" Ruth asked, and when Elise nodded, she added, "But how did it end up here?"

Suddenly, Elise had a purpose. She looked up at the name of the gallery: The French Collective. The sign said it opened at ten the next morning, an hour before the bookstore. "I don't know," Elise said, her throat dry. "But I intend to find out."

The next morning, Elise passed by the gallery and approached the closed bookstore just past 10 a.m., pausing to peer inside. It was still and quiet, but in the light of day, the store's troubling similarities to the original bookshop in Boulogne were even more staggering than they'd been the night before. She blinked, a headache already coming on; she would deal with that in an hour. First, she needed to figure out how her husband's stolen painting had ended up here in New York.

The bell above the gallery's door tinkled as she entered, and a tall, slender woman with a blond Marilyn Monroe hairdo and stacked-heel calfskin pumps strode over with a tight-lipped smile. "Can I help you?" she asked, looking Elise up and down.

Elise knew she didn't look like the typical art collector who wandered into a high-priced gallery like this one; she was dressed in a narrow wool skirt with seamed nylons and a simple V-neck lambswool sweater, her old wool coat over it. She hadn't bothered to do more that morning than run a brush through her hair and swipe on red lipstick, and she imagined she looked like a bit of a disaster, as she had barely slept the night before. But how could she, knowing that the day would hold a reunion with Juliette and a confrontation here at the gallery? She took a breath, drawing herself a little taller. "Yes, you can. I'd like to know the provenance of that Olivier LeClair painting in your window."

The woman squinted at her as if she'd been speaking another language, though she was quite sure she'd said the words in English. "The provenance?" she repeated.

"Yes," Elise said. "I'd like to know how you came to have that painting. You see, it is mine, and it was stolen by the Germans during the war. If you're doing business with former Nazis . . ."

The woman's eyes narrowed further. "The painting belongs to the gallery, ma'am."

Elise recognized the tone in her voice as the one people used with those they suspected of minor lunacy. Monsieur Vasseur sometimes spoke to her that way, a now-familiar mix of skepticism and pity. But Elise had no time for that today, and her patience had run out years ago. So much had been stolen from her, but here, like a gift from God, was something that she could take back.

"Actually, it does not," Elise said calmly. "Now, I'd like to speak to the gallery's owner, please, or I'll be forced to make a scene."

The woman looked her up and down once more and then, seeming to assess that she was serious, turned on her heel and walked away. Elise figured there was a fifty-fifty chance that she was calling the police rather than fetching the owner, so she moved toward the smaller second room in the back of the gallery to buy herself some time. She was muttering to herself, but then she stopped short in the doorway as she saw the four limewood sculptures, each of them lit by a single light from the ceiling, spaced around the center of the room.

The air rushed from Elise's lungs and she reached for the wall as she wobbled on her feet. Surely she was mistaken. Surely these were simply works that looked eerily like hers.

But no. As she moved closer to the statue nearest the door,

she knew every curve, could remember every stroke of her chisel, every sinewy scrap of wood shaving that had peeled away to reveal the shapes and turns on display here. She could remember sculpting the curve of an arm, chiseling the plump little legs, the tiny fingers, the wide eyes of her infant daughter. She could almost hear Mathilde's tiny coos from the bassinet as she slept beside her, oblivious as her mother finalized the finite angles of her own little face.

It was one of the first carvings she'd ever done of Mathilde, sculpting a moment in time, her daughter held in her own arms. She had titled it *L'amour d'une Mère*, or *A Mother's Love*, but the title plaque beneath it read, *A Babe in Arms*, by Anicette Rousselle, which made no sense at all. She had read about Rousselle in *Cahiers d'Art*, had heard that her wood carvings were commanding obscene prices, but this wasn't a Rousselle. This was *hers*. As she moved closer and reached out a hand to touch it, she felt drawn to it like a magnet, her fingers itching to make contact with the wood that she had brought to life twenty years earlier, when Mathilde was still alive.

"*Ne touchez pas!*" a man behind her snapped, and then, switching from French to sharply accented English, he added, "Those carvings are not to be touched! That is an extremely expensive piece of art. The artist died during the war!"

She knew who it was before she set eyes on him, and already, the pieces had fallen into place in her mind, rearranging themselves from a confusing jumble of questions into a sickening portrait of certainty. "Did she?" she asked as she turned around, deriving some satisfaction from the way his eyes widened like those of a rat in the kitchen when the lights are suddenly turned on. "Or did you *steal* these pieces from her like the opportunistic little bastard you are, Monsieur Bouet?"

Though she hadn't seen him in eighteen years, during which his hair had gone silver and he'd doubled his previous number of chins, Olivier's art dealer was unmistakable. He was dressed as immaculately and expensively as he'd always been, and a sudden spear of white-hot rage shot through her as she realized that at least a portion of his ample income these past years was likely due to the sale of her own work, which he'd been passing off under a different artist's name.

"Madame LeClair," he said after what seemed like an eternity. His voice was barely audible.

"Monsieur Bouet," she replied, looking him straight in the eye as her voice shook with rage. "What have you done?"

He glanced around nervously. She followed his eyes to each of the other three wood sculptures, too—all of them hers, all of them pieces she had created when her hands couldn't stop wringing her sweet baby girl from the wood, all of them priced astronomically. Finally, his gaze landed back on her. His face was red now, and a bead of sweat was trickling slowly down his forehead, just left of center, headed for one bushy eyebrow. "Madame LeClair, I can explain."

But he didn't say anything else, and an eerie sort of calm settled over her. "Is Anicette Rousselle real, Constant?" she asked, her voice even. "Or was she simply a figment of your imagination through which you could sell my work?"

"You can't . . . you must . . . please understand . . . but I—" He sputtered, then went silent.

"I deserve an answer, you monstrous little man."

"The latter," he mumbled, then, seeming to gather himself, he added in a low voice, "I—I made Anicette Rousselle up. You must understand, though; I could not have sold work under the LeClair name at the time because of your husband's political activities. There was no harm intended; it was purely pragmatic."

"Pragmatic," she repeated, fury swirling in her like a storm. "Oh, well, that explains everything."

"Madame LeClair, you must let me—"

She had no interest in his excuses. "And the German looting of my apartment? That was a lie, too?"

"No! No, that really happened! I swear it. It occurred all over Paris, and of course your husband was on their list." He looked down. "They did take some of your sculptures along with his work."

She narrowed her gaze. "And they just pleasantly handed them back to you after the war since they were such grand fellows?"

His face went redder. "I do not know what happened to those pieces, Madame LeClair. The ones here . . . They are the ones the Germans left behind, you see. Your husband was dead. I was certain you had not survived, and . . ." He trailed off, spreading his hands wide to indicate how helpless he'd been over the course of events that he himself had set into motion.

She stared at him in disbelief, nausea rising within her. "So all of these years that I've believed your friend Monsieur Vasseur was doing me a favor by selling my work so I could barely scrape by . . . you've been selling my pieces for thousands?"

"It isn't how it looks," he said, seemingly finding his voice. "At first, I thought you really were dead. What harm was I doing, then? By the time Monsieur Vasseur alerted me to the fact that you had come back, I had already created the persona of Anicette Rousselle, had begun to build her profile as one of France's greatest artists, lost tragically to the war. I'd already sold several of her—er, your—pieces. And well, you see, it had taken on a life of its own."

"Monsieur Vasseur was in on this, too?"

"No. He did not know a thing." He hung his head. "I understood from him that he was selling your work in Paris, and I was glad. I knew you were making enough money to live. It . . . It eased the guilt a little."

"And it never occurred to you perhaps to reach out and let me know that I had become a highly regarded artist? And that you owed me a great deal of money for work you *stole* from me while I was running for my *life*?" Her shock was turning to rage.

"Madame LeClair, I will make all of this right." He was sweating more profusely now. "I promise you that."

"*How?* How, Monsieur Bouet? You will give me back the past fifteen years of my life? You will tell the world what you've done? You will retrieve all the beloved pieces that you took from me?"

He cleared his throat and wiped away a bead of sweat that had dripped into his right eye. Now he was blinking wildly. "I will find a way, Madame LeClair. I give you my word, I will find a way. Please, don't call the police."

It hadn't occurred to her to do so, but perhaps it should have. He had stolen her art, her reputation, her money. But worst of all, he had stolen all she had left of her daughter. There wasn't an adequate penalty on earth for that. No, the things he had taken she could never get back, but in the rubble, something surged within her, a shot of pride at the realization that she wasn't a washed-up woodworker or a talentless hack as Olivier had once told her.

For years she'd had the career she'd always dreamed of, even if she hadn't known it.

Suddenly, she couldn't be here anymore. She felt weary, her world turned upside down once again—and she still needed to do what she'd come for, which was to find out the truth about her daughter, and to help Juliette and Lucie if she could. The bookstore would be opening soon; she couldn't stop now.

"You will tell the world the truth, Monsieur Bouet," she said, trying hard to keep her voice from shaking. She just needed time to collect herself, to breathe, to figure out her next move. "And you will return all the work you've stolen—mine and my husband's—or I *will* press charges. For now, though, I cannot stand to look at you. You are a man with no talent and no morals, and soon, the world will know."

And with that, she turned and walked out of the room, back into the main gallery. The blond woman was staring at her with an open mouth, and Elise supposed that she'd overheard the whole conversation. She was just about to storm past her when she realized she was forgetting something. She walked back into the smaller room, brushed past the trembling Constant Bouet, and picked up *L'amour d'une Mère*. Then, with her daughter tucked under her arm, she walked out of the gallery without looking back. It was only when she was on the street outside, shaking with rage, that she recognized the tears coursing down her cheeks, falling like rain onto her daughter's smoothly carved face.

CHAPTER THIRTY

Juliette felt her before she saw her, the ghost from the past darkening her door. She had just arrived at the bookstore and was going about her morning routine—dusting the shelves, straightening the books that customers had touched the day before, telling Paul about her evening, when the bell above the door chimed.

Juliette checked her watch and cursed, even as the hairs on both arms stood on end, alerting her of darkness and danger coming her way. She had become attuned to such things in the past several years, and she knew it was Paul sending her signs. Once, he had saved her from absentmindedly stepping into traffic, and she had narrowly missed being hit by a speeding Oldsmobile coupe. Another time, he had talked her back from the edge as she'd stood on the Brooklyn Bridge, staring at the water below, wondering if there was any reason at all not to jump. So she could feel it now, the breath of Paul's warning against her skin. What seemed more pressing, though, was the fact that she'd apparently left the front door unlocked. The sign outside stated clearly that

La Librairie des Rêves did not open until 11 a.m., and according
to her wristwatch, it was only 10:50.

"We aren't open yet!" she called out, trying to keep the anger
from her voice. "Come back at eleven!"

But instead of a mumbled apology and retreating footsteps,
Juliette heard only silence. Even Paul—who had been reminisc-
ing a moment earlier about the night he'd first kissed her, in a
crowded French café—had gone quiet, waiting for the intruder
to speak.

"Do you hear me?" Juliette called out again. "We don't open
for another ten minutes."

There was silence for another few seconds, and then a choked
voice asked, "Juliette?"

Time froze, for Juliette knew the voice in an instant, the
American accent coated with the rich honey of time spent in
Paris. Her name had never sounded as musical as it had when
Elise LeClair spoke it, pronouncing the *J* like a native English
speaker, and the *-ette* with the effortless lilt of the French. But
how could Elise LeClair possibly be here, in New York, an ocean
away from her trail of devastation?

"I told you she would come," Paul whispered in her ear. She
should have listened, should have prepared for this. But now, the
past was here, uninvited, and there was nothing she could do to
brace herself.

"Paul?" she said, but he had gone silent as he often did when
customers entered the store.

"Juliette?" came the familiar voice again. "Are you there?"

For a second, Juliette considered hiding. But if it really was
Elise LeClair, she would know all the spots that Juliette went to
seek solace and privacy. She closed her eyes briefly and was surprised when the image that flashed through her mind was not

the one in which Elise irresponsibly abandoned her daughter, but rather the one in which Elise found her one day, curled under the counter, sobbing. It had been just two months after she'd given birth to Lucie, and Lucie had been going through a phase where she never seemed to stop crying. Juliette hadn't slept in days, and she was at the end of her rope. When Lucie's squawks had escalated to a siren wail that morning, Paul had been out with the boys, and something in Juliette had simply shut off. Instead of going to her daughter to comfort her, she had put her hands over her ears and hidden under her desk with her eyes closed, repeating to herself again and again, "I'm a terrible mother."

It was Elise who had stumbled upon her, and Juliette had opened her eyes to see her friend standing before her, Mathilde on one shoulder and Lucie on the other, both babies calm and quiet. "Sometimes, I wish I could hide, too," Elise said with a smile that didn't seem to hold any judgment or accusation about Juliette's failures. "Lucky you, having a counter just your size."

Juliette had blinked at her friend in confusion, but after a few seconds, she had unfolded herself from the space and reached out her arms to take Lucie, who was cooing contentedly now. "How did you do that?"

"I have a little screamer myself," Elise had said, kissing Mathilde's head. "I can't explain it, but bouncing Mathilde around while I sing 'Night and Day' in my head always seems to calm her down. Somehow, it's just the right rhythm."

"The Fred Astaire song?"

"That's the one. Try it next time." Elise had smiled and abruptly changed the subject. "There's a book I'm looking for, for Olivier. Can you help me find it, Juliette?" And just like that, Juliette had felt normal again, like a mother capable of soothing her daughter, like a woman capable of running a bookshop.

Now, when she opened her eyes, she found Elise standing before her once again. "Juliette, it *is* you," Elise said.

Juliette was so dumbstruck by the strangeness of it that for a moment, she couldn't speak. Of course it had been eighteen years since she had seen the woman who had once been her best friend, and she knew that she herself had changed, too. But somehow, she had expected Elise to remain frozen in time, just as Paul and the boys had. Instead, Elise had aged, although even Juliette had to admit she'd done so gracefully. Her hair, though still long and thick, had gone gray at the temples, and there were lines on her forehead and between her brows, a new pair of parentheses framing her mouth. She looked as tired as Juliette felt, and the light had gone out in her eyes the way it did when one had lost something irreplaceable. Juliette felt a jolt of recognition. Was it possible that Elise was just as lost as she was? But no, that couldn't be; Elise had abandoned her daughter. She had no right to be sad. Having reminded herself of that, she pulled herself up to her full height and said, "Elise. What brings you here?"

From the way Elise blinked at her, Juliette had the sense that she'd taken the wrong tone, one far too casual and detached to use with someone who shouldn't logically be standing here. But then she noticed that Elise's face was tear-streaked, and that she appeared to be clutching a wood carving of a pair of arms holding a baby. Juliette looked at the piece of art in confusion. Was Elise coming unraveled? That would be an interesting development. It gave her a strange jolt of pleasure to consider it.

"Juliette," Elise said after a long, awkward pause. "Ruth said you were here. That you'd re-created La Librairie des Rêves. Still, I didn't quite believe it until . . ." She let the sentence trail off as she looked around the room, and Juliette could feel a swell of pride rising up within her.

"It's perfect," Juliette said, forgetting momentarily that she'd spent nearly two decades nursing a grudge against this woman. "It's just as you remember it, isn't it?"

"Indeed it is," Elise said, drawing the words out, and Juliette had the strange sense that they weren't intended to be a compliment.

"Why have you come?" Juliette asked, cutting right to the chase.

Again, Elise blinked at her, and Juliette had the feeling again that she'd said something wrong. "Because I want to know," she said. "I—I want to know what my daughter's final months were like. I—" Elise seemed to be having trouble speaking. "Please, Juliette. I know I have no right to ask anything of you. But if you could do me that kindness . . ."

Juliette could feel a storm gathering inside her. She could hear Paul whispering to her, telling her to calm down, but the anger was too great, and his voice faded into the dark clouds and thunderclaps. "You do recall, don't you, that you chose to leave your daughter with me?"

Tears formed in Elise's eyes, which startled Juliette. "Yes, I did," Elise said, her voice breaking. "I can never thank you enough for taking her in. I know how difficult it was for you, and what it meant that you did that for me in the midst of a war. It has haunted me for nearly twenty years that I haven't been able to thank you properly, or to return the favor."

"Return the favor?" Juliette's skin felt like it was crawling. "How could you return a favor like that?"

Elise took a step back, visibly startled. "Well, I—I couldn't possibly. I only mean that if there's anything I can do for you and Lucie . . ."

"Lucie is fine." Juliette could hear the ice in her own voice now, and she could see in Elise's face that she could hear it, too. Something tugged at her, a sense of unease.

"I'm glad you think so," she said, and Juliette bristled at her choice of words. Juliette was Lucie's mother! She was the only one who had the right—and the insight—to determine whether her daughter was well. "Please, Juliette," Elise went on after a short pause. "It has already been a very difficult morning. It would mean so much to me if we could—"

"What is that, anyhow?" Juliette asked, cutting her off. Her full attention was now on the carved infant in Elise's arms. "Why are you carrying that around with you?"

Elise lifted the piece and gazed at it with fresh tears in her eyes. "It's a piece I carved long ago. Of Mathilde."

She turned it around slowly, and Juliette gasped. It was beautiful; she had seen Elise's birds and a few of her abstracts, but she had never seen anything like this. Elise had captured the exact curves of a baby Mathilde's face, and the wood, so smooth and pale, seemed to be almost alive. "I remember," she whispered without meaning to as she stared at the tiny Mathilde. She remembered when the girls had been this size, only a few months old, so tiny and helpless, but already on the way to becoming themselves. Lucie had been wide-eyed, inquisitive, and a chatterer; Mathilde had taken the world in more slowly, more quietly, like she was thinking about every-thing. Juliette remembered marveling to Elise about how two little girls who looked so similar could be so innately different from the start. "But what on earth are you doing with the carving now?"

"The gallery on the corner had it," Elise said, her voice tight.

"I don't understand."

"It's a long story." Elise suddenly looked very weary. "Please, Juliette, would you talk to me? There's so much I want to know and—and so much I owe to you."

Juliette wasn't sure whether it was Paul murmuring in her ear, the familiarity of the carving, or the intense sadness in Elise's eyes, but she found herself nodding, and before she could stop the words from coming out, she had agreed. "I'll close the store, but only for a little while," she told Elise, already hating herself for what she was about to do. "We can talk in the back."

Juliette could see in Elise's eyes that she recognized this area of the bookshop, too; Juliette had taken great care to duplicate not just the public part of the store, but also the private room behind the register, where she and Paul took their morning coffee and where the children played when Juliette needed them to keep their voices down. It was the room where Juliette had first taken Elise that day she saw her in the park, the day Elise had gone into false labor, and in the years after that, they'd had countless conversations there.

"Even the table is the same," Elise said in awe, finally setting down her carving of Mathilde and running her hand along the uneven wood. "Juliette, how did you do it?"

Juliette felt a surge of pride. "It was difficult, Elise, but I knew I had to bring it all back. For them."

She didn't miss the flicker in Elise's eyes, and she reminded herself to be more careful. She already knew that Ruth and Lucie, perhaps even Arthur, frowned upon what she had done here. They thought she was burying herself in the past rather than living in the present, but for Juliette, the two were one and the same.

"And Paul and the boys are still . . . here?" Elise asked.

"Yes," Juliette said without elaborating. She knew Ruth had walked in and heard her talking to Paul a few times, and it was clear the woman had blabbed to Elise. There was really no more to say. She certainly didn't need to explain herself to Elise LeClair of all people.

"How about Mathilde?" Elise asked after a long silence. "Is she here in the store, too, Juliette?"

Elise's voice cracked with pain, and Juliette was startled by the depth of anguish there. It shook her own confidence in the narrative; it had been so easy to tell herself over the years that Elise had been monstrously selfish to leave her daughter behind.

"No, Elise," Juliette told her. "Mathilde is not here."

Elise looked down and nodded her acceptance of this. When she looked up again, there were fat tears running down her cheeks. "Please, Juliette, can you tell me what I missed? I know it's painful for you because of what happened . . . after. But when I was gone, I lay awake imagining her every night, thinking of the things she must be learning, the way she must be growing. Anything you could tell me, even after all these years, would mean the world."

Juliette hesitated, for she knew she didn't owe Elise a thing. But the pain in the other woman's eyes was impossible to look away from, and after a moment, she found herself speaking haltingly. "She was so bright, Elise. But you know that. She loved to sketch, just like you and Olivier. I think Lucie learned it from her; the two of them were like peas in a pod, always coloring something or another."

Juliette paused as Elise flinched, like Juliette had struck her. "Go on," she said, her voice choked. "Please. This is—it's what I need."

Juliette felt like she'd swallowed glass, but she forced herself to continue. "I remember Mathilde wanted to ride a bike. Something she'd seen in a book, I think, but we didn't have a bicycle small enough for the girls, and anyhow, it was too dangerous for the girls to ride outside, with all the soldiers . . . She and Lucie spent hours pretending to ride a bike around the store, and the boys would laugh at them and pretend they were on bicycles, too. I'm sure they looked crazy to customers, but their imaginations were so big . . ."

Elise was sobbing now, and to Juliette's surprise, there were tears coursing down her own cheeks, too. How long had it been since she had talked about her memories, since she had cried like this? It felt like a release, but it also felt like a dam within her was breaking, and there was so much the barrier was holding back that she couldn't afford for that to happen.

"Please, tell me more," Elise said, her voice strained.

Juliette looked at the table. "She was learning to read. Both girls were. Claude and Alphonse were teaching them. They could recognize short words, two or three letters, in French and English, and they were so proud of themselves. Lucie, she was always saying she was going to write a book one day, that I would sell her book in my store. Mathilde was going to write books, too. They were so like each other; what one did, the other one had to copy immediately."

Elise made a noise that sounded like it was something between a gasp and a sniffle. "They were so young, Juliette. And your boys . . . I'm so terribly sorry."

The warmth that had filled Juliette suddenly dissipated, and familiar anger took its place. "Well, you should be sorry. You left her, Elise! How could you?" The words exploded from Juliette like little bombs. "How could you ask us to protect her when you knew that it would mean we could not protect our own children? How could you put us in a situation like that? How can you sit there across from me pretending that you care about the child you abandoned?"

"Abandoned?" Elise breathed. She blinked a few times with such force that tears seemed to fling themselves from the corners of her eyes. "You think I *abandoned* her, Juliette? You can't possibly believe that's what I did! Every day of my life I regretted it, but you knew the situation. If I had taken her with me, we would have been killed."

"Yes, well, perhaps it would have been better that way," Juliette shot back, and from the sharp intake of Elise's breath, she immediately knew she'd said something terrible, something she could never take back, but it was too late to turn around now. "I loved your daughter, Elise, just as you loved mine. So did Paul, you see. And on the day the bomb fell, we both made the mistake of treating her like one of our own without thinking, trying to protect her just as we protected the others. If she hadn't been there with us, Elise, my children would have lived! I wouldn't be here, an ocean away from their graves, living this life I never asked for! Do you understand, Elise? *You* did this to us! You took my family from me! And now you have the nerve to show up here and ask me to tell you about your daughter? *Your* daughter is the reason *my* children are dead!"

Elise was sobbing now, her face blotchy, her eyes red. She had flinched at each of Juliette's blows, her deep sadness rising so clearly to the surface. "Juliette," Elise said. "I'm so sorry for all you lost, sorry for any position I put you in. It was never ever my intention."

"Yes, well, sometimes, our lives don't work out the way we intend them to, Elise." Juliette was practically spitting the words at her. "But decisions have consequences. And your decision took everything from me."

Elise stood, gripping the table. She was visibly trembling. "I don't know what to say, Juliette. I never imagined that you felt this way." She picked up the statue of a mother's arms cradling Mathilde, and Juliette felt another flash of white-hot rage. Even Elise's art was a lie; the love between mother and daughter was so clear in the gentle curves and angles of the mother's hands, but Elise hadn't loved Mathilde the right way. The right way meant never abandoning your children. Never leaving them behind. Never forgetting that first and foremost, you were their mother. It was why Juliette had found a way to bring Paul and the boys with her to New York, why she still spoke to them every day, why she was so adamant that her remaining child should live to honor the ones who never had a chance to grow up. *She* was a good mother. And good mothers did not deserve to have their children taken away.

Still, as Elise walked back shakily through the store to the exit, Juliette felt an unfamiliar pang of regret. Elise didn't look like the monster she had become in Juliette's mind. How could someone that culpable be so wounded at the same time? Juliette trailed behind her and struggled to put together the pieces in a way that made sense, and by the time she looked up again, Elise had reached the door. She put her hand on the handle and paused.

"I know you hate me," Elise said, her voice shaking as she turned back to Juliette. "But please know that I'll never forget the sacrifice you made. Thank you for watching over my daughter, Juliette. And I'm deeply sorry—for both of us—that things turned out the way they did."

And then, Elise was gone, and Juliette stared after her, pain and loss roiling in the pit of her stomach. Long after Elise had disappeared, Juliette turned, walked calmy into the back room of the store, and threw up in the trash can.

"Paul?" she asked into the silence, after she'd wiped her mouth and taken a sip of water. The bitter taste of bile lingered. "Paul, are you there?"

But the bookstore was silent, the ticking clock on the wall the only indication that time was moving forward at all.

CHAPTER THIRTY-ONE

Lucie knew something was wrong the moment she entered the gallery, and all at once, the excitement that had been bubbling up within her dissipated like smoke in a wind-whipped sky.

Last night, she had dreamed more vividly than ever of the Paris sky that seemed to be part of her every waking thought these days, the sky that stretched above the park near their apartment where her mother had taken her and the other children for long walks. "Every time I close my eyes, I see it," she told Tommy that morning as he unloaded Christmas trees from a truck his cousin had borrowed, stacking them in rows in the abandoned lot on Sterling Place. "But it's not the real world I see. I can't explain it. It's like when I dream it, it's a painting already, like my mind has already figured out the brushstrokes for me." She'd shot him a sideways glance. "You think I'm crazy, don't you?"

He'd laughed and shaken his head. "No. I think maybe it's like how soldiers get shell shock, you know? Maybe you've got some shell shock, and the painting is helping you to remember things."

"So maybe the more I paint, the less confused I'll feel about why my mother hates me so much?"

"She doesn't hate you, doll. Who could hate you?"

She didn't answer that, because he could never understand. He came from a family that was whole and overflowing with loud, boisterous love, not one full of ghosts and regrets.

"Look, Luce, I gotta get back to setting up the lot. Ten days until Christmas! And there's no use in both of us freezing our tails off out here."

He'd kissed her goodbye and jogged over to Domenico, who waved at her and called, "See ya, Lucie!" the words forming clouds in the twenty-five-degree morning.

She'd waved back and hurried to the subway, rubbing her arms to stay warm.

Now it was nearly noon and she had shown up at the gallery, eager to tackle the walls of studio six once again. Her mother had the bookstore to commune with her ghosts, and maybe this was Lucie's way of doing the same. She couldn't hear the voices of her father and brothers, but the more she brought the sky over Paris to life, the more it felt like everything was falling into place. Somehow, emptying the contents of her mind's palette onto the walls freed her up to tackle the blank canvases, too, and in the past week, she had painted Tommy's tree stand during Sunday's snowfall, and the French bakery across the street, its windows lined with baguettes still whistling with steam. Maybe if she got enough practice in, she could summon the courage to show some of her work to Mr. Fitzgerald.

But though the front door was unlocked, the lights were out inside, and the place appeared to be closed, which was unusual for the middle of a weekday. The LeClair that had hung in the window was gone, as were the ones that had lined the walls. It seemed impossible that the gallery could have sold all of them since her last visit, just three days earlier. "Mr. Fitzgerald?" she called out hesitantly, and when there was no answer, she tried the name of the other owner. "Mr. Bouet?" Even the snooty blond gallery assistant was nowhere to be found.

She headed tentatively toward the back, but she stopped short when she entered the smaller of the two rooms, which normally housed the Anicette Rousselle carvings, part of the collection that had put this gallery on the map. They were gone, all four of them, the pedestals where they'd sat empty, one of them slightly askew. Had the valuable artwork been stolen?

"Mr. Fitzgerald?" she called out again, her pulse accelerating in concern. Should she call the police? "Mr. Fitzgerald?"

Suddenly, Mr. Fitzgerald emerged from the back office, both hands on the back of his own neck, like he was trying to rub away an awful muscle cramp. "Lucie?" he asked, looking dazed. "Is everything all right?"

"Thank goodness. I was going to ask the same. Was the gallery robbed, Mr. Fitzgerald?"

He looked around the room, and from his throat erupted a noise that sounded like a chuckle, but with no mirth behind it. "No." He rolled his head forward and dropped his hands, then he sighed and pinched the bridge of his nose. He made the same joyless laughing sound. "We're in a bit of a mess, Lucie."

"Did someone steal the Olivier LeClairs and the Anicette Rousselles?" she asked, still trying to piece together what was happening.

"Well, yes." He finally looked directly at her. "It appears that *we* did."

"What?"

"Lucie, neither those carvings nor the LeClair paintings were ever ours to sell. Everything I've done for this gallery, for the artists, for the past decade . . . It's all been built on a foundation of lies. And now we'll likely owe more money than I could possibly pay out. Not to mention the guilt I feel over this . . ."

She stared at him. "Mr. Fitzgerald, whatever happened, I'm sure there's a logical explanation."

"Yes, in fact, it seems there is. The logical explanation is that my business partner is a thief, and I'm a fool." He didn't elaborate, but after a few seconds, he gestured for her to come into his office. "You may as well know the truth, Lucie. I'm afraid we'll have to close the gallery soon anyhow."

Lucie's stomach lurched as she followed him. He'd have to close the gallery? That meant closing the artists' spaces on the second floor, too. She should have known it was too good to be true.

In his office, he indicated that she should take a seat, and he sat down heavily in the chair behind his desk. For a few seconds, he didn't say anything. "I thought I was doing so much good here, Lucie. And the irony is that it was those Anicette Rousselle pieces that made me agree to open the gallery with my business partner. I wouldn't be here without them, and they were never his. There's not even an artist named Anicette Rousselle. He stole the pieces from some poor woman and invented a story about someone who never existed."

Lucie's mouth fell open. "So who is the real artist?"

He shrugged. "He didn't get that far. He just said he'd made a terrible mistake, that he had stolen the pieces from the artist because at first he'd believed she was dead. But this morning, she showed up at the gallery demanding an explanation." He pinched the bridge of his nose. "Constant walked out immediately afterward. He told me he had to go to the bank, but it's been hours and he hasn't returned." He gave a wry laugh. "I'd imagine he's probably boarding a ship to Europe right about now. Or maybe he's used the last of the gallery's money for a first-class ticket on one of those new transatlantic flights back to the Continent."

Lucie didn't know what to say. "And the LeClairs? Were those real?"

"The pieces are real, yes. Constant really was Olivier LeClair's art dealer in Paris. But the pieces we've been selling here, well, I fear he didn't obtain them legally."

"He stole them?"

"I don't know all the details. Sandra only overheard some of the conversation, and she was so upset she left in tears after telling me what she knew." He put his hands over his face, rubbing his eyes. "I should have listened to my gut."

"Your gut?"

"It's all we have as artists, right? But when Constant came along, he seemed to be an answer to all my prayers. I was about to lose my gallery, and he was offering me this great opportunity for an infusion of cash and a fresh start." He paused and scratched the back of his neck. "I almost said no. There was something about him that seemed off. But then he showed me photographs of the Anicette Rousselle carvings, and I *felt* something. I felt the way you're supposed to about really good, honest art. And when Constant took me to the warehouse where he was keeping a few dozen of her pieces, well, laying my hands on them did something to me, too. And I suppose I was moved by the tragedy of her story, an artist cut down in her prime."

"But it was all a lie?"

"The pieces were carved by an artist who is very much alive, and she had no idea he had taken them from her." He looked up. "Lucie, how will I ever live with myself?"

"But you didn't do it," she reminded him. "And she has every reason to be hurt and angry. But she'll have to understand that this had nothing to do with you."

"I'm afraid it won't be that simple, Lucie. I've been Constant's business partner for over a decade. Legally I'm just as responsible for all of this as he is. I simply don't see any way to move past it. All of the good I tried to do here . . . I'm afraid it means nothing."

"Mr. Fitzgerald," she said quietly. "It means everything. To someone like me, the good you've done means everything."

He looked at her, his face drawn. "Thank you, Lucie."

She hadn't intended to share any of her art yet, but it was time. Art was meant to make people's lives better, and perhaps she could do that here by offering her pieces to Mr. Fitzgerald to help pay off his debt. "What you've done for me, well, I can never repay you. You gave me a place to work, and a reason to feel that maybe one day, I could do important things. You can have everything I've painted so far. Maybe you can sell it and make back a bit of the money you'll owe the real Anicette Rousselle."

"Lucie, that's very kind. But to be honest, even if we sold a hundred pieces, I don't think it would be enough."

"Oh. Right. Of course." Lucie's cheeks flamed as she looked down at her lap.

"Lucie." He waited until she looked up. He appeared exhausted, but he was smiling at her now. "I didn't mean that your pieces aren't valuable, only that I owe the real Anicette Rousselle hundreds of thousands of dollars, and there's nothing I can sell to bridge that gap. But you know what would help me the most right now? To see the work you've done, if you're ready to show me. Knowing that you found some inspiration here means a lot to me."

She immediately regretted her offer, for if the money wouldn't make a difference, what was the point? And besides, what if her paintings were terrible, and they made Mr. Fitzgerald regret his decision to offer her his help? It would only make him feel worse.

But he was already standing, looking at her with an encouraging smile, and, despite the butterflies flapping around in her stomach, she forced herself to smile back before following him out the office door.

Upstairs, the scents of turpentine and linseed, wood shavings and wet clay combined in the heady aroma of artists at work. Down the hall, Lucie knew, there was a sculptor who always worked with her door closed, and in one of the other rooms, a heavyset woman chopped at big blocks of wood, making strange, abstract pieces while she sang Broadway show tunes to herself. But today, the floor was empty, and time seemed to slow as they approached Lucie's studio.

She used her key to unlock the door and then paused for a second before going in. "What if you hate what I've done?"

"Lucie," he said, his expression soft, "I'm certain I won't."

"But what if you do?"

"Then you should tell me I have no taste whatsoever."

She could hear the levity in his words, but they sank like stones within her. It was an entirely realistic thought that he might hate her work, but it was too late to turn back now. She took a deep breath, pushed the door open, and went in.

The fourteen canvases she had completed were propped against the wall in a neat row, and as Mr. Fitzgerald followed her in, his sharp inhalation made her chest tighten. Was it a sound of approval or of dismay?

She forced herself to turn to look at him. But his eyes weren't on her canvases; they were on the walls, the ceiling, and it took her a half second to realize what he was seeing. She had gotten so accustomed to painting the scenes she was remembering from her childhood, bit by bit, that her surroundings had become second nature to her. But Mr. Fitzgerald was seeing it for the first time. What if he thought it was terrible, juvenile? Or what if he hadn't really meant it when he told her that she could paint the surfaces of the room? What if he'd been joking, and she hadn't understood that? The longer his silence dragged on, the more foolish she began to feel.

"I'm sorry," she said when the quiet had grown uncomfortable. "I thought you meant it when you said I could paint whatever I liked, but obviously I—"

"Lucie," he cut her off. "This is spectacular."

"Pardon?" She was sure she'd heard him wrong.

"Maybe you're wasting your time on canvases," he said, almost to himself, but it felt like he'd punched her in the gut.

"You . . . think my art is a waste of time?" she asked, trying not to cry.

"What? No!" He chuckled. "No, Lucie. What I meant is that this is incredible. What you've done here with the walls and the ceiling . . . Well, it's so much more than a painting or even a mural. You're created a world. It's a completely different experience, and I think it's extraordinary."

She could feel herself blushing. The walls had never been intended as art; they were just the things she had to paint to clear her head before the rest could come. But she had to admit that the more detail she'd added, the more she had felt comforted by the world she'd created. "Oh. Well. Thank you."

His eyes roamed around her studio, alighting on each of her canvases in turn. "You're enormously talented, Lucie, and even if this gallery doesn't remain open, even if I can't give you your first show myself, I'll make sure someone does."

It took a second for his words to sink in. He was telling her exactly what every aspiring artist wanted to hear: that her work was worth something. "Do you mean it, Mr. Fitzgerald?"

"Of course I do, Lucie." He massaged his temples for a few seconds and then smiled again, but the light didn't reach his eyes.

"Look," she said after a moment. "I know it's not much, but my boyfriend, Tommy, he's running a Christmas tree lot with his cousin and a few friends on Sterling Place and Seventh, over in Park Slope. I bet he'll let me work there on commission if I ask, Mr. Fitzgerald, and I'll bring you the money I make. You can't lose this gallery."

His smile was gentle and sad. "Lucie, I'm not sure it's something either of us can stop. And I appreciate your offer, but you don't need to do that. You're an artist; you should be painting, not working a Christmas tree lot for a few extra bucks. Just keep doing what you're doing, and I see nothing but a bright future for you."

"Thanks, Mr. Fitzgerald." The words made her cheeks heat up again. "But I'm going to help you figure this out. It's the least I can do."

When Lucie walked out of the gallery a half hour later, she felt changed, like something had shifted within her. Maybe it was why, buoyed by thoughts that she wasn't crazy, that she might actually be able to make a career from art, she walked the half block to her mother's bookstore and went in before she could stop herself.

She had tucked the smallest of her paintings under her arm before she left, an image of a woman walking through a storm on a stretched canvas the size of a novel. She had painted it last week, and she hadn't realized, until she was midway through, that she had been painting her mother. The central figure was obscured by sheets of falling rain, and her black raincoat seemed to melt at the edges into air. All around her, clouds swirled. If you looked closely enough, you could just make out the silhouettes of a man, two little boys, and a baby girl in those wisps of condensation. There was a little girl there, too, for although her mother seemed not to care that Mathilde LeClair had also died that day, Lucie couldn't forget. Lucie's brush had brought out the shapes almost on their own, but as she'd been painting them, it had felt like the right thing. It was her way of saying, "I know. I know you talk to ghosts. And even though I worry about you, it's *okay*."

Now she walked briskly toward the back of the store before she could chicken out. Lucie knew that her mother resented her for living while the others died, and she hoped that with this painting, she could show her that she, too, missed her lost family terribly.

"Maman?" she called out, and when her mother didn't emerge, she tried again, a bit more loudly. "Maman?"

There was a rustling in the back, but still, her mother didn't come out, so Lucie steeled herself and headed through the door behind the register.

She stopped short as she entered the room. Her mother sat at the table, her head in her hands, and when Lucie came in, she didn't look up.

"Maman?" Lucie asked, rushing forward. She set the canvas on the table and bent to grasp her mother's shoulders. "Are you all right? What is it? What's happened?"

Her mother continued to stare at the table, but then slowly, she raised her gaze to meet Lucie's. "What are you doing here?" she asked dully, almost like she didn't recognize her.

"I—I came to show you something." Lucie hesitated. Something was wrong; her mother barely seemed to register the words. "Maman? Should I call a doctor?"

Finally, something sparked in her mother's eyes. "A doctor? What would a doctor do?"

"A doctor might help you," Lucie said carefully.

"I don't need help." Her mother's eyes narrowed as she stared at Lucie. "Is that what this is about? Did *she* send you?"

"Who?" Lucie was beginning to grow alarmed. Her mother often behaved oddly, but this seemed strange, even for her.

"And now you're playing dumb?"

"Maman, I have no idea what you mean."

Her mother laughed, a rough, bitter sound. "She has no right! Did she come to see you and fill your head with lies?"

"*Who*, Maman?" Lucie leaned forward and put a hand on her mother's arm. "Who are you talking about?"

Her mother recoiled like she'd been burned. "Don't pretend you don't know. Elise LeClair, of course. Is that why you're here? Is that what this is all about? My God, did she *paint* this?" She had zeroed in on the painting Lucie had set on the table.

"No, Maman, I did. It's—it's you," Lucie said as her mother continued to stare at the painting. "You're saying Elise LeClair is here? Mathilde's mother? In New York?"

But her mother didn't answer. She picked up the painting and gazed at it, and when she looked up again, there were tears in her eyes. "You painted *them*," she whispered.

"They're always with you, aren't they?" Lucie bit her tongue, but the next words rolled out anyhow. "It's not my fault, Maman.

I didn't get to choose. I had nothing to do with them dying."
Her mother made a noise under her breath, but she didn't dispute
Lucie's words. For a second, Lucie thought that was a good thing,
and so she pressed on. "May I meet her, Maman?"

"Why would you want to meet Elise LeClair?" Her mother's
voice was strangely flat as she lifted her gaze.

"I—" Lucie hesitated, for wasn't the answer obvious? The
more layers of the past she peeled back, the less sense it all made,
but her mother refused to talk about anything. She just needed
someone who had known her before the explosion, someone who
could fill in the missing parts that her mother refused to discuss,
for the more the puzzle came together, the more Lucie realized
she was missing all the vital pieces. "Because maybe," she said at
last, "she can help me understand everything."

Her mother's silence felt ominous. The grandfather clock
ticked loudly behind her. "What on earth is it that you feel you
need to understand?" her mother asked. "You are clothed. You
are fed. You are *alive*. What part of that do you have a quarrel
with?"

"It's just that the more I remember, the more confused I feel."
Lucie searched herself for the right words. "I—I just want to
know who I am."

"Who you are?" Her mother was on her feet, her face red, the
transformation having happened in the space of an instant. "Who
you *are*? You are my *daughter*!" Spittle flew from her mother's
mouth, landing on Lucie, and alarmed, she stood, pushing away
from the table. Her mother stepped closer, her eyes gleaming with
an anger that Lucie couldn't understand. "You are the daughter
God saved for me. For me, Lucie. For *me*!"

"No, Maman, I am myself," Lucie said quietly. "I am your
daughter, but I am also myself." When her mother simply stared

at her, she took a deep breath and went on. "I am myself, and I am a person who grieves the life you refuse to talk about. I grieve my brothers and my father and the baby sister I never knew. And I also grieve Mathilde." Her mother gasped and stepped back like Lucie had slapped her, but Lucie went on. "She was my friend, Maman, and she died that day, too. None of it was her fault, nor was it mine. And I want to tell Madame LeClair that her daughter was happy and loved and cared for, just like I used to be."

The words felt like a release, for Lucie had never said them before, had never pushed back at the black cloud that followed her, the coterie of ghosts pointing their fingers at her. Would her brothers have blamed her for living? Would her papa have hated her the way her mother did? She had spent her whole life since the day the bombs fell paying the price for a mistake that wasn't hers, absorbing like a sponge her mother's overwhelming grief and anger. Over time, that sadness and rage had become a part of her, a burden that she could barely shoulder.

But these past weeks of unleashing everything inside her with a paintbrush had done something to her. She was swimming up from the deepest part of the ocean, and with just a few more kicks, maybe she could break the surface and breathe again. Just last week, she had painted what little she remembered of the day their world had been destroyed, and though it had been painful to see the fire and ash and destruction on canvas, it had been cathartic, too.

"How can you hold Mathilde and her mother blameless?" Lucie's mother asked, her voice quiet.

"Because Mathilde was just a child. Because her mother couldn't have seen the future. And because she has lost a great deal, too."

Lucie wasn't sure how she expected her mother to react, but

she didn't expect her lips to curl into a sneer and her eyes to narrow at that. "Is that why you're trying to become a duplicate of the LeClairs?" Her mother took a few steps toward Lucie, moving around the table until she was standing just inches from her daughter. She reached out and touched Lucie's long hair. "You even look like her," she said, and Lucie fought the urge to recoil. "You look like a goddammed LeClair, like you're trying to spite me."

"I—" Lucie couldn't formulate an answer.

"Just go, Lucie." Her mother stepped back, her eyelashes fluttering rapidly. Once again, Lucie wondered if she should call a doctor, but she suspected that all her mother needed was to retreat back to her solitude so she could speak to Papa and the boys. The ghosts were always able to reach her in a way that Lucie never could.

"Maman," she tried one more time, but her mother was no longer listening. She was staring at the canvas Lucie had painted, a woman in a downpour, surrounded by ghosts.

CHAPTER THIRTY-TWO

As Elise knocked on the door to an apartment on the Lower East Side, on the third floor of a building that housed a kosher butcher, a pizza parlor, and a Chinese restaurant at ground level, she began to doubt her decision to come. After leaving the bookshop, she had returned to her hotel and tried calling Ruth, but there was no answer. After thirty minutes of pacing her room, she had gone downstairs and asked the concierge for subway directions to the address south of Houston Street where Ruth lived, and the concierge had recommended a taxi instead. At first, Elise had hesitated, weighing the cost, but then she'd realized that if she could manage to track down Constant Bouet, she would be a very wealthy woman. Certainly one of the most renowned wood-carvers of the twentieth century could afford cab fare.

But now, as she waited for Ruth to answer the door, she wondered why she was here. Perhaps Elise needed to let the past go in order to fully embrace the future, or she'd risk getting stuck in her grief, like Juliette. Then again, maybe she was already sinking; after all, had she not stayed in the same apartment for almost twenty years, sculpting a long-dead daughter over and over? What if she was just as unbalanced and unmoored as Juliette?

But then the door opened, and it wasn't Ruth standing there. It was Suzanne, now in her twenties, and something inside Elise cracked. She could remember Suzanne playing with Mathilde in the bookshop when the children were young, but she could also see clearly in her mind's eye the very moment she spotted Suzanne and Georges at the orphanage just after the war, when she hadn't known if they'd lived or died. She could remember holding Suzanne as she cried, comforting her when nightmares woke her, and feeling an overwhelming blend of joy and loss when their mother returned. Ruth and her children might be a piece of her past, but they were also her family, and she couldn't escape that. Nor, she realized with a start, did she want to. There was a difference between honoring the past and being trapped by it.

"Madame LeClair!" Suzanne exclaimed, her eyes filling with tears as she stepped forward and embraced Elise. After a startled second, Elise hugged her back, squeezing the child who had become a woman in Elise's absence. Where had the years gone?

"Suzanne," Elise whispered, pulling back to look at her. Her hair was styled in a smart bouffant, and she had filled out with the curves of a woman. Elise could remember so clearly how thin and frail Suzanne had appeared after the Liberation, how the lack of nutrition during the war years had made her hair stringy and lifeless, the lines of her face as sharp and pronounced as a jagged cliff side. But here before her was a rosy-cheeked, healthy woman, and Elise glanced skyward for a second and thanked God. "Look at you, my dear," she added. "You're absolutely beautiful."

Suzanne blushed. "Well, I could stand to go down a dress size or two."

Elise met her eye. "Don't you ever say such a thing. I was just thinking how happy it makes me to see you healthy and well."

Suzanne's blush deepened, turning the swells of her cheeks into little apples. Elise smiled at her and thought she might try to carve her from wood one day; it was time she tackled something other than the ghost of her daughter. Maybe this was the beginning of a way forward.

"Was my mother expecting you, Madame LeClair?" Suzanne asked, moving aside to let her in. "She told us you were here in New York, of course, but I'm afraid she must have forgotten if she had plans with you today; she went out to the store."

"No, Suzanne." Elise followed the girl in and marveled at how American the apartment looked, a Formica table in the kitchen nook, a threadbare pea-green sofa and matching armchair facing a small television in the corner, a framed painting of the Empire State Building above the mantel. Ruth and her children had successfully left the past behind and started anew. Why couldn't Elise do the same? "I told your mother I would call her later, but, well, something has happened."

Suzanne's brow creased in concern. "Come, sit down, Madame LeClair."

A moment later, Elise found herself pouring out the story of discovering her carvings of Mathilde in the art gallery, and of her troubling reunion with Juliette in the bookstore. "Was I—" She hesitated and cleared her throat. "Was I a terrible mother, Suzanne? Should I have taken Mathilde with me? Did I make a selfish decision? Is Juliette Foulon right? Am I the reason Mathilde is dead?"

The words sat between them, and Elise was afraid to see the truth on Suzanne's face. What if there had been a part of her that knew it would be easier to move on alone? She couldn't remember thinking of it that way, but what if she had? The mind plays tricks on us, and sometimes we recast the past in the way we need to see it in order to live with ourselves. Was that what Elise had done?

Finally, shaken by Suzanne's silence, she looked up and was startled to see tears rolling down Suzanne's round cheeks. "Suzanne? What is it?" she asked, and Suzanne choked out a little sob.

"Madame LeClair," she said, "you were a wonderful mother. You must believe that."

"Wonderful mothers don't leave their children."

"Then was my mother a terrible mother?"

Elise blinked quickly. "No, that's not what I meant, of course."

"I know. But think of what you're saying. My mother left us because she had to. Because if we had stayed with her, we would have been arrested and sent to that camp with her. We would have died, Madame LeClair. Georges and I would have died. Instead, my mother made what must have been the most difficult decision of her life. She sent me and Georges away, not knowing where we would go, not knowing whose roof we would sleep under, not knowing who would feed us or love us or look after us. But she knew it was our best chance of survival. Our mother made the decision to be separated from us, not because she was a terrible mother but because she wanted us to live. Are you telling me you didn't feel the same? You didn't want more than anything in the world for Mathilde to survive?"

Elise closed her eyes. She could remember the terror throbbing through her body as she walked briskly west that day, the urge to pick Mathilde up and run with her, the deep certainty that if they stayed together, they'd both perish. Leaving her with Juliette hadn't felt like a weight removed from her shoulders; it had felt like severing her soul from her body, like ripping her own heart out of her chest and leaving it beating and bleeding in someone else's care. "But Mathilde died anyhow," she said at last.

"You couldn't have foreseen that." Suzanne's voice was firm. "Nor could Madame Foulon. Terrible things happen in wars, Madame LeClair. And a terrible thing happened to Mathilde, and to Madame Foulon's family. But it was not because of you. You were a wonderful mother."

"How do you know that?" Elise wiped away a tear. "How could you know, Suzanne?"

"Because you were a mother to us when we needed one," Suzanne replied instantly. "Because even in the midst of your own grief, you didn't hesitate, not for a second. Your heart was broken, and yet there was enough love left to make Georges and me feel safe and wanted. You didn't just give us a home, you gave us your love. Our mother returned, thank God, but you were the one who brought us back to life while we waited. The way you cared for us is the way a mother cares, Madame LeClair." She hesitated and added, "Do not let Madame Foulon change the way you see the past. Mathilde was a very lucky girl to have had a mother like you."

"Lucky," Elise murmured. It was a strange thing to think of, that Mathilde had been lucky at all. But for each and every day of her life—all 1,188 days she had lived on this earth—she had been loved deeply. Elise had never fallen asleep without whispering to her, had never passed a day without begging God to protect her, hadn't passed an hour without thinking of her. Elise had done her very best to protect her, and the rest had been simply a cruel twist of fate.

"Madame LeClair?" Suzanne said after a moment. "Are you all right?"

"I will be, Suzanne." She breathed in and out. "I think I will be."

Ruth came home an hour later, and though she looked surprised to find Elise sitting in her living room, she welcomed her with a hug and insisted she stay for dinner. It was the third night of Hanukkah, and she was planning to roast a chicken.

"Think of how happy we would have been to have a whole bird during the war, Elise," she said with a smile, nudging her friend. "It would have been a *seudah*, a feast! I try never to take it for granted. Please, have a meal with us. Georges will be here soon."

And so Elise stayed and hugged Georges tightly when he came through the door, and fought back tears as Suzanne lit the third candle on the menorah, for Ruth and her children had not only survived but had kept their religious observances intact after all that had happened. They ate roasted chicken and potatoes and drank sweet red wine, and Elise teared up several times as she watched Suzanne and Georges laughing with their mother. What a gift that they had one another.

By the time dinner was over, it was pitch-black outside, the moon obscured by clouds, the streets dusted with snow. "You should stay the night," Ruth said, but Elise shook her head.

"I need to get back to my hotel. I have to go by the gallery in the morning."

"The gallery? Which gallery?" Ruth asked, and Elise realized she had been so caught up in being a part of the family tonight that she hadn't told her friend what had happened.

"I'll explain later."

"Shall I come with you?" Ruth asked. "Make sure you get back safely?"

Elise smiled at this, her friend's urge to protect her. "I'll be fine."

A few moments after saying her goodbyes to the children, Elise stood outside with Ruth as the older woman stepped toward the street, her hand raised to flag down a cab.

"Juliette doesn't want anything to do with me," Elise said as they waited. "But now that she has told me about Mathilde, now that I'm here in New York, I think I should try to see Lucie, too, just once. I have to make sure she's all right. I owe it to Juliette, even if she's no longer the person I remember."

"We're all the people we once were, my friend," Ruth said, giving Elise a sad smile. "Even if life transforms us, we are all who we are at our core, our whole lives through."

Elise woke just after dawn the next morning, and she peered out the window at a fog-draped city street. New York was just waking up: lights turning on behind curtained windows, the groan of a garbage truck, the first notes in a symphony of car horns that would escalate as the sun came up. It was snowing again, the flakes gently drifting down, though the dark clouds in the distance portended a coming storm.

Elise felt lighter this morning, more herself, and she knew it was due, in large part, to the conversation she'd had with Suzanne the day before. *You were a wonderful mother,* Suzanne had said, and there was finally a piece of Elise that could believe that. It's difficult to look at one's own past with clarity, but Suzanne had seen her for who she was. Ruth had, too.

Now, Elise just had to find a way to see herself. She had to reclaim the past, and she would begin by settling things with Constant Bouet. She dressed quickly in a wool dress, nylons, and her overcoat, and pulling a toque on to shield her from the cold, she left the hotel.

She didn't realistically expect the gallery to be open yet; it was just past 8 a.m. She was prepared to wait until Constant waddled down the street in one of his expensive suits, but as she approached from down the block, she was surprised to see the lights on, and a figure already moving around inside. She pressed her face to the glass and looked in. It was a man, though he was younger and in much better shape than Constant, dressed in faded black slacks and a shawl collar gray wool pullover. It must be Constant's business partner. A confrontation with Constant would have been more satisfying, but this man owed her, too, and she was ready to give him a piece of her mind. She tried the front door of the gallery, which was unlocked, and went in.

"I'm sorry, but we're closed," the man said, his back still to her as she entered in a burst of snowflakes and wind. She braced herself as the door swung closed behind her. She would not be dismissed from her own life anymore.

"I'm the artist whose work you've stolen," she announced, her voice shaking. "So don't you dare tell me you are closed."

She didn't recognize the steel in her own voice, and she felt a shiver of pride run up her spine. *You're stronger than you think*, Bernard had told her all those years ago, in a truck headed to Paris to reclaim her life. Maybe he'd been right after all.

She only had a second to enjoy this new, confident version of herself, though, before the man turned, and she had the sudden sense that she knew him, though she couldn't place who on earth he was. Though the wind was picking up outside, the snowflakes whipping around like angry bumblebees, one could have heard a pin drop in the gallery.

"You're the artist," he said, but his eyes didn't hold any malice, only deep sadness and regret. The words weren't a question but rather a resigned statement.

Elise nodded stiffly, her eyes drifting down to his sweater, which had a few drops of pale blue paint near the collar, and then to his fingers, where the same shade of paint was caked under his nails. "You're a painter?" she said, startled. She looked back up at his face. There was a flake of pale green clinging to his left temple, too.

He blinked a few times in surprise. "I am."

"And you would do such a thing to another artist?"

He looked pained. "Ma'am, I know you have no reason to believe me. But I had absolutely no idea. My business partner—"

"Constant Bouet," she filled in coldly.

He nodded. "It never occurred to me to question whether the artist was real, or whether Constant had concocted the story of Anicette Rousselle. The explanation made sense, since I knew he had been the primary dealer for several other prominent French artists. The irony is that Constant persuaded me to work with him by showing me photographs of your carvings. I was very moved by them. To know that it was all a lie . . ." He sighed. "I'm sorry. I should probably introduce myself. I'm Jack Fitzgerald. I co-own this gallery, which is something I was proud of until yesterday. Now, I feel only shame."

She studied him. His eyes were honest, kind. "Elise LeClair," she said, shaking his hand. His palm was warm against hers as he looked her in the eye.

"LeClair," he repeated slowly as he pulled his hand back. "Not Olivier LeClair's widow?"

No one had referred to her that way in a long time, and it sent a jolt of sadness through her. There were so many things lost, so many pieces of the past that were long gone. "Yes."

Mr. Fitzgerald's face went red. "Constant stole from his most famous client's *wife*? After his client *died*?" The shock and disgust in his tone was palpable, and it was enough to convince her he hadn't been in on Constant's scheme.

"You really didn't know."

He shook his head. "Hand to God, Mrs. LeClair, I don't know what to say. I'll make sure you're paid back, every single penny. I had no idea, I swear to you. I would never have—"

"Elise," she interrupted. "Call me Elise. I'm so tired of being nothing more than my husband's wife. And I believe you, Mr. Fitzgerald. Constant Bouet fooled me, too. But this—I don't understand it." She gestured around the gallery. "You seem like a . . . very different kind of man than he is. How on earth did you go into business with him?"

He gave her a weak smile. "Please, call me Jack. And you're right. I never cared much for Constant. But my own gallery was failing, and he came along at exactly the right moment. I opened this space with him on the condition that I could put in the artists' studios upstairs. It felt like the right decision at the time, even if I never had a good sense about him."

"Artists' studios?"

He pointed up at the ceiling. "Eight of them upstairs, free of charge. Every artist should have a place to find themselves, don't you think?"

"I do." She was quiet for a moment, thinking.

"Listen, I don't know how I can ever make this up to you, but I've already begun to put out inquiries to clients about getting your pieces back, and I can involve the police if you think—"

"No." She felt a peace settle over her. "Art is meant to be shared, isn't it? These people who bought my work, they must have felt something. The way you said you did. I—I don't want to take that back. I have to reclaim what is mine, but I don't think that means taking my pieces from people. I think it means learning to live with myself. *As* myself. I've spent too long being erased, Mr. Fitzgerald."

"Please, it's Jack. And I can't imagine anyone in their right mind trying to erase you, Elise." He held her gaze long enough that she had to look away.

"So these studios upstairs . . ." She felt like she was standing at the edge of a precipice, looking out at sea and sky. Should she jump? Did she have the courage to be a new version of herself, perhaps someone more like who she'd been before Olivier intervened and she'd let him mold her like clay? "Are any of them available?"

"Available?"

She took a deep breath. "Yes. To me. Maybe—maybe I need to start again. Maybe I need to come back to life—*my* life."

"*You* want to work here? After all that we've done to you?"

"Well, it's the least your gallery owes me, isn't it?"

The color rose to his cheeks again, and he looked away. "Indeed. Honestly, I can't tell you how sorry I am."

"Then don't. Give me a place to work while I'm in New York. Tell me you'll never deal with Constant Bouet again. And the rest, we'll figure out."

"You don't want to shut us down?"

"A few minutes ago, I certainly did. But then I walked in the door and saw the paint under your nails, and the look on your face, and I remembered that things aren't always exactly as they appear."

"I'm not sure I deserve your understanding."

"We all deserve a second chance." She thought of Olivier, the choices he'd made that had blown her life apart, the way she'd stood by him even when she knew better. "Especially when the mistakes we make begin with trusting the wrong people."

He stared at her. "I don't know what to say."

"Say you'll show me the studios."

He smiled slowly and nodded to himself. "Follow me."

In the hallway upstairs were eight closed doors and one other at the end of the hall. A few of the rooms had supplies or drying canvases propped outside. "Room number eight is yours, if you want it," Jack was saying, but she was no longer paying attention to him or the door he was unlocking, because right beside it were two canvases, one large and one small.

She bent to stare at them, her heart thudding, and Jack seemed to fade into the background. The smaller canvas was simply a dancing little girl, the wind catching her skirt as she twirled, but the background, clearly a street in Paris judging by the architecture of the building behind the spinning figure, looked exactly like *her* street. That was impossible, wasn't it?

But it was the larger painting that left her breathless. It was dark, filled with anguished gashes of black and gray, the image partially obscured by what looked like a thin layer of smoke. Pages of paper were suspended in the air, and the world burned, a single hole in the ceiling open to an incongruously blue sky above. In the center of the image were two little girls leaning against each other, their hands clasped. And though Elise couldn't see their faces, their little silhouettes were achingly familiar, and she recognized the backdrop, too—the leaning bookshelves, the Babar book lying facedown, its pages blown out. She'd been in this room before it had been destroyed, had stood in its eerie replica just yesterday.

"What is it?" Jack asked, and she could feel his arm brush against hers as he came to stand beside her, trying to figure out what she was seeing.

"I—I think this is my daughter in the paintings. My daughter and her friend." She wiped her tears away. She wondered if she was losing her mind. "But that can't be possible. Can it?"

Jack looked as confused as she felt, but there was a great sadness in his eyes. "Your daughter?"

She looked back at the painting. "She died seventeen years ago, during the war."

"My God. Elise. Of course. I'm so sorry."

She shook her head. "Jack, who painted this?"

"The artist is a young woman from Paris, though she's lived here in the States for many years. Her mother owns the bookstore just down the block."

Elise put a hand over her mouth. "This was painted by Lucie *Foulon*?" Her grief and confusion twisted more tightly together. She'd been right about the image, but what did that mean?

"You know her?" He looked surprised.

"This is her in the painting, with my Mathilde, when they were little girls. They were dear friends." Knowing that Lucie Foulon had become an artist, and a talented one at that, nearly broke her, for it was another reminder of everything Elise had missed with Mathilde. She thought of what Juliette had said about Lucie and Mathilde coloring together all those years ago. Would they have discovered their potential as artists together, encouraged one another, if Mathilde had lived? Elise would never know, but as she looked again at the painting, which screamed of grief and confusion and pain, she realized that one thing was clear: Lucie was struggling, too.

Of course she was. The girl had lost her father, her brothers, her best friend—and on top of that, her mother had withdrawn from the real world. Lucie had lived through not only those horrific losses but the traumatic event—a bomb falling from the clear blue sky on an April day—that precipitated them. And here she was, seventeen years later, trying to piece the puzzle together in her head by putting images of her past on canvas. It was exactly what Elise was doing each time she carved Mathilde's face from wood.

She took one last look at the painting before turning her attention back to Jack. "Do you believe in fate?"

He tilted his head, curiosity sparking in his expression. "I do . . ."

"You said it was *my* carvings that convinced you to open this gallery. And then, years later, you wind up giving one of your studios to my daughter's best friend, the girl who was beside her when she died. How could that be?"

"Lucie was beside her when . . . ?"

Elise nodded, and Jack's eyes welled with tears, surprising her. She wondered, suddenly, if he had sustained a similar loss.

"I think," he said slowly, "that sometimes, the roads we don't know we're walking are the ones that lead us to exactly where we're meant to be."

In that moment, she knew that he was correct and that she was right to have come, even if Juliette didn't want her here. Lucie needed to hear that it was all right to grieve the past, but also that she needed to let go of it in order to move into the future. It was a lesson Elise herself was only just beginning to learn, but she knew that something bigger than herself had brought her here to help the girl who had once been Mathilde's dearest friend.

"Jack, I have to talk to her. Do you know where she lives?"

There was something new in his eyes as he looked at her. "No. But I don't think she's home today anyhow. Her boyfriend's working a Christmas tree lot in Brooklyn, and she was going to try to pick up a few shifts to earn some money for the gallery. I told her she didn't need to do that, but—"

"Where in Brooklyn?" she interrupted.

"Park Slope." He paused, thinking. "Sterling Place and Seventh, I think she said."

"I—I need to talk to her."

Jack studied her for a second more. He couldn't possibly understand what was happening, for Elise didn't understand it herself. Still, somehow, he was with her yet the same. "Hang on," he said. "I'll grab my coat."

❧ CHAPTER THIRTY-THREE ❧

The fog was thick in New York, and it was already snowing when United Airlines Flight 826 lifted off from O'Hare Airport in Chicago that morning with a forty-six-year-old captain named Robert Sawyer at the controls. He'd gotten his job with United nearly twenty years before, on the second day of 1941, the same day that, across an ocean, Elise and Olivier had celebrated their daughter's first birthday.

Sometimes, fate and circumstance come together in an inexplicable storm of destiny. On a bright April day in 1943, something had happened in the cockpit of an American bomber with instructions to drop a load of explosives on the Renault plant on the Île Seguin, just across a narrow sliver of the Seine from Boulogne-Billancourt. The target should have been clear; it sat on an island, surrounded by the river on both sides. But instead, this particular bomber, as well as several others that had dropped beneath the clouds, missed their mark. One bomb fell on the Pont de Sèvres metro station. Others fell on the Longchamp racecourse as the horses prepared to run.

And one fell on the rue Goblet, on a little bookshop that held a family's hopes and dreams.

People die during wartime; it is inevitable. That April day, the death toll from the errant bombs topped three hundred. In France alone over the course of the war, more than sixty thousand civilians lost their lives to Allied bombs falling from the clouds, many of them missing their intended targets.

But mistakes happen in peacetime, too.

There were no signs that morning that Captain Sawyer's DC-8 jetliner would veer slightly off course, just as an American bomber had done seventeen years before. The fog was thick, the wind picking up, but Captain Sawyer had flown this route often, as had his first officer, forty-year-old Robert Fiebing, and the flight's second officer, Richard Pruitt, a thirty-year-old flight engineer. If you were flying from O'Hare to New York International Airport in the snow, these were the type of men you wanted at the controls—calm, intelligent, experienced. There were seventy-six passengers aboard, four young stewardesses. It should have been a routine day of travel.

At 10:22 a.m., Flight 826 radioed air traffic control. "If we're going to have a delay, we would rather hold upstairs than down. We're going to need three-quarters of a mile. Do you have the weather handy?"

"No, but I'll get it," a controller from New York Center radioed back. "There have been no delays until now." A minute later, the man was back with a weather report. "Fifteen hundred feet overcast, half mile. Light rain, fog, altimeter setting 29.65."

"We're starting down," came the reply from the flight deck.

Eleven minutes later, New York Center prepared to hand Flight 826 off to the airport's flight control center as the plane approached. "Eight twenty-six, roger, and you received the holding instructions at Preston. Radar service is terminated. Contact Idlewild Approach Control."

"Good day," the flight crew replied before radioing Idlewild Approach Control. "United 826, approaching Preston at five thousand."

"United 826, this is Idlewild Approach Control, maintain five thousand," the control center radioed back. "Little or no delay at Preston. Idlewild landing runway four right. ILS in use. Idlewild weather: six hundred scattered; estimated fifteen hundred overcast; visibility half mile; light rain and fog; altimeter 29.63. Over."

But the only reply was broken static and a sudden silence. United Flight 826 had already collided with another airplane, TWA Flight 266, a Lockheed Super Constellation with forty-four souls on board, over Staten Island. The wounded jet, one of its right engines missing, was now hurtling northeast toward Brooklyn.

CHAPTER THIRTY-FOUR

That morning, Juliette awoke in an empty bed with a feeling of dread in her stomach.

She'd had the same feeling on the morning of April 4, 1943, but she had dismissed it. Perhaps it had been something she'd eaten the night before, she'd told herself, or the onset of a minor cold. By the time she'd gotten out of bed that day, she'd felt better, and she'd continued to ignore the twist in her gut, the pain that told her something was wrong.

And now, she felt it again. She rolled over and looked at the clock. It was nearly nine. How had she slept so late? Paul would be wondering where she was.

She pulled on a robe and slid her feet into slippers, then padded into the bathroom and regarded herself in the mirror. She was always startled when she took the time to study her reflection, for it didn't match the way she felt. Paul and the boys remained the same age, and Antoinette was forever a baby. It seemed incongruous, then, that she should continue to move forward in time, the years turning her hair gray, life placing line after line on her forehead. She splashed some water on her face, then dried it, applied her cold cream, tissued it off, and finished with her Elizabeth Arden Eight Hour Cream, which the beauty magazines had promised would erase the years. It hadn't worked, but Juliette was a creature of habit, so on went the sticky cream, rubbed in until her face shone, followed by a dusting of powder. Blush, mascara, and a swipe of Victory Red lipstick made her feel like herself again.

Arthur was already at the breakfast table, the *New York Times* open in front of him, when she padded in. "Morning," he said.

"Where's Lucie?" she asked. Their conversations often went like this, an exchange of the barest pleasantries, the most basic facts. Most days, it suited her just fine, for she didn't need a husband; she needed a place to live and enough money to raise Lucie and run the store. Arthur had given her that in spades; he didn't need to provide conversation, too.

"Off with her Italian fellow, I think," he said without lowering the paper.

"She's still seeing that boy? Even after I told her not to?"

The newspaper came down, and Arthur peered at her over his bifocals. He looked like an old man, with white hair sprouting from every orifice. Sometimes she wished he would try a little harder. "Juliette, she's a grown woman. You can't control her choices forever."

"I certainly can as long as she's under *my* roof!" Juliette shot back.

"But it's not your roof. It's mine. And I, for one, think it's nice to see a young lady figuring out who she is."

Juliette felt like someone had poured hot water down the back of her robe. "What is that supposed to mean? She's my daughter. She's Lucie Foulon!"

He blinked at her as if her words didn't make sense. "Of course she is. Who else would she be?"

She waved her hands in exasperation. How could he not understand what she was saying? "She's not old enough to be dating, first of all. And that boy is probably the one encouraging her to paint. You know that, don't you? How can you condone this when you know it's not the future I want for her?"

"And what future is that, Juliette? You'd prefer she stay a little girl forever, that she move into the bookstore with you? That she continue living in the past?" Arthur snapped the newspaper back up, indicating that his side of the conversation was over. "It might be the life you've chosen for yourself, but it's no life for your daughter."

He flipped a page of the newspaper, and it made a sound like something ripping. Juliette thought perhaps it was the last shred of her patience, tearing in two.

"First Elise LeClair comes into the bookstore to tell me she's concerned about *my* daughter, and now you're criticizing my parenting, too?"

He lowered the paper again. "You didn't tell me that the LeClair woman was in New York. Was it nice for you to see her after all this time?"

"*Nice?*" Juliette repeated in disbelief. Arthur knew all about the LeClairs, and how Elise had deposited her daughter with the Foulons before running off to the south of France. "It was terrible, Arthur. She has no concept of how irresponsibly she behaved, and when I reminded her, she had the gall to look offended!"

"You told her—after seventeen years—that she was irresponsible? After she lost her daughter?"

"It was her fault," Juliette muttered.

Now Arthur looked worried. "Is that what you said, Juliette? It wasn't anyone's fault. It was a terrible thing that happened." He shook his head. "Is that why Lucie went off in such a huff this morning?"

"A huff?" A cold tingle began at the base of Juliette's back and began to creep slowly up her spine. "What did she say? Did Elise LeClair get to her?"

The worry line between Arthur's bushy white eyebrows grew deeper. "I have no idea. But she was upset. Something about art and people telling lies."

Juliette simply stared at him, her mouth dry. If Lucie was speaking of art and lies . . . If Elise was trying to find her . . . Abruptly, she pushed back her chair from the table. "Do you know where the Italian boy lives?"

"Juliette . . ." Arthur drew her name out like a warning.

She snapped her fingers. "Come on, Arthur. I know you. I know you checked him out." It was one of the things she both loved and hated about him. He had *people*, the kind of people who investigated things, who checked people's backgrounds. She had no doubt that he'd looked into her past before they'd married, and she knew that sometimes, a man dressed all in black with a mustache that looked like peach fuzz followed her to and from work. It would have bothered her more if she had anywhere secretive to go, but her life consisted only of coming and going from the bookstore. Arthur was burning his money having someone tail her, but if he knew where Lucie was now, well, it wasn't a waste at all.

He narrowed his eyes at her and seemed to think about it for a few seconds. "He lives off Mott Street with his parents. But he's not there today. There's a Christmas tree lot in Brooklyn he's running with a cousin of his."

"Where in Brooklyn?"

"Juliette . . ."

"*Where* in Brooklyn, Arthur? She's my daughter."

He sighed. "Sterling Place and Seventh Avenue. Are you happy now?"

"Thank you." Juliette didn't wait for him to interrogate her about her intentions. After all, what she had to do was perfectly clear. If Elise LeClair somehow found Lucie before Juliette could get there . . . Well, Juliette couldn't think about that right now.

Ten minutes later, wrapped in a long coat to shield her against the cold, she headed out the front door and hailed a taxi. She'd be late to the bookstore today, but Paul would have to understand.

The rain turned to light snow as the yellow cab hurtled across the Brooklyn Bridge twenty-five minutes later, and the knot in Juliette's stomach was rapidly becoming something more, the beginning of a terrible ulcer.

"Can't you go any faster?" she asked from the back seat.

"I'm going as fast as I can, lady." The balding driver didn't even glance at her. As he switched lanes, whizzing around a slow-moving pickup truck, Juliette gripped the door handle and closed her eyes.

"Tell her." Paul's voice was as clear and loud as if he'd been sitting right beside her.

Juliette's eyes flew open, and she swiveled her head, half expecting to see him beside her. But the back seat of the cab was empty.

"Paul?" she whispered.

"Tell her," he said again, but more loudly.

"I can't, Paul. How can you ask me to do such a thing?"

This time, the driver turned around to look at her. "You talking to me, lady?"

KRISTIN HARMEL

"No." She forced a polite smile. "Don't you think you'd better keep your eyes on the road?"

The man grunted and turned back around, but not before muttering something under his breath about always getting the crazy ones.

"*Tell her*," Paul repeated, and Juliette squeezed her eyes closed, willing him to be quiet. She needed to think.

Paul couldn't possibly be suggesting what it sounded like he was suggesting. *Tell her*. Tell whom? Tell Elise? Or tell Lucie that in the rubble of their bombed-out bookstore seventeen years earlier, with the world swimming around her in shadows and smoke, she'd made a mistake?

But if she hadn't pulled Lucie from the rubble that day, what reason would she have had to survive? She would have closed her eyes right there on that destroyed floor and walked toward the light with the others. She would have fallen asleep and slept forever; no move across the ocean, no New York, no Arthur.

Tell her.

And now Paul wanted her to rewrite history? How could he believe that it was the right thing when he knew very well that without Lucie, she had no reason to live?

But destiny, it seemed, had a way of righting itself, of throwing the dice again, of rerouting the road. It had begun with Lucie's willful disobedience as a child, her proclivity for crayons over Bobbsey Twins books, for doodling over reading. While other children ran like hellions through Central Park, hooting and hollering and pretending to be princesses and pirates, Lucie was always stubbornly bent over whatever scraps of paper she could find, trying to capture the shape of a blade of grass or the bulge and shadows of the clouds floating over her head.

Tell her.

It had made Juliette so angry, the girl's inclination to be someone she wasn't. She was Lucie Foulon. And yet her daughter remained independent, obstinate, choosing to listen to some drumbeat within her rather than her mother's loving guidance. This, despite the fact that Juliette had sacrificed so much to make sure her daughter's life was a good one. It had infuriated Juliette, the anger hardening within her over the years, twisting into a rock of rage that she kept in her stomach.

But the harder Lucie pushed, the more often Paul appeared to comfort Juliette, and Juliette knew, therefore, that she was doing the right thing. Lucie was twenty now, and somehow, it had all worked itself out, and things were fine.

But then Ruth Levy had stepped out of the past, her presence in the bookstore an inexplicable joke from the heavens, and it had been like someone pulling a thread. Round and round and round the unweaving had gone until somehow, one day, Elise LeClair was standing there, too.

How Juliette rued that day in the Bois de Boulogne that she had stopped to help Elise! What she'd set in motion, this friendship that was supposed to transcend time, had ruined everything.

Tell her.

"Tell her *what*?" Juliette snapped. "That I'm sorry I couldn't protect my own children? That I'm sorry I failed? That it's all my fault?"

Before Paul could reply, the cabdriver pulled over by the side of a shabby Victorian row house with a crumbling front stoop and grunted the fare, staring at her in the rearview mirror with narrowed eyes. As she handed over a few bills and stepped out into the foggy morning, the gentle snowfall had turned into something wet and unforgiving, and for a moment, she simply stood there, looking around as the cab screeched away.

There was a grocery store on the corner with a giant Pepsi-Cola bottle cap on its sign, buildings with peeling paint and broken windows, a church called the Pillar of Fire listing Sunday services, Sunday school, and Thursday worship on its sign. A whitewashed soda and candy store sat beside a funeral home, and nearby was the Christmas tree lot Arthur had mentioned.

Lucie. She had to be there.

Tell her, Paul repeated, but Juliette couldn't move, couldn't get her feet to cooperate with the voice in her head. As long as she stayed right here, rooted to the ground, nothing would change. Fate wouldn't be altered. She wouldn't have to do the thing she had come here to do.

She was dimly aware of a car pulling up to the curb behind her, the way the tires slung slush at her legs, the sharp slice of the slamming door, but she hardly noticed any of it until an incredulous voice cut into her thoughts. "Juliette?"

Slowly, Juliette turned and found herself face-to-face, quite impossibly, with Elise LeClair. There was a man who looked vaguely familiar standing a half pace behind her, and for a second, Juliette focused on that incongruous detail rather than the fact that everything was about to unravel, once and for all. "Who's this?" she asked, nodding at the man, who was perhaps fifty, with gray-streaked sandy hair, green eyes, and a friendly face.

Elise looked thrown by the question. "This is Jack Fitzgerald. He owns the gallery down the block from you."

The gallery, Juliette thought numbly. The gallery, which featured French art, had been the primary reason she'd chosen Fifty-Sixth Street for her bookstore. And yet somehow Elise knew one of the owners? She felt a rage slowly rising within her, anger at Elise for existing, and fury at the universe for continuing to push them together, even after all these years.

"Where is she?" Elise asked gently.

"Who?" Juliette asked, feeling suddenly dizzy. *Tell her.*

"Lucie." Oddly, Elise sounded terribly sad. "I saw some of her work, and . . . I think it might help if I talk with her." She hesitated. "Juliette, are you all right?"

Juliette opened her mouth to reply, but they were interrupted by a voice from across the street.

"Maman?"

Juliette and Elise looked up at the same time to see Lucie standing outside the Christmas tree lot, staring at them in confusion. Her eyes moved slowly from Juliette to the gallery owner before her gaze settled on Elise, and a strange expression passed over her face. Juliette could hear Elise's sharp intake of breath beside her.

Tell her.

"Maman?" Lucie asked again, but she was no longer looking at Juliette. She was looking at Elise, and in that moment, Juliette knew that the life she had spent the past seventeen years carefully constructing, brick by brick, was about to come tumbling down.

Juliette closed her eyes, wondering if she could freeze time, but when she opened them again, Lucie was already moving toward them. Her eyes hadn't left Elise's face. It was as if already, Juliette had ceased to exist.

Drawing a deep breath, Juliette turned to Elise. *Tell her,* Paul was saying in her ear over and over. *Tell her. Tell her!* "Elise," she began, nearly choking on the word, but Elise wasn't paying any attention at all to Juliette. Her focus was only on Lucie, floating across the street like a ghost. "Elise?" Juliette tried again, but suddenly, there was a sound to the south, the sound of a blast. Juliette dropped to her knees in the snow, cowering, her hands over her head, before she knew what she was doing.

"Is it a bomb?" she cried, panicked, still covering her head, though no one else had reacted similarly. All around her, people were looking up at the sky with curiosity, but none of them knew how easily airplanes could swoop down from the heavens and drop explosives into their lives. "Are they bombing us?"

The man from the gallery bent beside her. "No, ma'am." He pitied her; she could see it in his kind eyes. "There aren't any bombs here." She allowed him to help her to her feet, but she couldn't look at him, couldn't stand to see herself reflected in his gaze, so she turned back to her approaching daughter.

"Maman?" Lucie was almost across the street now. She came toward them, her eyes wide, and Elise took a step forward and then another, but as the sound from the south grew louder, Juliette knew that something was wrong, very wrong, no matter what Elise's friend had said.

Lucie and Elise were staring at each other, so they didn't see it, but Juliette did, and she knew with certainty now that she had finally lost her mind, for out of the gray sky, an airplane was shrieking toward them, here in a borough of New York City, just as one had seventeen years before, on an April afternoon in the suburbs of Paris.

Tell her! Paul was screaming now, but his voice was drowned out by the sound of whirring engines, by the cacophony of metal scraping brick, by the noise of the world coming down all around her. It was so familiar, so terribly familiar, and Juliette knew, in that moment, that everything she had done, everything she had tried so hard to believe, everything she had bent and broken and rebuilt, had caught up with her at last.

"Lucie!" Juliette cried. It was all she had time to say before the world came crashing down.

CHAPTER THIRTY-FIVE

Lucie felt it happening in slow motion, the collision somewhere to the south, the boom that shook the sky. It stirred something in her, a memory she hadn't been able to grasp, just out of her reach.

She'd been working the Christmas tree lot alongside Tommy, and she'd been thinking about other ways she might be able to help save the gallery. It was crazy, she realized now, to think that anything she painted would make a difference, and even if she sold a hundred trees a day between now and Christmas, it would barely make a dent in the problem. She would have to ask Arthur, even if it meant infuriating her mother.

She wasn't sure how much money her stepfather actually had, only that she and her mother had never wanted for anything material. And when her mother had asked to re-create the bookstore she'd once owned in France, he'd simply written a few checks and made it happen. He was cold and detached, nothing like the father she remembered from her early childhood, and if his treatment of her mother was any indication, he sometimes confused money with love. Well, let him confuse it one last time for her.

"Tommy?" she'd asked, stepping up beside him as he handed a customer his change. "I think I have to—"

"Hey," he'd interrupted, pointing across the street. "Is that your ma? And that man, what's his name, from the gallery?"

Lucie had turned to follow his gaze and was shocked to realize he was right. Her mother was standing there with Mr. Fitzgerald. What on earth?

"Maman?" she'd called out, confused.

But then she realized there was a third person with them, a woman who turned and looked at her, and suddenly the world froze. Lucie knew her immediately, for she'd been dreaming about her ever since she'd started painting the walls in her studio above the gallery. But she hadn't realized until now that the woman was anything but a figment of her own imagination.

The woman's mouth opened in an *O* of surprise as their eyes met. "Maman?" Lucie asked again. She could hear her own voice cracking.

She stared for a second more and then snapped herself into action. She had to know what was happening. Maman's face had gone as white as the snow, and she was looking at Lucie in horror as she began to cross the street toward them, but Lucie was barely looking at her. She couldn't tear her eyes away from the other woman. It was Elise LeClair, she was nearly certain, but Lucie was also acutely aware, with every fiber of her being, that she had never called her that, not when she knew her before the blast. She was almost all the way across the street when the sound of an explosion in the distance made the earth tremble and stopped Lucie in her tracks.

It made no sense. Bombs didn't drop in New York City. Was she imagining things now that her past had inexplicably shown up here on a Brooklyn street corner? She took a step forward, and then another, but the air was electrified, and she could smell fuel burning, and the sound of distant screams, and suddenly, though she knew just where she was, she was somehow back in France, too, three years old again, the girl who had become her sister clutching her hand. They had been smiling, laughing about something, when they'd heard the warning sirens, then almost instantly, an ominous rumble.

"Maman?" she heard herself say now, her voice like that of a child again, but the word was lost in the thick, cold air as the sky filled with sound.

"Run!" she heard a deep voice shout, but her feet were rooted to the ground, because it was all coming back to her in waves, the whistling overhead, the rumble of an approaching engine coming too close, the cold finger of terror running up her vertebrae like the keys of a player piano, the hair on her arms standing on end.

"Miss, come *on!*" yelled another man, his accent thick and Irish, and then there were rough hands on both of her arms, and she was being shoved away from her mother, toward the building beside the tree lot. But she didn't want to be inside, she realized. She had been inside a building the last time, the illusion of safety cocooning her just before the world exploded. She wriggled free of the stranger's grasp and stumbled away, against the tide of people. Away from the Christmas tree lot, where "Jingle Bell Rock" hummed obliviously from a small transistor radio, its cheery notes drowned out already by the screams that split the morning. Against the current. Toward her mother.

And then she saw it. It made no sense, but there was a jet—a passenger jet—coming right for them, red, blue, and black on white, sliding through the clouds like the blade of a giant's axe, its engines whistling, its glittering fuselage hurtling toward Sterling Place.

Then, in the next instant, it hit, one of its wings clipping the roof of the brownstone on the corner a frozen instant before the world exploded in a shower of shattered glass, slivered metal, and blasted concrete.

And in that split second before everything went black, in that balancing act between this world and the next, Lucie remembered. For the first time in seventeen years, Lucie remembered everything.

When she came to, Lucie was surrounded by smoke so thick she couldn't see, flames reaching for the sky, someone's suitcase open and spilling shirts and trousers onto the street. People were screaming, people were crying, a half-burned newspaper page was whipping violently in the wind.

But as Lucie's eyelids fluttered and she tried to get her bearings, that world disappeared, and suddenly, she wasn't in Brooklyn anymore, wasn't trapped under a fallen wall dangerously close to the dying engine of a jet that had fallen from the sky. She was in the charred quiet of the beloved bookstore in France, smoke and dust filling her lungs. She wanted to cry out for her mother, for her father, but she couldn't speak. She could see Papa's hand reaching up from the rubble, but it was stiff and unmoving, and she knew. She knew he was buried somewhere beneath the fallen books and crumbled stones. The boys were gone, and the little hand that still clutched hers was cold and stiff. She pulled away and forced herself upright to look down at the girl beside her. Her face was still and peaceful, her brown hair splayed out around her like rays from a golden sun, her eyes closed, her lips parted ever so slightly. "Lucie," she tried to say, but her voice made no sound.

And then, from the overwhelming silence came a voice. "Paul?" It was Maman. "Paul, what has happened?"

She tried to speak, to tell Maman that they were dead, all of them. But the words still wouldn't come, and her body wasn't cooperating.

"Paul? Claude? Alphonse?" Maman cried. "Where are you?"

"They are—" she tried to reply, and though she heard her own scratchy voice, Maman didn't respond.

She could hear Maman moving around, screaming the names of the other children, but no one seemed to be crying out for her, so she lay her head back down, exhausted. Her own mother was certainly dead; the woman she was supposed to call Maman had told her many times. *She's gone*, she would say, her tone soft and soothing. *But don't worry. You will always have a home with us.*

Perhaps that's why, when she finally mustered the energy to call out, she didn't protest when Maman called her by the wrong name. "Maman," she whispered, again and again. "Maman."

"Lucie, it's going to be all right," Maman said, though her face was streaked with blood, her hair matted crimson. "Maman will make everything all right."

And she had to believe that. She had to, because there was no other way. She understood, even then, that her entire survival rested in the hands of the woman who was sobbing and coughing as she pulled her from the rubble.

Later, she wanted to say something, to speak up. But surely Maman knew she was not Lucie, didn't she? And Maman was so very angry at Mathilde, so very relieved that it was Lucie who had survived instead. So how could she tell her? How could she protest? She tried once, sixteen months after the bombs, when people were dancing in the streets, celebrating the liberation of Paris. She and Maman had been living in a boardinghouse by then, part of a heaving mass of refugees with nowhere to go.

"Lucie," Maman said, pulling her close. "France is free."

"Maman," she had said quietly as a group outside their window sang "La Marseillaise." "I am not Lucie. I am Mathilde."

Her mother had pulled back and looked at her strangely. Was it possible that Maman was coming to the same realization, that she recognized Mathilde, too? But then, Maman's expression had tightened into something cold and unrecognizable.

"That isn't funny, Lucie," Maman said. "I never want to hear such nonsense from you again. There will be no supper for you tonight."

Later, after they were in America, Maman lay beside her each night and whispered to her, telling her that all her memories from the time before were just dreams. In time, Lucie came to believe it. Her first maman, who painted the ceilings of an apartment she barely remembered, her first papa pacing the parlor and giving fiery speeches about things she didn't understand, those were just things she'd made up, like the stories Maman had once told the children at bedtime. And in time, she came to believe Maman, for what reason could she possibly have to lie?

But now, here on her back in Brooklyn, buried under brick and dust, with smoke clogging her lungs just like all those years ago, it was all coming back, and she knew exactly who she was. Perhaps it was too late to tell anyone, to stand up from the rubble and reclaim a lost life. But in the end, no matter how many days we spend living the lives we are told are ours, it turns out that we are only ever ourselves.

"Lucie?" She could hear a voice in the darkness, calling to her, but it wasn't her name, was it? It never had been. And so she didn't answer. Instead, she closed her eyes and waited for the light to come find her.

CHAPTER THIRTY-SIX

Elise stumbled toward her hotel room door, tearstained, soot-streaked, and more exhausted than she'd ever been in her entire life. She'd been up all night, searching the rubble with Jack Fitzgerald beside her, an ally she'd never expected. She had called Ruth at some point, and Ruth had immediately volunteered to find the badly injured Juliette, who was barely conscious when an ambulance took her away, and to call Juliette's husband to let him know where she was. Elise didn't even know which hospital she'd been taken to, but she took some comfort now in knowing that Juliette was likely not alone.

But Lucie was missing. And Elise still couldn't understand what she'd seen in the seconds before the passenger jet fell from the sky, hurtling into a quiet city intersection.

"Maman," Lucie had said, and she'd been looking straight at Elise. Had Elise imagined that? Had she imagined that the point of Lucie's chin, the slope of her nose, the swell of her cheeks, the shape of her eyes, had matched almost exactly the face she'd been carving again and again for the past twenty years? Had she broken with reality for an instant, imprinted an image from her imagination on the face of a real girl? Or over the years, had she gotten the details of Mathilde's and Lucie's faces confused in her mind, somehow merging them into one person, whom she felt compelled to carve again and again, like an endless penance for something she could never repay?

The *New York Times* was reporting 127 confirmed dead, including at least three people on the ground, in a disaster that should have been impossible. Two planes, one apparently off its course, had collided. A TWA plane had come down in three parts in Staten Island, while a United jet had somehow wound up eight miles away, on a quiet street in Park Slope during a snowfall. More than two hundred and fifty firemen had responded to the seven-alarm blaze as the jet burned. A thirty-four-year-old sanitation worker who'd been unfortunate enough to be on the street was dead, the paper reported, as were two young men named John and Joseph, an uncle and a nephew who'd been working the Christmas tree lot. Missing were the ninety-year-old caretaker of a church and a twenty-year-old woman named Lucie Foulon, who'd been in the same Christmas tree lot as the two dead men, though her boyfriend, Tommy Barber, who'd also been there, had survived with only a broken leg. One passenger on the plane, an eleven-year-old boy, was fighting for his life in the hospital.

Elise and Jack had stayed at the crash site until the rescuers had pulled most of the dead from the wreckage, and a policeman had physically forced them back behind barricades and snapped at them that they were impeding the investigation.

"But Lucie," Elise had whispered, and though the policeman's face had softened with sympathy, he hadn't moved to let her through. "She's missing."

"Ma'am, if this Lucie is still here, we'll find her. But it's better you're not here if we do."

Jack had suggested going back to the gallery then, to start calling around to the hospitals, and Elise had allowed him to lead her away. But when the cab had neared midtown she'd asked if they could stop at her hotel instead. She had something she needed to show him.

"Here," she said now, unlocking the door to her room and pushing it open as Jack followed, a gentle hand on her back to steady her. Elise's throat was raw from smoke inhalation, her face so blackened with soot that she hadn't recognized her own reflection in the window as they entered the hotel lobby a moment earlier. "It's just here."

She crossed the room and picked up the bust of a grown Mathilde—the way Elise had been imagining her for years—and turned around to show Jack. This was the one she had carved just a few nights before, the one that had felt so alive to her, though she'd carved hundreds, perhaps thousands, of versions of the same things over the years.

Jack stared at it, and she knew he was seeing exactly what she had seen earlier that day. "But . . . that's Lucie Foulon," he said. He looked up at her in confusion. "You said you hadn't seen her since 1942."

"I hadn't." Elise set the bust down and stared at it. "But I've spent nearly two decades sculpting exactly what I thought Mathilde would have looked like at every stage of her life. These are my husband's eyes, Jack." She touched the carving of Mathilde just below the brow. "And the shape of her face was mine. I could see it even when she was a baby. Her lips were always like this, a rosebud bow. These were the features of my daughter's face, the pieces of my husband and me that came together to make her. I'm certain of it. How can this be Lucie Foulon?"

Jack stared first at the bust and then at Elise. She could see him tracing the lines, angles, and curves, putting the pieces together.

Finally, he stepped forward and touched Elise's chin, tilting her face toward his, and he stared at her for a second, taking her in like a piece of art. "Elise," he said, his voice choked. "She looks just like you. I don't know how I didn't see it before."

And then Elise's tears fell, because she wasn't crazy, she hadn't been seeing things, she hadn't let the past seep through the cracks and cast the wrong light on reality. Jack could see it, too. "But what does this mean?" She couldn't put words to the thought that was bubbling up inside her, for it made no sense at all.

Jack looked at her for a long time. "Let's go to the gallery," he said instead of answering her question. "Let's look at what else she has painted. She said that the more she painted, the more she felt like she was beginning to understand where she'd come from. Maybe there are some answers there."

Elise nodded, though exhaustion and grief were doing a familiar tango through her bones. When Jack put an arm around her, she gratefully leaned into him, accepting his support as they left the hotel room and headed out toward the gallery.

Ten minutes later, Jack was unlocking the gallery's front door and snapping the lights on. "Come on," he said. "Let's go upstairs."

Her whole body felt like it was breaking as Jack guided her up the steps to the second floor and led her down the hallway to studio number six, the small space that had given Lucie a place to paint. She placed a hand on Jack's arm before they went in. "Thank you," she said, "for this."

His eyes filled with tears as he unlocked the door. Elise took a step forward to enter, but then she stopped short.

There were a dozen canvases propped up against the walls, but they weren't what made Elise's heart thud in recognition. It was the fact that the ceiling was saturated in color, an all-encompassing rendition of a starry twilight hour in the Bois de Boulogne, the branches reaching for the heavens, the walls lined with intricately painted trees, perfectly detailed leaves. It wasn't exactly the same as the sky Elise had painted for Mathilde when she was a baby, but the differences were in the artistic rendering. The feeling was the same, though; standing in the center of the room made one feel nestled into the safety of the wood, but also a part of the endless universe stretching above.

And on the far wall, painted in script, was the phrase that Elise had repeated to her daughter every night as they sat in the room of trees and sky and looked up at the painted heavens: *Under these stars, fate will guide you home.*

She put her hand over her mouth. "Jack, this is . . ." Elise said, trailing off, and then there was a noise behind them, and she and Jack both turned at the same time. Elise gasped.

In the doorway was Lucie, or the girl who had grown up as Lucie, her face streaked, her hair black with soot. There was a gash on her forehead, a dried bloodstain on her neck. But she was here, alive, standing in a room that looked just like the one Elise had painted for her all those years ago.

"She—she told me you were dead," the girl said, and Elise had never heard a sound so sweet. "She told me my memories weren't real. But they were always here." She tapped her forehead. "Until they were *here*." She gestured around them, and Elise understood. The walls were wisps from the long-vanished past, brought back to life with the tip of a paintbrush.

Elise couldn't speak. Her tears were coursing down her cheeks like rivers. "My love," she finally managed to say.

"I—I think I'm Mathilde," the girl said. She took a step closer, her eyes never leaving Elise's face. "I'm Mathilde, aren't I?"

"Yes," Elise whispered. "Yes, my dear girl. You are Mathilde. And under these stars, fate has brought you home."

CHAPTER THIRTY-SEVEN

Juliette was dimly aware of people hovering above her as she drifted in and out of consciousness. The ambulance had brought her to Methodist Hospital; this much she knew, for the kind nurse who had stayed by her bedside the first night told her. "You're lucky to be alive," the nurse had said, though Juliette gave no indication she could hear her. She couldn't seem to move her limbs. She caught snippets of conversation. *Significant head trauma . . . Possible spinal injury . . . The little boy from the plane is dead.*

Yes, there had been a plane. She remembered that now. But it hadn't dropped bombs on them, as Juliette had expected it to. Instead, it had come crashing down, the tail splintering from the body with a giant crack, the rest of it bursting into flames. It hadn't been the same as having a bomb whistle through the ceiling of her store seventeen years ago, but it had been close.

Ruth Levy, the nice woman who used to frequent her store in Boulogne, had been there sometime during the night, and so had Arthur. He had murmured to her that he needed her to wake up, that Lucie needed her. But he didn't know yet that it had all come unraveled.

Juliette had never meant to hurt anyone. At first, she'd been so deep in her grief that she'd truly believed the girl who'd survived was Lucie. After all, it *had* to be Lucie, for if it wasn't, what did Juliette have to live for?

Later, there had been clues, things about Lucie that reminded Juliette of Elise, but she had pushed them away. And then Paul had begun whispering to her, and it was easier to look back than to look forward, easier to spend time with his ghost than it was to look Lucie in the face and acknowledge to herself what she'd done.

But the girl she'd saved from the rubble hadn't been Lucie after all. She knew that now with a great, sad certainty, for Lucie was here, in this room, bathed in white light, waving at her, looking just as she had on that day in April 1943, before the world exploded. Her hair was in pigtails, her pink dress a bit too small, her white knee socks slipping down her shins, her black shoes scuffed.

"Lucie?" Juliette said in disbelief, and she heard the voices above her again, murmuring about how she was conscious after all, and wasn't it a miracle. She recognized Elise's voice, and for a second, she considered trying to rise to the surface long enough to apologize. There was so much to say. But then there was warm breath on her cheek, and her friend's voice was in her ear.

"Thank you, Juliette," Elise whispered, and Juliette wanted to open her eyes and demand to know what Elise was thanking her for when all Juliette had done was to steal happiness that was never meant to be hers. But then, Elise's voice caught and she added, "Thank you for saving her. She will be my whole life from this day forward. I promise you."

And with a great sweep of sadness and joy, Juliette understood. She had done something worthwhile after all, but she couldn't turn away from the fact that the mistakes she'd made had far outweighed the good deeds. Life is a scale of wrongs and rights, and the balance of hers had tipped long ago.

As Elise pulled away, Juliette could hear the voice of Lucie, or the girl she'd raised as Lucie, and she felt a great peace settle over her. She wanted to reach for her one last time, to hold in her arms the child she'd spent seventeen years loving as her own, though she'd never had the right. But she couldn't move, and just as she was beginning to despair, she heard another voice, and suddenly, the world was awash in a strange glow.

"Maman?" It was Lucie speaking, but it wasn't the Lucie who loomed over her hospital bed like a specter, but rather the Lucie who was walking toward her now with her hand outstretched, the little girl she had lost so long ago.

"I'm so sorry, my love," Juliette whispered, and above her, in the hospital room, she heard crying, and she thought that perhaps the women there believed she was speaking to them. But she wasn't. She was apologizing to her three-year-old daughter for letting her die, and then for trying to replace her because there was no other way forward.

But little Lucie was smiling, and she didn't look angry, not at all. "Mathilde has her mother now, Maman. They'll be all right, both of them," she said, her eyes sparkling like the waters of the Seine. "Come. Papa and the others are waiting. It is time to go home."

And so, her heart overflowing with joy, Juliette Foulon reached out and, holding tightly to the tiny hand of her little girl, followed her into the light.

AUTHOR'S NOTE

When I sat down to write *The Paris Daughter* in the summer of 2021, the world seemed to be getting back to normal after the worst of the Covid-19 pandemic. I went on a book tour for *The Forest of Vanishing Stars*; businesses and schools were reopening; and we were reflecting, as a society, about having made it through a period of great darkness—the kind of trial by fire that is often a component of books about World War II.

I spent much of my book tour talking about how World War II novels remind us of our resilience in trying times, and I hoped, as I began to write *The Paris Daughter*, that this book would be another powerful affirmation of the human capacity for goodness, strength, and faith in the face of adversity.

I had no idea, though, that we would soon have an even stronger reminder of the terror ordinary people had to endure during World War II.

Of course you know by now that a huge part of the plot revolves around innocent civilians being bombed, which happened not just in France but all over Europe and Asia (as well as in Pearl Harbor, Hawaii, and even Dutch Harbor, Alaska) during the

Second World War. I spent a lot of time trying to imagine the fear and helplessness one would feel in the midst of war, knowing that any day, a bomb could fall from the sky, obliterating everything in its path.

And then, just after I wrapped up the first draft of the book, that situation suddenly became a reality for millions in modern-day Europe. Watching the heartbreaking events of 2022 unfold in Ukraine gave us all an intimate look at the price that so many innocent people, especially children, pay in wartime—but it also reminded us of the horrific cost of deadly weapons being deployed in civilian neighborhoods.

Such is the case in *The Paris Daughter*, which includes the real-life Allied bombing raids of the German-controlled Renault factory in the Paris suburb of Boulogne-Billancourt. In the book, Juliette and Paul Foulon spy strange-looking phosphorescent markers drifting down from the sky one dark night, in the way that many residents of western Paris realized, mere seconds before the first blast, that they were about to be bombed. That night, March 3, 1942, 235 RAF aircraft dropped 540 bombs, fewer than half of which fell in the target area, according to Lindsey Dodd's *French Children Under the Allied Bombs, 1940–45*, one of the many helpful books I used in my research. In Boulogne-Billancourt during that raid, 371 civilians were killed and another 317 were injured—but the Renault factory was back up and running again within six months.

Thirteen months and one day after that first bombing, the Allies came again, determined to wipe out the German-controlled factory. This time, though, it was the U.S. Air Force, arriving in broad daylight just as the famed Longchamp racecourse opened for the season. Eighty-eight aircraft dropped 650 bombs that day, with only 41 percent hitting their targets, according to Dodd's book. Three hundred twenty-seven civilians died as a result of the raid, and more than five hundred were injured in Boulogne-Billancourt alone. Like the Foulons, many were simply at home, going about their daily routines, when they lost everything.

I was still trying to understand what it would feel like to be a child under constant threat of bombing when I got an intriguing email. It was from a Holocaust survivor named Herb Barasch, who had lived in Belgium when World War II began, and who had just finished reading my 2020 novel, *The Book of Lost Names*. "I am a child survivor, hidden during the Holocaust," he wrote. "Your fiction is truly the reality of what happened during the Holocaust."

Fascinated, I wrote back, and we set up a time to chat by phone. During our call, he told me about the wrenching decision his parents made: they sent him off to live under a false identity at a Catholic orphanage, similar to the decision Ruth makes to send her children off with strangers in *The Paris Daughter*. "I was taken by a group of Underground people who placed the children in different locations," he told me. "My parents had no idea where I was going to be. The arrangement was that you won't know where your children are, and if you can't agree to that, we can't go forward."

Much like Elise in *The Paris Daughter* when she leaves Mathilde with Juliette, Barasch's parents left him behind knowing that they'd have no control over his safety—and heartbreakingly, no way to know, until the war ended, that he was all right.

"Their inner strength was unbelievable," he said. "They allowed someone to come take their son, knowing that they might not live, but they wanted me to survive. It was a lot for them to do that. It really scarred them for life."

Barasch stayed hidden for more than two years, and not only did he make it through, but so, too, did his parents, hiding in a basement. The family moved to the United States in 1948, and he now lives in San Francisco. Though the war is nearly eighty years in the past, Barasch still has clear memories of what it felt like to know that a bomb could fall from the sky at any moment.

"We had a bomb shelter in the monastery where I lived," he explained. "Sometimes you'd be there for seven, eight hours, because the Allies were bombing. We were all scared. If the bomb hit the building, chances were you wouldn't survive."

In addition to talking to Barasch, I read numerous firsthand accounts from people who lived in the suburbs of Paris and grew accustomed to grabbing gas masks and running for shelter whenever the air raid sirens sounded. Such stories and documents are vital in preserving our collective memory of the events that shape our world.

There are many other historical threads that run through this book, too. Those of you who have read *The Book of Lost Names* might recognize the town of Aurignon, where Elise winds up after leaving Mathilde behind, as well as Père Clément, the priest at the Église Saint-Alban. The town, which featured heavily in that book, is fictional, but it's based closely on the real-life escape lines that ran through south-central France, relying on forgers to create identity papers to move Jewish refugees—many of them children—to safety. In *The Paris Daughter*, Elise works briefly with this very same based-on-reality network—which was in part a nod to the many readers who asked for a follow-up to *The Book of Lost Names*. I generally don't write sequels, but it was wonderful for me to revisit Aurignon for a few chapters, and to see what became of some of the children who survive thanks to the escape lines that ran through France.

When Elise returns to Paris after the war and desperately tries to find Ruth's children, she works with a suburban orphanage that really was part of an Oeuvre de Secours aux Enfants network to reunite Jewish children with their families. And when she takes the children to the Hôtel Lutetia to search for their mother, she is walking in the footsteps of real people eighty years ago who visited the grand hotel, which had been converted temporarily into a center for returning refugees.

Later, Elise sails to America aboard the SS *United States*, which was in transatlantic service from 1952 through 1969. According to a 2008 article in *Popular Mechanics*, the ship was four city blocks long and seventeen stories high—and it could speed through the water at forty-four knots, or more than fifty miles per hour. On its maiden voyage in 1952, it crossed the Atlantic in just three days, twelve hours, and twelve minutes, a record that has never been broken.

Sadly, the plane crash that occurs late in the book is also very much based on reality. In fact, the quotes from the cockpit in the novel are pulled directly from the U.S. Civil Aeronautics Board's Aircraft Accident Report, released on June 18, 1962, roughly eighteen months after the tragic midair crash. At 10:33 a.m. on December 16, 1960, TWA Flight 266 from Columbus, Ohio, and United Flight 826 from Chicago collided in the air over Staten Island, New York. The TWA plane, a Lockheed Super Constellation, fell on Miller Army Field, near where the planes had struck each other. The United plane, a Douglas DC-8, flew for several minutes over the city, badly damaged, until it finally slammed into the corner of Seventh Avenue and Sterling Place in Park Slope, Brooklyn. Only one passenger—an eleven-year-old Boy Scout named Stephen Baltz—survived the initial crash, but he was badly burned and died from his injuries the following day, after staying conscious long enough to see his parents, who hadn't been on the flight with him. All 128 people aboard the two planes were killed, as were six people on the ground, two of whom were selling Christmas trees, as Lucie and her boyfriend are in the book. I still burst into tears (I'm crying now as I write this!) thinking of little Stephen—a sixth-grader who played Little League Baseball and sang in the church choir, and whose sweet face looks out at readers from a photograph on the front page of the December 17, 1960, issue of the *New York Times*.

In writing *The Paris Daughter*, I also went way down the rabbit hole of wood-carving research, reading such books as *Carving Award-Winning Songbirds* (Lori Corbett), *Carving Faces Workbook* (Harold Enlow), and *Chris Pye's Woodcarving Course & Reference Manual: A Beginner's Guide to Traditional Techniques*. I particularly loved *The Lost Carving: A Journey to the Heart of Making*, a beautiful memoir of wood carving by David Esterly, a renowned master carver who died in 2019. Esterly wrote with passion about the carver being shaped by the wood; I found his words very inspiring and illuminating. If you're interested in learning more about the art of wood carving, I would absolutely recommend his book. I'd also suggest checking out MaryMayCarving.com, the website of wood-carver Mary May, who quite generously spent time answering my questions about wood carving and helping me make sure that the wood-carving scenes in the book were accurate. If you're interested in learning how to carve wood, I highly recommend Mary May's classes, some of which are free. You can learn more about her and those classes on her site.

As always, any errors are my own.

A few other historical notes: Elise meets Olivier at an Artists Union meeting in New York; these weekly meetings really did happen between the early 1930s and 1942, and the group was instrumental in advocating for federally funded work for artists during the Great Depression. In Paris, Olivier allies himself with French communists, who had a complicated path during World

War II. The encounters with Pablo Picasso and his circle of artists are based on reality—I found the book *Life with Picasso*, by French artist Françoise Gilot, fascinating and illuminating. Gilot and Picasso, who met when she was twenty-one and he was sixty-one, had two children together over the course of a relationship that spanned nearly ten years. As a side note, Gilot, an accomplished painter, later married Jonas Salk, who developed the polio vaccine! What an interesting life she has led, and in this memoir, she speaks very frankly of what it was like to be by Picasso's side during and after World War II. The book *Inventing Downtown: Artist-Run Galleries in New York City 1952–1965* (Melissa Rachleff) helped me to create the gallery Jack Fitzgerald runs in New York (though the majority of these galleries were located downtown).

Now I'd like to emerge from these ruminations on the past and share a more personal note with you.

I never lose sight of how tremendously lucky I am to get to write novels for a living. It's a remarkable privilege to be welcomed into your life for a brief time to tell you a story, and I appreciate the trust you place in me to do just that. I take my job very seriously, and I research historical events to the best of my ability, not just because I care about accuracy, but because the idea of turning real history into fiction fascinates me.

People often ask why I'm so drawn to writing about the past. My reasons are numerous, but perhaps the most important one is that if we don't learn from history, we run the risk of repeating it. Too often in recent years, those of us who read frequently about World War II have seen shadows of that long-ago war in current events, and it's difficult seeing versions of past horrors happening again. When I write my novels, I'm not explicitly trying to teach you a lesson. Rather, I'm hoping that you're reminded of our place in the grand scheme of things—both in the events that have come before us, and in the events that are yet to come. I think that when we know more about the past, we are better prepared to face the future, whatever comes our way.

I also hope that when you read my books, you're reminded of our incredible human capacity for love, resilience, and survival, even in the midst of terrible times. We all go through dark periods in our lives. We all know anguish, just as we all know joy. But I hope that in reading books like mine, you're reminded that managing to pick ourselves up and put one foot in front of the other is always a victory—and that there is always light in the darkness, even if that spark is sometimes hard to see.

Finally, I am not only a writer, but also (like many of you) a passionate reader. That's one of the reasons I'm so honored to be a host of *Friends & Fiction*, an online community for readers that I cofounded and run with fellow *New York Times* bestselling authors Patti Callahan Henry, Kristy Woodson Harvey, and Mary Kay Andrews. Each week, we interview authors on a live Wednesday-night show, which has been such a joy. We talk about the authors' books, but also about the world behind their writing: the obstacles they've faced, their fears, their joys, their lives. And on the Facebook page we run, tens of thousands of readers engage with each other and with us every day, talking about the books and authors they're interested in. If you love to read, I hope you'll join us; we're on Facebook and YouTube, and you can learn more at FriendsandFiction.com. *Friends & Fiction* is, in my opinion, one of the friendliest corners of the internet, and we'd love to welcome you. I hope to see you there, and in the meantime, thanks so much for reading *The Paris Daughter*, and for trusting me to tell you a story that I hope moved you and made you think just a bit differently about the past—and about the world outside our doors.

ACKNOWLEDGMENTS

The acknowledgments are always the last piece of a book I write, probably because they're the hardest—harder than writing the novel itself! There are so, so, so many people who do so much to bring my books into the world, and every year I am paralyzed with fear that I'll forget someone. So deep breath—here it goes!

As always, I am forever indebted to my agent extraordinaire, Holly Root; my incredible editor, Abby Zidle; and my superstar publicist, Kristin Dwyer of Leo PR. Heather Baror-Shapiro continues to be a miracle worker of foreign rights, and Dana Spector at CAA has been my wonderful longtime partner in the film/TV world. I'm so excited to have added two new rock stars to my team this year, too: Jessica Roth, my in-house publicist at Gallery Books and world-class connoisseur of delicious pies; and Jonathan Baruch of Rain Management, my film manager, who has an incredible ability to make me feel capable of things I wouldn't have dreamed of earlier. And, of course, Jennifer Bergstrom remains not only the best publisher in the United States, but also inarguably the best person to drink champagne with. To all of you: I can never thank you enough for your friendship or your faith in me.

My team at Gallery Books/S&S is an incredible one; I don't know how I got so lucky. I've been so grateful to get to know Jen Long, Aimée Bell, Eliza Hanson, Sally Marvin, and Chelsea McGuckin even better over the past year. I'm also grateful to Jonathan Karp, Chrissy Festa, Lesley Collins, Tracy Nelson, Sarah Lieberman, Wendy Sheanin, Paula Amendolara, Heather Musika, Lisa Litwack, Hydia Scott-Riley, Lexi Dumas, Gaby Audet, Anabel Jimenez, Teresa Brumm, Michelle Leo, Tom Spain, Gary Urda, Nancy Tonik, Faren Bachelis, Tyrinne Lewis, Michelle Podberezniak (I miss you!), Hannah Moushabeck, Susan Kovar, Colleen Nuccio, the Book Club Favorites team, and the rest of the fabulous team at S&S, especially the incredible sales force, who have been so supportive. Special thanks to Molly Mitchell at Leo PR, Alyssa Maltese at Root Literary, Christine Hinrichs at Authors|Unbound, Kathie Bennett at Magic Time Literary, and the incredible producer Anna Gerb, who continues to fight for *The Book of Lost Names*. A special thank-you to Madeleine Maby, who always does such a beautiful job of narrating my books, and to Christina Sivrich, a dear friend who took on the audio narration of my novella, *How to Save a Life*, last year. And, of course, too, I adore my team at S&S Canada, which includes Natasha Tsakiris, Rebecca Snoddon, Felicia Quon, Adria Iwasutiak, and Shara Alexa. I also have to mention the extraordinary Nita Pronovost, vice president and editorial director at Simon & Schuster Canada, who perhaps has the best not-so-secret identity of anyone I've ever met.

You may know that, in 2020, I cofounded *Friends & Fiction*, a Facebook group and weekly web show with four other bestselling authors. It is still going strong, and I'm tremendously grateful to our flourishing community of more than one hundred thousand readers, and especially to my F&F besties,

New York Times bestselling authors Kristy Woodson Harvey, Patti Callahan Henry, and Mary Kay Andrews; managing director Meg Walker of Tandem Literary; our F&F Writer's Block podcast host Ron Block of the Cuyahoga County Public Library; and our self-proclaimed "AV Nerd" (and on-air producer/legit rock star) Shaun Hettinger. Thanks, too, to Rachel Jensen and Grace Walker, who work behind the scenes, and to my friends Brenda Gardner and Lisa Harrison, who run the Friends & Fiction Official Book Club, along with JoDena Pyscher. Thanks to the many F&F members who go the extra mile to support authors and readers, especially the Friends & Fiction Official Book Club Ambassadors: Annissa Armstrong, Irene Weener, Susan Seligman, Rhonda Perrett, Molly Neville, Nicole Fincher, Debby Stone, Bubba Wilson, Jill Mallia, Francene Katzen, Sharon Person, Dallas Strawn, Linda Burrell, Michelle Marcus, and Dawne McCurry (as well as Barbara Wojcik, Maria Lew, Sarah Grady, and Marlene Waters).

I'm also grateful to the many fellow authors who have taken the time to join us as guests. Kristy, Patti, Mary Kay, and I host a live web show every Wednesday night (you can watch it in our Facebook group or on our YouTube channel), and we've had the chance to chat with some truly extraordinary writers, many of whom are very open with us about the challenges they face in both their writing and personal lives. I've been moved to tears more than once, and I've also found myself laughing so hard with other guests that I can't catch my breath. Let's just say it's often the most emotion-packed hour of the week for us! If you're not part of Friends & Fiction yet, please do join us. You can find out more at FriendsandFiction.com. We are also now doing in-person "Friends & Fiction: LIVE" events; I hope you'll come see the four of us at one of our fun tour stops on the road!

To Kristy, Patti, Mary Kay, and Meg: Thanks for always having my back, and for giving me a safe place to vent, brainstorm, and share while letting me know that above all, I'll always be loved. I love you, ladies, and I'm in awe of your talent and your goodness.

Special thanks to the many librarians and booksellers all over the world who go out of their way every day to make sure the right books find their way into the hands of the right readers. Thanks especially to Lauren Zimmerman (Writer's Block Bookstore), Laura Taylor (Oxford Exchange), Cathy Graham and Serena Wyckoff (Copperfish Books), Rebecca Binkowski (MacIntosh Books + Paper), Zandria Senft (Bethany Beach Books), Susan Kehoe (Browseabout Books), Peter Albertelli and Maribeth Pelly (BookTowne), Olivia Meletes-Morris and Dallas Strawn (Litchfield Books), Polly Buxton (Buxton Books), Linda Kass (Gramercy Books), June Wilcox (M. Judson Booksellers), Stephanie Crowe (Page & Palette), Susan McBeth (Adventures by the Book), Tim Ehrenberg (Nantucket Bookworks), Jessica Osborne, Melissa Taylor, and Annie Childress (E. Shaver, Bookseller), Jamie Southern (Bookmarks), Easty Lambert-Brown (Ernest & Hadley Booksellers), Meredith Robinson (Little Professor Bookshop), Gary Parkes and Karen Schwettman (FoxTale Book Shoppe), Alsace Walentine and Candice Anderson (Tombolo Books), Terra Dunham (Book + Bottle), the wonderful booksellers at Steimatzky in Israel, the lovely folks at my local Barnes & Noble on Sand Lake Road in Orlando, and all the other booksellers around the country and world who have been so enormously supportive and wonderful. I can't wait to get back out on the road to tour this book and reunite with old bookseller friends and meet new ones. If you have a bookstore near where you live, lucky you; you're just a short journey away from a little slice of heaven on earth. It's no coincidence that in *The Paris Daughter*, one of the main characters owns a bookstore; it's hard to imagine a more magical place to spend one's days.

I mentioned my foreign rights agent, Heather Baror-Shapiro of Baror International, earlier, but what I didn't add was that she (along with the wonderful Farley Chase, who sold my foreign rights earlier in my career) has made it possible for my books to be published in more than thirty languages. It gives me a little shiver of delight and gratitude each time I receive an email from a reader on another continent; it's astounding to think about the incredible ability of words to reach around the globe and to connect us across cultures. Thanks especially to Hilit Hamou-Meir at The Armchair Publishing House in Israel (who has not only been an astoundingly wonderful publishing partner, but also sent me a beautiful basket from her village in Galilee this year), and to Rosa Schierenberg at the Welbeck Publishing Group in the UK. And a huge thank-you to the publishers and readers in countries around the world who are willing to take a chance on me and my books. Words can't adequately express how grateful I am.

To my mom, Carol; my siblings, Karen and Dave; my dad, Rick; and to the rest of my family, including Janine, Barry, Johanna, James, William, Emma, Donna, Steve, Anne, Fred, Janet, Courtney, and all the cousins. I'm also fortunate enough to have the most fun in-laws in the world; the Trouba family rocks, and our family reunions are epic. Thanks especially to Wanda and Mark, Grandma and Grandpa Trouba, and all the Trouba aunts, uncles, and cousins, along with Jarryd, Brittany, and Chloe; Bob and JoAnn Lietz, and the Rivers family.

To the many authors whom I respect enormously and who have made me feel supported over the years, including Wendy Toliver, Allison van Diepen, Linda Gerber, Emily Wing Smith, Alyson Noël, Jay Asher, Kristina McMorris, Nguyễn Phan Quế Mai,